Trigger Warning
An Academic Thriller
Sid Stark

Want to keep in touch and hear about news and special offers first? Sign up for my mailing list and get your FREE novella by scanning the QR code below:

1

IT'S REALLY DEPRESSING how even small pieces of good fortune are followed so often by their reverse.

I had plenty of opportunity to contemplate this universal truth as I sat, stood, and walked through the interminable orientation process for my new job at Crimson College. I had spent all of the spring semester trying to get this job, and all summer making plans for what I would do when I started it. But now that I was finally here, I was hoping that this portion of the job, at least, would be over. And the future wasn't looking too good either.

In marked contrast to my previous faculty jobs, which had been notable largely for their professional neglect, my current position as a VAP (Visiting Assistant Professor) of Russian involved a multiday onboarding process. Over the previous two days I, along with the largest and most contingent-heavy group of new faculty in Crimson College's history, had toured the campus and the dorms, done several exquisitely humiliating team-building exercises, and attended lectures and orientation sessions on the library, IT facilities, campus security, and the zeitgeist of the current crop of undergrads.

Which apparently was stressed out. We were given several training sessions on how to recognize drug abuse, binge drinking, suicidal ideation, and potential warnings that a student was about to flip out and commit a mass shooting. As part of that, campus police did a short session on what to do during an active shooter event, from which I gathered that if anyone *did* come strolling into your classroom with their finger pressed down on the trigger of an AR-15, you were well and truly fucked.

"Nothing," we were assured by several different deans, "like that is going to happen at Crimson, *of course*, but it's always better to be prepared. Everyone is *very* happy here. The worst we have to deal with is the Gang of Six."

The first dean who brought up the Gang of Six then skipped on merrily to talking about town-and-gown outreach without seeming to notice the excited murmur that went through everyone at the sound of this intriguing name. The second dean who mentioned it hastily corrected himself and refused to answer any questions about it. By the time it came up again, during the session with campus police, everyone was burning with curiosity, and when the particularly mousy-looking dean who had dropped the name tried to pretend that she hadn't said anything about it, several of the new faculty members insisted that we be informed what was going on.

"It's an anonymous group with an anonymous website," said Brian Michaels, the chief of the campus police force, when the mousy dean gulped and refused to say anything more. "We're keeping an eye on them."

"Are they making death threats? Planning mass shootings?" demanded several voices at once.

The mousy dean gulped again.

"No," said Brian Michaels. He was a big burly man in his fifties, with pale blue eyes, the kind of skin that puts the "red" in "redneck," and hair that had once been blond now going to gray and buzzed almost completely off. If I had to guess, I would have said that he wasn't much for book learning, but that he was clever and shrewd about "real world" things. I had the impression that he was having a hard time not snorting or rolling his eyes.

"They're, uh, how shall I put this, writin' blog posts about social justice issues," he said. "We have no reason to believe that they pose any threat of violence at all. But they've expressed some, uh, discontent with certain aspects o' campus life, so the college administration has decided to keep an eye on 'em. We always get a few unhappy customers—the Men's Protection Alliance has been blatherin' on for months now—but they never actually cause trouble."

This led to a fierce debate amongst the incoming faculty about the ethics of monitoring student groups and student social media activity, and for a moment it looked like a shouting match might break out between someone from the B School (business) and someone from English, until Brian Michaels broke it up and told everyone we needed to finish up, because we were on a strict schedule, and he wasn't going to get in trouble for making us late for our next training session.

The day was capped off with an outdoor picnic where we hobnobbed with two fresh deans, the Provost, and the President. That had been so much fun I had seriously considered bursting into tears afterwards, and wondered why I had ever agreed to take this job. Oh right, because I needed the money.

Now, at quarter past eight in the morning, I was pushing my way through the Georgia August heat in search of Lee 032, where the mandatory diversity and inclusivity training was scheduled to be held.

I had parked in the faculty parking area on the far side of the athletics center and hoofed it past the tennis courts, around the outdoor track and the football practice field, over the beach volleyball area, filling my shoes with sand in the process, past several dorms, and across the back quad to Lee, the main administrative building. Which may or may not have been named after Robert E. Lee. The college was cagey on that subject.

Sweat was trickling down my sides, soaking my bra and panties, by the time I found an open entrance to Lee. The chill of the air conditioning hitting my wet clothes was welcome at first. By the time I had circled the first floor twice and found the stairs to the basement, where Lee 032 was housed, I was feeling distinctly chilled. And I still had four more hours in here to go.

Lee 032 was a windowless basement space that looked kind of like a church rec room. Round tables, laid with tablecloths in Crimson College colors (crimson and cream, a combo that looked sort of but not exactly like Harvard's), had been set out around the room.

"There are name tags and place cards." A woman in a uniform-y non-uniform of a crimson blouse and cream pencil skirt stopped me at the door. Her name tag said *Tanika Scott, Assistant Dean of Faculty Development*. She looked at a table diagram in her hand. "What's your last name?"

"Halley," I told her. "Rowena Halley. Russian."

"Goodness! That's not something you hear every day. Welcome to Crimson, Rowena. Here's your name tag. You're at table four. Over there."

I took the name tag and followed her pointing finger to a table in the back corner of the room. The back corner was fine with me. Maybe I could catch a brief nap or at least check my email while I was there.

Another woman was already sitting there, scrolling through her phone. She was tall and fit and looked about my age, so mid-thirties, and had weathered skin and dark blonde hair that had been cut in a very short pixie that flirted with the boundary between attractively gamine and aggressively mannish.

Lesbian, ex-military, I guessed.

"Oh hey," she said, looking up from her phone as I approached. "Take a seat." She pulled out a chair for me. "Mel," she said as I sat down. "Well, Melissa Wilson, but everyone calls me Mel. Arabic."

"Nice to meet you," I said. "Rowena Halley. Russian."

"Nice. Oh hey, are you at our table too?"

A short, slightly plump woman was hovering uncertainly behind me, like she wanted to join us but didn't quite have the nerve. She was wearing big glasses, an oversized blouse and maxi-skirt, and was the only black person in the room other than Tanika Scott and the woman standing in the background wearing a caterer's uniform.

"I think so," she said diffidently. "I'm, uh, Chloe. Chloe Taylor. Chinese."

"Well don't just stand there, take a seat," Mel told her. "And welcome to the torturers' and terrorists' table."

I laughed. Mel winked at me. Chloe swallowed and sat down without looking at either me or Mel. Up close, I could see that her big glasses hid beautifully clear smooth skin, marred only by scars on her temples, presumably from a lifetime of aggressive hair straightening.

I had just opened my mouth to say something comforting to her when my phone *pinged* at me. I glanced at the screen, and my heart skipped a beat. It was a WhatsApp message from Dima.

"Everyone turn off your phones, please!" a heavyset woman called out in a singsong voice. "And welcome to Crimson!"

2

I JUST WANTED TO LET you know before you heard it from anyone else, Dima had texted me. *I was covering the shelling around Mariupol and I was lightly wounded. Nothing to worry about)) By the time you get this, it will have already healed up. Good luck with the new job))))*

My God, I texted back. *Where were you wounded? Have you seen a doctor?*

It's not worth it. We don't have enough surgeons here, and there are lots of others who need them more. I'll just have to tough it out)))) Don't worry, it'll heal by the wedding))))

I stared at that text, searching for subtext and wondering how to interpret it. "It'll heal by the wedding" was a common Russian folk saying when someone got injured, but in this case it felt fraught with meaning. I just wasn't sure what that meaning was.

Dima and I had once been engaged, but he had broken it off more than a year and a half ago. Dima was an investigative reporter, a job that in Russia had a high death rate. Some "serious people" had taken exception to a story he had been following, and had decided to stop him by kidnapping me and holding a gun to my head. Dima had not taken it well.

After he had neutralized them, he had broken off the engagement, sent me back to the US while running off himself to the Donbass to cover the war there, and refused to speak to me for a year. We were now very tentatively back in contact, but he always insisted that he had no intention of getting back together as a couple. Plus, I was seeing someone else, and the relationship looked to be turning serious. But every time I got a message from Dima, the rest of the world ceased to exist.

There's always a danger of infection, I typed back furiously. *I really think you should see a doctor. Can't you go to Kiev—"*

"Phones away!"

It was the woman with the singsong voice. She was looking straight at me, beaming a smile whose saccharine falsity made my cheeks ache just to look at it.

"I know we all have a *ton* to do," she went on, still speaking directly at me without acknowledging that she was doing it, "but this is *important*. After all, we all want to learn how to create a healthy, *inclusive* environment, don't we? So unless there's a war on—"

"There is."

She stopped, flustered.

"I mean, yes," she said after a pause. "But it doesn't affect us *directly*, now does it?"

"No, but a good friend of mine was just wounded in a shell attack."

Beside me, Mel sucked in a sharp breath.

"So I'm sorry for texting while you're talking," I continued, "but this is quite literally a matter of life and death. I promise I won't be disruptive, but I have to take this text."

The woman with the singsong voice was already opening her mouth to say something, even though it was clear she didn't have an appropriate response lined up. That so rarely stops people, though.

"Was it in Afghanistan?" Mel asked loudly, interrupting whatever the other woman was about to say.

"No, although my brother was there for most of last year. It was the Donbass. Eastern Ukraine."

At the next table, a heavyset woman with a bad dye job whipped her head around and stared at me.

"You are from Ukraine?" she demanded, her accent harsh.

"No, but I have a friend there."

"I have many friends there too. I am from Kiev, but half my family is from Lugansk. We must talk." She caught the eye of the woman with the singsong voice. "Afterwards," she said.

The woman with the singsong voice had recovered herself by this time. "I'm *so* glad that we are having this little discussion right now," she said. "It's the *perfect* example of what we are going to talk about today, which is how to be sensitive to other people, even when it seems like they are working at cross purposes to what we want. But all we have to do is adjust our attitude and make the necessary accommodations. For example"—she peered over at me—"what's your name?"

"Rowena Halley. Russian."

"Oh! You're *that* table."

"*Torturers and terrorists,*" Mel hissed at me, with a grim smile on one side of her face.

"Everyone," the singsong-voiced woman was saying, "I'm thrilled to introduce our new—what do you call them? 'Less commonly taught languages,' isn't it?—our new instructors for the Russian, Arabic, and Chinese programs we're so *proud* to be building here at Crimson."

She paused expectantly. After an awkward silence, there was some scattered applause.

"And of course, who better than the instructors of our brand-new less commonly taught languages to model diversity and inclusion, as well as respect for others and their differences? So, in the spirit of that, Rowena, would you mind please taking your texting outside. It creates such a, well, *disruptive* atmosphere to have even one person texting when we're trying to build a sense of community, don't you think?"

Out of the corner of my eye I saw Chloe stare down at her hands like she wished she could sink through the floor, and Mel lift one corner of her mouth in something that couldn't be called a snarl only because faculty members at selective liberal arts colleges didn't snarl at each other like wolves.

"Sure," I said. "Thanks for being so, um, understanding and accommodating. I'll be back in a bit."

3

I GOT UP FROM THE TABLE and, with all eyes focused on me, made my way past the woman from food service, who was staring ahead impassively like she was a hair's breadth away from snapping and calling all these assholes on their pretentious bullshit, and Tanika Scott, who gave me a smile that was probably supposed to be encouraging but came out as stricken, and left the basement. Even though I tried to close it soundlessly, the door slammed behind me. Good thing I wasn't being disruptive by texting silently.

I checked my phone as soon as I was out the door. Three more texts had come from Dima while I'd been sitting there getting lectured on sensitivity and consideration. I figured this was as good a reason as any to go all the way outside and get out of the oppressive basement for a while, so I did.

By the time I got out onto the sidewalk, a fourth text had come from Dima. A shell fragment had lightly grazed his shoulder, he said, but it was absolutely nothing to worry about. He'd been bandaged up and pumped full of antibiotics, and was already back out on the front lines. Best of all, it was his left shoulder.

Now I'm balanced, he wrote. *A wound on my left shoulder to counterbalance the one to my right hand.*

I don't think that's a good kind of balance, I replied. While covering the battle for the Donetsk Airport in December, Dima had gotten three fingers on his right hand snapped by Ukrainian forces who thought he was a separatist, not a journalist. Luckily he'd convinced them of his journalistic bona fides before the torture had gone any further. He'd even gotten an interview with Dmytro Yarosh, the leader of the paramilitary Right Sektor, out of the bargain, so he considered it all worth it. I was less sure.

No worries! he texted. *Like I said, it'll heal by the wedding. Meanwhile, not sure whether to stay here around Mariupol, go up to Donetsk city, or check out Stanitsa Luganskaya. There's so much action I'm spoilt for choice!*

How long have you been on the front? I texted back.

Oh, you know how it is.

Yes, I do. How long have you been on the front without a break?

You know I can't go home.

I know. Dima's home was Moscow, but he wasn't welcome there anymore.

You can go to Kiev, I pointed out.

True. I was there just...well, I guess it was six months ago, at least. No, more. Before New Year's. I came out here to greet the New Year with my comrades, and I guess I haven't left since.

That's eight months on the front! After another year already. You need to take a break. At least go to Kiev for a few days. Or maybe you could go somewhere else. Have you done anything about Israeli citizenship?

Dima's maternal grandmother had been Jewish, so there was a chance that he might qualify for Israeli citizenship. It was something he'd talked about on and off for years, but never actually done anything about. Dima might write blistering diatribes against the corruption poisoning the Russian Federation, but the homemade tattoo over his heart that read "Russians Don't Surrender" was the real expression of his one true faith. I suspected that the only way to get him to renounce his Russian citizenship would be to pry it from his cold, dead fingers.

Not yet, he texted back. *Someone I know in Kiev said he'd look into it for me, but I haven't heard anything about it yet.*

I ground my teeth a little. *What about American citizenship?* I texted. *You could probably qualify for political asylum.*

Still trying to get your stars and stripes on me, Inna?))))) Actually, no fooling, I did ask about that the last time I was in Kiev. They told me officially maybe, but they told me unofficially I'd need to do something like marry a native-born American citizen to be sure.

I stared at the phone for a long time. Was it the heat of an August morning in Georgia making me feel sick, or was it a rush of crazy emotion at those words? I wanted to laugh, cry, vomit, kiss someone, and punch someone in the face all at once.

You know that would be easy enough to organize, I texted back.

Really? Who'd you have in mind for the bride?))))) Kim Kardashian?))))))

Is that who you want? I meant to add some smiley faces to help keep the tone light and joking, but my hands were clumsy on the phone, and I accidentally sent the text instead.

No thanks. Armenians are nice to look at, but I've never wanted to marry one)))) I'm afraid there's only one American woman I've ever considered worth a second glance, Inna, and that's you.

Why was my heart beating so fast? I must have gone soft after a few years up North, and now I was getting heatstroke from a little warmth and sunlight. It wasn't even that hot yet.

*This might not be the best moment, and I don't...*I erased that text, started another one, erased that one, tried again, erased that one too, and went back to my original words. *This might not be the best moment to say this, and I don't want you to feel, I don't know, awkward or obliged, but you **know** that if you ever need an American bride in order to get an American passport, that can be arranged.*

There was an excruciating eternity of waiting before Dima's next text came through.

Are you offering?))))

Of course, if that's what you need.

There was another excruciating eternity of waiting.

Oh, Innochka. My little Decembrist's wife. Don't waste yourself on me, Innochka, my silly little girl. Aren't you still with that American? What's his name?

Alex. Yes. But we're not married. We're not even engaged. It's just a...thing.

Does he know that?

I don't know.

Is he a good man?

Yes.

Better than me?

Different.

That means he's better. And I hope he is. Because I want you to marry him.

Who are you, my father? Do you also have a dowry you're prepared to offer along with my hand and heart to the first suitable suitor?

))))) Still as witty as ever, Inna)))) But no fooling, Innochka, if he's a good man, you should marry him. Didn't you just turn thirty-five? You're not getting any younger, and old age is not a pleasure, especially when you're alone.

And what about you?

Let me take care of myself, Inna.

You don't seem capable of taking care of yourself. You just got hit by a shell!

A shell fragment. If it had been a direct hit, I'd be smeared from here to Rostov))))

You know what I mean! You say you can take care of yourself, but you're not doing a very good job of it. For the love of Christ, Dima, go see a surgeon about this wound. And take at least a little break from the front. Go to Kiev, go to Lvov, go to wherever the hell you want, just get out of the Donbass for a while. At least until your shoulder heals.

I obey, Comrade General!!!!)))))

Naughty boy!

You know it))))) Wait: aren't you supposed to be at work? Some kind of training?

They kicked me out for texting.

They kicked you out for texting?!??! What is this, a strict regime of freedom deprivation? Are they going to send you to do corrective labor next?!?

So it seems. But with a paycheck.

A paycheck—that's good. Get back in there and earn it!

I obey, Comrade General!

*Akh, Inna, what **am** I going to do with you?))))) Look, I have to go. My phone's about to die. Try not to get into trouble, okay?*

I'll promise if you will, I wrote. But there was no reply.

4

THE CHILL HIT ME SO hard when I stepped back into Lee Hall that I instantly got an ice cream headache. Weird. I had gotten them while walking around on very cold days in Russia, but never just from AC. Of course, I never had liked basements. Probably I should get counseling or something for my basement phobia.

"Oh, *thank you* for rejoining us, Rowena."

It was singsong-voiced woman, dashing my hopes of slipping back into the session unnoticeably.

"I trust everything is taken care of?" she said. "Nothing further you need to do? You're ready to give us your undivided attention now?"

Everyone was staring at me, some with prurient curiosity, some with hope that I might relieve a little of the boredom that was already setting in, and Mel and the Ukrainian woman with sympathy.

"It was just a flesh wound," I said, loud enough for the entire room to hear. "He's already been bandaged up and given antibiotics. Nothing more I can do right now."

In the silence that followed, I went over and sat down between Mel and Chloe. What had gotten into me? I was normally so mild-mannered. Making myself the center of attention had never been my style. But I could feel the dragon of don't-fuck-with-me rising to the surface, stretching out her massive wings, flexing her sinuous neck, and baring her razor-sharp teeth. I had spent so long kowtowing to other academics, and the brutal pressures of the job market, that I had started taking them as seriously as they took themselves. But they were just straw men. I had been fearless when very frightening people had held me at gunpoint. I had been calm when the man I had thought for a long time was the love of my life had gotten wounded in a war zone—again. Suddenly the singsong-voiced woman and her ilk appeared to me for what they really were, which was pathetic. Okay, the pathetic holders of my paycheck, but still. Maybe I *should* start pushing back at them more. Maybe they had a lot less power over my future than either they or I thought.

"*I'm glad he's not hurt too bad,*" Mel hissed in my ear.

"*Thanks,*" I hissed back. "*What are we doing now?*"

She indicated a handout in front of me. "Welcome to Crimson College!" was emblazoned in big letters across the top of the first page, with "New Faculty Orientation 2015, Diversity and Inclusivity Training, 8:30-12:30, Lee 032" underneath that.

"*That's her,*" Mel hissed, pointing at the name "Dorothy Talbot, Associate Dean of Diversity and Faculty Development," at the bottom of the page.

I wondered how many deans Crimson College had. For a place that had less than three thousand students, it seemed awfully well supplied with deans and other senior administrators.

Out of the corner of my eye I sensed that Dorothy was giving us a sideways look. I looked up from the handout and tried to focus on what was going on.

"And so," Dorothy was saying, as brightly as a bad kindergarten teacher, "I'd like us all to start by breaking out and discussing what intersectionality means to each of *us*, and how we can all work to become more aware of the effects of intersectionality in our everyday lives, how we can be more aware of it in our students, and how we can best serve their unique, intersectional, needs." She gave us one final false smile. "Tanika and I will be circulating the room to help answer questions, facilitate discussion, and provide ideas. Tanika, could you please start at that end?"

Tanika followed Dorothy's pointing finger to scurry over to where Mel, Chloe, and I were sitting in the back corner. "So, ladies," she said, with the painfully irritating smile of someone who doesn't actually know how to connect with other people, "who would like to start the discussion? Does anyone have any examples of intersectionality in their own lives?"

There was an awkward moment of silence while I wrestled with the temptation to point out that she probably shouldn't call us "ladies." "Everyone" would be better, or maybe nothing at all. I mourned, as I often had before, that Americans were not in the habit of calling each other "comrade." Many Russians had told me that one of the greater tragedies of the fall of the Soviet Union was that addressing everyone as "comrade" had gone out of fashion. It was the perfect form of address for a multicultural, egalitarian society. Probably telling Tanika that would not win me any points.

"Well," said Mel, when it became apparent that neither Chloe nor I was going to speak up, "I'd say I've got lots of intersectionality going on." Her voice had a flat, hard edge to it, rather than the treacly tones I could hear dripping in from the rest of the room. "I'm a woman *and* gay *and* from the South *and* a first-generation college student. Oh, and a veteran. Air Force."

I knew it! I congratulated myself, while Tanika said, "That's *great,*" as if those were good deeds Mel could take credit for, rather than mostly things that had just happened to her. "And can you give any examples of how a better understanding of intersectionality has helped you out?"

"When people start giving me shit about one thing, I just start playing some other minority card," said Mel.

I laughed. Tanika gave me a reproachful look. "I don't think that's how we're supposed to be using it," she said.

"I know." Mel flashed her a smile. "And I don't. I'm just messing with you. I guess I'd say that I know how it can be to love my country and my home state of South Carolina, even when big parts of it don't love me back."

Now Tanika was nodding encouragingly. "That's very good," she said. "What about you, uh"—she glanced at the nametag on Chloe's chest—"Chloe?"

"Um." Chloe looked down at her hands, and then, taking a deep breath and visibly steeling herself, looked up and said, "Well, like, I'm, like, a woman. And I'm black, obviously. But my family's, like, middle-class and educated, so I'm not, like, everyone's stereotype of the poor black ghetto girl. I'm really just a huge nerd from a stereotypical nuclear family. So I guess that's, like, been a thing, like, pretty much my whole life. And I've always loved East Asian cultures, and I went into Chinese even though I'm not Chinese at all. If you're Chinese everyone takes it for granted, and if you're white everyone accepts that you get to study other cultures, but since I'm black, I'm always having to explain and justify my choice to go into something other than Africana Studies."

"That's really *good*," said Tanika, nodding and giving Chloe a sickly-sweet smile. Maybe that's what was causing the low-level nausea rising up from my gut to my gorge. "So you really *know* what it's like to have people make incorrect assumptions about you."

"Um, yeah," said Chloe, not meeting Tanika's eye.

"I'm sure your tablemates will get a lot of benefit out of continuing this conversation after I leave you, but first I'd like to hear from you, Rowena."

Tanika fixed me with an expectant smile. I knew I was supposed to say something about how I was a cisgender heterosexual white woman, and then roll around on the floor in sackcloth and ashes, tearing at my hair and beating at my breast and declaring what an unredeemable sinner I was for all the unfair advantages I'd been given in life. Funny how, say, minority men were not expected to do the same in order to atone for their original sin of male privilege. Oh, wait, that's because they were men.

"I grew up on a commune in rural Georgia," I said. "Lots of my Russian acquaintances mistake me for Pashtun rather than my real ethnic background, which is Irish. I've always been an outsider in my own culture, whatever you want to say that culture is."

"Oh. That's, um, that's *very*, um, interesting, Rowena." Tanika gave me an uncertain semi-smile. "I'll just, um, leave you to discuss this further. And then at the end we're going to ask all the tables to tell the rest of the group your ideas for how to increase the awareness and practice of intersectionality in the college."

She scurried off to the next table, leaving behind a distinct lack of lively intellectual discussion.

"Well," said Mel, once the silence at our table had stretched on too long for decency, "what *do* you think about intersectionality, *ladies*?"

I didn't say what I was really thinking, which was that intersectionality was the work of people whose intentions were so good that they were going to pave a highway straight to hell for all of us.

"I think it's good to be aware that most people's lives are more complicated than they appear at first glance," I said.

"For sure," said Mel. Chloe nodded in what looked like genuine agreement.

"Speaking of which," said Mel. She looked over her shoulder. Tanika was two tables down from us, favoring its lucky inhabitants with another sickly-sweet smile. Dorothy was still on the far side of the room. Just looking at her caused a flash of rage to heat up my chest. Jeez. I needed to get this under control.

"Okay, all clear," said Mel. "So, speaking of things being more complicated, I assume you heard all that stuff about the Gang of Six?"

Chloe and I both nodded.

"Have you read any of their posts?"

Chloe and I both shook our heads.

"Check it out."

Keeping one eye cocked for Tanika and Dorothy, Mel pulled out her phone and brought up a website. Holding the phone under the table, she angled it so both Chloe and I could read it.

It was a free WordPress site with a very amateur banner that read "The Gang of Six" in knockoff crimson and cream across the top. "BLACK BLOOD MONEY FOR GEORGIA'S MOST RACIST COLLEGE?" screamed the headline of the top blog post.

"Holy crap," murmured Chloe. "Oops, sorry. Didn't mean to swear."

"Don't fuckin' worry about it," said Mel. "'Holy crap' is right. I don't know if what they're saying is true, but if it is…"

"Time for sharing, everyone!" Dorothy sang out.

5

WE MUST NOT HAVE BEEN sufficiently surreptitious in our phone-reading, or maybe we had just already been marked out as bad apples. Dorothy was giving our table a treacle-laden death glare from across the room.

"I know *some* of you are having very productive conversations, but since *some* of you seem to have already finished your discussions and moved on to other things, I want us all to go ahead and share our insights. Rowena, would your table care to start?"

"Yes," said Mel, cutting me off before I could respond. "We talked about how everyone's lives are more complicated than they seem from the outside. And then we moved on to a specific example from here at Crimson College, and how we might apply the lessons of intersectionality and inclusivity in our work here. Specifically, we were looking at the allegations of the Gang of Six, and how we might work to mitigate some of the injustices they have been shining a spotlight on."

Dorothy's nostrils flared. She opened her mouth and closed it without saying anything. Red spots were blooming on her cheeks.

"I don't think we need to concern ourselves about the Gang of Six," she finally managed to say. "They represent a very *small* minority of the Crimson community. The *vast* majority of our students, staff, and faculty are extremely happy to be here. We really *are* like one happy family. So, um, Melissa, is it? What would *you* suggest to help foster that kind of close, family atmosphere?"

"I think," said Mel, "I'll defer that question to someone who's actually from a happy family."

"Oh. Um." Dorothy looked as wrong-footed as a wrestler caught off guard by a sheep.

"I have some thoughts." It was, surprisingly, Chloe. Her voice was barely above a whisper, but in the silence after Mel's declaration it rang out louder than she had intended. She ducked her head when everyone looked at her.

"*Wonderful.*" Dorothy brightened. "I'm *so* glad you're so willing to make a *productive* contribution, um,"—"*Chloe,*" hissed Tanika—"yes, thank you, *Chloe.* Could you share your thoughts with the rest of us?"

"Um, yeah." A bead of sweat rolled down Chloe's neck, but she straightened her shoulders and carried on. "In my family we always have this rule, I guess you'd call it, that you always have to remember that the other person has, like, love in their heart for you. So if they do something that, like, hurts you, you're supposed to start with the best interpretation of it you can, instead of jumping to the worst conclusion."

"*Lovely,*" said Dorothy, ruining what was otherwise a beautiful sentiment. "And I think"—she looked around the rest of the room meaningfully—"we can *all* take Chloe's *excellent* suggestion to heart, and use her wisdom to guide us in our collegial interactions here on campus as well as with our loved ones at home. Now, table two, what do you have to say? You, yes, you? What's your name again?"

"Olena," said the Ukrainian woman. "Economics."

"Oh, yes. Now, correct me if I'm wrong, but you're one of our new international faculty members, are you not? Can we get a show of hands? Can all the international faculty members raise their hands?"

Olena, looking incredulous, raised her hand. After a moment, a couple of Chinese men at table four very tentatively did the same.

"Oh, *wonderful*. Would you all introduce yourselves?"

Awkward silence filled the room, allowing me to focus on how my sweat-soaked underwear had now picked up the air conditioning's icy chill, making me shiver.

"I already introduced myself," said Olena. "So I do not think I need to do it again. It is your turn." She pointed her chin at the Chinese men.

The two men exchanged a nervous look, each trying to get the other to go first.

"You can call me James," one finally said. "Mathematics."

"And you can call me Randall," said the other. "Also mathematics."

"Oh, surely there's no need to take on Western names," said Dorothy. "Part of fostering an inclusive atmosphere is accepting names from *all* cultures, and not forcing people to change their names in order to fit in."

"It is better if you call me James," said James. "Easier. You cannot pronounce my real name properly."

Randall nodded in fervent agreement.

"Oh. Oh. Well...of course." Dorothy turned to face the entire room and said, with that tone of voice that bad teachers use when they're belaboring a painfully obvious point, "Of course, the *most* important thing is to respect the other person's wishes. So if someone says they wish to be called by a particular name, that's what you should do. Thank you for helping share that insight, uh, James and, um, Randall."

"You are welcome," said James. No doubt he meant it to be polite, but to American ears it sounded condescending. Dorothy bridled, but then, with a visible effort, decided to move on.

After that we spent an unnecessarily long time hearing from every table on what they thought about how to foster an atmosphere of diversity and inclusion and family togetherness. Which, as Mel hissed to me when Dorothy had her back to us, were often mutually incompatible. But whatever.

The next block of training involved a PowerPoint presentation about different communication styles, broken down by culture. We were lectured for a while about how African-Americans and Eastern Europeans might come across to middle class white Westerners as overly confrontational, but that was just a cultural difference, and so we shouldn't get offended. Then Olena confronted Dorothy about the use of stereotyping in a course about diversity, and Dorothy got offended. So that was amusing. Then we were lectured for a while about how East Asians tended to be soft-spoken and non-confrontational, and Dorothy called on James and Randall to confirm her words.

"I suppose this is correct," said Randall softly, looking like he wanted to add something, but was too polite to do so. Which was also amusing.

It was coming on towards 12:30, and I was beginning to feel a faint hope that I might make it out of there without dying of headache, chill from the air conditioning on my wet clothes, or sheer boredom, when some B School-looking person from the middle of the room raised his hand.

"Fuck, no," whispered Mel. "Just let it go, man, just let it go."

"What if it's someone who's *not* from one of these protected classes we just learned about?" the man asked. "What if it's, say, a male student who feels that he's on the receiving end of sexual discrimination or sexual harassment? What if he feels that the Women's Studies classes"—"WLGBTQA classes," Dorothy interrupted him—"yeah, those. What if he feels like those classes have created a hostile atmosphere for him, and he can't express himself without being subjected to microaggressions or outright silencing?"

"I'd tell him he's finally having a learning experience," muttered Mel.

"Yeah," I muttered back. "But I doubt anyone else will. Was it in *Between Men* that Sedgwick talked about the extreme sensitivity of male feelings, or *Epistemology of the Closet*?"

"I don't remember, but I think you just triggered a flashback to my comps. Now if you'd just bring up some Kristeva, I'll have a fullblown PTSD attack. Which might get us out of here."

"Sorry. Oops. Looks like people are staring again."

We shut up and tuned back in to the awkward discussion that was taking place between Dorothy, the B School person, and various other faculty members who couldn't resist chiming in on the issue of what to do when members of a privileged class felt threatened and silenced. Since this was a problem with no easy answers, everyone was ready to lay down the law on what to do.

"Didn't they say there was some kind of men's rights activist group here during one of the sessions yesterday?" someone at the next table put in. "Maybe we'll get to find out if we get some of them in our classes."

"God, I fucking hope not," said Mel, *sotto voce*. "But I probably will. Whaddya think: if I show them my war wounds, will that shut them up?"

"Worth a try," I whispered back. I rubbed my temples. The argument that had flared up over whether men's rights and white supremacist groups should be allowed to operate in the name of free speech, or shut down in the name of public safety, was wrapping another layer of pain around my head. Especially once it devolved into a lament on the plight of the modern male and how we had to be sensitive to that.

"'Cause otherwise we'll get shot," said Mel, still *sotto voce*. "Remember, *ladies*, it's on us not to provoke them into attacking us. It's our fault if they're unhappy. I think I'm going to do some digging, see how many of these little shits are roaming our fair campus."

"Lots," I said.

"Too damn right. Oh, thank God. Looks like we're breaking up. Finally. Freedom, sweet, sweet freedom. At least until the faculty meeting—I mean meetings, in the plural—tomorrow."

"Oh boy," I said. "See you there."

6

MY HEADACHE DISSIPATED as soon as I stepped back outside, and by the time I got home I was feeling almost myself again. I even got some unpacking done.

"One of these days," I told Fevronia, my tan long-haired cat who was my not-so-long-suffering companion in my moves, "we're going to settle down and not have to move every few months."

Fevronia gave me a doubtful look and disappeared behind a pile of empty boxes. She seemed to be settling into our current domicile better than she had all our previous ones. Or maybe she was still traumatized by the road trip I'd taken her on out to California to visit Alex. It had seemed like a good idea at the time, and it had been, but maybe next time I would leave Fevronia behind. She didn't enjoy being in the car, she didn't enjoy new places, and she didn't really like Alex. Not for any flaw of his own, but just because like any self-respecting feline, she didn't really like people, especially men.

Well, she was safe from him now. After ten days in California with him, mainly helping him set up his new apartment and get psyched up for his new job teaching Arabic at the DLI (Defense Language Institute), I'd driven all the way to Georgia, showing up last weekend and moving into my new apartment. Between the stress of moving and starting a new job, and the knowledge that Alex was now a four-day drive away, I had not been in a good mood when I arrived. Maybe that was why everything about this new job that I had been so thrilled to get now seemed so bleak.

At least my current place was much nicer than my previous apartments. I had moved up in the world financially with this job and was now earning almost enough to live on. Still considerably less than the price of attending Crimson College, but enough that I might be able to splurge and shop at real grocery stores instead of the dollar store.

Left to my own devices I might have chosen a living situation a little more in line with the slum chic I'd spent most of my adult life in, but my grandmother had picked the apartment out for me while I'd been working in Indiana over the summer. I had a sneaking suspicion that she'd either haggled down the price, or put up some of the deposit money behind my back. It was humiliating for a thirty-five-year-old PhD to have to take her grandmother's charity, but it wasn't the first time I'd been forced to rely on her, and it probably wouldn't be the last. Most of my almost-enough-to-live-on salary was going to go to paying off all the credit card debt I'd racked up while working my previous jobs, and there were still conferences to attend and (fingers crossed!) interviews to go to, and my car was on its last, last legs. Or wheels.

Still, it was pleasant to be in an apartment that had working fixtures and didn't reek of mildew and old cigarette smoke. And the internet was decent, too.

After a couple of hours of unpacking, I took advantage of the decent internet to research the Gang of Six. I wondered how much of a spike in traffic their site was getting because of the college's attempts to warn faculty about them. Probably they were rubbing their hands with glee at all the free advertising.

The site looked just as cheap and amateur on my laptop as it had on Mel's phone. I read the most recent post, about BLACK BLOOD MONEY FOR GEORGIA'S MOST RACIST

COLLEGE, which I thought was a bit harsh. Georgia had lots of racist colleges. I discovered that the Gang of Six had a strong dislike for the college's recent donor, Security Solutions, which they accused of "profiteering off the blood and sweat of our Black brothers and sisters, like generations of Georgians before them."

I thought about researching Security Solutions and finding out what they were up to, but got sidetracked by the next post down, which was a rant about the Men's Protection Alliance and its plans to protest a guest speaker. Piecing together the hints dropped in the post, I gathered that Crimson had invited one of the women caught up in Gamergate to come speak at the college later this fall, and the Men's Protection Alliance had demanded that they be able to invite a Men's Rights speaker as well. When that had been denied, they had kicked up a tantrum and were threatening to protest the scheduled event. The Gang of Six poster hinted darkly at plans for violence.

"Welcome to college," I said, and shut down my computer.

7

THE NEXT MORNING STARTED off a little less bright and early than the previous day, but I still had to show up on campus for a 9:00am college-wide faculty meeting, followed by a meeting of the Department of Foreign Languages. At least, unlike my previous positions, I was on the payroll for this. I hadn't actually gotten a paycheck yet, but I was already officially on the books as a Crimson College employee.

I reminded myself of that happy thought as I hotfooted it across the back quad until I found Bedford Hall. Presumably named after Confederate general Nathan Bedford Forrest, although the college was even cagier about that than they were about the provenance of Lee Hall.

The faculty meeting was in an auditorium in the basement of Bedford Hall. Just like yesterday, the air conditioning hit me like an arctic blast when I stepped inside, triggering an instant headache and making me shiver as the temperature of the sweat soaking my underwear dropped thirty degrees in the space of seconds.

I looked around as I entered the auditorium, hoping to catch sight of Mel or Chloe so that I would have at least one friendly neighbor during what was guaranteed to be a trying experience. No luck. Mel hadn't come in yet, and Chloe was cornered between two very earnest-looking faculty members in the front row, one of whom I recognized as a dean. No doubt the college was going to be running her off her feet, using her as their poster child for diversity. I considered trying to go down there and rescue her. Awkward, and the aisle was blocked by a knot of faculty members gossiping about their summer vacations. I gave it up as a bad deal, and sat down in the first available seat, next to a no-nonsense-looking woman with a weathered face and blonde hair going to gray.

We managed nothing more than a quick exchange of glances before a small gaggle of deans and deanlets got up on the stage at the front of the auditorium, and declared the meeting open.

"I'm *so* delighted to welcome all of you here to the Fall 2015 semester," said a woman I recognized from my Skype interview. "Of course many of you already know me, but let me introduce myself to the rest of you: Theresa Mayfield. Formerly from French, and of course French will always hold a special place in my heart, but now, thanks to everyone's generous support, leading my first faculty meeting as the Dean of the College of Arts and Sciences. So please everyone, be patient as I fumble my way through this. I've spent the past month reading and re-reading *Robert's Rules*, but I still don't think I've got it down pat. Cathy, do we have a copy of *Robert's Rules* on hand?"

A deanlet-y-looking woman nodded and held up a paperback copy of *Robert's Rules of Order*.

"Oh good. We all need our security blankets, even deans. Now, I, um, officially call this meeting to order. Is that right?" She looked over at Cathy.

"Right enough!" called Cathy.

"Very good. You all should have gotten emails with the meeting agenda. There isn't a huge amount of business to take care of, which I'm sure you're all glad to hear, since I just know you're all thirsting to attend your department faculty meetings."

There was some scattered laughter.

"So, item one. I'm thrilled to say that, with the generous donations we have received from Security Solutions, we should be able to break ground on the new football stadium this semester."

The woman sitting next to me huffed loudly enough to break through my growing headache. "Security Solutions, my ass," she murmured.

I looked over at her.

"You didn't know?"

I shook my head, causing a nasty spike of pain to drive through my left eye and then spread to my temple.

"Security Solutions is a for-profit prison company," the woman whispered. "Georgia has the highest rate of incarceration in the country, and private prisons are now a multi-billion-dollar business in Georgia alone. They've started donating to schools and colleges. To 'give back to the state'"—the woman made air quotes that were even snarkier than her voice—"and they say that they'll have no influence over college decision-making processes, but it sure sounds suspicious, doesn't it?"

"It does," I agreed, massaging my temple.

"But that's education these days. The factory farming of America's youth. So I suppose it's only fitting that we get funded by for-profit prisons. Do you have a headache?"

"A bit," I admitted.

"Yeah, me too. These meetings will do it to you. I swear, I get a headache as soon as I even step in this auditorium, even if there's no meeting going on. Julie! Julie, what's wrong?"

A skinny woman with faded red hair and a look of deep distress on her face was stumbling past us in the direction of the exit as fast as her worn black pencil skirt would allow her. "Panic attack!" she hissed.

"Oh God. Not again. You need help?"

Julie shook her head and continued stumbling up the aisle.

"Poor Julie," whispered the woman sitting next to me. "Generalized anxiety disorder. She gets panic attacks sometimes when she's teaching or in meetings. She had one in here last semester, too. She's tried every anti-anxiety med under the sun, but she says they're just getting worse and worse."

"How awful," I said.

"Yeah, she says even though she knows it's 'just' a panic attack, every single time it happens she's convinced that this time is different, this time she really is going to die. Plus they cause terrible diarrhea. I'd better go check on her. I'm Diane, by the way," she said. "Biology."

"Rowena. Russian."

"So they finally got around to hiring a Russian instructor? That's great." Diane shook my hand and then climbed over my legs and scuttled in a half-crouch down the row of seats to the main aisle and out the exit.

I turned my attention back to the faculty meeting. "We have a motion to change the description of the F-ART major," Theresa was saying.

I looked at the agenda. Indeed. Fine Arts was F-ART. Subdivided into M-ART (Music), D-ART (Dance), G-ART (Graphic arts), and T-ART (Theater).

"Motion to change the name," said a man at the other end of my row promptly.

"I know." Theresa emitted a small half-sigh. "Thank you for your input, Darryl. Your objection is noted, as it is every semester. I'm sure we'd all love to change the course identifier, but you know that the last time we tried, the Dean's office got a petition signed by every student on campus not to. So they've decided to keep it for the foreseeable future."

"Goddamn undergrads," muttered Darryl.

"Indeed," said Theresa. "But since keeping them happy is what pays our salaries, it has been decided to allow the little pipsqueaks to keep their F-ART major if that's what it takes. But the Fine Arts faculty have put forth a motion to add the phrase 'competence in both traditional and modern forms' to the major description. All in favor, please say aye."

The motion passed unanimously, and the meeting continued its plodding way forward. If anyone else took exception to the money from Security Solutions, they didn't voice it. There was discussion of a proposed Physical Engineering major, and some discussion about a proposal to break up the Department of Modern Languages into multiple departments. Spanish had gotten so big that it already had its own department, but the question was what to do with the other language programs. Keep them all lumped together? Keep French with Spanish as a Romance Languages department, or put it in with the other program-ettes? Create a separate LCTL (Less Commonly Taught Languages) program, or put Arabic and French, and Russian and German, together, as most colleges did? And in that case, what to do about Chinese?

To my surprise and horror, I was called upon to weigh in on this issue. I voted for a separate LCTL program, which Mel (who had slipped in at the back) and Chloe both seconded. The rest of the faculty seemed surprised by that.

"Less Commonly Taught Languages have their own special needs," I said. "For starters, they normally require much more time to learn than more commonly taught languages."

"Oh, I think that's an exaggeration," said a man I recognized from my interview as Klaus, from German. "Everyone says how difficult these languages are, but that's not very helpful, is it? We don't want to scare away students."

I was still formulating a response to that when Theresa said she was going to table the discussion for now.

"I think this is something best discussed first by the language programs themselves," she said. "Goodness knows we've had plenty to say about it already, but I think we need the input of our new LCTL instructors before we can move forward. So let's bring it up again for the end-of-semester general meeting. And now, I'm glad to say, we're already on our last item on the agenda."

"You're missing something!" a scruffy-looking man who was probably from Math shouted from two rows in front of me.

Theresa looked doubtfully at her printed-out meeting agenda. "No, I don't think so," she said, after a moment of careful perusal.

"The Gang of Six!" the man said. "Aren't we going to discuss them at all?"

There was a wave of nods throughout the auditorium.

"Well, I really don't think..."

"They've posted *again*," said the man. "Just last night! More about Security Solutions!"

Theresa pursed her mouth. "I am sorry to hear that, but we cannot just ban them from posting. Especially since we have no idea who they are."

"Can't IT track them down?" demanded the scruffy man.

"Alas, this is not a thriller movie," said Theresa. "I didn't understand all the details, but IT has informed me that they do not actually have those kinds of capabilities. I'm afraid if we want to find out who they actually are, we will have to rely on old-fashioned sleuthing. So, everyone, I ask that you keep an eye out for...anything that might be indicative of discontent with your students. Not just because we want to find out who the Gang of Six are—not because we want to punish them, of course, but because we want to *talk* with them—but because we really do care about *all* our students, even the...difficult ones."

There was more scattered laughter.

"So anyway, everyone, please keep an eye out for, I don't know, 'Gang of Six' t-shirts or something on your students. Meanwhile, I'm not sure there's much else we can or should be doing about them. Students will be students—unfortunately."

More scattered laughter.

"And the little darlings will be moving in tomorrow, which brings me to the last item on our agenda, which are the move-in celebrations. As you recall, we voted last year to do something new and special to show our new students just how much we appreciate them, and consider them part of the family. So we will have a welcoming committee waiting for them as they drive in at the front gates, and faculty members helping them move into their dorm."

For a moment I couldn't believe what I had just heard, but when I looked around, I saw everyone else giving resigned nods. And then I remembered that this was the "New Student Welcome Event" I had gotten an email about and put into my phone calendar for tomorrow. I just hadn't realized we would be working as bellhops. I wondered if they would tip us. I was sure I wasn't the only one who could use the money.

"So," continued Theresa briskly, "I—well, actually, Tanika and Cathy—have created a duty roster for our younger, fitter, faculty to participate in this fun activity. Move-in starts at 8:00am tomorrow and continues until 2:00pm. We've broken it down into shifts so that no one has to spend too much time doing heavy lifting, or, on the other hand, standing in the sun in full regalia."

"Are we still going to do that thing we talked about?" someone called out from behind me.

"What thing?" asked Theresa.

"You know, the...what was it called? Separating...no, that's not it...something about putting the students in different houses...from *Harry Potter*."

"Sorting?" Chloe said tremulously into the silence.

"Yes, that's it," said the person who had asked the question, at the same time as Theresa said, "Yes, all the incoming students have been, I believe the correct term is 'Sorted,' into 'Houses.' We had them do some kind of a test that's supposed to match their personality with their 'House,' but really it's just a way to split them into groups so that they all get funneled to the correct entrances to the freshman dorm. Anyway, the greeting committee will be representing the different 'Houses.' That sounds like something that maybe our younger faculty might have a better idea of how to handle than us old fogies. Let's see...Rowena, there you are. Is that something you think you could handle? Organizing the different 'Houses'? I think we're supposed to have, let's see"—she looked down at her notes—"'Heads of Houses' to greet the students. So I suppose you could be, um, let me see, the Head of, um..."

"Ravenclaw, obviously," I called out.

Half the faculty burst out laughing. Half looked befuddled.

"I suppose, if you want to," said Theresa. "Judging by the way some of you are laughing, I suppose there's some kind of a joke here?"

"The founder of Ravenclaw was also named Rowena," I explained. "And she was supposed to look kind of like me, too. Only I graduated from Indiana. My robes are Gryffindor red, not Ravenclaw blue."

Theresa looked even more confused. "I'll swap you," Mel shouted from the back. "I graduated from UNC. My thousand-dollar robes are celestial Tar Heel blue, which could also pass as Ravenclaw colors."

"Oh! That's very kind of you, um..."

"Mel. Melissa Wilson. Arabic."

"Oh, great. And I have you and Rowena down in the same shift, as well. So...let's move on to actually organizing this thing. If I call out your name, please come to the front of the room. Rowena and

Mel, consider your names already called. The rest of you are free to go."

Mel came and joined me as we made our way to the front of the auditorium. "Didn't realize I was going to be playing fucking dress-up for this," she said. "But whatever. As long as they're paying me. And you *do* look a bit like Rowena Ravenclaw."

"Yeah," I said. "I do. And like you said, whatever. As long as they're paying us."

8

AFTER A SHORT HUDDLE at the front of the auditorium with several of the other lucky winners of the Harry Potter Sweepstakes, we got ourselves Sorted into Houses and got shifts organized so that no one would have to spend all day standing in full regalia in the blazing sun, while also making an idiot out of themselves.

Mel and I agreed that she would take Ravenclaw and I would take Gryffindor, despite the felicitous circumstance of my name, since that seemed easier than swapping regalia. Coming up with Slytherin and Hufflepuff robes was a little more challenging, but we eventually found grads from Tulane (green) and Johns Hopkins (yellow) who were willing to take a shift at the front gates.

"I really feel like this is a productive use of my training," I said to Mel as we double-timed it from Bedford Hall to Saunders Hall, where the Department of Modern Languages was holding its pre-semester faculty meeting.

"Yeah," said Mel. "Hey, do you think Saunders Hall is named after the same Saunders as at UNC? Who was supposedly the head of a KKK chapter?"

"Highly possible. Would fit in nicely with Bedford and Lee."

"Yeah. Let's maybe not say anything about it to Chloe. Bet she's got enough on her plate already. Wouldn't want her to get all principled and quit and ruin her career."

"Okay," I said.

"She told me yesterday she was tenure-track. That the college got slammed a couple years ago for having, surprise surprise, zero African-American tenure-track or tenured faculty members, so they created a special position just to hire one. One. I'm sure that will erase centuries of injustice. And I think that's also kind of how I got hired. Not to a tenure-track position, unfortunately, but as part of this they also had it brought to their attention that they had, shall we say, a hostile atmosphere towards their gay students, and they decided to fix this by creating a task force to study the issue, and also, incidentally, to hire me, so that I can singlehandedly solve this problem for them. Not loving my chances, but at least it got me a job. The first time that being out, loud, and proud has ever gotten anything good for me, to be honest."

"Well, that's nice," I said. "I hope they don't take advantage of you too badly. It wouldn't surprise me if they wanted you for every committee and student outreach event they can cram into your schedule, even though you're contingent. Are you a VAP?"

"VAP," confirmed Mel. "And the pathetic thing is how fucking grateful I am even for that. You know how it is. The more qualified I got, the less they wanted to pay me. I was working as an adjunct last year while I was applying for every job I was remotely qualified for, and a bunch I wasn't as well, and it got so bad I was sure for a couple of months there I was going to be panhandling for spare change this fall between classes. You know, standing by the side of the road with a cardboard sign saying 'Homeless Iraq vet, please help.' Maybe in my doctoral robes and hood. They say the hoods were originally worn so that students could throw coins in them after their classes. Maybe we should start that tradition up again."

"I was just thinking that maybe the students would tip us tomorrow when we're bellhopping for them."

"Here's hoping. What's the time?" Mel pulled out her phone and glanced at it. "Oh shit. I think we're late. Is that Saunders up ahead?"

I squinted. "I *think* so."

Mel grinned. "Race you?"

"You're on."

9

"FUCK." MEL HELD THE door open for me, panting and wiping sweat off her face with her free hand. "You wiped the floor with me. Where the fuck did you learn to run like that...oh, hi, um, Theresa."

"Oh, there you are, Melissa, is it? And Rowena. We were just sending out a search party for you, in case you'd gotten lost and were wandering the back quad, sending out distress signals and flipping coins to find out who should eat whom."

"Nothing that dire," said Mel. "We just got held up by all the infighting over who had to represent Slytherin."

"I suppose that's another *Harry Potter* reference?" said Theresa. "I really must read those books one of these days. Maybe when my granddaughter is of an age to make it appropriate. Anyway, I trust you got it all sorted out? You both do seem like very capable young women. *And* excellent runners. I caught sight of that little footrace you ran across the quad. Quite impressive, both of you. And I must repeat Melissa's question, Rowena: where *did* you learn to run like that?"

Theresa winked, like maybe she had heard Mel's bad language and had found it amusing.

"It's a long story," I said. "But the short version is that my boyfriend—well, ex-boyfriend—used to make me go running with him."

"Until one day you outran him?" said Mel.

"Something like that."

"I'm sorry to hear that, but sometimes that's for the best," said Theresa, into a silence that was threatening to grow melancholy. "But what I was going to say to the both of you is that we have interdepartmental running competitions every semester. I'm sure the Modern Languages department would be thrilled to bits to have two such strong runners on the team. I'm afraid that Math has left us and everyone else in the dust for the past three years running. Haha, pun intended. Anyway, although I'll be leaving Modern Languages—temporarily, I hope!—for the Dean's office, of course it holds a special place in my heart, and I'd *love* to see you clean Evelyn from Math's clock in the under-fifty women's division. Actually, from what I just saw, you might be able to clean *everyone's* clock, including the men's. Wouldn't that be sweet for Modern Languages to win the overall trophy?"

"Heck yeah," said Mel. "Count me in."

"Um, me too," I said.

"Oh, fantastic. Anyway, as I was saying, I got elevated rather suddenly to the Dean's office this summer, as part of all this reorganization we're going through, so I'm afraid I won't have the pleasure of working directly with you two. And I'm very sorry about that, because after your interviews I was *so* looking forward to it, but just remember that you'll have a friend in the Dean's office. And today I'll be running my last department meeting, before Karen takes over as chair of the department. Oh, and here we are."

We stepped into a seminar-style classroom that was filled to overflowing with a table that had been designed for some other, bigger, room. Mel and I squeezed in and sidled sweatily past other faculty members until we got to the two remaining chairs, which were at the widest part of the table and thus could not actually be pulled out. After some acrobatics and sucking in our stomachs to Victorian corsetry proportions, we managed to sit down.

There was a round of introductions. Klaus, Akiko, and Jessica from my first interview were all there, as was Darryl from my second interview. There were half a dozen other people whose names I forgot as soon as they were uttered. Having a bad memory for names is a failing in a teacher, but it was a failing I had yet to overcome. Then there was a quick review of this semester's schedule, and other related business.

"Well, I think we're all well on our way to having a wonderful semester," said Theresa. "And so now I'd like to move on to discussing curriculum development. Oops, I'm sorry, Karen, I really should be turning the chair's duties over to you." She gave a smile to the woman sitting next to her at the head of the table.

Karen failed to smile back. Karen was short and squat and had wispy gray hair and the expression of someone suffering from terminal ill nature. She had only said half a dozen words, and already I was regretting the fact that she was replacing Theresa as chair. Theresa struck me as little bit silly, perhaps, but basically decent and even somewhat competent. Karen was already making my fists itch. I reminded myself that as an academic I was above such petty things.

"Yes, thank you, Theresa," said Karen, not sounding very grateful. "Of course we're all glad to have you here, supporting the department you've served so faithfully all these years, but I'm sure we can do very well without you. Oh! I didn't mean it like that." It was obvious from Karen's expression that she had meant it *exactly* like that. "I meant that we wouldn't want you to feel obliged to fit our department meetings into your busy schedule. I'm sure you'll find that the Dean's office provides you with more than enough to do." Karen's mouth, which I couldn't help but notice was wrinkled and sunken, pursed in resentment.

"I'm sure," said Theresa. "But I hope you'll continue to indulge me if I slip in occasionally. Anyway, I see we have curriculum development next on our agenda, and rightly so. I'm sure, especially with these up-and-coming young scholars we've just had the good fortune to hire"—she favored me, Mel, and Chloe with a warm smile—"that we can revamp our, to be honest, rather tired curriculum and turn it into something that will have the students flocking in like flies."

"Yes," said Karen. Her mouth pursed again, displaying all its wrinkles. How was it possible she was so unattractive? She couldn't have been much older than my mother, and I still saw my mother as a vigorous and, inasmuch as I could be aware of such things about my own mother, attractive woman. But Karen looked like she was already collapsing into herself, even though she was unhealthily plump. "Dave?" said Karen. "Why don't we start with you?"

The man sitting across from me twitched. He was small and tweedy and wore glasses that cried out for the application of the adjective "bespectacled."

"Well, you know that I've been working on creating more interdisciplinary course offerings for years, and expanding German into a number of cross-listed areas. Right now I'm working on a course on Social History and Industrial Technology," he said earnestly.

"That sounds promising," said Karen with a frown, while Mel jotted something down on her meeting agenda.

"I think so," said Dave, swelling up at this faint praise. "Owen—Owen Hughes—from Engineering and I are planning to create a course proposal for it this semester, to submit for approval next semester."

Mel turned her meeting agenda so that I could see what she had written, which was:

Social
History and
Industrial
Technology.

I hastily turned a laugh into a cough.

"Sorry," I said, when everyone looked at me. "Sometimes the AC makes me cough."

"Of course," said Karen, radiating a total lack of sympathy and understanding. "Well, if you're done coughing now, um, Rowena, is it? You'll want to listen carefully to the next item on the agenda, since it affects you. We're going to be revamping the FUCC—"

"The *what*?" I interrupted before I could stop myself.

"The FUCC." She was pronouncing it letter-by-letter, but still. "The French Undergraduate Core Curriculum," she explained. "And we'd like to have something similar developed for Russian."

"Um, sure," I said. At least it would be RUCC rather than FUCC.

"Arabic and Chinese, too," she said, giving Mel and Chloe stern looks, like she was expecting them to skive off this critical task.

"Sure," said Mel, while Chloe muttered, "Of course." Out of the corner of my eye, I could see Mel sketching "FUCC," "AUCC," "RUCC," and "CUCC" on the corner of her meeting agenda. She smiled to herself and drew a little line between FUCC and CUCC.

Karen was going on and on about the college's upcoming SACS accreditation and how we needed to prepare for that. Mel started sketching a surprisingly realistic, given her loudly declared sexual proclivities, cock and balls around FUCC and CUCC. I forced myself to look away and focus on Karen.

After we had all promised to redo or come up with a curriculum for our respective programs, there was an entirely pointless argument about the coffeemaker in the department common space. This was followed by an argument about whether or not to install new locks in the classroom doors.

"Campus Police are encouraging all the departments to install new locks that lock from the inside," said Theresa, who had taken over the meeting again after the coffeemaker argument had gone on long enough. "In case of active shooters."

"Surely that's not going to happen here," objected several people at once.

"No, of course not, but it makes Campus Police feel like they've done something about the problem," said Theresa.

"And you never know," put in Darryl. "Maybe the Gang of Six *will* decide to come after us filthy faculty members after all."

There were some groans and eye rolling. "I don't see why Campus Police haven't caught them already," said Darryl. "I mean, they're undergrads. How wily can they be?"

"Undergrads can be surprisingly wily," said Theresa. "But that's not the point. They have the right to free speech, just like everyone else. We can't sic the police on them just because we don't like what they're saying. Although I *do* cringe every time I see all those comma splices they litter their posts with. It makes me wonder *what* the English department is doing, if this is the kind of writing our students turn out."

"Maybe they're not actually our students," suggested Darryl.

"That *would* be a welcome development," said Theresa. "But in the meantime, keep an eye out for them, everyone, just in case. You'll recognize them by their comma splices."

There was a group laugh.

"And more seriously, I see that rumor has it that our darling little Nathan Willoughby is heading up the proposed Men's Protection Alliance protests against our Gamergate speaker this fall. Darryl, I believe he's in your Advanced French class this semester?"

"Yes, God help me," said Darryl.

"Well, keep an eye on *him* for sure, and see if you can, I don't know, lead him into the light or something. What that little pissant pipsqueak thinks he has to complain about, I don't know"—"Being called a pissant pipsqueak, presumably," said Darryl—"Yes, but, not to use a cliché, he was *asking* for it. Anyway, I don't know if there's anything we can do for or about him, but it makes me cringe to know that he's one of our majors. So see if you can make him see some sense, or, failing that, drive him out of the department. Let English have him."

"Where there are even more girls than here," said Darryl.

"I know. Funny thing, isn't it? How he's chosen to surround himself with women wherever he goes? And yet he *still* can't get laid, or so he claims in all his blog posts. You'd think he'd at least have the decency to shut up about it. Anyway, Mel, Chloe, Rowena, I don't want you to think that *all* our students are like this. Most of them are lovely. You just have to keep an eye out for the very occasional bad apple."

"No problem," I said. And then, at last, all the meetings were over.

10

AT 7:45 THE NEXT MORNING I was trotting across campus from the faculty parking behind the back quad to the main entrance in front of the front quad. In full regalia. It was a mere 75 degrees now, but temperatures were slated to hit the upper 90s by noon. So a fine day to stand outside in ankle-length polyester robes and a velvet tam.

I stopped to adjust my hood. A purely ceremonial item, it was supposed to drape across my shoulders and hang down below my waist in the back. There was a little claspy thing in the front to hold it in place. But the little claspy thing was totally inadequate for the brisk pace I was setting, and the hood kept slipping off.

"Rowena, right?" A middle-aged man in green Tulane robes stopped beside me to do some similar adjustments.

"Um, Keith, right? History?"

"You remembered! We must not be working you hard enough yet."

"Um..."

"I voted against this nonsense when it came up last semester, and so did everyone else with even a grain of sense, but somehow we got overruled. I don't even know how. I don't know any faculty members who thought it was a good idea. But seems like our power is being eroded more and more every year. I'm sure a fiat came down on high from Recruitment and Admissions or Student Development or the

Office of Babysitting and Spoonfeeding or whatever it's called now, so here we are. I don't see any of *those* people out here at the crack of dawn, prepared to spend the morning humiliating themselves and getting heatstroke."

"Yeah," I said. "Funny thing. And thanks, by the way. For agreeing to be Slytherin."

Keith shrugged. "Whatever. I've never actually read the books, although my kids made me take them to one of the movies. But I have no emotional involvement in this BS." He looked at me sideways. "I suppose you're going to tell me they're your favorite books in the world?"

"I'm a Russianist," I said. "My favorite books in the world were all written in Russian. If you're looking for something with magic in it, I recommend *Master and Margarita*. But these books are pretty good too, and the kids might get a kick out of this."

"Yeah," said Keith. "Too bad they're here for a rigorous liberal arts education, not to get a kick out of seeing their professors cavort around in garish costumes. Oh, hey. Is this all of us?"

Mel, in her sky-blue Tar Heel getup, and Daniel, a gangly man from Political Science in bright yellow Johns Hopkins robes, were hurrying towards us. Mel had a stack of posterboard in her arms.

"Call me an overachiever, but I thought if we're gonna do this, we should do this," she said. "So I stopped by the store last night and got posterboard and markers. I figured we could make posters for each of the houses, with—and this is why we want to do this—instructions for how to find the correct entrance to the dorm that they're supposed to use."

"Oh, right," said Keith. "We're supposed to working as traffic cops as well. Does anyone remember where the little buggers are supposed to go?"

I wrestled a copy of the instructions out from under my voluminous robes. Somehow I had ended up in charge of this ill-advised venture, which was probably supposed to make me feel good about myself as a go-getter who was fitting in well with the campus community, but actually boded very ill.

"All first-year students are housed in Jackson Hall," I read. I wondered if Jackson Hall was named after Andrew Jackson. So not a Confederate general, just a slave owner. Of course, in the US, as in Russia, pretty much anyone who had done anything worth naming a building after had been a slave owner. I wondered what future generations would say about us, and which of our actions would trigger outrage and furious revisions of history. I had my guesses, but there was just so much to choose from.

"Yeah, poor little kids," said Keith. "That place has no air conditioning, and there are constant complaints about mold. But it's tradition. Plus the college doesn't have the money to renovate anything. It's all going to hiring more Deans of Donations. Oh shit. Is that our first customer of the day?"

A car was pulling up to the entrance. It was decorated in crimson and cream streamers and balloons. A teenage face, barely visible behind all the braces and acne, stuck itself out the passenger side window.

"Whoa, this is *awesome!*" he said. "I'm Jacob. Wait, am I supposed to tell you my House? That's *sooooo* cool. Gryffindor."

I bounded forward. "Great to meet you, Jacob! I'm Professor Halley, the head of Gryffindor House, here to welcome you to Crimson College. First years are housed in Jackson Hall, and Gryffindors should check in at Entrance A. Which is, um..." I looked over at the others.

"Drive straight ahead and take a right at the T," said Keith. "There will be signs leading you straight to Jackson Hall from there. Entrance A is the first entrance you'll come to. There will be people there to direct you and help you unload your things."

"Wow, *really*? This is incredible! Thank you guys so much! I think this is the best day of my life! Hey, are you professors? Any of you from Math?"

"No, but when you get to the dorm, ask around for Professor Irving and Professor Arlington. Oh, and I think Professor Li will be there too. They're all from Math," Keith told him.

"Whoa, thanks so much! Man, college is overfulfilling all my expectations already! Did you get that, Mom?"

Jacob's mom nodded, and, with an almost equally manic grin as her son, pulled past us and headed in the direction of Jackson Hall.

"Does anyone else feel like Goofy welcoming the kiddies to Disneyworld?" asked Keith.

"Maybe a little," I said.

"Well hey, as I was telling Rowena yesterday, at least it's not *actual* panhandling, which was what I thought I was going to be doing this fall," said Mel. "Still got me some extra posterboard, though, just in case I need that 'Homeless Iraq Vet, Please Help' sign after all. I figure if nothing else, this'll be good practice for that. Okay, who likes to draw?"

It was quickly ascertained that the only person who liked to draw, or was even able to draw, was Mel herself. In short order she had turned out four very creditable posters, with the House logos and directions for check-in on each one.

"Yeah, whatever," she said, when we remarked on how good the posters were. "I'm lefthanded *and* a lesbian. Of course I have artistic talent. Oh shit. Is that another student?"

An SUV large enough to raise the global temperature by at least half a degree all on its own was pulling through the gates. It, too, was decorated with crimson and cream streamers and balloons, but the excited teenage face looking out the passenger window was holding up a Ravenclaw sign that was almost as good as Mel's.

"Guess this one's mine," she said. "Wish me luck!" And she danced up to the side of the car, waving her poster with enthusiasm that almost seemed real.

11

AFTER THAT THERE WAS a steady stream of cars that soon backed up into a logjam. A good half of them were decorated with Crimson College colors and/or the colors of the House the student had been Sorted into. The other half were resolutely not decorated, and the students and their parents let us know just how ridiculous they found all this. Several of the Slytherins refused their designation, and demanded to be allowed to check in at the Gryffindor entrance. When we told them they needed to check into their proper entrance, there were some toddler-style meltdowns, especially from the parents.

"Imagine teaching grade school," said Keith. "At least we only have to deal with parents once or twice a year. Is it ten yet? Can we go?"

The welcoming committee had been organized into two-hour shifts. It was now 9:55, and our relief shift was trickling in. We arranged robe swaps one by one behind a tree—wouldn't want the students to see us out of regalia, even though we were fully dressed underneath—and by 10:10 I had handed the reins of the welcoming committee over to Evelyn (Professor Irving) from Math.

"Thanks, everyone, for letting us use your robes," she said, trying to get my Indiana/Gryffindor robes to look a little less sweaty and crumpled. "We promise we'll take good care of them. Oh crap, is that a student?"

"They just keep on comin'," said Mel. "Shit, I think I feel something crawling up my leg." She pulled up her pant leg. "Gross! A tick." She flicked it away. "Maybe you better stand on the road instead of the grass."

We all looked at the heat shimmers that were already building up on the blacktop.

"I think I might take my chances with the grass," said Evelyn.

"Have fun," I told her, and set off in the direction of Jackson Hall to put in my shift as a bellhop.

It was already well into the 80s, and humid, even though the sun was beating down. So, your typical August day in Georgia. I wondered if we could arrange some kind of a shade tent for the poor suckers who would be working the 12-2 shift by the front gate. A golf cart from Facilities Services was driving towards me. I flagged it down.

"Sorry," said the man driving it. "We can't give rides to faculty. Our insurance won't let us. Plus we're going the wrong way. Jackson Hall is that way."

"That's fine," I said. "I was just wondering about getting some kind of a tent or shade pavilion set up by the front gate."

"Yeah." The driver sucked on his teeth a little. "We're supposed to start running them a regular supply of ice water starting now, but a tent wouldn't be a bad idea. I'll look into it...what the hell! Watch it!

A black SUV with a conspicuous lack of school decorations, Crimson or otherwise, shot past us, so close it almost clipped the golf cart.

"Jeez," said the golf cart driver. "What's the rush, man? It's not like you're going to get into your dorm any faster." And indeed, the SUV was now stopped and waiting in line to pull forward to the unloading zone, stuck behind ten other cars.

"Some people," said the golf cart driver, shaking his head. "Always gotta hog the road. I'll look into the tent."

"Thanks," I told him, and continued plodding up the hill to Jackson Hall.

"You're late!" What was Dorothy doing here? Actually, now that I thought about it, she was probably the mastermind behind this scheme.

"We had to do a changeover of the robes, and then walk over," I told her.

"Well...I suppose so, but...some people are *very* tired! We've been here since eight this morning, and it's already almost ten thirty!"

"Yeah," I said. "Where should I go?"

"Weren't you at the front gate? What House were you representing? Let's put you at that entrance, in case you get some of the same students."

"Gryffindor," I said. "Entrance A. Is that it?" I walked over to where a long line of cars was waiting to get to the unloading zone in front of doors festooned with crimson and cream signs that said "Welcome Gryffindors! Welcome to Crimson College! Entrance A" before Dorothy could irritate me any further.

When I got there, I found Chloe holding a chilled water bottle to her forehead. Sweat was beading up around the scars on her temples, and soaking the back of her blouse.

"How's it going?" I asked.

"I'm pretty sure I didn't go through all that college to be a bellhop," she said. "Maybe tomorrow I can dress up in a maid's uniform and serve all these white kids some hors d'eouvres, and say 'That's okay honey chile, you just come to Mammie,' when they fall and hurt themselves."

"Yeah," I said. "So what's the procedure?"

"We take turns greeting them when they pull up to the unloading zone, and offer to help carry their stuff into their dorm room. They're supposed to know what room they're in, but we've got a list somewhere too…here it is." She fished a damp printout out of her pocket. "Don't know if they've got one for you somewhere, but I'm guessing not. This whole thing has been a, I don't want to say what, from beginning to end, and I'm here till noon. I volunteered to take two shifts at the unloading zone so I wouldn't have to dress up in robes and make a fool of myself by the front entrance. How was that, by the way?"

Apparently heat and aggravation were making Chloe more voluble than usual. "Hot," I said. "Humiliating."

"I imagine. Oh jeez. That next car pulling up is mine. You can shadow me for the first one, see what we do, and then start taking your turn on your own."

A Lexus SUV pulled up into the unloading zone. A family of five poured out, looking around with mingled exhaustion, trepidation, and excitement.

"Welcome to Crimson College," said Chloe, deadpan. "I'm Professor Taylor. Do you need help with your bags?"

12

"MY NAME'S TAYLOR TOO! Only it's my first name."

"That's nice." Chloe was too hot and exhausted to summon up a smile. She had the body of a true academic, meaning unfit. If she were a sidekick in a Nancy Drew story, she'd be labeled "pleasantly plump." But as the heroine of her own story, she was just obviously overheated and sick of hauling baggage for overprivileged white kids, no matter how friendly and well-intentioned they were. I could practically see the thought hanging over her head that she hadn't spent the last decade becoming an expert in Chinese characters and pitch tones in order to work as someone's servant.

"Do you know what room you're in?" I asked Taylor. She was also "pleasantly plump," with blonde curls ringing her face. After one minute outside, she was already turning a sweaty pink.

"Ummm...149, I think..."

"The first floor is for boys," said Chloe, less patiently than maybe she would have liked. "Is it 249?"

Taylor pulled out a pink smartphone that probably cost as much as my entire grocery budget for last year. I reminded myself that this year I would be able to splash out and buy real food, including fresh vegetables, and the reason I would be able to do that was because of this job. She scrolled through her messages with a frown of concentration, and said, "Oh, yeah, 249. Is that on the second floor? Is there an elevator? Because I've, like, got a lot of stuff."

"It's on the second floor, but the elevator's been shut down for move-in," Chloe told her.

"Oh my!" Taylor's mother was like a larger, older version of her, right down to the blonde ringlets that danced around her face when she shook her head. "Why on earth would they do something like that?"

"The elevator can't take the strain of hauling everyone's stuff up and down," said Chloe. "That's why we're here. To help you out."

"Well, that's very nice of you," said Taylor's mother. "And you say you're professors?"

"Uh-huh," said Chloe. "I'm from Chinese. And Professor, um..." She looked over at me desperately.

"Hi," I said. "I'm Professor Halley. Russian."

"Oh *wow*," said Taylor. "Then I think you must be my professor, Professor Taylor! I signed up to take first-year Chinese, and I remember that the professor had the same name as me! Is that you?"

"It is," said Chloe. "Shall we get your stuff moved out? People are waiting."

And in fact, the line backed up behind Taylor's SUV was getting ever longer. The incoming first year class was only about 750 students, which was nothing by the standards of the colleges I had attended, but they were all trying to move into one dorm on one Friday morning.

Taylor's family started unloading the car. Soon there was an impressive pile of suitcases, boxes, and crates stacked up on the sidewalk.

"Wow," said Taylor. "I didn't realize I had so much stuff. Now I'm wondering how it's all going to fit in my dorm room."

"I'll go see if I can get a cart," said Chloe. "And if that's everything, you can pull your car forward and make room for the next person in line."

Chloe disappeared into Jackson Hall. Taylor's father hopped back into his SUV and pulled it forward, into the line of cars heading off to the parking lot.

As soon as the space in front of the loading zone was clear, the same black SUV that had almost run me down on the walk over here pulled into it with a screech of tires, coming to a stop so close to the curb that Taylor and I instinctively jumped back.

"Goodness!" exclaimed Taylor's mother. "Watch out!"

A heavily tinted window rolled down. "Why are you just standing there!" a woman demanded, sticking her head out the passenger window. "People are waiting!"

"We're waiting for our cart," Taylor's mother told her.

"Well, go get it! Chris. Chri-is! Christopher. Stop fooling around with that damn game and start unloading your crap."

Taylor's mother made an involuntary face. I could feel my own face copying her.

"Taylor, honey," said her mother. "Why don't you go see if you can help Professor Taylor get that cart. And maybe find a Resident Advisor so that you can check in and get your keys. You can't get into your room without keys!"

"What, she's not an RA?" the woman in the black SUV demanded, pointing at me. "Then what's she doing here?"

"I'm part of the welcoming and unloading committee," I said. "Professor Halley. Russian."

The back door of the SUV opened and a skinny—actually, the more appropriate term would be "weedy"—boy peered out. He was so fair his blond eyebrows disappeared into his skin, which had an unhealthy pallor that took on an overheated pink tinge as soon as he stuck his face out into the open air.

"Russian?" he asked. "Are you my professor? I'm registered to take first year Russian."

"In that case yes, you'll be in my class," I told him. "Welcome to Crimson. Do you have a lot of stuff?"

The boy shrugged and poured out of the SUV. When he unfolded onto his feet, he revealed himself to be about my height (5'10"), but much less fit. Everything about him screamed "gamer," from the pasty skin to the oversized phone he clutched like a precious talisman in his right hand.

"I'm Chris," he mumbled, looking down at his feet.

"*Lovely*," said Taylor's mother, with forced enthusiasm. "Maybe you and Taylor could go check in together, while the rest of us unload your car. I'm sure your mom will appreciate the help."

"She's not my mother," Chris muttered, while the woman in the front laughed, not very mirthfully, and said, "Oh, I ain't his mother. I'm just his stepmother. Well, what are you waiting for, Chris? Go check in! Room 116, remember? Go get going before you forget!"

She made impatient shooing motions with her hand. Chris looked at her, then at me, then at Taylor, swallowed, and started off uncertainly in the direction of the entrance to Jackson Hall. Taylor trotted over to join him, and, smiling with what sure looked like genuine warmth, told him how excited she was to be starting college. Chris muttered a one-syllable response and looked the other way.

"I swear to God, I don't know what to do with that boy," said his stepmother, getting all the way out of the SUV. "Least he don't have a lot of stuff. And what he does got, is only 'cause I made him take it. If it'd been up to him, he woulda showed up here with nothing but his damn games."

Taylor's mother gave her an uncertain smile. "Why don't we help you unpack while they check in," she said.

"Why don't I go see if I can get you a cart," I suggested.

Chris's stepmother ignored me, which I took as tacit acceptance, and so I left them to go explore the glories of Jackson Hall.

After the blazing sun on the pavement outside, the lobby of Jackson Hall was blindingly dark. Unfortunately, it was not frigidly cool. Apparently the rumors that it didn't have air conditioning were true. Astonishing that students and their parents put up with that.

I saw Taylor and Chris standing nervously in front of the lobby desk, which was unstaffed. Over in the corner, Chloe was having an argument with a boy holding an RA-looking clipboard over a shabby hotel luggage cart. I went over to them.

"Well, what are we supposed to do?" Chloe was demanding. "Haul all their stuff up there with our bare hands?"

"It's the second floor," the boy told her. It was a rare student who could irritate me on first sight, but this boy had already managed to. There was something about his smile that made me want to wipe it off his face, and then wipe the floor with him. "We've been over this before. You won't be able to take the cart up the stairs anyway."

"Yeah, but we can use it to haul all their stuff into the lobby in one go," Chloe argued. "That makes it much faster to clear the loading zone."

"I'm sorry, but that cart is reserved for first-floor residents only," said the boy. His smirk conveyed just how much he was enjoying telling her no.

"Are you supposed to be checking students in?" I asked him. "Because there are a couple of students waiting to check in. And I've got a student waiting to move into a first-floor room. Can I have the cart?"

His gaze slid from Chloe over to me, lingering just a little too long on my breasts. I took mean-spirited pleasure in the thought that I was wearing my most supportive sports bra. Combined with my natural state as an A cup, that meant there really wasn't anything to see in that department, even with my shirt soaked with sweat. When his gaze finally met mine, I held it for a second before giving him a similar "elevator eyes" perusal.

"Nathan Willoughby," I read off his name tag when I was done. "We were *just* talking about you in yesterday's faculty meeting. I'm sure everyone will be happy to hear how helpful you've been."

"Um, yeah." The self-satisfaction in his expression slipped, to be replaced by something much needier and weaker. "Um, yeah, you can, um, like, have the cart, I guess."

"*Great*," I said. "Now why don't you get over to the desk. I think Taylor and Chris have been waiting long enough."

"Um, yeah," said Nathan, and scurried off. I tried to pretend I didn't feel satisfaction over my victory in this meaningless pissing contest, and failed. I did like to win.

13

"LET'S GO," I HISSED to Chloe as soon as Nathan had gone, with ill grace, to go check Taylor and Chris in. I grabbed the cart and started dragging it towards the door.

The cart turned out to be almost as annoying as Nathan, with wheels that all wanted to wheel in opposing directions. It took me and Chloe three tries to get it moving in the right direction.

"I don't know what's wrong with that boy," said Chloe, as soon as we were outside. "He's been a complete pain in the you-know-what since he came on shift an hour ago. The other RAs will let anyone use a cart, but he has this rule about only for the first floor, since they can't go up the stairs."

"Whatever," I said. "*We're* the professors. Let's get Taylor's stuff loaded onto it, and then I'll hang onto it for Chris."

But that plan ran into snag when Chris's stepmother, now joined at the curb by Chris's equally unpleasant father, tried to commandeer the cart for themselves. When I refused to argue with them anymore and started loading Taylor's stuff onto the cart, Chris's father flushed so bright red I thought he might be about to have a stroke. Instead of collapsing, though, he made to grab the cart away from me.

"Dad!" Chris came shuffling over. "Dad, it's okay. She was here first." He pointed his thumb at Taylor, carefully not looking at her.

"That cart is for the first floor!" Nathan came bustling over, waving his clipboard and directing outrage in every direction except at me.

"You see!" Chris's father actually began unloading Taylor's stuff from the cart. "This is *our* cart!"

"Dad..." Chris was practically melting from mortification.

I contemplated confronting Chris's father. Did I want to get into a screaming fight with a student's parent my first week on my new job? No, no, I did not. Guile and shame seemed better weapons.

"Why don't we start moving Taylor's stuff into the dorm?" I said. "Chris, would you be gallant enough to help us?"

"What?" Chris looked like he'd never had the adjective "gallant" applied to him, which was probably true. "Um, yeah, I guess. Sure. What do you, like, want me to do?"

"Just start carrying stuff up. Room 249, right?"

"Right," said Taylor. "Come on! Thanks so much, Chris! That's so nice of you."

"Very nice of you," repeated Taylor's mother. "You see, Taylor? You've only just gotten here, and already you've made friends!"

Chris looked lost, like he'd never been called someone's friend before, but, ignoring his father's demand that he help unload his own stuff, he gathered up an armful of plastic crates and followed Taylor back into the dorm.

By the time we all got back from our first run to Taylor's room, Chris's father and stepmother had loaded all his stuff onto the cart, and, with Nathan's help, were trying to guide it through the front door.

"Here," I said. "Your front wheel's gotten twisted around. Let me straighten it out for you." I tried to nudge the misbehaving front wheel into the correct position. Just as I got it almost straight, Nathan gave the cart a sharp push. My shoe caught in the wheel, which suddenly jumped forward, giving my leg a hard twist and sending me staggering against the door frame.

"Oh my! Are you okay?" Taylor's mother, who was right behind me, caught me, saving me from going sprawling full-length on the floor. "Stop!" she shouted at Nathan. "Stop pushing!"

Nathan and Chris's father jerked the cart back away from the door, sending me staggering again. "Stop!" shouted Taylor's mother. "Stop, stop, stop!"

I was now hanging onto the door frame with both hands, my left leg twisted in a ridiculous position that, if I fell, looked guaranteed to twist my knee beyond all repair. "My shoe," I said to Taylor's mother. "Can you slip my shoe off?"

Nathan and Chris's father had finally stopped monkeying around with the cart and were standing there, doing nothing to help me. Taylor's mother gave them a disapproving look, and then hurried over to kneel down and untie my sneaker.

"The laces are caught in the wheel," she said. "Just a second...there we go! Are you all right?"

I pulled myself upright and put my foot gingerly down onto the floor. "A little sore," I said. "Not too bad."

"Well, thank goodness! You could have really messed up your knee. Let me just get the lace out of the wheel...here you go. Good as new. Well, almost. The lace is all black and dirty."

"That's okay," I said. "That's hardly the worst thing that's happened to it."

I limped over to an elderly couch in the middle of the lobby and, trying not to wince, carefully put my shoe back on. I hadn't felt or heard anything tear, but my knee had definitely been twisted more than was healthy.

"He did it deliberately!" Taylor's mother whispered in indignation, once Nathan and Chris's father had trundled the cart past us and down the first-floor corridor. "They both did! I *saw* them do it!"

"Yeah," I said. "Real prize specimens there, huh?"

"And honestly..." Taylor's mother was still speaking in a half-whisper, "I know it's very nice of you to come help us out and all, and we really appreciate it, but it seems a little, I don't know, *undignified,* I'd say, to have professors unloading students' things. And even a little inappropriate, frankly. I mean, you and Professor Taylor seem perfectly nice, and I'm sure Taylor is in good hands with you, but what if you'd been men? I don't like the idea of men, even professors, knowing where her dorm room is, not to mention going into her room and messing with her stuff. What, is she supposed to have a bunch of weird old men—sorry, I don't mean any offense to professors, but you know what I mean; I mean, some of them *can* be very weird, or at least, mine were—a bunch of weird old men unpacking her underwear and toiletries and hanging up her summer dresses? It's just, I don't know..."

"I know," I said. "It's creepy, that's what it is. *I* certainly wouldn't have wanted any of my professors coming into my dorm room and messing with my things when I was an undergrad. But I don't make those kinds of decisions. They just pay me to carry them out."

"I'm sure, honey—I mean Professor Halley, I'm *so* sorry, I just, it just slipped out..."

"It's okay," I said. "I'm a Georgia native. I answer best to 'honey,' followed closely by 'darlin',' and 'oh, Rowena, bless your little heart.' 'Professor' sounds like it belongs to someone else." I pulled my shoe on and stood up. "Shall we go check on what they're getting up to in our absence?"

"Oh, Lord, honey, I'm sure it's nothing good," said Taylor's mother. "Let's go rescue them before they go unpacking in the wrong room entirely. Room 249, right?"

"249," I confirmed, and, limping, headed up the stairs.

14

WE GOT TAYLOR AND CHRIS moved in, and then there was Braydon, and then there was Noah, and then there was Emma, and then there was Caitlyn, Katie, and Katrina, and then there were some more, but I was no longer in a state to remember names. My knee was aching continuously by that point, with sharp jolts of pain whenever I tried to turn while putting my weight on it. I was also soaked in sweat, and had a pounding headache. My only consolation, if consolation it could be called, was that Chloe looked worse.

"Not sure this is worth it," she said. "Not sure even tenure is worth this. I thought I would do *anything* to get tenure, but I'm already full of doubts. And you're not even tenure-track, right?"

"Right." I limped out to the curb by the loading zone. No new cars were approaching. "Just a VAP on a nine-month appointment. Are we done? Can we go yet? Who's in charge here?"

"Didn't they put you in charge?" said Chloe.

"Yeah. Of the faculty welcoming committee, at least. So I'm declaring us done with welcoming people." I limped over to where a knot of people from Residence Life and Facilities Maintenance were standing in a small patch of shade. "Is that it?" I asked.

One of the Facilities Services men gave me a look full of pity. "I reckon it is for you, hon," he said. "You go on and get out of here. If anyone shows up late, we'll take care of 'em."

"We still have three more students to move in." It was Nathan, who had appeared out of nowhere, wielding his clipboard.

"Have they shown up?" I asked.

"No, but we can't just *leave*," said Nathan. "You're supposed to be the faculty welcoming committee! What kind of example are you setting for students by just leaving?!"

"One called to say they got caught in traffic in Atlanta and won't be here for another hour," said Tricia, the representative from Res Life who was running Entrance A. "I don't know about the others."

"It's already after three," I said. "We were supposed to be done here at two. And I'm injured, and Chloe—Professor Taylor—is about to collapse from heat stroke, and we've got classes to prep for Monday. We need to leave."

"Students have class on Monday too," said Nathan.

"Yeah," I said. "As someone with more than ten years of college under my belt, I can tell you it's a very different thing. If any of the other faculty want to hang around for the stragglers, that's fine, but unless you really, really need us here, Chloe and I are leaving."

"Well...you *have* stayed more than hour past when you were supposed leave...I suppose we could manage..." said Tricia.

"Thanks," I said before she could rescind her statement, and limped back to Chloe with the good news.

"Now I just need to go down to the entrance and tell everyone to go home and get my robes back," I said.

"You look like you shouldn't be walking on that leg," said Chloe. "Do you want me to, um, get my car and give you a ride or something?"

"Well...if you don't mind..."

"Professor Halley! Professor Taylor!" It was Taylor's family, in their SUV. Taylor's mother had rolled down the window and was calling to us.

"Are you still here?" she asked.

"About to leave," I told her.

"Well...your leg looks pretty bad. Do you need a ride?"

"Are you going anywhere near the main entrance?" I asked.

"We're about to go get some lunch. We can drop you off there, easy as pie. Do you need a ride there too, Professor Taylor?"

"That's okay," Chloe told us. "My car's around back. See you all later." She turned and started walking away, her shoulders drooping from exhaustion.

"Dean—my husband—can move into the back if you'd like the front seat, Professor Halley," said Taylor's mother.

"That's okay," I told her. "The back is fine."

"If you don't mind. It might be a bit of a squeeze—we're giving Chris a ride too."

It was indeed a bit of a squeeze. Taylor's two younger siblings were in the far back, and Taylor and Chris were in the center row of seats, with an empty middle seat between them. After some awkward negotiation, Taylor scooted over into the middle, right up against Chris, giving me the seat by the door. Although it was roomy enough, I still was acutely aware that I was sitting there drenched in sweat while practically touching a student. Taylor appeared unfazed, but Chris was giving me sideways looks of doubt from the other side of the vehicle.

"Do you have any suggestions for good places to eat, Professor Halley?" Taylor's mother asked, once we were all buckled in and moving again.

"Actually, no," I admitted. "I'm almost as new here as you. I just got here last week. Although I've heard there's a sandwich shop called O'Reilly's that's good. Might be busy right now, though. If they're still open, that is."

"I know, it's past three o'clock. But we'll take our chances. Dean, honey, can you look up O'Reilly's on your phone? We like to avoid the big chains, try out local places when we can. And can we invite you to join us? You look like you could use some lunch or whatever we want to call this meal yourself. I know Taylor's about to pass out from hunger, aren't you, sweetie? And Chris too. His parents already left...I guess they had to get home right away, didn't they, hon? So we said we'd take him out with us. That RA, the one who wasn't, well, very nice, he told us the campus cafeteria is open today, but they'd already closed by the time we were done unpacking and getting everything put away. Apparently there's some kind of a little store where you can get snacks and stuff, and that RA, he offered to share his lunch with Chris, but there wasn't anything for the rest of us, and after all that we wanted a real meal, didn't we, everyone? And we wanted to see a bit more of Greenfields while we were here. So since Chris's parents had already left—well, they had to leave, I understand, I really do, but it must be very hard for you, Chris, to be just dumped here by yourself, your first day of college and all."

"It's okay," muttered Chris. "I'm used to it."

"I know, but that's no reason not to try to make this day a little bit more special, is it? And it *was* nice of that RA, what's his name—"

"Nathan," muttered Chris.

"That's right, Nathan, I mean, it was nice of him to offer to share his lunch with you, but I know how boys eat, and frankly, he doesn't seem like the kind of person you want to get too close to, Chris, honey, if you don't mind me saying so."

"He seemed nice enough to me," muttered Chris, looking down at his lap.

"Yes, well, I'm sure he has plenty of good points, but he was *quite rude* to his professors, and, well, women in general, and that's just not something I can tolerate. Taylor, I hope he's not your RA while you're here, or if he is, try to stay away from him. If it's a problem, don't hesitate to ask for a new room, somewhere outside of his jurisdiction, sugar."

"Hopefully it won't come to that," said Taylor, who looked torn between apprehension and hilarity at the prospect.

"Yes, of course, moving is such a pain, and it's so nice that you've already made friends in your wing of the dorm—we're *so glad* to get to know you better, Chris—but if it does, don't hesitate. I won't hear of anyone harassing my little girl! And Professor Halley, I know it's a lot to ask, but if you could keep an eye out for her..."

"Of course," I said. "And, just between us, I've already heard, shall we say, unhappy murmurs about Nathan amongst the faculty. I don't think he has a lot of friends there. So falling in with him and his crowd might not be the best thing to do if you want to build good relations with your professors and have a smooth time of it here."

"Wow! Thank you for telling us that, Professor. You see, Taylor, that's why it pays—*one* of the reasons why it pays—to build good relationships with your professors. They'll give you handy little tips like that that can make things a lot easier for you."

"And we'll write good letters of recommendation for you when it comes time to apply for scholarships or study abroad programs or grad school," I said.

"That too! So anyway, we'd love to have you join us for lunch, Professor Halley, if you're free."

"That's very kind of you," I said. "But I'm afraid I've got to rescue my robes and get them home. I'll probably see you tomorrow at the welcome picnic, though."

"Oh, of course! Rescue your robes?"

"My doctoral regalia," I explained, pointing to where the welcoming committee by the front gate was packing up. "The red robes are mine. I need to get them back. I wonder if they can be dry cleaned?"

"Gosh, yes, I hadn't thought about that," said Taylor's mother. "I suppose they're not cheap, are they?"

"The ones in university colors normally come in at about a thousand bucks," I told her. "So I hope nothing bad has happened to them. If you could just drop me off here, that would be great. Thanks so much for the ride."

"No problem, Professor Halley, and see you tomorrow at the picnic!" Taylor and her mother both waved goodbye as they drove past me. Chris watched me without waving, his head turning to follow me until the SUV pulled through the gates and disappeared onto the main road.

"Jesus, what happened to you? You look like shit." Mel came over, her arms full of posters.

"An unfortunate incident with a cart. Twisted knee."

She winced. "Ouch. Look, I've got your robes over there with mine. You want to watch over them while I go get my car? I can give you a ride back to the parking lot. Oh, and hey: I bet you could use this." She overhand-tossed me a chilled bottle of water.

"Wow. Both would be great."

"Drink up, then. I'll be back with transport before you're done. And then this whole thing will be behind us. We can look back on it and laugh."

"Yeah," I said. "I'm laughing already."

15

BY THE TIME MEL PICKED me up in a Jeep Cherokee that had seen better days, and probably better decades, my knee was so stiff I wasn't sure I was going to be able to shift gears.

"You okay to get home?" she asked.

"What's the alternative? Walk? I'm sorry. I didn't mean to snap. I'm just tired."

"First of all, that wasn't snapping. That was just a normal conversation. Do you even know how to snap?"

"I was going to say yes, but I guess not."

"Yeah, I didn't think so. Where do you live?"

"Peachtree Estates."

"No shit? Me too. I guess it's the only decent place in town for someone on a contingent faculty budget. Surprised we haven't seen each around before now."

"I'm on the back side of Building G."

"Okay, I'm in Building A. But still. Once your knee heals up, we should go running together. But in the meantime, why don't I give you a ride home, and then I can pick you up tomorrow and bring you over for the picnic."

"Gosh," I said. "That's really nice. You don't have to do that."

"Well, maybe I'm treating others as I'd like to be treated, if the need should ever arise. So no pressure, but the offer's open."

"Well..." I flexed my knee and hissed involuntarily in pain. "Okay. Jeez. This is really bothering me."

"You want me to drive you straight to Urgent Care?"

"What are they going to do that I can't do myself? I don't think anything's broken. I don't even think anything's torn, at least not badly. It's just strained in the wrong place. I'll go home and put it up with some ice on it...scratch that. I don't have any ice. I'll just go home and put it up."

"I'll bring you some ice," said Mel.

"You really don't have to do that."

"I'm not doing it because you're compelling me, like some dark vampire lord or something. I'm doing it because this is already looking like a major shit show, and I figure we could both use someone to watch our backs. So that's what I'm offering to do."

"Um, okay. Much appreciated."

"Great. Let's go."

We drove back through campus and out the front gates onto College Drive and through the main drag of Greenfields, Georgia, past the big box stores, the car dealer, and the random collection of marginal businesses that got sketchier and sketchier as we drew closer to Peachtree Estates.

"I never asked," Mel said abruptly, as we waited at the light to turn onto Peachtree Avenue. The street sign was new and had a large peach painted on it, making an almost obscene contrast with the smoke shop to our left and the rundown pawn shop to our right. "Your friend. The one who got shot. How's he doing?"

"Okay, I guess. I haven't heard anything from him since. He's not...ours is a fraught relationship."

"Yeah. One of those." The light changed and Mel took a left. "Being deployed doesn't help," she said once we were on the brand-new blacktop of Peachtree Avenue.

"Yeah...he's not deployed, technically. He's a journalist. An investigative reporter who specializes in war crimes. He used to be in OMON; you know, the Russian riot police/special forces units, until he got disillusioned and joined the opposition. Now he's reporting from the war in the Donbass, and he can't go back to Moscow. There are some people there who have issued some pretty credible death threats. Plus he's on the government's shit list."

"Fuck," said Mel.

"We used to be engaged," I told her. "Until he broke it off. You know the drill: 'I'm doing it for *you*, I'm thinking of *you*, it's not safe so you have to leave, blah blah blah.' We didn't speak for almost a year. But now we're back in communication. At least sometimes. I don't know if that's better or not. No, that's not true. Not knowing what was going on with him was torture. Anything would be better than that. But he doesn't want to get back together as, you know, a couple, and I already kind of have another boyfriend anyway. No, I *definitely* already have another boyfriend. Who also teaches Arabic, by the way. He's just starting a job at the DLI."

"No shit? That's where I started out. I ran away from home—you can imagine what it was like; my family's total trailer trash from South Carolina, and they didn't know what to do with me any more than I knew what to do with them—so I got the hell out of there as soon as I could and did the one thing I could think of, and enlisted. I know, such a cliché, right? The butch lesbian who ran off and joined the military. And a lot of it sucked, it really did. But they sent me to the DLI and taught me Arabic, and...here I am. Oh, and here we go. Building G, right?"

"Right. Apartment 303."

"Shit. That's the third floor, right?"

"Yep."

"I'll carry your stuff up for you."

"Um...thanks."

"You sit down with your leg up and don't move," she said, after shepherding me into the apartment. "I'll be right back with some ice."

"I really appreciate it."

"Yeah, and I know you'd do the same for me."

"Well...yeah."

"No worries, then. And you can pay me back by reading up on the latest exploits of the Gang of Six while I'm off running errands. I heard they put up a new blog post today, but I haven't managed to read it yet. I wonder if they know they've gotten a new fan? Though it sounds like a lot of the faculty are glued to their blog at this point. And the best part is that we never would have heard of them if they hadn't made such a point of refuting everything they're saying at all the meetings and training sessions."

"Maybe it was their secret plan all along," I said. "Maybe they're really from the Dean's office, and this was their way of getting themselves some free publicity."

"I'd like to think that anyone from the Dean's office, even an assistant dean, would know how to write without all those fucking comma splices, but maybe not. They are deans, after all."

"Or maybe it's part of their cunning disguise," I said.

"Yeah. Tell you what: you put your literary training to good use and analyze the latest post, and tell me what you think when I get back."

"It's a deal," I said.

16

ONCE MEL LEFT, FEVRONIA came creeping out from under the bed, gave me a sideways glare for lying on the floor with my foot propped up, and disappeared back to her hiding place. Resigning myself to not getting any affection from my pet, I got out my phone and brought up the website for the Gang of Six.

It looked even more amateur today than it had previously, with poor-quality graphics that had been distorted to fit into the header, and yellow text in an almost unreadable font. I wondered if that was a deliberate aesthetic choice on the part of the creators as a way of making a statement about the opacity of information or textual representation or something like that, or they just thought it looked cool and hadn't considered its ability to fulfill its communicative task, i.e., being read.

In glaring red block caps, the headline of the latest blog post read:

GUNS ON CAMPUS! GAMERGATE HEROINE'S VISIT MAY BE CALLED OFF

In an obvious attempt to cover up their problems with diversity and inclusion the campus administration invited Miriam Chen to speak on campus this fall. Miriam Chen was one of the women targeted in the Gamergate scandal, her boyfriend posted nude pictures of her online after she broke up with him, she was targeted by other gamers after joining Anita Sarkeesian in criticizing the portrayal of women in games and gamer culture. Miriam had to leave her house, she was doxxed by her boyfriend, angry gamers or people claiming to be gamers because we believe that REAL gamers would never act like that started sending her rape and death threats.

Now Crimson College is trying to rebrand itself as a diverse "safe space," it invited Miriam to speak this fall about contemporary feminism and gaming, but the event might be canceled because of protests by the Men's Protection Alliance which is claiming that Miriam and discussions of sexism are sexist. We also just heard word that there MAY have been a threat to shoot Miriam, some anonymous students are threatening to bring guns to the event. According to our sources they claim they are saying they will only carry the guns as a symbolic protest but guns on campus often turn into school shootings.

WILL OUR COLLEGE ADMINISTRATION DO ANYTHING TO PROTECT US? OR ARE WE GOING TO BE GUNNED DOWN LIKE THE STUDENTS AT VIRGINIA TECH, SANDY HOOK AND TOO MANY OTHER SCHOOLS TO COUNT?

"Holy fucking shit," I said out loud. No wonder the campus administration was getting their collective undies in a bundle. One could almost hear the sound of screaming brakes as applications from the children of wealthy parents came to a screeching halt.

"You might think that this isn't our problem," I said to where Fevronia was hiding under the bed. "But it is. Not only would being shot put a real crimp on my ability to buy cat food, but if I want to keep my job, crappy as it is, I need the college to stay solvent."

Fevronia came out, gave me a firm head butt, and skulked off to the kitchen. The sound of her gulping down cat food was followed shortly by the sound of her barfing it all back up.

"That's the spirit!" I called to her. Then I continued to lie on my back and wait for Mel to return.

Mel, showing that she was actually an angel in disguise, not only brought me ice and a knee brace, but cleaned up Fevronia's vomit as well.

"It's just a little cat vomit," she said. "Hardly the worst thing I've dealt with. Besides, I owe you for making me laugh"—I had read the blog post out loud to her in my best reciting-Russian-poetry voice—"and you look damn cute lying on the floor. Oh shit. That probably counts as sexual harassment, doesn't it?"

"That's okay," I said. "In my experience, only men are capable of sexual harassment. In women it's mainly harmless."

"Jeez. I don't know how to take that. I was hoping for tough."

"You're tough," I said. "Just not in a creepy way."

"Okay. I'll take that. You gonna be okay here by yourself? You need me to get you some supper? Do a safety check later?"

"Now you're just being sweet," I said. "Almost girly."

"Shut your mouth," she said. "Okay, I'm outie, but I'll check up on you later tonight, and I'll come pick you up tomorrow and take you to campus for the glorious picnic."

"I can hardly wait," I said.

After she left I dragged myself to my feet and made supper and surveyed the bedraggled mess that had once been my thousand-dollar doctoral regalia. I wondered if I could get compensated for having it cleaned or replaced. Almost certainly not. I wondered what would happen if this knee thing turned out to be serious. I almost certainly wouldn't get any kind of compensation for that either.

"I guess we're back to plan B," I told Fevronia. "Hoping for the best."

17

THE NEXT DAY MY KNEE was noticeably puffy and caused a nasty bolt of pain to shoot through me every time I stepped on it wrong. Mel took one look at my hobble and declared that we were going to stop back at her apartment and pick up a hiking pole on the way out.

"Thanks," I said. "You really don't have to..."

"Yeah, I do. It makes me cringe just to look at you. Come on."

Hiking pole in hand, we drove over to campus, which was more chaotic than we had been expecting.

"Oh, right," said Mel, as we sat parked in the middle of campus, trying to get past a turn-off to one of the dorms. "Upperclassmen are moving in over the weekend."

"I don't think we should be calling them 'men' since well over half of them are women," I said. Crimson, like most liberal arts colleges, was becoming heavily female. No doubt poverty and degradation—more than we already had—were not far behind.

"Yeah. Goddamn English. The use of 'men' for 'people' is so embedded in the language that we don't have a lot of elegant options. 'Course, I was an 'airman' for years. Still haven't gotten the taste out of my mouth."

"Yeah, I bet. We could go for 'upperclassers,'" I suggested. "Like 'freshers' for 'freshmen.' Or 'upperclassters,' to use the feminine form."

"Yeah. Bummer that 'ster' has become humorous and derogatory."

"Funny that," I said. "Maybe 'trix' and 'trices' could make a comeback. 'Upperclasstrices' sounds nice."

"I like it," said Mel. "But I think we'd be crucified for excessive PC-ness."

"We're not being PC," I said. "We're being linguistically precise."

"Yeah. Oh hey, we're moving again."

Mel dropped me off at the front quad, which was already teaming with balloons, banners, and uncomfortable first-years. Using my borrowed hiking pole, I limped over to where a small knot of equally uncomfortable faculty were gathering by a set of barbecue smokers.

"Rowena! What happened?" Theresa, wearing a sundress that showed off her lean figure, but also made me feel that faculty, especially deans, should not wear sundresses, came over. "Beer? Or are you on painkillers?" She offered me a spare bottle from the pair she had in her hands.

"Um, yeah, sure. I mean, no, I'm not on painkillers. A beer might help. It was from move-in. Someone kind of...ran over me with their cart."

"Oh no! How awful for you. And for them. I bet they felt terrible."

"Actually," I said, "I think they kind of did it on purpose. They certainly didn't apologize afterwards."

"Oh. Really? That's...that's weird. Well, um...I hope this won't keep you from representing the department in our interdepartmental races."

"We'll see," I said.

"Gosh, well...oh, hi, Karen."

Karen, wearing a purple flowery muumuu thing that accentuated the plump squatness of her figure, came over. Her mouth was as pursed as if she'd just bitten into an unripe persimmon.

"Did you read it?" she demanded, addressing Theresa and ignoring me.

Theresa took a slug from her beer before responding. "I assume you're referring to the latest post by the Gang of Six," she said when she had swallowed.

"We have to put a stop to them! I've already had three students—*and* their parents!—ask me about it."

"Yes, of course it's just the kind of publicity we don't want, but what can we do? They're not doing anything illegal, and we don't even know who they are."

"They're violating the Honor Code!"

"How?" asked Theresa. "They're not plagiarizing papers or cheating on their exams—or, as I just said, breaking the law. They're exercising their First Amendment right to free speech. I agree that it would be nicer for all concerned if they just shut the heck up, but we can't *make* them do that."

"The Honor Code specifically says that students are not supposed to do anything that will bring the college into ill repute," said Karen.

"Yes, well, I suppose you could make that argument—but I'm afraid we might be bringing the college into even worse repute if we try to shut them up, tempting as it is. But don't worry," added Theresa, seeing that Karen was about to protest again. "The Dean's office is drafting a response to the latest post as we speak. We're planning to do a press release about it tomorrow."

"One should have been done yesterday, as soon as the post went out!"

"We had to get into contact with Miriam Chen and get her response first," said Theresa.

Karen pursed her mouth even more tightly, as if the unripe persimmon had been followed by antiperspirant. She shook her head in Theresa's direction, and turned to me.

"I heard that Miranda Arenson is one of the Gang of Six," she said.

"Um, okay," I said.

She made an impatient gesture. "Miranda Arenson is one of your students! Haven't you checked your course rosters yet?!"

"The names don't really mean much to me until I have faces to go along with them."

"The rosters have photos!"

"Live faces," I said. "I have to actually meet the student to know who they are."

"*I* always memorize all my students' names and faces *before* the first day of class," said Karen.

"That's, um...nice. So have you had Miranda Arenson in your class before?"

"She was an advisee." Karen turned back to Theresa. "Why aren't the new faculty acting as advisors? It's not fair to the rest of us."

"I'm sure you remember how stressful the first year at a new place was," said Theresa. "And we decided that faculty couldn't advise incoming students without some experience with the college themselves first. Besides, most of these new faculty members, like Rowena, are on visiting positions."

"It's an imposition on the rest of us! Having to pick up their slack. Anyway, I had Miranda as an advisee last year. I moved her on to another faculty member this year; I couldn't deal with her anymore. She always had such a bad attitude. And now she's a photographer for the *Crimson Champion*. I take it you've heard of the *Champion*?"

"Um..."

"The school paper! Of course, it's mainly online now. But really, um, Rowena, right? With all you new faculty, it's hard to keep track of who's who. But I would expect you to take more of an interest in your new school! Especially those of you starting new programs. You're not just ordinary incoming faculty; you've been entrusted with the creation of a whole new line of study. Responsibilities and expectations are consequently high. The department is counting on you to make a good impression, and the students will be looking to you for guidance."

"Uh-huh," I said. "So it looks like I'll be working with this Miranda?"

"Well, I *know* she registered for Russian. As chair I consider it my *duty* to be acquainted with the enrollments for *all* our department's course offerings, even now that they've grown so much. So Miranda's name jumped out at me. If there's trouble, you can be sure she's part of it. And I'm sure she's the ringleader of the Gang of Six."

"Well, I'll, um, keep an eye on her," I said.

"You need to do more than *keep an eye on her*," said Karen. But what exactly she expected me to do was drowned out by a PA system cutting on with a crackle of static.

"Oh, I'm up," said Theresa. "Enjoy yourself, Rowena. Hope your leg gets better soon."

She hurried off, and joined a queue of deans and other administrators welcoming us all to Crimson College and the picnic. There was a description of the festivities planned for the evening, including fun things like "Dunk Your Professor." I thanked my lucky stars I hadn't been volunteered for that. Maybe only tenured faculty had to put up with that kind of thing.

"And since we're in Georgia, of course we've got a watermelon eatin' contest!" finished off Dorothy, who was the one introducing all the activities. "Come join our newest hire, Professor Taylor from

Chinese, and see how much watermelon you can chow down in one minute!"

For a moment I thought I must be having an aural hallucination. Then I looked in the direction that Dorothy was indicating, and saw that indeed, Chloe, flanked by the same blank-faced woman from Food Services, was presiding over a table covered with slices of watermelon, and a big sign inviting everyone to a watermelon eatin' contest.

Driven by the same compulsion that sends people running in the direction of a really awful car crash, I hurried over towards the table as fast as my limp would allow.

Focused on wielding my hiking pole and not falling, I instead crashed into someone who had come to an abrupt halt in front of me, muttering, "Holy crap, they're not gonna frickin' *believe* this at the paper."

"Oh, sorry!" I said, grabbing her to keep both of us from thudding ignominiously to the ground in front of most of the faculty and administration and the entire first-year class.

"Hey, watch where you're...oh, sorry. Didn't realize you were, like, disabled."

"I'm not," I said. "Well, I guess actually I am right now." I took in the girl's real camera, as opposed to a phone, and her badge, which she had clipped ostentatiously to the front of her shirt, that read **PRESS: CRIMSON CHAMPION.**

"Hey, are you Miranda?" I asked.

She gave me a suspicious look out from under her bangs, which hung, goth-rocker style, in an asymmetrical slice over her left eye. Her roots were a dark auburn, but the rest of her chin-length bob was died an aggressive black, except for a patch of lavender at the longest point over her left ear, and a kind of chalky robin's egg blue in the buzzed undercut at the back of her head.

"What makes you think that?" she demanded.

"We were literally just talking about you...well, about Miranda Arenson, the new photographer for the *Crimson Champion*."

"Who was talking about me?"

"Karen, the new chair of the Modern Languages department. She was telling me...well, anyway, I'm the new Russian instructor, and she was telling me about, um, my students."

"Oh. Yeah. That's me. So you're the new Russian professor? You don't look old enough to be a professor."

"Looks can be deceiving," I said. "So are you going to do a story about this?" I gestured to where Chloe was now setting up two students to face off over a plate of watermelon slices.

"Oh, hell yeah. I mean, not the story that needs to be done about it, obviously, because we'd never be allowed to print *that*, but there'll be pictures for sure, and we'll try and work something in to make it clear how bad this looks. I mean, can you frickin' *believe* this?"

"Unfortunately, yes," I said.

"Yeah, I guess so. Well, I better go get some photos. See you Monday, Professor..?"

"Halley," I supplied. She slipped off to get a better angle for her shot before I was able to ask her if she was behind the Gang of Six. I told myself I'd do it on Monday. Not because I wanted to get her in trouble, but because I wanted to protect a troublemaker like her from a little bit of the trouble she was going to draw down on herself. The world, especially small liberal arts colleges, needed a few lords and ladies of chaos, and Miranda looked like a lady of chaos par excellence.

I made my way over to where Chloe, her mouth set in a grim line, was setting up another watermelon face-off.

"Hey," I said. "Are you okay?"

"What? Oh, I'm fine."

"How on *earth* did you get roped into this? To be honest I, um...well, when I heard the announcement and saw you here, I thought for a minute I was having a stroke or something."

"Yeah, me too. First bellhopping, then working a watermelon eatin' contest. But they told me that it was a tradition for the youngest incoming tenure-track faculty member to oversee this event, and they couldn't give me special consideration and put an extra burden on others just because I'm black."

"Yeah, but that's bullshit."

All the students at the table gaped at me. I thought the woman from Food Services almost cracked a smile.

"You want me to, I don't know, take over for you?"

Chloe gave the offer a moment of serious consideration, and then shook her head. "You're just a VAP, right? I mean, not 'just' a VAP, but you know what I mean."

"Yeah, I know. And yeah, I'm a VAP, but whatever. It'll be massively less humiliating for me than for you."

"You already stood out there at the gate in full regalia waving a big sign saying 'Welcome to Gryffindor.' I think you've humiliated yourself enough for one day. Besides, you're injured. And I'm live-texting the event to my uncle Ralph, and I'd hate to disappoint him. He loves laughing at stuff like that."

"Well, if you're sure," I said. "But don't hesitate to let me know if it gets too much and you want me to take over."

"Thanks. That's really nice of you. But I'm hoping that if I get this over with once, there won't be any hazing after this."

"Good luck with that," I said.

18

AFTER AN HOUR OF HANGING around getting progressively hotter and more sore, and refusing multiple offers of barbecue, I tracked down Mel and asked if she'd mind running me over to my car.

"Sure, no problem. It'll give me an excuse to leave anyway. I always hate functions like this. And I think I found another tick crawling up my leg."

"Yuck! Let's get the hell out of here."

Mel drove me back to my car, and watched with concern as I maneuvered my way in.

"Driving stick," she said. "That's hard-core."

"Insert double entendre here," I said.

"Haha, yeah. Even if it's not a very lesbian-friendly one. You sure you're okay to shift gears?"

"It's only a couple miles down the road, with no hills. How hard can it be?"

"With a bum knee? Pretty damn hard. Tell you what: I'll be right behind you, so if it gets too much, just pull over and I'll chauffeur you the rest of the way home. And hang onto the hiking pole."

"Jeez," I said. "You seem to think I'm made of spun glass or something."

Mel flashed me a self-conscious smile. "Yeah. I, um, I might have a little problem with being overbearingly nurturing and protective.

All the worst qualities of a woman and a man, rolled into one. I'll try to lay off. But seriously, don't hesitate to ask for help if you need it. It'll make my day, it really will."

"Okay," I said. "I will, I promise. But I'm pretty sure I can make it home."

Shifting gears was more painful than I would have liked, but I drove myself home even so, and walked myself into my apartment, promising Mel that I would take care of myself, and call her if I needed help for anything.

"But really, I should be fine," I told her. "I'll be in lockdown at home, doing last-minute prep for Monday. Although it shouldn't be too bad. It's just two sections of first semester. I'm basically ready for it, no matter how much Karen tried to guilt me into feeling bad about my lack of preparedness."

"Oh God." Mel rolled her eyes. "I've only met her once, and I already hate her. What did she do?"

I filled her in on Karen's passive-aggressive guilt trip, and the whole Miranda story.

"Well, good for Miranda," said Mel when I was done. "What do you think: *is* she the mastermind behind the Gang of Six?"

"Maybe. Or maybe not. Too soon to tell. I'm getting way too sucked into this, but I can't help myself. I'll be interested in seeing if a new post goes up tomorrow. Maybe that'll tell me something."

"Yeah, like if she uses the photographs she took from the event tonight," said Mel.

"Although if they're posted on the campus paper website, the bloggers could just lift them from there and use them for their own site."

"True. Sounds like some fun sleuthing, in any case. Much better than lesson prep."

"Especially since I'll be teaching stuff I've taught a dozen times already," I said.

"Yeah, same here. Are you on a two-three schedule?"

"Yep. Two sections of first semester in the fall, and then I guess two sections of second semester in the spring, plus a culture class. I think someone else already wrote up the description for it; something about 'Introduction to Slavic Civilization' or something like that. But I have to choose all the readings and create the syllabus and all the assignments and so on. Which is better. Trying to teach someone else's class is a nightmare."

"Yeah, same here. On both counts. I'm on the same two-three schedule, and I've also got to come up with an Intro to Middle Eastern Civ class according to someone else's description for the spring. Shouldn't be too hard; I taught a couple of classes like that in grad school, so I have a pretty good idea of what readings and stuff work and what don't, and doing it my way'll be a hell of a lot easier than trying to do what someone else wants. I've always sucked at that. The military didn't cure me of it, and neither did grad school, even though they both tried as hard as they fucking could. Hey—you want me to bring you dinner tomorrow? You need me to go shopping for you?"

I opened my mouth to tell her to stop hovering, and then said, "I'd love to get together for dinner tomorrow." Then I mentally kicked myself, because I could feel our relationship careening off in a direction that I'd never wanted to go with another woman, especially not when I had a boyfriend. A boyfriend who was literally a continent away, but still definitely a boyfriend, and one who had made it clear that he was looking for something serious. As serious as it could be when we were on opposite coasts. Meanwhile, I was alone and injured, and Mel looked like she needed a friend too. So instead of backing out of my agreement, I said, "I don't eat meat, FYI."

"Really? I keep trying to give it up, and then falling off the wagon. Maybe you can be a good influence on me. Tell you what: I'll bring over a selection of delicious meat-free Middle Eastern dishes, and you can keep your leg up, and we can both dig into the Gang of Six website. Maybe we can solve that little problem for the administration before the semester even starts, and they'll be so grateful they'll offer us tenure."

"Sounds like a plan," I said.

19

BY SUNDAY I THOUGHT the pain and swelling in my knee might have reached its peak and was considering going back down again. I spent Sunday morning sitting with my leg propped up while I printed off my syllabi—on my own dime, of course—and finalized my plans for tomorrow's lessons. Not that there was that much to do. It was two sections of RUS 101, using the same textbook I'd used many times before. The main challenge would be to keep myself from falling asleep.

Sunday evening Mel came over, bearing, as promised, a selection of Middle Eastern dishes. When I asked her where she'd found them, she said she'd made them all from scratch.

"Very impressive," I said.

"Yeah, well, I like to cook, and I don't get a chance to cook for other people very often, not since my girlfriend left me."

"Ouch. Sounds painful."

"Yeah, you know how it is. I was too much of an obsessive pain in the ass who wouldn't settle down and do something sensible like take that job working reception at her hair salon. God, she was such a lipstick! A complete girly-girl. Makeup, hair, nails, dozens of matching outfits—the whole nine yards. And I was totally head-over-heels for her, but I guess she didn't feel the same about me.

"She broke it off last winter, when she found out my contract for my adjunct positions hadn't been renewed and I was applying for more academic jobs instead of getting a 'real job'—her words—like she wanted. Said"—Mel tried to smile, and then looked off into the corner instead—"that I was like some entitled rocker musician sponging off his girlfriend while pretending to chase his dreams, and she deserved better than that, and she wasn't going to let me use her like that anymore and I had to move out the next day. There was a whole packing-up-and-moving-out scene like in a fuckin' R&B music video or something. I broke down and cried three times, and begged her to take me back on whatever terms she wanted, while she kept telling me she needed to do this in order to take care of herself and be her most authentic self and one day I'd look back on this and realize that she was pushing me towards self-sufficiency and responsibility and all that shit. All the neighbors were watching. It was the most gut-wrenchingly humiliating day of my life. At least until last Friday."

"Double ouch," I said. "I'm sorry."

"Well, it wasn't you who did it, so don't apologize for whatever shit Jewel—that was her name—felt she had to pull. And I'd like to say I've moved on and I'm better off without her, but I can't. But whatever. It's over, whether I wanted it to be or not. And that's the long version of why I wanted to go all out and make something special for tonight."

"Well, I appreciate it," I said. I repressed another twinge of concern that I was inadvertently leading Mel on. Maybe in this high-stress situation I was being too friendly and needy and clingy, and giving the wrong impression. Or maybe Mel was in a high-stress situation herself, and feeling friendly and needy and clingy, and clinging to me because I was the only person currently available. Maybe it would all blow over without any hurt feelings once the semester started.

"Do you want to look at the Gang of Six website?" I asked.

We spent a good hour perusing the Gang of Six's rudimentary website. The first post dated from the beginning of the previous semester, and introduced the Gang's mission, which was "To speak Truth to Power and expose the Dark Reality behind Crimson College's cozy Appearance." That post had zero likes, as did the next one, about Crimson College's use of contract workers for its food service, janitorial, and grounds crew staff as a way of getting around its commitment to paying all its employees a living wage.

There had been posts at a rate of about one a week for the first half of the semester. None of them had any likes or comments. Maybe people were reading them anonymously, but it certainly looked like the blog hadn't gotten much traffic in the first couple of months of its existence.

That all changed the week after spring break, when they put up their first post about the proposed funding from Security Solutions for the new football stadium. There was a flurry of comments on the bottom of that post, and it was followed up by a post saying that they'd gotten over 100 hits and quadrupled their number of followers.

"Yeah, from one to four," said Mel, reading that.

"They've got over four hundred now," I said, looking at the follower count on the sidebar.

After that, their posts appeared to get steadily more popular. In the final post of the previous semester, they thanked the Dean's office and the Office of Student Wellbeing for sharing their posts in multiple campus-wide emails, and promised to return in the fall with even more explosive exposés.

"I don't see what the college is so worked up about," said Mel, after we had reread the most recent posts. "Yeah, they're critical, but they're not making any threats of violence. And it's not like what they're saying is news. I mean, some of the specifics were news, but not the general gist of the problem. The only thing really shocking is the stuff about Security Solutions, and it's not like that's a secret, especially since they're going to have their name on the side of the new football stadium. And the blog's reach is miniscule. The only reason they're getting any attention at all is because the college administration keeps telling people about them. If they'd just ignored them, ten to one they wouldn't even have bothered restarting the blog this fall."

"Yeah, well, people tend to panic in the face of truthful accusations. And all those deanlets and administrators have to justify their paychecks somehow. The real question"—I clicked over onto MensProtectionAlliance.com and brought up the most recent post, about protesting Miriam Chen's speaking engagement—"is why the Men's Protection Alliance has been allowed to operate unchecked, when they *have* been making actual threats."

Mel raised an eyebrow at me. "Fuck, Rowena, I didn't think you were that naive. They're *men*. Well, actually, they're still boys, but you get what I mean. And they're only saying what everyone else, in their heart of hearts, really thinks. Most people, even the ones who would swear on a stack of Bibles that they don't, feel deep down that women are evil and dangerous and have all kinds of unfair advantages and hidden powers that we use to manipulate those around us.

"And, you know, in a way women *do* have a lot of power. If you're ever the only woman in a group of horny, sex-deprived guys, you'll realize just how much power you have over them—and how helpless you are, how meaningless you are to them as a person. It's like being a pile of chicken nuggets, or hell, a live chicken, tossed into a group of starving people. They'll fight to the death for you, and then they'll tear you apart until there's nothing left of you but a pile of shit. But that's not how they see it. To them, you're the most important thing, the most powerful force, on the planet. So the language of social justice rings false in most people's ears when applied to women, but true as a bell when applied to men.

"Plus, they're not criticizing the college. They're whining about how hard things are for them, not shouting about how the college is making things hard for other people. That's a lot easier for the administration to justify protecting as an expression of free speech."

"I hate how right you are about all of that," I said.

"Yeah, me too. So whaddya think? Is this Miranda chick the mastermind behind the Gang of Six?"

"I mean, I only met her for a second, but she did seem like the kind of person who *could* be. But that doesn't mean that she *is*. Especially since she's affiliated with the campus paper. I'd like to think that anyone working for a news service, even a student-run campus paper, could do a slicker job than *this*. And I didn't see anything on the website to indicate who the real people are behind it, did you?"

"Nope. Amateur as they are, they've covered their tracks well enough that way. They've got a cartoon for an avatar, GangofSix as their username, and GangofSix@gmail.com for their email, if anyone wants to contact them. Are they on Twitter?"

"Let's check." I did a quick search on Twitter and discovered that they did indeed have a Twitter account, with a grand total of 300 followers. It had the same blurry cartoon avatar, and linked back to the blog and the Gmail account.

"They may have provided a real phone number—unless they used a burner phone—as a security measure for their account, but there's no way of getting it without doing some much more advanced hacking than I feel up for right now, and frankly, it doesn't seem worth it," said Mel. "Let the undergrads have their fun. It gives them something more meaningful to do than taking drugs and chasing tail, and maybe they'll actually do some good in the process. Personally, I'm 100% on their side."

"Yeah," I said. "Me too. If it does turn out that Miranda is their ringleader, I'll probably just give her tips on how to make things more professional, and maybe how to use some of the more popular academic hashtags to try and get the attention of the people on #AcademicTwitter."

"That's the spirit," said Mel.

20

MEL OFFERED TO DRIVE me to campus the next day, and after some hesitation, I accepted. Even though I recognized the clear financial and environmental benefits of carpooling, I liked my independence so much I'd never been able to bring myself to do it. Public transport was fine; getting a ride in someone else's car was not.

But with my knee still sore and swollen, the drive would be painful, and the hike from the faculty parking lot to Bedford Hall would be excruciating at best, and permanently disabling at worst. So, since we had similar teaching schedules, I accepted Mel's offer.

She dropped me off as close as she could to Bedford Hall at 8:30 the next morning. My hobble must have been even worse than I thought, because she rejoined me, having parked her car and slogged over from behind the football stadium, just as I was finally reaching the front door.

"It makes my knee hurt just to look at you," she said, holding the door for me.

"Thanks. I mean, for holding the door, not for telling me how bad I look. Although I know what you mean. It's not actually that bad, really, as long as I don't twist it or jar it the wrong way. So that's why I have to shuffle along so carefully."

"If it doesn't start getting majorly better in another couple of days, I'd go see a doctor about it. I know that's an expensive pain in the ass, but they could get you one of those full-leg braces that might protect it a little better than the one you've got, and a set of proper crutches."

"Yeah," I said. "I know. I'm just a wimp about stuff like that."

"Who isn't? You need help getting into your classroom?"

"I'm fine," I told her. "I know you need to go get set up."

"If you're sure." She gave me a look of doubt before setting off to her classroom, at the far end of the hall.

My classroom was right near the front door, and only a couple doors down the hall from my office. Which was a good thing, because I wasn't sure I could have made it to the far end of the building, at least not without spilling my bags full of stuff all over the floor.

Its proximity to the main entrance was the only good thing about the classroom, where I would be teaching two back-to-back sections of RUS 101, at 9:00am and 10:00am, Monday, Tuesday, Wednesday, and Friday. As a teaching schedule it wasn't that bad, although more than what a research-intensive position would be. At least in theory. In practice, my friends with research-intensive positions were still teaching similar schedules, or more.

The classroom itself was billed as a "seminar room," which meant that it was about the size of my bedroom, but filled to overflowing with a table that barely left any room for the chairs, let alone the people. The students had to get out of their chairs and go stand by the door to let me edge sideways, sucking in my gut, to the head of the room by the board and the smartroom console.

By 8:59 all nine of us—me and eight students—were in place. I suggested leaving the door open in order to get a little air, but Miranda told me that other instructors considered that disruptive. Besides, campus tours came through here several times a day and tended to stop right in front of this particular classroom in order to brag about Crimson's small class sizes, so we'd want the door closed unless we wanted a bunch of "weird randos" joining us.

"You never know," I said. "Sometimes weird randos make the best people. But let's leave the door closed for now, and see how it goes."

How it went was smelly. Some of the students had a relaxed attitude towards personal hygiene, at least for their 9:00am classes, and some wore enough perfume, body spray, and scented hair products to choke a horse. Underneath it all was the faint but unmistakable bass note of mildew, rising up from the elderly carpet. By 9:30 I was already developing a killer headache.

Other than that, I couldn't complain about the class too much. Of the eight students, Miranda and Chris were the only ones who stuck out as potential troublemakers. The other six were so clean-cut I felt like I was getting papercuts just from looking at them. All of them seemed smart and enthusiastic. By the end of the first fifteen minutes, I could already tell that Chris was going to be a problem when it came to group work, and Miranda would argue with me if she thought I was making a mistake or not living up to her standards, and the others would go along with the flow. None of that was likely to cause me any major problems. They were just students like any other.

I hadn't been able to go to the bathroom beforehand, so I was hoping to make the hobble there and back in the ten minutes between my two classes, but Miranda came over and cornered me before I could escape.

"Cool lesson," she said.

"Thanks."

"So, I wanted to ask you..." She fidgeted with her hair for a moment, pushing the pointed slice of her bangs back behind her ear, revealing both her eyes. Behind the black eyeliner, they were large and amber and looked like they belonged to someone less edgy and more sweet-natured than the person Miranda was trying to pass herself off as. I was willing to bet that by graduation she'd shed the goth-rocker getup in favor of something earthy. Five years down the road she'd probably be doing something worthy and a little bit risky in a developing nation, and ten years from now she'd probably have a graduate degree in something like Peace Studies. I recognized the type, because that's who I had been too. Minus the dyed hair and makeup. I'd always been too lazy, and, to be honest, maybe a little bit too vain, to spend all that time and money making myself look weird.

"Yes?" I said.

"So, you know, I'm with the *Crimson Champion*," she said. "And we'd like to do a feature about our new faculty, especially the ones coming in to teach new languages. So since I'm already in your class I said I'd, like, ask you if you'd be willing to do an interview with us."

"Of course," I said. "I'd be happy to. Just let me know when."

"Great!" She smiled in relief at my easy agreement. Underneath all that dye she was just another shy nerd who hadn't yet learned how to let her press pass shield her from the assault on her overly sensitive feelings that any interaction with strangers would cause.

"I'm sure that Professor Wilson, the new Arabic instructor, and Professor Taylor, the new Chinese instructor, would be happy to talk to you as well," I said.

"You think so?"

"I'm sure of it," I said. "And I'll tell them that I'm doing it, too. That should make them even more likely to agree."

"Really? Thanks!" Miranda gave me a genuinely sweet smile, and left.

21

A QUICK CHECK OF MY phone after Miranda left showed me that there was only five minutes until the start of my next class. I poked my head out the classroom door. Students were already congregating in an impatient knot outside. Down at the far end of the hall there was a line snaking out of the women's room. Even without a bum knee I wouldn't be able to make it there and back in time. But my headache was getting worse and worse. Maybe splashing some cold water on my face would help.

While I was standing there watching and wasting time wondering whether I could make it there and back without being too egregiously late, Chloe came out of the bathroom, looking harried and a little lost, like maybe she was also trying to make it to her 10:00am class but wasn't sure where it was.

Just as her gaze fixed, with a look of intense relief, on the door of the seminar room across the hall from mine, a student called out to her. She paused to say hi to, I saw, Taylor, who was sitting on one of the padded benches in the open space where the hall made a T with a perpendicular hall running along the back of the building.

Sitting next to Taylor on the bench was Chris. At first he was, as he had been for most of his class with me, looking at the floor. But as Taylor spoke to Chloe, her face animated with enthusiasm, his eyes slowly raised from the floor to the side of Taylor's head. For a moment, as if a shutter had been lifted, a look that could only be described as mad infatuation lit up his face. Then it shut down again, and he went back to staring at the floor.

"Well, well, *well*," I started to say, and then stopped myself. The students for section two of RUS 101 were pushing their way into the classroom. I made a note to mention it to Chloe later as something that might cheer everyone up, and, sucking in my gut over my increasingly full bladder, squeezed my way back to the front of the classroom.

22

AFTER THE EXCITEMENT of the first day of class, things settled down to something calm, almost boring. The most interesting thing that happened was that my knee improved to the point that I was able to start driving again.

Mel and I had agreed to carpool, so on Wednesday morning of the second week I was parked outside her apartment, ready to pick her up. Normally she was waiting for me by the curb when I pulled up, but not today. She only showed up after I texted her that I was there.

"Gosh," I said when she finally got in the car. "You look like death warmed over."

"Really? Good. I mean, that's how I feel, so I'm glad people can tell. Maybe they won't hassle me. Is something going around? I feel like shit. Like I'm coming down with a really nasty flu."

"It's only the second of September. Hardly flu season. But if you think you're coming down with something, for heaven's sake go back home and lie down. You're no good to anyone like that, and, frankly, I don't want you in the car with me."

She tried and failed to grin. "I look that bad, huh?"

I gave her a once-over. "You're *green*," I told her. "You look like you're transforming into a lizard. Get the heck away from me."

"I don't have anyone to fill in for me."

"I'm sure the students would rather miss a class or two than get whatever disgusting plague you're carrying. I know *I* would, and I think I speak for the rest of the department as well."

"I dunno. Karen was just moaning on the other day about people who miss class because of head colds, or take the whole day off for dental surgery."

"Karen," I said, "is an asshole. Go back inside, and I'll let everyone know you're sick with the flu and won't be coming in. Everyone will thank you for your consideration, even if they don't know it yet."

"Maybe." Mel shivered and rubbed her forehead. "I feel...weird. Like I've got ants crawling under my skin, or someone's hooked me to a taser and is slowly ramping up the power. And I hurt all over. Old injuries are flaring up, and my thumbs hurt so much I could barely stand to pick up a glass of water."

"Get out of my car right now! I'll check in on you this afternoon, okay? Meanwhile, get back to bed!"

"Yes, *ma'am*." Mel tried to roll her eyes at me and give a cheeky salute, but instead winced and rubbed her forehead again. She was limping noticeably as she walked back into the building, and it took her three tries to get the right key in the lock and open the door.

Once I was certain she had made it safely back inside, I opened all the windows and slathered up with hand sanitizer. Whatever Mel had, it looked miserable.

I texted her just before class to see how she was feeling, and again after my classes were over to see if I needed to rush over and carry her off to urgent care.

I'm not feeling any worse, she texted back. *And no vomiting or crazy coughing or anything like that. I just hurt all over like I've been hit by a truck. I'm going to lie here in bed and hope it passes.*

Let me know if you need anything, I wrote. *Do you want me to drop off some supper for you? I can leave it on the doormat :)*

Jeez, you're a real pal :) :) But I'm good. I've got some leftovers waiting for me if I feel like eating. I think I just need to rest.

Then rest, I wrote. *I'm about to meet with Miranda for our interview, but I'll check in later.*

Copy that.

Encouraged by the fact that Mel wasn't getting any worse, and was even able to make jokes via text, I went to my meeting with Miranda in a cheerful frame of mind. So far, Miranda was my favorite of my students, and I was genuinely happy to help out the student paper and also get a little free publicity for the college's fledgling Russian program.

Plus, it would give me a chance to feel her out about the Gang of Six. Not that I had any intention of reporting her if she *were* part of it, but the part of me that had always liked mysteries and spy stories was enjoying the thought of her having a second identity as the college's anonymous public enemy. Another blog post had come out over the weekend, excoriating the college for its use of toxic herbicides and pesticides in its landscaping.

That had triggered a sharply-worded response from the Office of the Provost itself, claiming that 1) health and wellbeing was the college's number-one priority, 2) all products used on campus were FDA-approved for safety and effectiveness, and 3) the landscaping was done through a privately contracted firm, so the college bore no direct responsibility for their actions.

This last claim had caused the Gang of Six to post a vigorous follow-up, in which they rehashed the issue of colleges, including but not limited to Crimson, contracting out their landscaping and janitorial services in order to avoid paying the workers a living wage. The Gang of Six's instincts and research skills were spot-on, even if they couldn't seem to write without comma splices to save their lives. The articles in the *Crimson Champion* were generally comma-splice free; I didn't know whether this was because the editorial staff went in and fixed them, or because we were dealing with two completely separate sets of people.

Anyway, I was looking forward to my talk with Miranda, even if it meant spending an extra hour in my stuffy office. I'd always had a problem with claustrophobia, and the office was making it worse. I'd much rather have been put in a busy shared space that had windows and plenty of open floor, rather than this musty, airless closet.

"Gosh," said Miranda when I showed her in. "They didn't give you much of a room, did they? I thought professors had better offices than this."

"It depends on the professor," I said. "I'm new *and* contingent, so they obviously stuffed me into whatever broom closet they could find on short notice."

"Oh. So, do you think that, like, the college isn't fully supporting the Russian program?"

"I think the fact that they've started a Russian program at all shows way more support than most colleges are giving to the subject," I said, looking for that balance between a palatable truth and an unacceptable level of forthright honesty. "I'm sure they're doing the best they can, given that this is the program's first semester, and no one knows how successful it's going to be."

"Makes sense, I guess. Although I still think they coulda given you a better office. So, can you, like, tell me a bit about how you became a Russian professor?"

I spent a while talking about my past working at an NGO that investigated election fraud and human rights abuses in developing democracies. Miranda sat there with her mouth open the whole time, and confessed when I was done that she'd never even heard that such a thing was possible.

"How do you even get *into* something like?" she asked. "I'd have no idea even where to start!"

"There are job postings for that, same as for anything else," I told her. "If you're interested, I can point you in the right direction. Lots of people do a stint of NGO work after graduation, especially people who study Russian. It's a natural progression."

"That's...that's just *so cool*," said Miranda, shedding her own facade of coolness and revealing her natural state of warmhearted activist and enthusiastic dreamer underneath. "I'd *love* to learn more about that, Professor Halley."

"Sure. I'll send you some stuff this afternoon. And I can put you in touch with some people on the ground if you want to learn more." In the back of my head, I could hear Alex telling me that here I was, grooming another student to follow in my saintly footsteps. But what else was I going to do? It was what I knew about, and it was what they wanted to know about too. Intelligent, idealistic young people needed an outlet for their intelligence and idealism, and if they didn't do something like this, they'd end up taking drugs or joining ISIS or something. A few years digging wells or rescuing orphans or saving whales or whatever seemed like a much better outcome, for them and everyone else. They might not make a ton of money, but maybe they'd find their passion, and at the very least they'd get some eye-opening experience in how the world worked.

"So are you very involved in activism?" I asked. "*Is* there a lot of activism at Crimson? Thus far it hasn't seemed like that kind of a place."

Miranda made a face. "It's not. It's, like, somewhere to the right of my grandma's Bible group, but with less ambition and real-world smarts. The administration just wants the college to look all cutesy and cozy and safe, and most of the students just want to have a good time, or get in good with the good-ole-boys network and score a cushy job after graduation. Most kids with real smarts go somewhere else."

"Don't sell yourself short," I said.

Miranda shrugged. "I'm just here because I'm a legacy student. My mom and my grandma went here."

"Really? Mine too!"

"Really? Well, that's cool, I guess. And you gotta hand it to 'em: this was a women's college back when women couldn't go to most colleges. My grandma wanted to go somewhere like an Ivy League school, but most of 'em didn't start admitting women till years after she would have graduated. So she came here instead, and so did my mom. And so the college offered me a pretty sweet scholarship to come here, and so my parents said I had to come here and not Bryn Mawr, which was the place I got into that I really wanted to go to. So"—she shrugged like she didn't care, when really she did—"here I am. So I gotta figure out what to do about it, how to get a real college education at a place like this."

"You can get a real college education here," I told her. "You can get a real college education *anywhere*. You just have to take charge of your learning."

"Yeah, I guess," said Miranda. "Anyway, no one does *anything* political here. Well, except for the Gang of Six. Have you heard of them?"

"Yes," I said. "Faculty keep getting emails about how we shouldn't pay any attention to them. So of course now we're all glued to their blog."

"Yeah." Miranda cracked a half-smile. "Students too. The paper's trying to figure out who they are, or at least get in touch with 'em so that we can interview 'em, but so far no luck. Actually, that's one of my assignments for the semester: see if I can find 'em and get an interview. But to be honest I have no idea even where to start."

Miranda delivered all this with a frustration that was either genuine, or the product of such prodigious acting talent that I would have no chance of getting past it to the truth. Which was a bit disappointing. I had had high hopes that she would be our ringleader, and I would have the secret consciousness of having the most notorious person on campus in my classes. Alas, it seemed not.

"Faculty have been asked to keep an eye out for them too, and report anyone we think might be suspicious," I told her. "So if you *do* find them, let them know, will you? I know a lot of us are rooting for them, but some people really have it in for them."

"Yeah, I'm not surprised," said Miranda. "But thanks for the tip, Professor. That's really cool of you to pass that on. And I'd better let you go, but can I contact you if I have any further questions? Sometimes my editor likes to do follow-ups."

"Sure, no problem," I told her, and escorted her out of the office, watching her aggressive dye job as it made its strident way down the hall and out the building.

23

"OH, ROWENA, THERE YOU are. I've been looking for you." Karen's expression, as she collared me in the hallway outside my office, made it seem as if I had been deliberately avoiding her, or at least slacking off on my duties, instead of coming in for all my classes and office hours as scheduled.

"Well, here I am," I said.

"Yes...can you come into my office?"

"Um, okay." I followed Karen down the hall to the chair's office. Since she walked in front of me, not looking back at me and not making any conversation, I had plenty of time to wonder what this was all about. I couldn't think of anything that she would need to talk to me about, and especially not something worth dragging me into her office for. Unless she wanted to ask how Mel was doing? But surely she could have just asked me that in the hallway, or better yet, emailed Mel herself. Maybe she wanted to congratulate me on having garnered free publicity for the Russian program by talking to the *Champion*, and brainstorm with me on how to further raise the program's profile.

I looked at her back, moving stiffly in front of me. For someone so plump, she managed to emit a powerful air of brittleness and rigidity. I couldn't imagine her brainstorming with anyone, or even congratulating them on a job well done. She was too insecure even to mouth proprieties about other people's success.

Her office, while much more spacious than mine, felt at least as crowded from all the piles of paper stacked higgledy-piggledy on the desk, chairs, bookshelves, and floor. The sloppy mess matched her flyaway gray hair and unflattering muumuu. I told myself that thinking such thoughts was unkind, but I couldn't stop them from coming to me.

We had to remove piles of ungraded essays and homework off a chair so that I could sit down. Then she went over and spent a while fussing with her chair and starting up her computer, all without speaking to me. I resisted the urge to check my phone for texts from Mel or Alex or Dima or anyone, or just to find how much of my time she was wasting, while I waited.

"I wanted to talk to you about your contract renewal," she said, once she had gotten everything about her desk set up to her satisfaction. Well, "satisfaction" was too strong a word. She was sitting there staring at the computer screen instead of looking at me, her lips pursed in distaste at whatever she was seeing.

"Um, okay?" The contract I had signed had been for two years, with the possibility of renewal for a third year. Discussing it the second week of my first semester seemed a little premature.

"As you know," she said, speaking severely but still not looking at me, "your initial contract is for a period of two years, but the first semester is a probationary period. If the department finds your performance to be unsatisfactory, we will terminate the contract at the end of the probationary period."

"After one semester or one year?" I asked.

Now she did look at me. It was a look full of confusion, by someone who hadn't expected to be called upon for clarification and was panicking over this simplest of questions.

"The probationary period is one semester," she repeated.

"So what happens to the program if you decide to terminate my contract after one semester?" I asked. "What happens to all the students signed up for the spring semester?" I didn't ask what would happen to me. Leaving me broke and homeless, with no hope of employment until the next summer at the earliest, didn't seem like it would bother her at all. If anything, she would probably cheer the repo crew on when they came to get my car and my few remaining pieces of crappy furniture.

She made a helpless movement with her mouth, that then firmed up into an expression of supercilious displeasure. "Of course we would provide the students with a suitable instructor," she said. "I'm sure we wouldn't have any trouble finding one."

"Mmmmm." In theory she was all too depressingly correct. Overqualified instructors of Russian and every other subject were easy to come by. In practice, though, finding someone on short notice who would be willing to move to small-town Georgia would be a bit of a challenge.

"Of *course* the welfare and intellectual development of our students is our first concern," said Karen, her mouth taking on such a sucking-on-an-unripe-persimmon expression that her plump face looked almost gaunt. "Which is why we have instituted this policy. We wanted to ensure that *all* our instructors are working according to the high standards we expect at Crimson."

"Uh-huh," I said.

"So we need to start the review process soon, in order to have it finished well before the end of the semester, in case we *do* need to hire someone else."

"Mmm-hmmm," I said.

"You'll need to submit your syllabi and a sample of your teaching materials. And we'll need to do at least one teaching observation."

"Oh." I stifled an intense desire to groan, or maybe rail against the stupidity of the universe. Teaching observations were torture. Not only were they nerve-racking to the instructor, but they put the students off their game and tended to disrupt the entire week. And then you had to pretend to be grateful for the observer's suggestions for "improvement." Along with evaluations and all the other bureaucracy of the modern university, it was yet another attempt to turn teaching into widget-making. I took a certain dark pleasure in the absolute recalcitrance of education to bend to anyone's will and become a standardized, automated process, but the frequent and aggressive attempts to do so left teachers miserable and students uneducated.

"So," said Karen, trying to speak briskly but still just sounding insecure, "I need to find a time to observe your class. I'll definitely be doing an observation, and Darryl might as well—*if* he can fit it into his schedule." Her forehead wrinkled into a frown almost as impressive as the one that was turning her saggy mouth into a drawstring purse. "Tenured faculty have *so many* demands on their time. With all these contingent faculty members coming in, the burden on us tenured faculty has gotten impossible."

"Sounds like you need to hire more tenure-track faculty," I said. "And give them tenure."

Karen's entire face almost disappeared into a mass of lines, she frowned so hard at that suggestion. "We have to maintain standards!" she snapped, once she'd extracted her face from its collapsing hole of ill-natured wrinkles. "We can't just hand tenure out to anyone and everyone who wants it! Which is why it is imperative that we conduct these teaching observations now! Let's see..." She rooted around on her desk until she found, hiding under a pile of coffee-stained tests from—I surreptitiously craned my neck just enough to read the heading upside-down—last semester, a day planner. Also coffee-stained.

"Let's see..." she said again, leafing through the day planner, dislodging a number of scraps of paper and what looked like cough drop wrappers in the process. "When do you teach? Nine?"

"Nine and ten," I confirmed.

"I teach at ten...The chair gets a teaching exemption, but not nearly enough of one...If I had known how much trouble it would be to be chair, I wouldn't have agreed, but *someone* had to step in after Theresa decided to leave us for the Dean's office at the last minute...I certainly can't come observe you right before my own class, which meets Monday-Wednesday-Friday, so it will have to be Tuesday...I have a 9:00am chairs meeting next Tuesday...it will have to be the following Tuesday, the fifteenth. Make a note that I'll be observing you at 9:00am on Tuesday the fifteenth, Rowena, and please be sure to send me your lesson plan and teaching materials at least a day in advance so that I can acquaint myself with them before the actual observation."

"Um," I said. "Okay. I don't think we have a test that day."

"You should *know* when you have upcoming tests, Rowena," said Karen. She tried to fix me with a stern glare, but ended up looking back at the computer instead. "Otherwise assignments will constantly be catching you by surprise, and you won't be able to prepare your students adequately for them." She delivered that speech to the computer screen. I wondered how much she always fell behind each semester, and how many of her own tests caught her by surprise. She seemed like that kind of person.

"Okay," I said. "Tuesday the fifteenth sounds great. I'll be sure to send you my materials in plenty of time."

"Don't forget," she said, still speaking to the computer screen. "And where's Mel? I need to speak with her about her teaching observation as well." She sighed heavily. "These new programs are turning into a real headache. I hope they turn out to be worth it."

"Um, yeah," I said. "Mel's out today with a really nasty case of the flu."

"There's no one to fill in for her!"

"That *is* the problem with very small programs," I said. "Well, one of the problems."

"If she's going to be sick all the time..." said Karen. "We can't have an instructor, *especially* from one of these new, tiny programs, who's constantly out sick!"

"I doubt she did it on purpose," I said. "And since she stayed home, hopefully the rest of us won't get sick too."

"She had better be ready to return to class by Friday! Cancelling *two* classes in a row, *especially* so early in the semester, is unacceptable!"

"I'll be sure to let the influenza virus know that," I said. Then, when Karen made no response, I left.

24

I TEXTED MEL BEFORE I set off for home, asking how she was doing and if she needed anything.

*If you're really offering...*she texted back.

Of course! Anything I can do.

In that case, could you pick up some epsom salts? I'm still not coughing or anything, but Jesus Christ am I in pain. My hands hurt so much I'm whimpering like a baby just texting you this, and now my elbows are killing me. And I don't want to talk about my knees. Maybe a hot soak in epsom salts will help.

Emergency supply of epsom salts, coming right up! I texted. *Although I'll probably just drop them off at the door.*

You do that. I'd hate to spread this around.

I picked up epsom salts at the grocery store and dropped them off on Mel's doormat, with a text to let her know they were waiting for her. Then I went to my own apartment and, with extreme reluctance, started going through all the job websites.

One of the many wonderful, wonderful things about having a two-year appointment was that I had thought, erroneously as it turned out, that I wouldn't have to go back on the market this year. I had planned to apply just for any likely-looking tenure-track positions that came up, and focus on writing a book proposal. But now it seemed I could be out on my ear as early as next semester. I knew that a lot of Karen's threats had just been bluster, the result of insecurity and poor leadership skills, but that didn't mean she wouldn't terminate my contract if the spirit moved her. So I needed to start sending out applications again.

By suppertime I was feeling so nauseated I was worried that I was coming down with whatever had laid Mel low, but I had a list of jobs to apply for. A pathetically short list. Since it was only September, I knew that more jobs would be posted, but as it was, the list I'd made was worrisomely meager, while also promising hours of tedious effort that would almost certainly be a complete and utter waste.

Food settled my stomach some, which suggested that maybe I wasn't coming down with the flu, just a bad case of the job market blues. I texted Mel and got the news that she was still feeling lousy, but didn't seem about to die. I thought about starting work on the first application on my list. Then I texted Alex instead.

Instead of texting, he called back.

"You sounded pretty down in your text," he explained. "Plus, I wanted to hear your voice. When was the last time we actually talked?"

"Um...this weekend? No, the weekend before that. A whole ten days ago."

"Shit," said Alex, "We've done exactly what we said we weren't going to do, haven't we? We've let the semester take over and put it first, instead of each other."

"Yeah," I said. "We suck."

"No—although I'd be happy for you to suck on anything you wanted to, the next time I see you in person, baby—we're just stuck in harmful patterns of behavior. And as usual, you think you should be able to break out of them, no problem, but you can't."

"I know. And speaking of harmful patterns of behavior, looks like I'm going back on the market this year."

"What? Why? I thought you had a multi-year position."

I outlined the probationary semester situation, and how I felt like I needed to go back on the market and apply for temporary positions as well as tenure-track ones, just in case.

"Dammit," said Alex. "That's pretty cold, even for academics. I was hoping Crimson would be better than that. I was hoping it could turn into something long-term for you, if you liked it there."

"Yeah, me too. But they've got this whole too-sweet-to-be-true exterior, with a festering underbelly of meanness. Like a lot of places. I don't know that anywhere else I ended up would be any better. I'm just so sick of being on the market. And even if I do get a job for next year, if they terminate my contract this semester, I'll be unemployed all spring."

"You found a spring position last year."

"Yeah, but how likely am I to get lucky like that again? 'Lucky,' hah. That was a crap job at a crap school, and it didn't pay enough to live on."

"I remember. But, you know, if you do need a place to crash next semester, you can always come crash with me. I know it's far away from home, but it could be okay, right? You liked California pretty well when you came to see me here last month, didn't you?"

"I did." And I had. Mainly I'd liked being with Alex, but I'd also liked being in California. It was pretty and exotic and practically a foreign country to someone from Georgia, but without the hassle of visas and foreign currency fees and learning a new language. I could feel its warm and sunny pull working on me from all the way across the continent. Even though Monterey was not actually that warm and sunny. It was more cool and Pacific Northwest-y. But it still had that California glow.

"I know it's not your first choice of what to do next semester, but the offer's definitely open. And maybe it would be, you know, a good thing."

"Yeah," I said. "And you're right, it wouldn't be my first choice, but that's because I dislike the idea of being unemployed and dependent. If I had some way of supporting myself, spending a semester with you in California would be a really attractive option."

"Really? That's great. Really great."

There was a pause while we both contemplated the possibility of me moving out to California and moving in with Alex. Right then, sitting by myself, with the sound of his voice and his breathing so intimate in my ear, but his body a continent away, the thought of giving up all the daily hassle of my current existence and my search for jobs I was less and less sure I even wanted and being with him was so tempting that I wanted to say, "Let's do it, and let the job-chips fall where they may."

But I didn't. I was 50%, maybe 75% sure that that was the right decision, or could be some day. But right now I felt too dangerously desperate to make a decision like that. I wanted Alex to pull me out of this dark place I was in and up into the sun. The problem was that he wanted the same thing from me. And I wasn't sure either of us could give each other what we both wanted and needed. Maybe that was beyond anyone. Other people can make you unhappy, but only you can make yourself happy. Of course, being with Alex made me happy, but I felt, with that kind of bone-deep instinctive feel that made you choose puppies over snakes, or snakes over puppies if that's where your inclinations lay, that I needed to come to him because it was my first choice, not my last choice.

"If I come live with you, I want it to be because that's what we both want more than anything, not because I don't have any better options," I said out loud. "I'd rather give up a good job to be with you than move in with you because I've lost a bad job and don't have any other even worse jobs lined up."

"Yeah," said Alex. "That's what I'd like too. But things don't always work out optimally. And probably this is just more bullshit hazing, and they'll re-up your contract no problem, and it'll be me coming to crash with you instead of the other way around, but I just wanted to make it clear that you had that option, okay?"

"Okay," I said. "So how are things going there? Do you really think you'll be out on the street soon too?"

"Who the fuck knows? I'm on a twelve-month contract, and after that it could get renewed, or I could be left with my dick in the wind. The sucky thing, sort of, is that the DLI doesn't operate on a regular academic schedule. They get their orders from the agencies they serve every year, and then they figure out how many classes they need and when they're going to start, but it's not a fixed semester schedule like it is for a regular school. My contract this time around just happened to start at the time as the regular fall semester, but they could find out they don't need me next year, or not need me for another six months, or whatever. In a way it's a more honest system, but it doesn't give me a lot of confidence or stability."

"Oh," I said. "Well, do you like it other than that? Would you want to stay?"

"All the students remind me so much of myself at that age it makes me sick," said Alex. "And there are other things. I already knew some people here, which is a mixed blessing, to fucking say the least. But it could be worse, and it's a paycheck and a legitimate use of my very expensive skillset, so there's that."

"Those are all good things," I said.

"Yeah. I guess. But enough about job shit. If I were there, I'd give you a kiss, but since I'm not, I'll just have to wish you a good night."

"Good night," I said, and, feeling profoundly unsatisfied, hung up.

25

I SPENT THE NEXT DAY alternately working on application materials and checking in with Mel, who told me that she was on the mend. Reassured on that front, I was able to focus all of my angst on the fact that I was back on the market. At least I wasn't going to apply to the big postdocs again. Some of them limited you to applying only once, and the rest, I had decided, were a giant waste of time and money. I would only apply to jobs that I might have an outside chance of getting, and hope that something worked out.

I was all set to tell Mel about my resolution, and give her a heads-up about the probationary semester and the teaching observations, but when she got in my car Friday morning, I blurted out, "You look like shit," instead.

"Jeez, thanks," said Mel.

"You said you were better. You don't *look* better."

She made a face. "I'm better. Well, a little bit better. And Karen has been riding my ass for the past two days about how there's no one to fill in for me, and how the department's counting on me, and how this is a probationary semester and I need to be making a good impression and demonstrating my commitment, blahdeefuckingblahblah, so I decided fuck it, I was coming in this morning. If I get you sick, I promise you I will bring you soup every single day."

"Okay," I said. "And let me know if you need to go home early."

"And cancel both our classes? I don't think so."

"You may not have a choice," I said.

"I don't think I'm *that* sick," said Mel. "I mean, I feel shitty, but I'm not vomiting or anything. I just hurt like a motherfucker."

"Maybe you should see a doctor."

"They'll tell me I have the flu and send me home. No, first they'll go on for a while about fucking PTSD and how I need a psych evaluation and counseling and maybe this is all psychosomatic, and *then* they'll tell me I have the flu and send me home. This ain't my first rodeo with the medical profession. If I think there's something they can do, I'll go see a doctor, I swear to God, I really will, but dollars to donuts they'll just make the current situation worse."

"Well...okay. But seriously, don't hesitate for a minute to tell me if you need to leave early."

"If I promise to do so, will you stop bugging me about it?"

"Maybe," I said.

"Okay, then, *maybe* I'll tell you if I think I need to leave early. That good enough for you?"

"I'm going to choose to believe all that snark means you really are on the mend," I said. "But I'm dropping you off as close to Bedford as I can manage. Don't argue! I saw how you limped on the way out the door."

"Well...okay."

Arguing with me seemed to have taken Mel's current supply of sass, and she sat in silence all the way to campus, only nodding occasionally as I ranted about going back on the market. She hissed from pain as she climbed out of the car, and hobbled into Bedford like she'd been badly beaten. I doused myself in hand sanitizer before putting the car back into gear and again after parking it and getting out. Whatever she had, I really didn't want it.

When I got into Bedford, Mel was nowhere to be seen, but Chloe was sitting on one of the benches in the main hall, her head hanging.

"Hey, are you okay?" I asked, coming up to her.

She jumped as if I'd stuck her with a pin. "Oh, sorry," she said. "You startled me."

"Not sure why *you're* apologizing to *me*, then," I said.

"Yeah. I just...do you ever get panic attacks?"

"Um...no, not really. Why? Are you having one?"

"I was," she said. "I walked into my office and...it's not the first time, either. Actually, pretty much every time I go into my office I start to feel weird, I start sweating, my heart starts to race, and I just want to get out of there as fast as possible. But this time was the worst. I was thinking on the way over—have you heard about the teaching observations? Are you on a probationary semester too?"

"Mmmm-hmmm," I said.

"Really? Gosh. I thought you were a VAP on a short-term contract. Not that there's anything wrong with that—I mean, not that that reflects badly on you; it reflects badly on them—but what's the point of having a probationary semester if they're just going to get rid of you in a couple of years anyway? I didn't mean it like that! I just...when I get panic attacks, I get, like, I go into a Tourette's state or something, I blurt out all kinds of stuff I shouldn't."

"It's okay. And you're right. I'm a VAP on a short-term contract. Having a probationary semester seems ridiculous, especially if they do actually end up getting rid of me halfway through the academic year. But I didn't know they were doing that to tenure-track faculty as well."

"Yeah, me neither. I knew there would a two-year and a four-year review before I went up for tenure, but no one said anything to me about a probationary semester until Karen pulled me into her office on Wednesday and starting going on about it. Well, first she said it was a probationary semester, and then she said it was my two-year review. I said it was more like my two-week review, seeing as that's how long I've been here, and she told me I obviously didn't have a lot of experience with how academia worked, which was why they needed to do the review now, to help set me on the right path. To be honest, I kinda got the feeling she was talking through her butt—oh crap, did I just say that out loud?"

"It's okay," I said. "I've heard worse. Have I told you about my brother, the career Marine? Every other word out of his mouth starts with F. If not something worse."

Chloe produced a small smile, and started massaging her temples, her fingers moving around the scars left from too much hair straightening.

"I can imagine," she said. "Anyway, does it seem to you like Karen doesn't know what she's doing?"

"Only in every aspect of her job that I've witnessed so far. I'd feel sorry for her if it weren't such a big problem for us."

"I don't feel sorry for her," said Chloe. "I think she's a big bully. And she's taking it out on me."

"Well, yes." It was all too unfortunately common. Women from previous generations had fought hard to forge a place in academia, smashing down barriers and forcing their way in. Now they were fearful and mean and virulently misogynistic, and determined to ensure that the current crop of younger women flooding into the ivory tower suffered at least as much as they had.

"I'm pretty sure this is how the cycle of hazing and abuse perpetuates," I said.

"It's because I'm black. Or fat. I don't see her doing it to anyone else."

"How you look sure could be part of it," I said. "I wouldn't be surprised if Karen doesn't know how to act around someone who isn't white. Although Mel and I are both white and thin, and she's been pretty shitty to us so far too. I bet she mistreats everyone. Bullying and exploitation are endemic to education. It just gets refracted through the lens of racism or sexism or ableism or homophobia or whatever."

Chloe gave me a sideways look. "Karen seems nice enough to *you.*"

I opened my mouth to say *Are you blind?* Then I reconsidered. "Have you had a problem with panic attacks in the past?" I asked instead.

"I had terrible problems with them in undergrad. Same as here, actually: I showed up to school and bam! Panic attacks. I was all looking forward to college, too. That's probably what the problem was: I thought it was going to be so great, and I got myself all worked up over it. Then they went away in grad school, and here they are again. I was just so happy to get this job, you know? I knew how lucky I was, even if it wasn't my first choice. A tenure-track job straight out of grad school! I'd won the lottery, or something even better. And I guess...my office is probably symbolic of this new stage in my life, and all the hopes and dreams and terrible, terrible stress around it, or something like that, and that's why every time I go in it I start to panic. Oh, hi, Taylor."

"Hi, Professor Taylor! And you too, Professor Halley!" Taylor waved at us as she walked past, moving practically in lockstep with Chris.

"Were they secretly holding hands?" Chloe whispered once they'd gone by.

"It kinda looked like that, didn't it? I'm not surprised, though. Well, I am, but only because I didn't know Chris had it in him. But they sure seemed sweet on each other right from the beginning."

"Well, that's nice. I guess. Although I thought Nathan was the one with a crush on Taylor."

"Nathan...as in Nathan Willoughby?" I asked. "The jerk from move-in day?"

"Mmm-hmmm. His French class gets out the same time mine does, and he's been hanging around and meeting up with Taylor every day, trying to get her to go do stuff with him."

"Gosh," I said. "Does she seem interested?"

Chloe shrugged. "She's the kind of bubble-headed blonde who always seems interested when a man—or a boy—looks her way."

I bit back a comment on the sexism inherent in that statement, and, checking my phone, said, "Gosh, it's 8:55 already. I'd better get going. Are you okay to get to class?"

"Yeah. The attack's pretty much over. I should probably get some counseling, though. It didn't do much for me last time, but I wasn't really committed to it the way I should have been. But this time will be different. I can't let this derail everything I've worked so hard for over a decade to get. I'll get it under control, no matter what."

"Sounds like a good plan," I said.

26

MEL MADE IT THROUGH the day, and recovered enough over the weekend to drive us to campus on Monday.

"I'm almost sorry to be getting better," she said. "Now I won't have an excuse to get out of this fucking teaching observation and review I've got for my eleven o'clock class."

"Yeah," I said. "Although I think anything serious enough to get you out of it would be infinitely worse than a stupid observation, loathsome as it is."

"I guess. But it looks like I won't be finding out, which I guess is a good thing. You haven't come down with it yet, have you?"

"Nope." I remained flu-free, and so did everyone else in the department.

"Well, I hope it was just some passing freak thing I picked up from visiting my family last weekend. I shoulda known better than to go see them. Can't wait to get completely over it. I'm feeling a lot better than I was last week, but fuck, my knees *still* hurt. And so do my elbows. And my right thumb's still killing me. I dislocated it a few years back, and it's like it's been injured all over again. But hopefully I'll be good to go for my fucking observation. When's yours? Mine's tomorrow."

"Next week," I said.

"Well, I'll be sure to give you the skinny on it, let you know what kind of shit Karen gets up to."

"Thanks," I said. "I appreciate it."

The skinny, which I got the next day, was that Karen had come into Mel's class five minutes late, forced half the students to move in order to give her the seat by the door, spread out her papers on the table with lots of rustling and loud sighs, and proceeded to take notes very ostentatiously the entire time. The students had spent most of the class looking at her sideways instead of concentrating on the lesson, which, Mel said, had as a consequence been the one truly lousy lesson she'd given here so far. Karen had then gotten up five minutes before the end, told Mel loudly that she expected to see her in her office as soon as the lesson was over, and then bustled out, as disruptively as she'd arrived.

"And then—wait for it—when I *did* go to her office, she led with some bullshit about how I should organize my seating for better classroom flow and student engagement. I literally didn't know how to respond to that. First of all, my classroom is a windowless hole that's so small we can't walk around it at the best of times. Second of all, she made the students move when she came in! If I *had* had a seating plan other than 'Squeeze in wherever you can,' she would have totally fucked it up. I thought about pointing all that out to her, but I know her fucking type: they make suggestions that seem reasonable but are actually impossible to implement, and then when you tell them that their suggestions are impossible, they accuse you of having a bad attitude. So I was all like, 'Oh, thanks, that's a *great* idea. How would you suggest I organize my seating to optimize classroom flow and student engagement?'"

"What did she say?" I asked.

"She told me one of the things they'd hired me for was my supposed experience and expertise in teaching, and it was my responsibility to come up with appropriate lesson plans and classroom management techniques, not hers."

"Gosh," I said. "I'm surprised she didn't take the opportunity to hold forth for half an hour on best practices in classroom management. Many people I know in her position wouldn't be able to shut up about it."

"I know. And I wish she had. At least then I could have nodded along and pretended like I was grateful for what she was telling me. But instead she went on to my choice and presentation of materials, which she said were 'opaque.' She went on and on about how she couldn't follow what was happening in class, and I wanted to be all like, 'Yeah, 'cause you haven't been to any of the previous classes and you don't speak a fucking word of Arabic, plus you seem to be a self-important moron, so you, unlike my students, can't keep up.'

"And she complained about me writing in Arabic on the board, which she said was confusing, since some of the students asked to have words explained to them, and she also complained about me using English on the board, because I'm supposed to be creating an immersive environment from day one. I could literally feel my hands itching to reach out and throttle her while I shouted 'Jesus fucking Christ, woman, make up your damn mind! Either we avoid all confusion, or we create an immersive environment, but it's kind of an either/or situation.'

"Plus, I got the feeling, although fuck knows she's hardly the only one, that she'd, like, never taken or taught a language class before. I mean, I know that's not true, but her suggestions made it sound like she had no idea what goes on in a language classroom."

"Maybe that's true," I said. "Maybe she's spent her entire career so confused and incompetent that she genuinely doesn't know what normal, competent language teaching looks like."

"Yeah, I guess. I couldn't figure out if she's genuinely that stupid, or it's all a, like, fucking clever ruse to enable her to bully me more effectively."

"I get the feeling that she's genuinely that stupid," I said. "Stupidity and incompetence combined with ill-will can produce amazing simulacra of cunning conspiracies."

"Too damn true. So anyway, to top it all off, she started asking me about my goddamn sex life. Like, she was trying to come across as all friendly and such, you know, the concerned mentor, and so she started asking me how the dating scene was here for 'people like me,' and whether I'd been able to get out and 'meet people' and such. I guess it would have sounded innocent enough on a transcript or something, but the look in her eye as she said it turned my stomach. And then she told me to be sure to submit my syllabi and teaching portfolio by the end of the week. I wanted to point out that I'd *already* submitted my teaching portfolio when I applied for the damn job, and it hadn't changed much since that was just last semester, but I was just all like, 'Sure, Karen, no problem, I'll get right on that.' And then I got the fuck out of there."

"Ugh," I said.

"And now I don't know if she's being such a gross bitch to me because that's who she is to everyone, or if she just hates me because I'm a lesbian."

"My guess is that she's a horrible bully to everyone she thinks she has power over, but she expresses it in different ways to different people," I said. "So she'll bully you in a homophobic way, and Chloe in a racist way, and so on and so forth. It's individually tailored bullying."

"Yeah." Mel gave me a sideways look. "You'd better watch out for yourself, Rowena. I think she's got a real fucking bee in her bonnet about you. She started going off at one point about how we can't all charm our students with our good looks like Rowena Halley can, so those of us who aren't so lucky need to develop actual technique in order to teach."

"Gee whiz," I said. "I don't know whether to be flattered or appalled."

"Yeah, I know. Once again I literally didn't know what the fuck to say. I mean, were we really gossiping about another instructor's personal appearance behind her back? I kept wondering if this was really happening. But I'd watch out, if I were you. I think she's got a Sapphic *thang* for you that she can't bear to acknowledge."

Mel was silent for a moment. "Jewel was real pretty," she said after a bit. "Different from how you are—she was half-Latina, half-German—but the same in that everyone who saw her thought to themselves, 'Now *there's* a pretty woman.' She had the same strong and fit but also super-feminine thing that you've got going on."

"Um," I said.

"Sorry if that made you uncomfortable. What I was trying to say was that it caused her a lot of problems. Everywhere she went she caused a reaction, and everyone wanted a piece of her. She could just be sitting in the corner minding her own business, and three men and two women would come up and hit on her before she could order a drink. Before she started her own business, her bosses and coworkers were always saying she got everything because of her looks, not because she was good at what she did. No one could ever see anything in her other than her looks, and people were always trying to get something from her, with no thought of the person behind the pretty face and the hot body.

"Or they were trying to punish her for making them feel bad just by existing. And of course, I was out of my mind about her too. I couldn't just be a friend to her because she was so fucking pretty. So anyway, Rowena, I just wanted to say...I guess I just wanted to give you a heads-up. I know I'm probably not telling you anything you don't already know, but Karen & Co. might try to really fuck things up for you just because they can't stand how you make them feel."

"Gosh," I said. "That makes me feel bad. I certainly don't want to make other people unhappy. But I appreciate the heads-up."

27

ALL TOO SOON, MY OWN observation was upon me. Maybe nature sensed what was going on, and brought the rainstorm that drenched me and everyone else to the bone on our way to class on Monday morning as a prelude to the delights to come.

I dutifully emailed my lesson plan to Karen Monday afternoon. This triggered an immediate response complaining about my tardiness, since she had requested that I send her the lesson plan and materials "a FULL 24 hours prior to the class!"

I emailed back with an apology for my unpardonable lateness, but said I wanted to make sure she had the most up-to-date version of the plan and the materials, and since I always waited until after teaching the preceding class to finalize my plan and materials for the upcoming class, in case something came up that needed to be addressed, I'd had to wait until Monday morning's classes were done to create my plan and materials for Tuesday.

The expectation is that you will be more organized than that, Rowena, Karen emailed back. *And when I make a request to a junior faculty member, I expect it to be fulfilled to the letter.*

I spent a moment indulging in fantasies of bloody mayhem. Then I went home through the dreary rain and sent out another job application.

I woke up the next morning feeling a similar low-level dread to what greeted me on the day of an interview. Only this time it was tinged with a sour, smoldering feeling that I could only characterize as hatred. I'd been working with Karen for three weeks and already I hated her, even though she hadn't done anything actually bad to me. Yet. Maybe she was like a fledgling serial killer, building up to her main crime. In fact, I was willing to bet that's exactly what she was like.

Mel dropped me off outside of Bedford Hall so that I'd have a few extra minutes to prep for my class while she parked the car. I was still chewing over my simmering rage at Karen as I walked across the corner of the quad and entered the building. My preoccupation with other things made the sudden wave of dizziness that swept over me as I stepped into Bedford all the more surprising.

What is going on?!? The dizziness was already receding, leaving me doubting that it had even happened. I must have overdone it on coffee this morning. Sometimes it affected me like that if I had it on an empty stomach while I was in a severe state of nerves. I thought I was more angry than nervous, but maybe not. Maybe I was having an anxiety attack. Chloe's story of panic attacks every time she went into her office had freaked me out a little bit. Especially on the heels of the woman who'd had a panic attack during the faculty meeting.

None of that's going to happen to you! I told myself. *Not unless you let it. You're not prone to panic attacks. You've been chased by armed thugs, and held at gunpoint, and all kinds of other bad things, and never felt so much as a twinge of panic. You'll be fine!*

But as I was walking down the hallway, I suddenly had the peculiar sensation that "I" was walking next to my body, not in it. By the time I got into the classroom, I was having a hard time recognizing my body as my own. And when I closed the classroom door, the door and the walls and the chairs and the students all seemed weirdly far away and alien, like I was looking at a picture of a different planet and couldn't figure out what I was seeing. The only thing I could sense with clarity was the smell of mildew filling the room, stronger than ever with all the rain we'd just had.

"Good morning!" Was my voice always this loud? Or maybe it was super-quiet and I was just hearing it wrong.

"Good morning!" said the students. Then they started to ask me questions, and the weird sensation passed.

It returned when Karen came bustling in five minutes late, just as she had for Mel's class, and stayed with me for the entire session. I kept feeling like this wasn't actually happening to me, it *couldn't* be happening to me, and I was helpless to do anything about it. Like a rape victim. Probably brought on by Karen's outrageous behavior.

Just as she had with Mel, she made several of my students get up and move so that she could have the seat by the door. She took up three spaces' worth of room with all the pens and pieces of paper she spread out on the table, and rustled her materials loudly as she took ostentatious notes for the duration of the class. On several occasions she cleared her throat in a manner that suggested she was doing it not because she was trying to clear phlegm, but because she disapproved of what I was doing.

And when I broke the students into small groups for the final exercise, and suggested that she make up the third member in the group that was a person short, she told me, sniffing loudly as she did so, that it would be *highly* inappropriate and a breach of protocol. Several of the students stared at her in surprise, and Miranda fixed her a death glare that would have shriveled a more sensitive woman to ash, but the only reaction that provoked was a small, satisfied smile.

Just as the students had finally settled down after all the disruptions and started to get into the swing of telling each other what they had in their suitcases, Karen stood up, and, with much loud shuffling of paper, said, "Come see me in my office after class, Rowena," and attempted to stride commandingly out of the classroom. She was hindered in doing so by dropping first her folder, and then, after she had scrabbled all the loose papers off the floor and jammed them back into her folder, her pen, which broke and started pouring red ink onto the classroom carpet.

Several of the students suppressed titters. Those nearest to her offered her tissues. Karen accepted them with a peevish air, as if they were bothering her rather than helping her, and dabbed at the carpet for a second before saying, "Rowena, be sure to get someone to come in and clean this up," and making another attempt at striding off commandingly. This time she was hindered only by her own dumpy figure, but that was a pretty serious hindrance.

"Who *was* that?" demanded Camden, a blond boy who had thus far always come across as friendly and easy-going. "Is she *always* such a bitch?"

"Oh yeah," said Miranda. "Crimson's Bitch Number 1, that's her. She used to be my advisor, until she dumped me because of my 'bad attitude.' And thank God for that. Totes fucking nightmare."

"Yes, well, there's no need to worry about it," I told them. "She's not your problem, so let's not waste another second on it. We should be able to fit in one more—oops, actually, we're already almost out of time, and I guess I should find someone to call about the red ink on the carpet before my next class."

"I thought your next class was in ten minutes, Professor," said Miranda.

"It is. Hopefully I can find the right number on my phone."

"I can do it," she offered. "I have the campus directory bookmarked, because of my work with the paper. I'll give Facilities Services a call as soon as we get out."

"Would you? That'd be great. If you think they'll listen to you."

"I'm sure they'll listen to me as much as they'll listen to you, Professor. They don't really do much, although for what they get paid, who can blame 'em? But I'll put in the call right now."

"Thanks. Let's get out of here, everyone."

A run to the bathroom between classes made me feel a little better, although the close, moldy-smelling air of the classroom seemed particularly claustrophobia-inducing when I came back into it. By the end of my second class, a sharp pain was building behind my left eye, and blue and gold lights sparkled and flashed whenever I turned my head.

"Headache?" asked Karen as I entered her office.

I took my hand away from where I was rubbing my temple. "A bit," I said. Half of me thought that admitting any kind of weakness to her was a terrible idea. Half of me, the more optimistic half, said that maybe that would make her more sympathetic towards me. Worth a shot, at least. "I used to have migraines in undergrad. They mostly went away when I moved to Russia, and they've been pretty low-key ever since, but they've really flared up since I came here. Must be something about Georgia. Or maybe I'm just hungry."

"You need to get that under control, Rowena," Karen told me sternly. "As I've *already* had to remind Mel, you are each running what is essentially a one-person program. The college is depending on *you* to run your respective programs in a responsible and reliable manner, which is why it's so important that we do these observations and evaluations. We want to be sure that you're capable of teaching at the level we expect at a place like Crimson, and also that you're able to fit in with the department and the campus in general. You certainly can't be canceling class or missing activities just because you're feeling a little under the weather."

"Uh-huh." I sat down on the nearest shabby upholstered chair, which was the only one not overflowing with random scraps of paper and last year's final exams. I hoped it was my imagination making me think that it reeked of mildew.

The feeling of unreality returned with redoubled strength as I sat there. I wasn't sure whether it made Karen's haranguing more or less easy to tolerate. As with Mel, she dragged the meeting out for the better part of an hour. She referred repeatedly to all the notes she'd taken, except that half the time she was unable to read her own handwriting, and would sit there puzzling over what she'd written, before saying, "Well, it doesn't matter anyway. The *point* is that that's not the way things are done at Crimson."

"But that's the exercise the book has for that grammatical point," I said, somewhere around the third or fourth time.

"Really, Rowena, I'd expected better from you. Everyone knows that textbook exercises are totally inadequate. You should be making your own exercises, ones that are more interactive and communicative."

"Well," I said, "I *did* also have an exercise that I created myself, a conversation exercise..."

"One is insufficient," Karen cut me off, maybe because she liked interrupting me, maybe because she didn't want to give me a chance to remind her that she'd interrupted the homemade conversation exercise, first with her churlish refusal to participate, and then her hyper-embarrassing exit. "*All* your exercises should be communicative and conversation-focused, rather than drill."

"Most Russian instructors find that their students need a fair amount of grammar drill," I said.

"Students should be picking up grammar through conversation exercises! Really, I don't see what's so hard about it. *My* students do it all the time."

"That's nice," I said. "But most Americans can't pick up Russian grammar without explicit instruction and drill."

"That's not how we do things here at Crimson, Rowena, and I expect you to put in the effort needed to make sure that that's what happens."

For a moment I thought I was going to scream at her. Then I thought I was going to burst out laughing at the thought of

English-speakers plucking the rules of Russian grammar out of thin air. Then I was afraid I was going to vomit. The air in the office was sickeningly close.

"Okay," I said, instead of doing any of those things. "Sure."

Karen harangued me for a little while longer, and then made me sign a statement saying I'd had that meeting with her and acknowledged all the areas which she'd noted for improvement. Then she went on for a while about how I needed to do more committee work.

"Like what kind of committee work?" I asked. "And I thought that as a VAP, I wasn't allowed to do committee work."

"Well...we're expecting more and more from our VAPs, Rowena. You need to show you're committed to the program and willing to do your part."

"Sure," I said. "What kind of committee work did you have in mind?"

"What kind...you can't expect *me* to arrange everything for you, Rowena! That's something you need take responsibility for yourself."

"Okay," I said. "How do I find out more about volunteering for committee work?"

That question released an avalanche of complaints about the heavy burden of committee work at Crimson, and the incompetence of most of the committees. Even though Karen was the one saying it, I had to believe most of it was true.

It took a good quarter of an hour before the flood dried up. I was just getting up to go, thinking it was finally over, when she said, "Have you made any progress in finding out the link between Miranda and the Gang of Six, Rowena?"

I froze in mid-crouch. "As far as I can tell, she doesn't have anything to do with them."

Karen's face turned an especially unpleasant shade of gray. "That's not possible! Really, Rowena, you shouldn't let yourself be fooled so easily by your students."

"Well, I spoke with her about the Gang of Six at some length while she was interviewing me about the Russian program, and she specifically said that she'd been assigned to research them for paper, but she wasn't making any progress."

"She's lying," Karen snapped out instinctively.

"What makes you think that?" A stab of pain went through my left eye, making my words come out more sharply than maybe they should have. Or maybe they weren't nearly sharp enough.

"Really, Rowena! Just *look* at her!"

"I did. I look at her four days a week, plus the lengthy discussion I had with her about the Russian program for the paper. She's not your typical Crimson student, that's true. But as far as I could tell, her confusion about the Gang of Six was genuine. And frankly, anonymous blogging doesn't seem her style. I'd guess she works for the paper and wears all that makeup and that flamboyant hairstyle for a reason. She wants to be noticed. I think if she were to write up criticisms of the college, she'd sign her name to them."

"You're so *naive*, Rowena. One of the things you need to learn if you're going to succeed here is that students lie. They lie so much that half the time they can't tell the difference between truth and fiction, and they'll insist on their truthfulness when you catch them out in a boldfaced lie. They're *always* looking to get something out of you, so you can't believe a word they say."

"It's certainly true that many people can't tell the difference between truth and fiction," I said. "And there are plenty of people who lie all the time, and some of them believe they're telling the truth. But it's also true that if you spend all your time looking for lies, you can stumble right past the truth without seeing it. Like everyone else here on campus, I'd love to find out who the Gang of Six are, at the very least in order to assuage my curiosity, and I'll keep an eye on Miranda, as I would for any of my students, but if she's the ringleader behind them, she's doing a dang good job of concealing it."

Karen swallowed. Her face was so puffy and droopy that the action made her look like a bullfrog about to burst into song. "I think we're done here," she said.

"Have a good day," I said, and left.

28

I HALF-EXPECTED TO be fired on the spot for talking to Karen like that, or maybe just because she didn't like the cut of my jib, but instead all I got was a snippy email demanding that I submit a teaching portfolio, my syllabi for this semester, and syllabi for next semester. I wanted to believe that the demand for next semester's syllabi was a good sign that my contract was not about to be terminated, but it was all too possible that it was just more sadism and busywork. American education has turned busywork into high art. Extremely intelligent, highly educated people spend hours of their time every week producing PowerPoint slides and fill-in-the-blank exercises and multiple choice quizzes so that our best and brightest young people can spend hours of their time pretending to learn instead of actually learning.

The following week it was Chloe's turn to be observed. At Mel's suggestion, the three of us got together for lunch the Friday before at O'Reilly's Sandwich Shoppe in order to give her our insights into the process. Unfortunately, the only insights we were able to give was that Karen was mean, and possibly crazy.

"Oh no," Chloe said. She picked a little at her Caesar salad, and then pushed it away. She'd announced that she was trying a new diet, and we were absolutely not to allow her to order fries or dessert or anything like that. But right now she didn't appear to feel like eating at all. I wasn't sure if it was because of nerves over the upcoming observation, nerves over the fact that everyone in the Sandwich Shoppe was giving her a double-take, as if they'd never seen a black person before, or just general nerves. "I don't know if I can handle something like that."

"You can," Mel and I said simultaneously.

"I just...I've just been feeling really fragile recently. These panic attacks...every time I think I've got them beat, they come back and grab me by the throat. This is the worst they've ever been. If they get any worse, I don't know what I'm going to do. I made an appointment with a therapist, but they couldn't fit me in until next month. I don't know if I can make it until then."

"You can," said Mel again. "Plus, what's a therapist going to do for you that you can't do for yourself?"

Chloe gave her a weird look. "You must not have seen a therapist before."

"Unfortunately, that's not the case. I've seen way the fuck more therapists and shrinks than I'd like. And so have a lot of my friends. And half the time, they ended up even more fucked up than they were before."

Chloe was shorter than Mel by a good six inches, but she still gave the impression of looking down her nose, ever so slightly, at her. "That's not how it's supposed to work. That's not how it works if you go to a *good* therapist."

"Maybe," said Mel. "Although in that case there aren't that many good therapists. The way it normally seems to work is that you go to the shrink and say, 'Doc, help me out, I'm so unhappy because I'm a queer little dyke and I'm afraid my family won't understand and my friends won't understand and my church will tell me I'm going to hell.' And the shrink will nod understandingly and tell you you have a brain imbalance and prescribe you antidepressants. So you'll start taking them, and soon you'll blow up like a prize sow and be a hundred pounds overweight."

The other people in the Sandwich Shoppe were giving Mel sideways glances too. She was always just a little too butch, and right now her voice was just a little too loud, to pass for straight in a place like Greenfields, Georgia.

"So you'll go back to the shrink and say, 'Doc, doc, you gotta help me, I'm so unhappy, not only am I queer little dyke, now I'm a fat queer little dyke and no one wants to go out with me and I'm afraid I'll never get to have the sexual experience that I want so badly. And the shrink will nod understandingly again and up your dosage, maybe put you on two or three different things at once."

We were sitting at a table by the front door. Two men came in, paused, glanced at the three of us, and then surveyed me carefully up and down. Mel, over whom their eyes had slid unnoticed, continued, her face flushed now under her tan.

"So then you'll blow up even more and develop diabetes and maybe some tardive dyskinesia, and then you'll be well and truly fucked for life, except no one will ever want to fuck a fat, twitching dyke like you, and you can't hold down a job either because you're constantly in a drug-induced haze. So the little bit of sadness you had at first will have turned into full-blown suicidal ideation, and rightly so, goddammit."

Most of the women in the Shoppe were now looking our way. Most of the men, I was pretty sure, were looking specifically my way. It was nice to know that I wasn't being left out of the attention that my friends were getting. If I mentioned all those male gazes being directed at me, I was pretty sure that Chloe would tell me how lucky and self-centered I was. A lot of my not-traditionally-pretty female friends were worse than men in thinking that unasked-for male attention was a compliment that I should be both grateful to receive, and repentant for getting when others didn't.

"That sounds awful," was what I said out loud. "But not surprising."

Chloe, meanwhile, had a look on her face like she didn't believe Mel, and was struggling to find a response, either to her words or her obvious pain. I had the sudden acute awareness that Chloe was a good seven years younger than Mel and I, and probably much more sheltered. She'd told us she'd gone straight from undergrad to grad school, and gotten this job straight out of grad school. Which was a stunning, unbelievable piece of luck. Although from everything I'd seen so far, Chloe also had to be given the credit for being an extremely talented scholar. She'd mentioned that she'd gotten an article published in the *PMLA,* one of the premier journals for literary studies, while she was still in grad school, and she already had editors from academic presses approaching *her*, instead of the other way around, about turning her dissertation into a book. It was hard not to be consumed with envy just sitting next to her.

But that meant that she'd spent her entire life from the age of five onwards in the claustrophobic confines of school, and been rewarded for it. She'd probably never thought about questioning its core values and ingrained patterns of behavior. She didn't seem like a rebel at heart, and she'd never had anything happen in her life yet to turn her into one. Of the three of us she was the most compliant and conformist, as well as the most inexperienced and naive. For now. Maybe Crimson would shake that out of her. Or maybe in twenty years' time she would be taking Karen's place as the bully in the department corner office.

"I've certainly heard plenty of horror stories, especially about drugs," I said, instead of any of that. "But if you find therapy helps you, that's great. And in the meantime, I'm sure you can get through the observation. It's never fun, and Karen is, well, frankly, awful, but it was so surreally terrible it was funny, you know? Just, I don't know, smile politely and let her say what she's going to say, because whatever it is, you won't be able to stop it, and just try to get out of there with your skin intact."

"That sounds terrible," said Chloe. 'That's not how it's supposed to be."

"No, but it's how it is," said Mel. "Just pretend you're at your comps or your dissertation defense again."

"Everyone was really nice to me at my comps and my defense," said Chloe. She paused, a reflective expression crossing her face. "Which maybe wasn't such a great thing," she added. "The first time I had a hostile search committee at an interview, I completely crumbled and fell apart. I'd never had to deal with anything like that before."

"See, there you go," said Mel. "Think of this as toughening."

"I don't think I want to be toughened," said Chloe.

"Nobody does, but it's gonna happen, so you might as well get something out of it," said Mel. "Besides, after a while all kinds of stuff just doesn't seem that frightening anymore. My committee was so gross to me at my defense that I seriously considered taking up cutting afterwards. And, remember, I was in a fucking war. I was in a fucking war, and one of the worst things I've ever gone through was an afternoon talking about my research to people who were supposed to be my mentors. I remember standing at the counter the next morning, cutting up an apple, and having this intense urge to start slicing into my wrists. I had this moment of clarity, where I thought, 'Oh. This is why rape victims cut themselves. And I could start down that path too.' And then I was like, 'Nah. I'm not gonna do that. I'm not gonna start down that road.' And I put the knife down, and walked away.

"But after that even the meanest interview committees seem like pushovers. They start to give me shit, and I just smile and think about the money they might give me. Trust me, that's what's going to happen here. Karen might be a prize bitch to you, and it'll suck, and then the next time someone's a bitch to you, you'll be like, 'Wait a minute, fuck you! You don't scare me.'"

Chloe shuddered. "That sounds awful. Maybe...I don't know, maybe if I'm just really nice to her, she'll be nice to me. That normally works. Although"—she frowned—"I kinda get the feeling she can't stand to be in the same room with me. She never looks straight at me. It's like I'm a crazy wild animal or something." Chloe laughed, not very happily. "I guess maybe she's never actually spent any time with anyone black before."

"Maybe not," I said. "And being nice to her isn't a bad strategy. It's normally my go-to first tactic. But don't beat yourself up too much if it doesn't work. Karen's a bully, and sometimes there's nothing you can do to get along with a bully. If you fight back, they'll smack you down even harder, but going along with what they want won't save you either. And you can't hide the fact that you're a rising star, any more than you can hide your skin color. She's probably going to hate you for both of them, and the ability to change that isn't in your hands."

Chloe looked so down at those words, and also so disbelieving, that I switched topics and asked if she'd seen any more signs of the romance I thought might be blossoming between Taylor and Chris.

"Not really," she said. "That Nathan boy is all over Taylor after every class—just like half the guys on campus. I'm telling you, that girl is a menace. She reminds me of a girl I used to have to teach in grad school. Just the same kind of bubble-headed blonde chick—well, you know how they are. A real flirt, *and* I always got the feeling she was about to say something racist. She certainly thought she was the center of the universe, that's for sure, and she always seemed to look down on *me*. Then she started dating a black guy in the class, and I kept hoping he'd teach her a good hard lesson, take her down a peg, but he just gave her puppy eyes like everyone else. What?" Chloe realized that both Mel and I were staring at her with open-mouthed horror. "I'm not saying I wanted him to, you know, *rape* her or beat her up..."

"That's pretty much what it sounded like, though," said Mel. I had been too busy congratulating myself on being right, and on having the foresight not to mention all the men staring at me, to say anything. "Especially to a blonde chick such as myself, who's been told more than once that she needs some man to take her down a peg and straighten her out."

"Oh. Oh, well, I guess...that's not what I meant *at all*, but, you know, she was *so* annoying, and *so* blonde, and I just wanted her to get her comeuppance...I mean, girls like that can cause a lot of trouble. That Taylor sure seems like she's causing a lot of trouble. Even for someone like Nathan. When, that is, he's not chasing after that punk-rocker girl in your class, Rowena."

"Miranda? You think he's interested in Miranda?"

Chloe shrugged. "I've seen them together more than once, and he always looked super-sweet on her. You'd think someone who keeps blathering on about Men's Rights and how women control everything wouldn't spend so much of his time chasing girls."

"I think you've put your finger on the crux of the problem," I said.

"Yeah. Have you heard the latest? They're now saying they're going to reschedule the Miriam Chen talk. There was so much outcry from both directions about the threats that they've bumped it back a month, to November. The Gang of Six posted a whole thing about it yesterday."

"I saw," I said. "Is it just me, or does it seem like they have a new writer? Someone who's even more hardcore?"

"I noticed that too," said Mel. "You're sure it's not your Miranda?"

"Not unless she's just been recruited to them. Which is entirely possible. I'll see if I can feel her out about it next week. Not because Karen wants me to, but so that I can warn the Gang of Six she's out to get them."

29

I HAD BEEN PLANNING to ask Miranda if she had heard anything more about, or had any thoughts on, the Miriam Chen talk, but she beat me to the punch. She came bursting into the classroom at 8:50 on Monday morning, demanding, "Have you heard, Professor Halley? About Miriam Chen?"

"I heard that the talk had been pushed back a month," I said.

"Yeah. The college issued some bullshit thing about accommodating Miriam Chen's schedule, but the Gang of Six put out a post saying it's because of more threats. They're saying that she's saying she got a whole series of death threats from people saying they're students here at Crimson. I've already tried to get in touch with her to confirm this, but she's not answering her email or phone, and I can't blame her, can you?"

"Not really," I said.

"Anyway," said Miranda. "I actually had, well...I wanted to ask you a favor, Professor Halley."

"Sure," I said.

"I was gonna ask you...are you on the committee for organizing Chen's talk? Or do you know anyone who is? 'Cause I was thinking...maybe that would be the way to get ahold of her."

"I'm not on the committee, and I don't know anyone who is, unfortunately."

Miranda's face fell.

"But," I said, "my department chair keeps harassing me about doing committee work, even though technically I'm not supposed to. But maybe I could say I wanted to, and *get* on the committee."

Miranda's face lit up. "Really? You'd do that, Professor Halley?"

I shrugged. "I really do need to do some committee work in order to get my department chair off my back. At least this way I'll be working to organize something I actually believe in, and maybe I can help you out as well."

"Yeah. I guess most committee work is pretty boring, huh?"

"If it were just boring, that wouldn't be so bad," I said. "The problem is that it's also pointless. Although maybe I'm being unfair. I haven't done a huge amount of it, or any here at Crimson, so maybe it's more worthwhile than I think it is."

"Nah," said Miranda. "I bet it's mainly boring and pointless. Most of the time I don't know what any of the professors or staff do here. It seems like they just go to meetings all the time without doing anything that actually helps students at all."

"I fear you may have a point," I said. "I'm afraid that helping students is not actually the prime directive of most universities."

Miranda looked interested, like she'd never thought about that before. "What is, then, Professor? 'Cause they're always talking about how they're here for us and here to help us out, but most professors and staff members, if you ask them for help, they'll tell you no, even if it wouldn't be that hard for them to do what you need them to do for you. It's like they're specifically here *not* to help you."

"Yeah," I said. "Because what they're really here for is to take money from you."

Miranda made a face. "Sounds about right, Professor, even though most of 'em aren't ever going to admit it."

"I know," I said. "And don't tell anyone you heard it from me. But I really would like to help bring Miriam Chen to campus. At least it would a concrete accomplishment, and she might have something interesting to say. Do you happen to know who's in charge of it?"

"I know I talked to Professor DeWitt from Sociology about it. I think she might be in charge."

"Okay," I said. "I'll get in touch with her and see if they'll let me join them."

"Sounds good. And thanks again, Professor."

The other students were now filing in and trying to find a decent place to sit. A doomed task in this room, but they always tried every time. Miranda took the seat in the corner by the board, the one where it was difficult to take notes and impossible to do anything else. I assumed that she was doing it in order to spare anyone else having to sit there. She really was a very sweet girl. Chris sat down next to her. He was holding his head turned slightly to the left, like he was trying to hide the left side of his face from me. When I went over to the board, which was to his left, I saw that he had a brand-new piercing in his left ear.

I thought about saying something about it. Then I looked at his nervous expression, and decided against it. He must have gotten his ear pierced in order to make a statement and get attention, but now that he was getting the attention, he wasn't enjoying it as much as he'd thought he would. Isn't that always the way, especially in college. Every single student wanted to be special, unique, and different. But there were so many of them. The world was so full of people now that it was impossible to be anything other than just another member of the herd, disposable and replaceable. And there was nothing like school to make you realize that.

"Is everyone ready for some pronunciation drills?" I said. "Repeat after me."

30

SANDRA DEWITT, ASSOCIATE Professor of Sociology, turned out to be more than happy to have me join the committee organizing Miriam Chen's talk when I emailed her about it that afternoon.

It's always wonderful when a new faculty member *asks* to join a committee, she wrote back. *And in this case, the more, the merrier! How's your event planning? I'm afraid the rest of us are pretty much hopeless about that kind of thing. And with all the complications surrounding Chen's talk, it's making it twice as difficult as usual.*

I'm not about to become a professional wedding planner, but I've put together guest speaker engagements and local conferences plenty of times, I wrote back. *I'd be happy to pitch in that way if that's what's needed.*

Fabulous! Will you be around and available to get coffee sometime in the next couple of days?

Coffee would be great, I told her. *I teach MTWF at 9 and 10, and then I'm available after that.*

Tomorrow at 11 work for you? Have you been to Brew's Up yet? It's surprisingly good for a campus cafe.

I haven't. I'd love to check it out.

Great! It's on the front quad, right by the bookstore. I'll get there at 11, and you can show up when you get free from your second class.

Looking forward to it, I wrote. Which was almost true. Sandra seemed, at least on email, to be a pleasant-enough person, and I really did want to help out with organizing the Miriam Chen talk, and coffee was always welcome. But first I had to keep Chloe from melting down in a puddle of nerves over her teaching observation, which was scheduled for 9:00am Tuesday morning.

She texted me Monday evening to say that Karen had already gotten on her case about not sending her the teaching materials in a sufficiently timely fashion.

Yeah, she did that to me, too, I told her.

I just don't know if I can do this!

You *can*. It might suck—it *will* suck, but you *can* do it. You will be as strong and as brave as you need to be.

I'm just having so many problems with panic attacks. And I still haven't seen my new therapist, and I don't know what to do. I think I need to go back on meds, but my old prescriptions have all expired, and I can't get new ones until I see my therapist and my doctor, and it's such a pain to get that kind of stuff arranged in a new place.

I know. And you'll get it straightened out. But first you'll make it through this observation.

What if I have a panic attack in the middle of class?

Has that happened before? I asked.

A couple of times, but they were just little ones. And I was able to sit down and take a few deep breaths and carry on.

Then do the same thing if it happens tomorrow. Do your students know?

Of course not! I don't want to give them any more reason to look down on me.

I'm sure they don't look down on you, I wrote. I left out the part about how thinking people look down on you has a tendency to be a self-fulfilling prophecy. That would only send Chloe into an even bigger tizzy. *And they might be more sympathetic than you think. Honesty has a habit of disarming people. And that way, if you have to sit down and take a few deep breaths or something, they'll know why, and they might try to help you out.*

Maybe you can get away with being friends with your students and admitting weakness to them, but *I* can't. And I swear this group hates me.

I'm sure they don't, I wrote.

They do! They just sit there and stare at me when I try to get them to do stuff. I just want to reach out and shake them sometimes! And I'm sure they're going to sabotage me tomorrow.

Now I was the one wanting to reach out and shake someone, although in this case it was Chloe.

Just try to be the kind of teacher you always wished you'd had when you were an undergrad, I wrote.

Oh God. That's so much pressure!

I don't mean to sound all New Age-y and positive thinking BS-y, but once you embrace your best self, becoming it is surprisingly easy, blahblahblah, I wrote. *And you *can* do it. You *can* make it through this observation, and all the rest, too.*

What if I don't? What if I lose my first real job before it even begins?

If they fire you at this point, you don't want to have anything to do with them anyway, I pointed out.

Yeah, but I'll be unemployed and unemployable, and I'm not even thirty!

That will suck, I agreed. *But you still don't want a job where people are that shitty to you.*

Easy for you to say! You're not tenure-track! You don't have that kind of pressure!

I took a deep breath, and exhaled it slowly through my nose. *True,* I texted back. *But I know a thing or two about pressure and sucky situations, and I'm telling you now that sometimes the only way out is through. Sometimes you just have to tough out the bad situations, and hope for the best.*

It shouldn't be like that!

It shouldn't, I wrote. *But it is. And in any case, you have to go through with this observation no matter what. Unless you just want to quit your job on the spot. And in eighteen hours it will be all be over. The whole thing will take two hours, tops, and then it will be behind you.*

Yeah, I guess. Can we get together afterwards?

I'm meeting with someone at 11, I wrote. *But anytime after that, sure. Do you want to do lunch?*

Maybe. I probably won't be able to eat tomorrow morning, so hopefully I'll be hungry afterwards.

Lunch it is, I wrote. *And in the meantime, stay strong! And I've got to go now—I've got a call coming in.* While I had been texting with Chloe, Alex had called.

31

"SORRY I MISSED YOUR call," I told Alex when I called him back. "I was texting with someone."

"Was it another man?" I could hear the vibrations come over the phone connection that meant Alex was trying not to laugh. It made the hair on the back of my neck rise. In a good way. How long since I'd actually heard his voice? Too long. Somehow just hearing it, flying all the way from the other side of the country and the continent, felt even more arousing than it would have if we'd been sitting face-to-face. Although face-to-face might be pretty arousing right now.

"No," I said. "Not in either of the senses you might mean. It wasn't a man, and it wasn't a lover. It was Chloe."

"Chloe...which one is she? The lesbian? Should I be concerned? Intrigued? Making plans for a super-hot threesome?"

"No, Mel is the lesbian. Although maybe Chloe's a lesbian too. But if she is, she's keeping herself pretty deep in the closet. And she's too stressed out about her upcoming teaching observation to be thinking about flirting right now, anyway."

"Ouch," said Alex. "Those things can be fucking brutal. Is she right to be worried?"

"Well, I told you about mine..."

"That you did. You think she's in for the same treatment?"

"Pretty much. I think Karen—our department chair—has to torture people. It's like a sick compulsion for her. And, I don't mean to be a pessimist or a wimp or anything, but I don't know how long all of us can stand it. She's been nothing but shitty to me, Mel, and Chloe since we've started here. We're only four weeks into the semester, and I'm already having to suppress fantasies about her getting hit by a truck or eaten by a T-Rex or something. Just being in the same institution as her is turning me into a bad person. And I think it might be even worse for Mel and Chloe. Especially Chloe."

"How so?"

I told him about Mel's bouts of depression and Chloe's outbursts against me and her students.

"I know you don't want to hear this, Rowena, but they're both big girls," Alex said, once I had finished. "They can take care of themselves."

"They don't seem to be doing a very good job of it!"

"Okay, fair enough. But they're still big girls, and it's on them to get their lives together. And how much trouble do you really think they're in?"

"Not very much right now. But I could see them both going off the deep end."

"Okay. Let's say that happens. What would going off the deep end look like for them?"

"I think it would be different for each," I said. "I think in Chloe's case it would mean becoming, you know, one of *them*. Turning into another mean-spirited academic bully. A few years down the road, and people could hate her as much as we currently hate Karen."

"That would suck," said Alex. "But mainly for her. It probably wouldn't be your problem at all, because chances are good you won't even be there anymore anyway, right?"

"Yeah, I guess. It just seems like such a waste."

"Of course it's a waste, but there might not be anything you can do to stop it, Rowena. Like I said, she's a big girl, even if she doesn't realize it yet, and she's gotta be the one who lives her life and makes her choices. And if she chooses to be a bully, well, that's on her."

"Yeah, but she might have really good reasons for ending up that way."

"Yeah. Just like everyone else. *You* have really good reasons to be a bully, Rowena, but are you?"

"I hope not," I said. "Every day I remind myself not to become one. Every day, I scan myself for signs of bullying, and try to nip any that I find in the bud. I think that's the only way to prevent it, if you're a teacher."

"Too fucking true. And you can be this Chloe's friend, because having a good friend is always helpful for not turning into a monster, and you can be a good example to her, but she's still gotta live her own life and make her own choices, and some of them might be bad."

"I know," I said. "I just feel sorry for her. And for Mel."

"So, what about Mel? You think she's gonna turn into a bully as well if she's not careful?"

"No," I said. "I think Mel is much more about self-harm than harming others. She's all tough and abrasive on the outside, but inside she's a cuddly lamb. Or something like that. She might tell you you're being an ass to your face, but I don't think she'd stab you in the back. But she might stab *herself* in the back. She's already mentioned having the urge to take up cutting."

"Well, fuck," said Alex. "I'm really sorry to hear that. But once again, you can be her friend, Rowena, but you can't stop her from harming herself if that's what she's set on doing. People who are set on self-destruction tend to get their way."

"I know. I know. I'm mainly just venting. I guess...I think I'm *pining* for you, and this is my way of getting close to you."

"Pining for me, huh?" said Alex. "Pining for me how bad?"

"Pretty bad," I said. "I know we agreed that I wouldn't come visit you for fall break, and I couldn't scrape up the cash for it anyway, and even if I did, I'd only be able to stay for about thirty-six hours, tops, but right now I'm wishing I could have even thirty-six hours with you."

"Yeah," said Alex. "Right now I'm wishing that too. And I'm trying to think of a way to come out and visit you. What about Thanksgiving?"

"I have Wednesday through Sunday off. Still not very long, and it's the worst week of the year for travel."

"Yeah, I know. And I've gotta go see my parents. I guess I could fly over to Pennsylvania Tuesday night, spend Wednesday and Thursday with them, fly down to Georgia Thursday night or Friday morning, spend Friday and Saturday with you, and fly back to Monterey on Sunday, and hope that I don't get stranded in Denver or something and miss Monday morning's classes."

"That's a lot of flying," I said. "That's a lot of money, and a lot of things that could go wrong."

"I know. It's probably a stupid idea."

"I just wish there were some way we could see each other sooner than Christmas," I said. "I was thinking...I don't know what your plans for Christmas are, but maybe I could come out and visit you over winter break? At least we'd see each other then. But that seems like a long way away right now."

"I know. How the fuck did we come to this so fast, Rowena?" he asked. "It's been more than a month since the last time we saw each other, and we're already making excuses for why we can't see each other next month, or the month after that. You know what? Fuck this. And fuck my parents. They've gotten me for every single Thanksgiving my entire life. Even the year I was deployed, I was home in time for Thanksgiving. And every year they make it excruciating. Maybe this year you should get me for Thanksgiving instead." He paused. "If you want me, that is."

"I do," I told him. "But it might mean having Thanksgiving dinner with my grandparents. And probably John."

"Not your parents?"

"They're still doing their Doctors Without Borders thing."

"Well, that's cool. I can't imagine my own parents doing anything like that. And I'd love to have Thanksgiving dinner with your grandparents, if you're okay with that."

"It might be a little awkward," I warned him.

"Because they'll keep bringing up other boyfriends whom you've brought home for Thanksgiving?"

"No, because I've never brought a boyfriend home for Thanksgiving before. The only serious boyfriend I ever had was Dima, and the commute would have been a little too long."

"Dima...this is *him*? The Russian guy?"

"Um...yeah."

"You don't have to hide him from me, Rowena. I know you were engaged to this guy, and he broke it off and sent you packing, and that's why you're with me instead of with him."

"You make it sound like I'm settling," I said. "I'm not."

"Maybe not, but you still have a past. Same as me. And that's cool. That's part of what makes you interesting. So don't feel like you have to hide it from me. Anyway, I'd love to come have Thanksgiving with your family. Even John."

"Wow, really?"

"Yes, Rowena. Really."

"That's great. Probably the easiest place to fly into is Atlanta. I could come get you at the airport."

"I'd like that. Almost as much as I'd like being with you right now. I need...I don't know, I need *something*."

"*I* think I know what you need," I said.

"Yeah, I bet you do." Even over the phone I could hear him smile. And then I could hear the smile fade. "I've just had a shitty couple of days, and I'd like to be around someone who could make me feel a little less shitty about myself."

"Why? What happened?"

"Oh, you know. The usual shit. Some buddy—actually, that's putting it much too strongly. Someone I knew slightly in the Navy was in town and wanted to get together with me and some other guys he knew. So we went out drinking last night, and I had to listen to them go on and on about all the firefights they'd been in, yada yada yada, until they demanded to know one of my stories, and...and...you know what? I'm not going to get into that shit. It's not important. Maybe someday I'll tell you, but...I can't. You don't need to hear my war stories. No one needs to hear my war stories. I didn't exactly cover myself with glory over there."

"I don't think anyone did," I said.

"Yeah, but...you know what? I'm going to stop whining about it right now. I don't want to blurt out something so self-pitying it'll make me regret it forever."

"You don't have to be afraid to tell me anything."

"Yeah, well...let's talk about something else. How's Fevronia?"

I filled Alex in on Fevronia's latest misdeeds. By the end of it, he was laughing.

"Thanks," he said. "That made me feel a lot better. It's pretty late there already, huh? I should probably let you get to bed."

"Glad to help. And sleep well."

"Good night, Rowena," he said. He was no longer laughing. "Sweet dreams. You, at least, deserve them."

32

AFTER THAT I WAS IN a bit of a state. Sorry for Alex and whatever mysterious thing he was going through, and suffering from frustrated arousal after hearing his voice but not being able to be with him or do anything about it, and still worried about Chloe, even though, as Alex had pointed out, she was a big girl and could look out for herself, even if she hadn't realized it yet. So I tossed and turned half the night.

Then, just as I was finally dropping into a real sleep, Fevronia came and threw up on the pillow next to mine, the one that was supposed to be reserved for lovers but most of the time was a cat vomit receptacle. Probably this was a symbol or a sign or something. I reminded myself that Fevronia was the one person in my life who was always there for me, even if she expressed it in unwelcome ways sometimes. Then I cleaned up the vomit and changed out the pillowcase and tried to go back to sleep.

My lack of rest must have been the reason behind my general feeling of lousiness when I got up the next morning, and the piercing headache that hit me as soon as I walked into my classroom. By the end of the first class, I was digging the knuckles of my left hand into my temple as I wrote on the board with my right hand, in a vain attempt to ease the stabbing pain behind my eyes.

It only got worse, though, when I ran to the bathroom between classes and got hit with a bright light right in the eyes as I stepped out of the stall. By the time I made it back to my classroom, a blurry gray blob was sitting in the center of my vision, and wouldn't go away, even when I closed my eyes.

I passed Chloe walking from her classroom to Karen's office, with the expression of a murderer on the way to the gallows on her face.

"How'd it go?" I asked.

"Poopy. Real poopy. And now I've got to meet with her and talk about it!"

"At least the first half is over. Do you still want to meet for lunch at noon?"

"I guess. At least that way—what's the matter with you? Why are you making that face?"

"Migraine," I said.

"Yuck!"

"I know," I said. "I'd better get to my second class, but good luck with everything, and you can tell me all about it in a couple of hours."

"Yeah," said Chloe, and, with an extreme lack of enthusiasm, trudged off in the direction of Karen's office.

When I stepped back into my classroom, the gray blob transformed into a kind of flickering castle-shaped thing, and then gradually spread out into a shimmering ring that filled the whole left side of my field of vision. Mindful of my own advice to Chloe about honesty and sharing, I told my students that I was experiencing a migraine aura and was having trouble seeing right now.

The good news, I told them, was this meant that they would get to be the ones to write on the board. And, just as I'd told Chloe would happen, they all expressed sympathy and went to work with a will, writing sentences on the board with considerable energy, if a certain lack of grammatical correctness, or even a basic grasp of spelling. But those things would come, I assured all of us, especially myself.

By the time the second class was over, the migraine scotoma had dissipated, leaving exhaustion and threatening whispers of the possibility of excruciating pain in its wake. I locked myself in my office and did a quick headstand before setting off to my meeting with Sandra, but even that normally sure-fire remedy did nothing for the throbbing gathering ominously behind my eyes.

The walk across campus to the front quad helped, though, as did the cup of coffee I ordered as soon as I got to Brew's Up.

"I thought coffee triggered migraines," said Sandra, when I found her and joined her at a rickety round table by the coffee shop's front window, and explained what was happening.

"It can. But it can also be a magical cure for them, too." Which seemed to be what was happening now. The pain was already washing away with each sip of coffee I took. "This is nice," I said, looking around. "Much less claustrophobic than most of the other buildings I've been in here."

"I know, right? The buildings look so cute from the outside, like the movie set for some film director's idea of what a neocolonial Southern college campus should look like, but inside they're just cheap modern prefab gone slightly to seed. Oops." She looked around. "I hope a dean didn't hear me say that."

"I don't *see* any deans," I assured her. "But it seems like there's so many of them that I can't keep track of them all."

Sandra laughed. She was a surprisingly friendly, normal, well-groomed person for an academic. Her hair had been expertly colored a dark blonde with lighter highlights, and cut into a stylish shag. She wore a beige linen pantsuit, and subtle makeup that emphasized the authority she'd gained by entering her fifties, while minimizing the lines and skin damage. Maybe there *was* hope for those of us who didn't want to spend the next thirty years becoming frumpy, unhappy bullies. Maybe it really was possible to get through a career in academia unscathed by its corrupting influence.

"We do seem to be suffering from a bit of a plague of deans lately," she said. "Along with a surfeit of contingent faculty. Are you tenure-track? Or a VAP? Or an adjunct?"

"A VAP," I told her. "But fresh off a semester of adjuncting elsewhere."

"At least you're moving up in the world. Although I was horrified, if not surprised, to hear that a full quarter of the faculty hired this year were adjuncts. And most of the rest are VAPs and postdocs."

"Yep," I said. "I heard that we're the first crop of faculty at Crimson to be majority contingent."

She shook her head. "You probably don't need me, or anyone else with tenure, to start going off in front of you about income inequality, and how universities are becoming ever more economically stratified, with deans and senior administrators proliferating at the top, and adjuncts and visiting faculty doing most of the heavy lifting at the bottom, but even we tenured old fogies are aware of what's going on—and we don't like it. Not only is it unfair, it means more pressure on us in the short run, and, if you'll pardon me for getting on my high horse and preaching to the choir for a moment, the destruction of American academia and our pre-eminent place in the world of higher education in the long run." The corners of her mouth, which was wide and mobile and only slightly blurred around the edges by age, turned down, and then forcibly turned back up into a smile. "But that's not what we're here to discuss," she said. "We're here to talk about bringing Miriam Chen to campus."

"Yes," I said. "So what's going on with that?"

What was going on with that, it turned out, was that the talk, which had originally been scheduled for October, had been pushed back to November after the first round of threats against Chen had been made. Now more threats had come in, and the talk was tentatively being pushed back yet again, maybe all the way to December and the last week of class, in order to give things more time to calm down.

"And we need to look into what kind of expanded security measures we can implement, too," Sandra told me. "In fact, Rowena, would you be willing to take point on that? I guess you'd start by talking to Brian—Chief Michaels, that is, the chief of campus police. Ask him what kind of security measures he recommends, and what venue he thinks would be most secure. We're going to have to move it anyway, with the rescheduling and everything, so we might as well see if we can get somewhere safer—if there *is* somewhere safer. I'm afraid we've never had to think about these kinds of things before. But this is what we're coming to: protecting guest speakers from being gunned down at the podium.

"Anyway, if you could start by contacting Brian Michaels and asking him for his suggestions, and then maybe getting in touch with Miriam and asking her what would make *her* feel better. I'm afraid she's rather high-strung, although I suppose we can hardly blame her for it. I just hope she doesn't back out entirely. I think she's starting to feel the pinch of being a real revolutionary. You know, standing up for what you believe in sounds all very well and good, until you actually have to do it."

"Yeah," I said. "Having the courage of your convictions is pretty rare, and for good reason. Most people can only do it when everyone else around them is doing it too."

"Yes, of course...I've heard that there's been an increasing crackdown on all kinds of things in Russia recently. Is that true? Do you know anyone who's been caught up in that? Because that could be a really interesting thing for the students to hear about. Most forms of political protest are so easy here in the US that most

Americans have no idea what it even means—and, although I know this is an unkind thought to have, I get the sense that most of our students have been so indoctrinated into being law-abiding that it wouldn't even cross their minds to protest anything, except maybe too long a line at the Apple store. I get the sense that a lot of them think that suffering for your beliefs is a sign of stupidity. But it sounds like the spirit of protest is still going strong in Russia."

"It is," I said. My phone *pinged*. A green WhatsApp message popped up on my screen. "And yes," I said. "I do know someone who's been caught up in the crackdown, and had to choose to stand up for his convictions. In fact, he's just messaged me."

33

ARE YOU BUSY NOW? Dima had texted.

I'm meeting with someone, I texted back.

A man?)))))

No. A professor.

Of course, professors aren't men))))) *They're asexual ethereal beings*)))))

This one's a woman.

"Sorry about this," I told Sandra, putting the phone down but keeping it face-up on the table, so I could monitor incoming texts. "I don't hear that often from this friend of mine."

Since being wounded in August, Dima had only texted me once, to tell me that he had, as ordered, seen a surgeon, who had laughed in his face and told him his only danger was from all the women who would be chasing him when they saw his war wound. I had texted a couple of times to check in, but those messages had gone unanswered, and the only reassurance I'd had for the past two weeks that Dima was still alive was the occasional appearance of his byline in *Nezavisimaya Pravda* (*Independent Truth*), the online opposition newspaper he worked for.

"It's no problem." Sandra was looking at me with sympathy, and more than a little shrewdness. "I can see this person must be important to you."

"We, um, we used to be engaged."

"But not anymore?"

"Not anymore. He felt like he had to choose between politics and me, and he chose politics."

Sandra made a small grimace. "People can be stupid like that sometimes. We chase the shiny things, and leave the things—or more commonly, the people—of real substance behind. And I hope you won't take it the wrong way, Rowena, if I tell you that I've seen a lot of keen young scholars come in and throw themselves into their careers, chasing that brass ring of tenure or even just the renewal of their contract. And then ten years later—*if* they make it that long—they're bitter and burned out and wondering why they don't have any friends or a family or a life of any kind outside of their jobs, which have turned out to be just the kind of pain-in-the-neck middle-management type of thing that they thought they went into academia to escape.

"So it's lovely that you're so eager to volunteer for things and help us out, and I do think that in this particular case what we're doing has meaning beyond a line on someone's CV, but don't throw yourself too hard into this kind of thing. If you prove to be even the tiniest bit competent, which I'm guessing you will, you're going to have people asking you to join committees and do service work every day, and they'll all have good reasons why you should, and they'll all try to guilt you and threaten you into helping them out, and you'll end up spending all your time and energy running around pleasing other people by running social events that no one comes to, instead of focusing on the things that really matter, whether that's making a significant contribution to scholarship, or getting back together with this man who has just sent you"—she glanced down at my phone—"*three* messages in the past two minutes."

She stood up. "I'll leave you to answer those messages, because I think that might be the most important thing you do all day, even if most of my colleagues would consider that statement blasphemous.

And while you're doing that, I'll email you Miriam Chen and Brian Michael's contact information, and you can let me know what they say when you hear back from them."

"I'll write to them this afternoon," I said.

"That would be lovely, Rowena. But *do* think about what I said. If you have to choose between campus politics and *him*"—she nodded at the phone—"there's a good chance that you should choose him."

I found myself smiling, even though it wasn't a very cheerful smile. "You don't even know him."

"No, and no doubt he's got plenty of problems, but so does everyone and everything. Crimson likes to bill itself as a little slice of trouble-free paradise for the middlingly-intelligent sons and daughters of the elite, but we have just as much trouble as anywhere else. Maybe more, because we turn our backs to it instead of facing it head on. I don't know what you're expecting to find here, Rowena, but if it's a safe haven from the troubles of the world, I'm afraid you're going to be highly disappointed."

"Mostly I like to plunge headfirst into the troubles of the world," I said. "I used to do non-profit work in Russia, after all. I'm just here because they're paying me, and I think they're paying me because I'm one of the few people even remotely qualified to do this job who would be willing to move to Greenfields, Georgia."

"Good. I'm glad to hear that, although I doubt many of my colleagues would be. I'll leave you to answer your texts, Rowena, and I look forward to working with you." She gave my shoulder a squeeze, which was probably a violation of some kind of college rule, and left.

34

I'M NOT BUSY ANYMORE, I texted back to Dima as soon as
Sandra had left. *Although I'm meeting with a colleague in a minute.
What's up?*

A male colleague?)))))

No, a woman. Where are you?

*Kiev, would you believe it? I took your advice and left the front.
Don't worry; I'll be back)))))* *But you were right: I needed a break.*

You should listen to me more!)))))

I obey, Comrade General! When do you meet with your colleague?

While I had been texting with Dima, Chloe had texted me to say
that she was already at Sullivan's, the restaurant on campus, and she
needed to tell me all about her meeting with Karen in order to do a
mental cleanse and pull herself back together.

She's already waiting for me, I wrote Dima. *But I can walk and
text.*

*Can you call? Video? You're supposed to be able to do video chat on
WhatsApp. I just...I just don't know. I just wanted to see you. Just for a
second.*

Okay.

Before I had even gotten up from the table, WhatsApp was
already sending me a video request.

"Allo?" I said. "Dima? Can you see me?"

Every head in Brew's Up turned and stared at the sound of Russian. I got up and hustled out the door before I made any more of a spectacle of myself, either by shouting loudly in Russian, or by bursting into tears.

"Inna? Can you hear me?"

"I can hear you." The video image was so grainy I could barely make out Dima's face, but his voice was coming through loud and clear. The sound of it was triggering a kind of tearful trembling, starting in the center of my chest and spreading out all over my body. Now that it was the end of September, it was pleasantly cool out on the quad, but my fingers were slippery on the phone, and sweat was trickling down my sides.

"Inna," said Dima. "Inna. You look...just like you always did. Only your hair's longer."

"I don't have the money to go to the hairdresser's."

"Don't they pay you?"

"Not enough to get my hair cut."

Dima frowned, or so I thought, as the video fragmented and then reassembled in pinky-brown blobs that may or may not have been his face. "That's not how it's supposed to be," he said. "That's not what I wanted for you when I told you to go back to America. I wanted you to be living the good life. After all, it's America."

"I know. But it turns out that the communists might have been right about America. At least in some ways. I've been poorer here than I ever was in Moscow. And people keep shooting at me here too."

Dima's face suddenly snapped into focus on the screen. "That's not acceptable, Inna," he said. "What about that man? The American? Why isn't he taking care of you?"

"He's poor too. And I can take care of myself."

"No one can take care of themselves all by themself, Inna." Dima's face pixelated and turned back into a random collection of pinky-brown blobs. "I think my connection is going," he said, his voice crackling and cutting in and out. "And I should leave before I spend all day talking to you. And..." Dima seemed to be trying to say something else, but the connection crackled and then cut out completely before I could figure out what it was.

35

CHLOE WAS SITTING BY herself, fidgeting and looking uncomfortable, when I stepped into Sullivan's. It was across the front quad from Brew's Up, and was an actual sit-down restaurant, albeit one that could only seat five tables at a time. I had been told on multiple occasions it was the nicest restaurant in Greenfields. I had resisted the urge to point out that the bar was very low.

"Oh, you're finally here," said Chloe, when I came over. "I asked Mel to come too, but she's got to finish her 11:00am class and then she's meeting with a student. I just don't think I could have stood sitting here by myself for another minute, especially after the morning I had. I'm *sure* everyone is looking at me."

I looked around the restaurant. There were only two other occupied tables. They didn't appear to me to be looking in this direction, but maybe they had been before I'd shown up. "At least it's over," I said, sitting down.

"For *now*. I still have to turn in a bunch more stuff. Did you?"

"Yeah. Syllabi and a teaching portfolio."

"Yeah, me too. Crazy, right? I mean, we just submitted all that stuff when we applied, or at least I did."

"I know," I said. "Me too. It's just busywork. They're just making you jump through hoops because they can."

"It shouldn't be like this!"

"No," I agreed. "It shouldn't. Have you ordered yet?"

Before Chloe could answer, a waitress came over with a glass of ice water and another menu.

"I'll have the Caesar salad, no croutons, dressing on the side," Chloe told her without looking at her or even waiting to be asked if she was ready to order. "No, wait: is the chicken breaded?"

"It is," the waitress told her, smiling a big smile. "It's real tasty!"

"I can't have anything with breading." Chloe didn't smile back, or even meet the waitress's eyes. "Can I have grilled instead? Or, wait, do you have fish? Some kind of grilled salmon?"

"We have catfish, hon, but it's breaded and fried too. It's real tasty, though."

Chloe stiffened. "I'm faculty," she said. "Not a student."

"That so?" said the waitress. She gave her another big smile, which Chloe resolutely refused to acknowledge. "You're so lucky, then! Such pretty smooth skin. I sure wish I looked as young as you did." The waitress was probably no older than I was, but her Scotch-Irish skin was heavily freckled and sun-damaged, and her mouth was already showing the wrinkles of a long-time smoker.

Chloe gave her an incredulous look. "Did you really just comment on my skin?" she demanded.

The waitress looked flustered. "I mean...yeah...it's so pretty...you really could pass for a student, hon..."

Chloe opened her mouth to say something, probably something unwise. "I'll have the fried PB & Nutella sandwich," I said loudly. "And we'll take a serving of fries to split. And why don't you go ahead and get something fried too, Chloe."

Chloe gave me a withering look.

"Like you said, it's been a hard morning," I told her. "Let's treat ourselves. And you'll feel better after you've had a decent lunch. Go back on the diet tomorrow."

The waitress smiled in relief. "There you go, hon. Two pretty girls out to lunch on a nice day like today? Might as well enjoy yourselves a little. I sure know I would if I was you! Get the fried catfish, hon. I'll go in and put in that order right away."

She hurried off. Chloe gave me another withering look.

"You didn't even let me order!" she hissed. "You totally...I don't know...disempowered me in front of her!"

My headache was starting to come back. "I'm sorry," I said. "But you were already disempowering yourself. You were being mean to a waitress!"

"You heard what she said to me!"

"She was trying to be nice."

"Yeah, but she called me hon! And talked about my skin, right to my face!"

"I know," I said. "And I can see why you might not like that. But she really was trying to be nice."

"But what she really was being was racist! And you wouldn't let me call her out on it!"

"She's a waitress," I said. "She probably makes something like two dollars an hour, and depends on tips to survive. She probably doesn't have a college degree, and is never going to get one. She's probably been poor her whole life, and is going to keep on being poor for the rest of it. And she waits on self-centered faculty members and overprivileged teenagers for a living. *You're* the one with the privilege and the power here. You can afford to be gracious. You have to be, if you want her respect."

I stopped to massage my temples. Chloe was staring at me.

"Wow," she said eventually. "I didn't even know you could talk like that. I thought you were too, I don't know, easy-going or something to tell it to people straight."

"I have a migraine. It went away, but now it feels like it's coming back."

"Oh. Do you...I don't know, do you want an aspirin or something?"

"That's okay," I said. "I'm sure I'll feel better once I eat something. So anyway, what happened with Karen?"

What had happened with Karen, it turned out, was pretty much the same as what had happened to me and to Mel. She had come in late, been rude and disruptive during the class, left early, and then spent an hour afterwards making criticisms of Chloe's teaching that were as nonsensical as they were mean-spirited. She'd also told Chloe that she was still on probation, and would have to be observed again in the spring, in order to see if the suggestions for improvement had been implemented.

"Ugh," I said. "What a pain. But at least that suggests she's not planning to terminate you immediately."

"No, but she might do it next semester!"

"Yeah, I guess so," I said. "I'm starting to wonder if they ever planned to have a critical need languages program at all. I mean, in a long-term way. Maybe they just wrote up some kind of a good-sounding proposal in order to get some external funding or something, and then hired us to show their good-faith effort, but they've been planning to terminate us and end the programs after one year all along. Then they can say that they tried, they really did, but there just wasn't enough student interest or they just couldn't get any qualified faculty members to come work here, and then once we're gone they'll put the money towards the new football stadium."

"Wouldn't surprise me," said Chloe.

"Although that suggests more organization and long-term planning than I've seen in evidence here so far. Far more likely is that Karen is just mean and incompetent."

"Yeah," said Chloe. "You know, I tried to be nice to her and get her on my side, I really did, but it seemed like the more I tried, the meaner she was to me."

"Yeah," I said. "That's how people like that are. Like I told you beforehand, you're pretty much damned no matter what you do."

The waitress came hurrying over, bearing our plates. She gave me a big smile and Chloe a nervous, uncertain look. "I, um, I went ahead and had them put chicken *and* catfish on your salad, hon," she told Chloe. "That way you can pick and choose what you want."

"Thanks," Chloe told her. "And, uh...sorry if I was a little short with you earlier. I've just been having a really tough morning."

"No problem, hon, no problem! I sure know how that can be myself. Especially if it's that time of the month, if you know what I mean. Well, enjoy your lunch, ladies, and if you need anything, just call me on over, okay?" She hurried off.

"Wow," said Chloe. "It worked. Okay, so she was still kind of weird and rude, but she was nicer than before. Why didn't it work with Karen?"

"Because," I said, "first of all, Karen is an asshole, and second of all, Karen is in a position of power over you. Neither of those two conditions apply with the waitress."

"Okay. So what about the students? Because, and this is the thing that's killing me, while a lot of what Karen said was just her talking out of her butt, if I'm honest with myself my class really wasn't that good. I feel like I did everything right, or at least I had everything set up right, but it still didn't work out like it should have. Actually, it never does. I think my materials are good and my lesson plans are solid, but something's missing. The students always seem bored or unhappy, and I can't blame them. Sometimes *I'm* bored or unhappy in there, so why shouldn't they be? I just...I don't know, maybe I'm not really cut out for teaching. I mean, I love learning stuff, and researching, and that whole side of it, but when it comes to teaching...I've always been shy, I've always had a hard time relating to people. My mother thinks I'm somewhere on the autism spectrum, and I think maybe she's right. Maybe teaching was the wrong career choice for me. Maybe this whole thing is completely wrong!"

"That seems a little over-dramatic for one bad day," I said.

"Yeah, but...do you ever feel like the students are laughing at you behind your back, like you're about to lose control of them at any moment and you have to hold onto the class with everything you've got to keep it from spiraling out of control?"

"Sometimes," I said. "But not often. And I generally find that students don't like being held under control."

"Yeah...I just don't know what to do. I don't know how to be liked. And I guess you'd probably tell me I'm the one in the position of power in the classroom or something like that, but it sure doesn't feel like it to me! It feels like the students are the ones who hold all the power, and they're the ones bullying me. What do you think? You think they're really the ones bullying us?"

"Maybe sometimes," I said. "Anyone can bully anyone: that's the thing about bullying. But in this case that seems pretty unlikely. In my experience, students might still have a fair amount of original sin in them, but it hasn't yet congealed into evil. Most of them are still capable of responding to authenticity and good will with authenticity and good will of their own."

"Except for the ones who flip out and shoot you," said Chloe.

"Yes, well, those are special cases. And I wouldn't exactly call that *bullying*. More like insanity brought about by the inhumane conditions we've created out of an excess of good intentions. Maybe school shooters are the canaries in the coal mines, warning us just how far astray we've gone. But they're the outliers. The vast majority of people will just engage in some petty, low-level, everyday evil. Someone like Karen probably isn't going to kill you, or even slap your face. She'll just do things to grind you down with the banality of her evil until *you're* the one who snaps."

"Ugh," said Chloe. "You ever feel like you're in, I don't know, *Schindler's List* or *Lord of the Flies* or something like that?"

"Yeah," I said. "I think modern-day academia might be as close as we can get to finding out what a *Lord of the Flies* situation would be if it were a society of women instead of boys. Although that's not quite right. It's more like a very, very genteel form of labor camp."

Chloe stabbed moodily at a piece of lettuce. "Sometimes I think I've spent years and years becoming an incredibly educated specialist in order to end right back up at the plantation that my ancestors wanted to leave. Did you know that Crimson used to be a plantation?"

"Yes," I said. "Although these days they try to keep that pretty quiet."

Chloe stabbed at another piece of lettuce. "I thought I would be coming here and making a difference, rewriting history or vindicating my family and my people or something like that. Instead, I'm kind of just back in a plantation all over again, except that I'm desperate to stay instead of desperate to leave, and according to you, I might be one of the overseers instead of the field workers. Although I kind of feel like a field worker too."

"Yeah, I know," I said. "Welcome to the cycle of oppression and abuse."

"You think we can ever break out of it?"

"Maybe," I said. "But I'm not holding my breath."

36

FOOD MADE THE MIGRAINE recede to nothing more than a faintly threatening throbbing behind my eyes, so after lunch I emailed Brian Michaels, chief of campus police, about the security for the Miriam Chen talk.

Sandra told me you'd be getting in contact with me, he wrote back. *Welcome aboard. Not sure if this is a good thing we're doing here or not. Miriam Chen's talk is putting Crimson on the map, but not in a good way. By the way, you any relation to John Halley? Was in the Marines?*

If we're talking about the same John Halley, then he's my brother, I wrote. *And he's still in the Marines. Doing his whole twenty years.*

No kidding? Good for him. My son served under his command. Only had good things to say about him.

I had heard similar things from pretty much everyone who had ever served under John's command. As his younger sister, I had a hard time believing this, but the verdict was unanimous. John was, despite all expectations to the contrary, an excellent leader. It was only to his family that he displayed his fucked-up drama queen side.

I'm very glad to hear that, I wrote back.

I heard he was deployed to Afghanistan again. How'd that go?

As well as it could, I guess. He's back now, at Camp Lejeune.

Good that he's back. My son never wanted to tell me the whole story, but I'm pretty sure your brother saved his life, so anything you need from me, you got.

Thanks, I wrote. *Right now I'm mainly looking for advice on how to make sure that Miriam Chen's visit to campus goes off as smoothly and safely as possible.*

The talk was booked in the library auditorium, but that's impossible to secure. Hundreds of people walking in and out of the building with big bags. It were me, I'd move the talk to the sports center. How many people you expecting?

I have no idea. Could be a few dozen, could be a few hundred. Normally guest lectures are pretty under-attended, but this one might be different. Or not.

You could put it in the auditorium in Lee Hall, but that's still not easy to secure. The reason I said the sports center was because we already have metal detectors there. See if you can get the basketball arena. They set that up for different size events all the time. Not nearly as much traffic there as the library or Lee, and easier to close down on the night. We can shut it down to anyone who isn't coming to the talk, shut all but one entrance to the arena, set up the metal detectors, and make everyone go through them. Goes without saying that I'll have everyone on duty that night. That's not very many though. I can ask the town police if they'll pitch in.

Are you really expecting trouble? I asked.

I think 99% of these a**holes are all hat, no cattle. But sounds like Miriam's been getting some pretty nasty threats, and I'd sure hate for Crimson to be the place where they get carried out. So we're going to act like we take them seriously. Plus according to Sandra she's a touchy thing and she keeps threatening to back out, so maybe this will make her feel better and not leave us in the lurch at the last minute.

Okay, I wrote. *I'll see if I can get the basketball arena for the talk. I'll be in touch once I have a venue.*

You do that. Meanwhile I guess I'll be looking for the Gang of Six some more.

Are the police really interested in them? I asked.

No. I think they're just a bunch of pipsqueak college kids playing at being bad. But the college administration wants us to investigate them, so that's what we're doing. And they're the ones who actually said they thought there was going to be a shooting at the Miriam Chen talk.

I didn't want to wish him good luck, since I didn't want anyone from the campus administration to find out who the Gang of Six were, so I just thanked him for his help and told him I'd be in touch.

37

I EMAILED MIRIAM CHEN right after I finished emailing with Brian Michaels, but she was not nearly so prompt in replying. She didn't respond to me until Wednesday afternoon, by which time I'd already tentatively booked the basketball arena for Tuesday, December 1st. Jillian, the woman in the Rooms and Scheduling department I'd spent most of an hour on the phone with after spending most of an hour trying and failing to make sense of the online venue booking system, told me that normally they wouldn't be able to accommodate such a late request, but as it happened they'd just had a cancellation, so I could have the basketball arena—*if* I booked it immediately. So I did, without waiting to hear back from Miriam if Tuesday, December 1st would work for her.

Maybe that was why she was in such a bad mood when I finally talked to her late Wednesday afternoon. I tried to explain the venue booking issue, but she didn't seem able to process that information. Finally, after an hour of fruitless emailing, I suggested that we hold a Skype call to hammer out the details face-to-face.

This required more negotiation, because she didn't seem capable of holding a spontaneous Skype call, but after another round of emails, we agreed that I would call her on Skype at 10:00am the next morning.

Accordingly, I called her up Thursday morning at exactly 10:00am. No reply. I tried again five minutes later, and when she didn't pick up that time either, left a message.

At 10:30 a message *blooped* onto my screen. *You ready to talk?* it said.

I forced myself to reply *Yes, absolutely!* and not *I've been ready for the past half hour*.

A few seconds later, and Miriam Chen's face swam onto my screen. I hoped the connection was still fuzzy enough not to betray my shock. I'd seen pictures of Miriam Chen, but it was hard to see the face currently on my screen as the same person. All the photos I'd seen of her showed a slender, nerdy-looking Asian-American woman in her twenties. I supposed that the Miriam looking at me now was also a nerdy-looking Asian-American woman in her twenties, and she had the same black glasses, but this Miriam must have been the better part of a hundred pounds overweight.

I remembered Mel's story about her friends who had been put on antidepressants and blown up like prize sows. Maybe the same thing had happened to Miriam. Maybe she'd been so stressed by all the rape threats and death threats and so on, which was understandable, that she'd been put on horse-sized doses of tranquilizers and other such drugs, and now we were all seeing the result. Poor thing. I thought that gaining all that weight would make me at least as depressed as death threats, if not more so. After all, I'd had death threats too, so I knew what it was like. Mostly they'd just made me mad. But gaining weight had made me miserable. I thought I'd probably go for the unmedicated experience, myself. Poor Miriam. Telling her what I thought probably would not be a good start to the conversation.

"Thanks for agreeing to speak with me," I said. "As I mentioned, I'm a new member of the committee organizing your talk at Crimson. I'm also very glad to be able to talk to you, since I've been following what you've been doing, and I have a lot of admiration for your work." Flattery was often a good technique to get people to agree to what you want them to do.

"Yeah." She didn't look flattered. She looked like she was about to burst into tears.

"I know a lot of us here at Crimson are very excited that you've agreed to come and give this talk. I think it will be an extremely interesting and beneficial experience for the students. In fact, one of my students works for the campus paper, and has said she'd love to do an interview with you, if you'd be willing to. Not only would it be an item of considerable interest to the campus community, but she's said it would be very exciting to her personally to talk to a feminist activist like you."

Now Miriam looked even more like she was about to burst into tears. "There's just no way I could do an interview right now," she said. "I'm in such a fragile emotional state right now! My anxiety is through the roof."

"Um, okay. I'm sure that must be very difficult, given the position you're in. Do you, uh, think you'll still be able to do the talk?"

"If I get my meds sorted out by then."

"Um, okay. So, shall we just go ahead with the assumption that you will for now? It's easier to cancel than to schedule something on the fly. So, as I said in my emails, I had to go ahead and book the venue for December 1st, but if that date doesn't work for you, we can try to find something else. When I spoke with the chief of campus police, he specifically recommended the basketball arena as being the easiest to make secure, and that was one of the few dates I could get it for..."

"It's not like I've got anything else to go to," she interrupted. "I'm pretty much under house arrest here. I haven't been outside in a week." She looked around the room, as if picking up signals from it the rest of us couldn't understand. "No, two weeks. And before that I hardly went out either. Just to give talks and stuff. And I had to double up on my meds to get through those. Then I had to leave my *home* and hide out here. At least I'm still in New York, but I had to leave my apartment, which I *love,* and now I'm stuck in this dump. I've got a couple talks coming up next month, but I don't know...and I don't know if I'll be able to make it to yours, either."

"Of course your safety should be your primary concern," I said. "We understand that. We will of course do absolutely everything in our power to ensure that the event goes off without a hitch, and we all, including our chief of police, believe the threat to be minimal, but I understand that you're getting threats from all kinds of people, and you naturally have to take that seriously. And I want to make it clear, as a personal message, that if you have cause to believe that you have a genuine threat to your life, you shouldn't feel obliged to put yourself into danger for our talk. I'll...I'll make a back-up plan in case you can't make it at the last minute. Maybe we can organize a panel discussion about, I don't know, violence in the media or something like that. That way, if you can't make it, we'll still have the panel discussion. So you won't have to feel that extra level of pressure about the situation."

"I can't believe you said that to my face. I can't believe you're putting your panel before my wellbeing!" Miriam still looked like she was about to burst into tears, but overlaid with a brittle veil of anger.

"Oh. Well, um, that wasn't my intention at all, so I'm sorry if it came across like that. I was trying...what I'd like to do is make it so that you can come, of course, but if something *should* come up, I wouldn't want you to feel obliged to put yourself in danger for the sake of the event. I just want to take that pressure off of you, so that you can make the best decision under whatever the circumstances are when the time comes."

"Well, you should have said so!"

I thought I did! But I only said that to myself. "Of course," I said out loud. "So *will* the first work for you? Or do you have something else scheduled then?"

"What else would I have scheduled? I'm under house arrest, remember?"

"Um, okay. Let's say we'll go ahead and do it on the first, then. So, um, what could we do to help make you feel more comfortable and secure?"

"Have you found those...what are they called? The Gang of Six? Have you found out who they are yet?"

"No," I said. "But, to be honest, Chief Michaels doesn't think they're a threat, and I have to say I agree. I've been reading their blog, and they seem pretty supportive of you. In fact, they've been openly critical of the Men's Protection Alliance for threatening to protest your talk."

"What kind of threats?!"

"Oh. Um. Well, once again, nothing that actually seems concerning. Just that they might, you know, have a small picket or protest outside."

"Oh my God! You have to look into this!"

"Of course," I said. "I know the police are keeping an eye on them."

"Not those idiot yokels! I mean you personally!"

"Um," I said. "Okay. I'll take a look at their posts and see if anything jumps out at me. Although maybe you should be the one..."

"I can't put myself through that."

"Yeah," I said. "I can understand that. To be honest, they're pretty obnoxious. But I haven't heard anything that suggests any real reason for concern."

"I heard that they might bring guns!"

"Yeah. Um, someone *might* have mentioned something about that, although I think that was an allegation made by the Gang of

Six, not a threat that's been tracked down as actually made by the Men's Protection Alliance. But they can't. That's why we want to have metal detectors at the door."

"Really? I thought in a place like Georgia, you'd just let any racist redneck wander in with a whole armload of guns. Don't you have, like, concealed carry everywhere you go?"

I took a deep breath. "Not in schools," I said. "And Crimson is a private college. We can ban guns however we want. So we're going to ban all weapons at the talk, and have everyone pass through a metal detector before they can come in."

"Really? I didn't think *Georgia* would do something like that."

"Georgia might surprise you," I said.

"Maybe," she said. "What about racism? I bet most of the people there are pretty racist, aren't they? Do you think they're going to harass me about that?"

"Um, probably not," I said. "This is a selective liberal arts college, after all. It's kind of like most other S-LACs. You're at least as likely to be called out for insensitive speech as you are to be the recipient of a racial slur."

"Oh. Really? That's not what I would have thought. And I guess it'll still be pretty warm then? That'd be nice. I don't know if I can handle being cooped up here much longer, especially once the weather gets cold and dark. I have really bad Seasonal Affective Disorder, on top of everything else. And claustrophobia *and* agoraphobia. You can't imagine how terrible it is, cooped up like this, knowing that people are out there who want to kill you."

"Actually, I can, " I said. "I've been the recipient of death threats myself. So I know exactly how much it sucks."

"Really? What did *you* do to earn death threats?"

"Well, it wasn't so much what I did. It was my, um, my boyfriend. I was just collateral damage, a way to get to him."

"Oh." Miriam gave me a supercilious look. "So you've never done anything *yourself*, then. Anything really meaningful, that is."

"Um," I said. "Maybe not in quite the way you mean. So, um, to get back to the threats, have you gotten any from anyone you think has any relationship with Crimson College?"

She shrugged. "You mean, full of misspelled racist threats?" She did an extremely bad imitation of a Southern accent. "'Y'all's in danger, ya yeller Chink cunt, so go back to where y'all belong.' Nothing like that. Just some people saying I shouldn't do the talk, and one guy who said he'd still have sex with me even though I won't keep my mouth shut. I set *him* straight! I told him I wouldn't let him near me if he was the last man on earth. But I get that kind of stuff for *every* talk. So I don't know if this one is special."

"Oh," I said. "Well, um, good, I guess. If you *do* get anything suspicious that you think has something to do with Crimson, be sure to let me know immediately, okay? Or Chief Michaels."

"I don't want to have anything to do with him. I'm sure he's just another good ole boy"—her attempt at saying "good ole boy" was almost as sad as her attempt at saying "y'all"—"just like all the others."

"Um," I said. "As far as I can tell, he's at least somewhat competent at his job. And he, um, feels like he owes me, so if I ask, he'll probably try to help me out."

"What'd *you* do for him?"

"Not so much me as my brother. Chief Michaels's son served under him in the Marines."

"Oh my God! Your brother is a *Marine*?" The way she said it made me think that this knowledge was filling her with disgust, not panty-melting lust. Maybe I wouldn't tell John about this. Well, only if he really annoyed me.

"Yep," I said.

"So *you're* one of them, too!"

"Um, well, I was never in the Marines, if that's what you mean. I avoided military service entirely."

"No, I meant, like, a redneck."

"Oh. Well, um, my family is largely of Scotch-Irish descent, that's true. And we're from Georgia. But we're really more intellectual than redneck."

"Huh," said Miriam. "I didn't think there could be any intellectuals in Georgia."

"You might be surprised," I told her again, and then, with relief, hung up.

38

ARE YOU FREE NOW? WANT to go for a run? I texted Mel as soon as I got off the call with Miriam.

How much of a run? she texted back. *I'm not sure I'm ready for the ass-kicking I know you could administer.*

Haha. My knee's still not 100%, so I don't think I'll be kicking anyone's ass anytime soon, especially not yours. I was thinking of a gentle jog around the block before I flip out and go crazy.

Sounds good. I've been working all morning on a fucking app for a job I'm not going to get because I've been too busy applying for jobs to do the research and writing I need to do in order to get the jobs I'm applying for. I should take a break before I blow a gasket and do something I'll regret. Meet you by the main entrance in ten? I normally just run up and down Peachtree Avenue. If I'm feeling really adventurous, I'll venture onto the main road, but it's up to you.

Let's decide once we start running, I wrote. *See you in ten!*

It was almost cool when I met Mel ten minutes later by the main gates to the Peachtree Estates. Not cool enough for either of us to switch from shorts to sweatpants for a midday run, but the warmth was pleasant rather than oppressive, the way it had been until this week.

"I can't believe it's been a month and this is the first time we're going running together," Mel said when I showed up.

194

"My knee's still twingey, so I've only been able to start back up running this past week. And I still have to be careful and take it really easy, so go gentle on me, okay? And don't let me do anything stupid."

"There are *so many* ways I want to respond to that. But I guess I'll just say that I'm still not 100% after that weird flu I got, so I'll have to go easy on you whether I want to or not. Actually"—she rubbed her right knee and grimaced—"my knee's bothering me too. And my hands are still killing me. Not all the time, but on and off. And I keep getting weird muscle cramps and stuff. Sometimes I think about going to the doctor about it, but just as I'm making up my mind to do that, the pain goes away. Then it comes back three days later, but in a different place."

"Weird," I said. "Have you ever had anything like that before?"

She shook her head. "The normal soreness from working out, of course, but nothing like this weirdness. It's getting better, but super slowly. But whatever. Ready to run?"

I started off at a slow jog down Peachtree Avenue, with Mel keeping pace easily at my side. I noted that she was running on my right, between me and any oncoming traffic. We were running down a sidewalk alongside a private road that got maybe two cars an hour, but I recognized the stance. Dima had always done the same thing. I thought about saying something about it. Then I didn't know what I would say. So I told her about my talk with Miriam Chen instead.

"Jesus," said Mel when I was done. "She sounds really fucked up."

"Yeah. I mean, I understand. She's going through a really tough thing. But she was just..."

"Your typical member of the Northeast liberal elite, full of good intentions, but incapable of interacting with someone not exactly like her without causing terminal offense?"

"I mean, basically. I guess I shouldn't be surprised. I was just hoping for better from her. I actually read some of what she wrote;

you know, the stuff that raised all the ruckus. She seemed really smart and thoughtful there."

"Probably she was," said Mel. "Probably she's a smart, thoughtful person who cares deeply about the causes she champions. But she's also, what: like, twenty-seven or something? And I'm guessing she's never had to deal with anything really tough before."

"She's written a number of times about encountering racism and sexism."

"Yeah," said Mel. "And I'm sure that sucked. Because wealth and privilege don't actually protect you from that. Black Harvard professors still get the cops called on them, and Daughters of the American Revolution still get talked down to and slapped around and treated like crap. But from what I've read about Miriam Chen, she's spent her whole life living in comfortable affluence, going to the best schools and hanging out with the best people. And I'm sure some of those 'best people' made her feel left out. But I don't think she ever spent much time wading around in knee-deep shit, or losing her fingers to a baling machine, or any of the things that my trailer-trash family all did. It doesn't sound to me like she ever had to deal with much straight-up physical suffering, or genuine fear for her life. And so now that it's finally come to her, she's not handling it well."

Mel said all this with an ease that suggested that, whatever she might say, she still had plenty of running in her. If this was her at half-strength, at full strength she must have been impressive. Or terrifying.

"Yeah," I said. "So now I don't know what to do with her. I'm a little afraid, to be honest, that she'll show up and piss everyone off so much that she'll create an incident where there wasn't one to begin with."

Mel shrugged. "That's on her, then. Your job is just to get her here, right?"

"Right," I said. "So I guess I'd better keep working on that. Which means"—I groaned—"I need to look into the Men's Protection Alliance, like I promised, and see if I think they're a credible threat. I just don't know if I can do that. I mean, of course I *can*. I just don't know if I'll be able to recognize a credible threat. Everything they say sounds like a threat to me."

"Yeah," said Mel. "Tell you what: I'll help. Two heads are better than one, and all that."

"Really? You'd do that? It might be pretty gross."

"Not as gross as some of those job applications I've got waiting for me," said Mel. "Hey—you ready to turn around? You look like you're starting to limp."

"Yeah," I said. "Don't want to re-injure the knee."

"Yeah," said Mel. "Me too. Come on. Let's go read what the little wannabe rapists we're teaching are thinking."

39

WE WENT STRAIGHT FROM our run—"run"; we'd jogged a mile, tops. But it was still more than either of us had managed in a month, so we agreed to declare it a victory—to my place to go through the Men's Protection Alliance blog.

"No point in showering beforehand," Mel said. "Since we'll just have to shower as soon as we're done, anyway."

"True," I said. "And I just want to get it over with. The sooner you go to jail, the sooner you get out, and all that."

"Is that some Russian saying? It sounds like some Russian saying."

"It is indeed."

"I like it. Good to know that somewhere in the world there are still people with a decently black sense of humor."

"I know," I said. "Sometimes even I, a native-born American, find the constant American optimism and good cheer to be sickening. And a lot of my Russian friends find it unbearably cloying. Sometimes they just have to sit down and read a sad story or watch a tragic movie to clear the taste from their mouth."

"I totally get that," said Mel. "I mean, if everyone's happy and spouting positive thinking around you, where do you turn when you're feeling bad?"

"I know," I said. "There's nothing like other people's optimism and positivity when you're feeling bad to make you realize you're well and truly fucked. Not only are you miserable and depressed and in a sucky situation, but everyone around you is lying to your face and trying to fuck with your sense of reality. Under other circumstances we'd call it gaslighting."

"No kidding," said Mel. "Well, speaking of lying and gaslighting, let's read this fucking blog."

The Men's Protection Alliance blog was, I was annoyed to note, somewhat slicker and more professional that the Gang of Six's. The prose was just as overwrought, though, and even harder to take, since I didn't sympathize with them at all.

There was some obligatory stuff in some of the earlier posts about the unfair advantages mothers had in the courts in custody battles. After my experience the previous semester, when I had found myself the unofficial mediator of an international custody battle, I was even less sympathetic to that than I would have been earlier. Especially since, jeez, courts were an institution created and run by men, and were still largely dominated by men. To think that they gave women any kind of unfair advantage was as laughable as saying that all-white juries gave black defendants an unfair advantage. Although no doubt there were plenty of people who would argue exactly that.

But since the producers and consumers—if there were any—of this blog were all college students, they quickly moved on from the unfairness of custody rulings to lengthy jeremiads on the cruelties of college girls, and the posters' difficulties in finding anyone to relieve them of their virginity and their pent-up sexuality, which was begging so painfully for an outlet.

"I mean," said Mel, after we'd read half-a-dozen posts on that topic, "I do feel a tiny amount of sympathy here, or I would if they weren't such selfish little creeps. I mean, the concept of 'incel' *was* created by a queer woman. If these little shits want to know something about how hard it is to get laid, they should come talk to us lesbians."

"Yeah," I said. "And it's not like even straight women, who I know are generally considered, and maybe with some justice, as having the easiest time finding sexual partners, are that well off in that department. I mean, it's pretty easy to get sexually assaulted, or probably to be used by someone in some kind of icky one-night-stand, but finding someone you'd actually want to have sex with, who wants to have sex with you, is no piece of cake. And then there's the whole love thing. When I hear men saying that they have to have sex *right now* or they'll just die—well, I don't really know what that's like. I mean, the need specifically to have sex with just any random stranger just for the sake of having sex.

"But the love thing...I've certainly spent plenty of time feeling like if I don't have love, if I have to spend even one more minute alone, I'll just start screaming and screaming and screaming and I won't be able to stop. Speaking in broad terms, I'd say that women are at least as desperate for love and a family as men are for sex. We certainly sacrifice way more for it, when it comes to money and health and safety and self-respect.

"So I also kind of get where they're coming from, because that's something you desperately, desperately need, something without which your life will fail to have meaning on some fundamental level, but that requires another person to agree to go along with it. I just don't think the government should ensure that everyone have access to sex. Although I kind of *would* like to see how these guys would respond if they were told they were being drafted into a program that would require them to serve as government-mandated sexual partners. Bet they'd run screaming back to their celibacy real quick."

"Yeah," said Mel. "Funny how that works. It's all fun and games until *you're* the one being forced to provide other people sexual favors. Oh shit. Is that a post about Miriam Chen?"

"Crap, yes, it is. I guess we'd better read it through carefully."

"Blech," said Mel, but settled down to read it with attention when I clicked on it.

FAKE "SOCIAL JUSTICE" WARRIOR COMING TO CRIMSON? WE SAY NO!!!!

The MPA has recently heard that Miriam Chen might be coming to campus. Of course all MPA warriors and incels everywhere have heard the name Miriam Chen, she is one of the "social justice warriors" who have made things so difficult for ordinary men like us. Miriam Chen published a series of blog posts complaining about how she was treated while playing online games, she alleges that she was a target for "sexual harassment" in the online gaming community.

WE SAY BULLSHIT!!!!!

The online gaming community is one of the few safe spaces (we are using that phrase ironically) for incels and other oppressed and mistreated males like us, it's UNFAIR for "social justice warriors" and stuck-up bitches like Miriam Chen to come in and colonize OUR space and force us to play by THEIR rules. WE CREATED THIS SPACE!!!! If Miriam Chen and girls like her don't like it, they can just leave!!! But that never occurs to them, they have to push everyone around and spoil things for everyone else by making everyone conform to THEIR rules, just like they do in meatspace! Girls like Miriam Chen are determined to emasculate men, ALL MEN, they won't stop just with putting us down and keeping us from getting the happiness we're OWED out in the "real world," they have to do in GameSpace as well!!!!

TIME TO SAY NO!!!!!!

So, brave MPA warriors, time to stand up for yourselves and let Miriam Chen and all the Stacys and Social Justice Warriors like her know what you think! If Miriam Chen or anyone like her shows up to Crimson College, let's all stand up and let her know how we feel! No

*violence please but if you want to display your best weapon ;) and let her
know what she's missing you'll be doing mankind a service!*

STAND UP FOR YOURSELVES, MEN!!!!!

"Oh God," said Mel. "Does that mean what I think it means? Are they really urging guys to flash her with their dicks?"

"That is my interpretation, yes," I said.

"Oh, Jesus. Well, I mean, I guess she won't be in much danger then, unless it's of upchucking all over the stage, or maybe laughing herself sick. And...I gotta ask..." Mel gave me a sideways look. "Do straight women *really* find dicks attractive? Like, do you enjoy perusing them just for fun?"

"Um," I said. "Not really. I think most of us don't think they're that, um, attractive just on their own. They have to be attached to someone you love to be attractive, or even tolerable. It's more about the emotions behind the, um, display, than the display itself, if you get my drift."

"Yeah," said Mel. "And I get it. I mean, I don't want to see a bunch of random clits being shoved in my face, either. Just the one that belongs to that special someone. Well, is this it? Or does it get worse?"

We scrolled through the rest of the posts, but aside from rather offensive sentiments, and even more offensive grammar and syntax, we couldn't find anything of concern. The MPA might be planning to flash Miriam Chen, but if they were planning to do anything actually violent, they weren't posting about it in public.

40

I EMAILED MIRIAM CHEN the next day with the information that I, personally, along with another woman whose judgment I trusted, had reviewed every single blog post on the Men's Protection Alliance site, and hadn't found a single word that seemed to threaten actual violence.

As far as I can tell, the only "weapon" they *might* pull out on you are their penises, I wrote to her. *Unappetizing, but hardly dangerous, I would say, haha.*

Apparently Miriam did not share my amusement at the thought of being flashed by a bunch of frat boys. She responded with a lengthy diatribe about the use of displays of male genitalia to enforce patriarchal systems of authority. Which was all too true. But by taking it seriously, she was giving it even more power over her. I tried to think of a way of telling her, as one feminist who'd experienced death threats to another, to lighten up and stop letting these low-level bullies control her life. But I couldn't come up with one that didn't sound dismissive and condescending.

And after all, she did have a point: it was from the oozing muck of groups like the Men's Protection Alliance that serial killers and school shooters were born, rising from the slime like orcs being birthed in Saruman's lairs. We *should* be taking them seriously. But that didn't mean that this particular threat from this particular group wasn't laughably pathetic.

Miriam demanded that we ban all the members of the MPA from the talk. I wrestled with how to respond to that as well. I was personally of the opinion that joining a Men's Rights/incel organization was akin to joining the Ku Klux Klan or some neo-Nazi group, and only half a step away from joining ISIS or al-Qaeda. But that didn't mean that we could ban them from attending a public event. Maybe we should be cracking down much harder on people like that, but from a legal standpoint, we probably couldn't, and from a PR standpoint we *definitely* couldn't. The publicity that would be generated by an outspoken feminist banning a group of Men's Rights activists would be so bad that it would entirely overshadow whatever good we might do by bringing in Miriam Chen to give a talk.

I tried to express this to Miriam in a helpful, non-judgmental way, but that only provoked an outburst that I was putting the college's reputation before her personal safety.

I closed my eyes and prayed for the strength and wisdom to respond appropriately. Half of me wanted to fire back a response that I didn't give a crap about the college's reputation and I would in fact be delighted to see it develop a few cracks. I certainly had no intention of jeopardizing Miriam or anyone else's safety for the sake of making the college look good.

The other half of me, though, wanted to give her a sharp lecture about how I had spent a lot of time with activists operating in a society that was much more dangerous than the one she was in, and if she wanted to play with the big girls, she needed to step up to the plate and be ready to put her money where her mouth was. Anna Politkovskaya hadn't whined and complained about the possibility of seeing a few unsolicited penises. She'd marched straight to her martyrdom with her head held high.

But then again, she'd maybe known what she was getting herself into a little better than Miriam Chen had. Miriam Chen was a gamer who had spent her entire life in safety and comfort. She might have been offended by the sexism and misogyny of the gaming world, but like most American women of my acquaintance, she had constructed an unrealistically friendly, cuddly image of what men, even raging misogynists, were. She hadn't grasped the Pandora's box of evil she was going to unleash by poking that snake. She hadn't realized she was going to make herself a martyr for the cause, and now that she had, she didn't know how to deal with it, or the kind of life she was going to have to lead in order to live up to the persona she'd created for herself.

Of course, being an American was a big hindrance there. Russians could accept self-sacrifice and suffering and giving yourself to a cause that was bigger than you. Americans seemed to have lost that. If someone like Miriam Chen announced that she was going to put herself in a crazed shooter's crosshairs, she would be seen as laughingstock, not a saint. But she didn't seem like much of a saint, either, and you couldn't make someone else become a saint through nagging.

I don't know if we can ban all of the MPA members, in part because we don't know who they are, I wrote. *But we might be able to corral the ringleaders a little.*

How can you not know who they are?! she demanded.

Because we don't track all our students 24/7, I wrote back. *We're not that totalitarian a dictatorship.*

I'm not coming unless the people who wrote those threats are banned! I can't put myself through that!

We might be able to do that, I wrote. That was still a sticky issue, but maybe we could arrange a special "free speech" zone for the MPA dipshits and whoever else felt the need to exercise their First Amendment rights of being an asshole.

Promise me that you'll keep them away!

I will definitely see what I can do, I wrote.

That's not good enough! I can't come unless they're definitely not going to be there!

Okay, I wrote. I wasn't actually sure that I would be able to do that, but I decided that saying I would was the easiest thing to do right now. *I'll get right on that.*

41

I STARTED BY CONTACTING Brian Michaels about Miriam's request to ban everyone from the MPA from her talk. I could almost hear his groan coming back over the email system when he replied.

Believe me, I'd love to ban those troublemakers permanently, he wrote. *But we **can't**. Not without expelling them, and there's no way the college is going to get that negative publicity by banning someone for activism. And we don't even know who they are. Nathan Willoughby is probably the head of it, but even he keeps his nose clean enough that we don't have reason to do anything about him. And we don't know if he's the one who wrote that thing about flashing their dicks at Chen. Sorry about the language.*

Don't worry, I wrote. *You should hear my brother talk :) :)*

Oh, I heard enough of that from my son. Damn near whupped his ass when I heard the way he was talking after he got back. But his grandmother took care of that for me.

So what should we do about the talk? I asked. *We've put so much work into it already, and it's already made the national news, and Miriam is on the verge of backing out. And I do share her concerns. Most of these troublemakers are just mouthing off, but there's always the possibility that someone might go off the deep end and do something terrible.*

Like I said, we can't ban anyone unless they've done something actually illegal, Brian wrote back. *But I like your idea of a free speech* zone. *I know other campuses are doing it. Maybe we can get all the troublemakers together where we can keep an eye on them. Other than that, the main thing will be to keep weapons out of the event venue. That's what we've got the metal detectors for.*

Makes sense. I just wish there were something else we could do.

*If you found out who these jackasses are, we could keep an eye on them better. And if they **do** put a toe out of line, we can arrest them or at least ban them from campus.*

I'll see what I can do, I wrote.

I said that just to say that, but the next weekend, as I was sitting at the computer staring at yet another cover letter for yet another job I wasn't going to get, I found myself scrolling through the MPA's website again, searching for clues about their intentions or identity. Reading their posts made me feel dirty, but not as dirty as job applications.

My attempts, alas, were no more successful than they had been with the Gang of Six. Both groups had a website, a Twitter account, and a small handful of followers, but nothing else. The MPA didn't even have an email address. My burst of enthusiasm for doing a little amateur sleuthing and hunting them down faded, and I went back to my job applications.

My ardor was revived, however, a couple of weeks later, when, as I was idly scrolling through the Gang of Six website in order to work myself into a state of indignation instead of working, I caught sight of the name "Miriam Chen."

MIRIAM CHEN UNDER MORE THREATS FROM MEN'S PROTECTION ALLIANCE???? screamed the headline.

*The **disgusting** recent post from the Men's Protection Alliance who can't seem to keep their dirty minds and other dirty things to themselves has once again gone unremarked and unpunished by the campus authorities. As usual these nazis are allowed to get away with MURDER! When are the campus authorities going to WAKE UP* *and stop them before they commit some terrible crime like they're threatening to do, they really are a menace and must be STOPPED! If the campus police won't do it then it's up to US! As you recall WE were the ones who reported the death threats the MPA made against Miriam Chen but WE were the ones who were blamed instead! It's no surprise the authorities think WE'RE the threat since WE'RE the ones wanting to change the foundations of our oppressive social structures but they're using that as an excuse not to investigate the very REAL threat the MPA poses to Miriam Chen and everyone else on campus! Sixers, be on your guard!*

Underneath was a series of comments condemning the MPA post. The last commenter, using the screenname LostAndFoundBoy, said they were going to "take the fight to the enemy" and speak out against the MPA post directly.

I immediately went over to the MPA's website, where I was greeted by a recent and very unflattering picture of Miriam that showed every single one of her extra hundred pounds, along with the caption *Miriam Chen, or fat hog?* This was followed by a short "exclusive" piece about Miriam Chen's weight gain, and how this is what happens to girls who call themselves feminists.

While most of the MPA's posts didn't get much attention, this one had garnered half a dozen comments. Most of them were to the effect that the posters no longer wanted to flash Miriam, since the very sight of her in her new, obese, form would cause even the hardiest erection to shrivel up into nothing. Although they put it in a way that emphasized their own virility and sexual prowess.

I used to fantasize about getting it on with Miriam Chen, a poster called "Nottagirl" wrote. *She was the hottest Becky to hit the gaming circuit in years. Too bad she was such a stuck-up bitch like the rest of them! But now even a desperate incel like me wouldn't touch her with a ten foot pole. Now if I found her staked out and begging for it I'd tell her Sorry Bitch and just keep walking. She had her chance and she blew it. I even wrote to her last month to tell her I'd fuck her even though she wouldn't stop running her mouth off but she told me she wouldn't let me near her if I was the last man on earth. Too late bitch! I'd pay good money to see her fucked by another fat hog like her though. That would be sweet. Face down in the mud and begging for mercy while taking it from behind from a pig is just what all the snooty Beckys like her deserve. Bet they wouldn't look down on us so much after that! Maybe we can arrange something like that for her when she comes here!*

"Becky," I noted with amused despair, meant an ordinary (white and/or middle class and/or straight) woman, just as it did amongst intersectional feminists. One of life's amusing little ironies, especially given how loudly my more progressive friends liked to proclaim that "words matter!" Incels and intersectional feminists had a lot more in common with each other than either side would like to believe. They were both products of the same zeitgeist, after all. Probably if I said that, it would provoke a response almost as nasty as Miriam Chen's appearance had amongst these guys.

There were four comments in support of Nottagirl's. True to their words, LostAndFoundBoy had written a condemnation of the post itself, and of Nottagirl's comment on it. This earned him—I assumed LostAndFoundBoy was male—an outpouring of outrage from the other posters. Oh well. Speaking out against injustice was so often a pointless task. Probably he wouldn't bother again.

I took a screenshot of the post and the comments, in case the posters came to their senses and deleted them later. I wasn't sure if this could be considered an actionable threat, but it seemed more sinister than anything we'd found so far, and genuinely vile enough to warrant some real action. I emailed it to Brian Michaels and asked what he wanted to do about it.

42

WHAT BRIAN MICHAELS wanted to do, it turned out, was nothing. Or rather, as he confessed, he'd like to go round up all those wussy mama's boys and turn them over to my brother and the good folks at Parris Island so they could get all the devil quarterdecked right out of them. But not only was it illegal to pressgang people into the Marines for a few ill-advised blog posts, we didn't even know who the posters actually were.

Find out who they are, and then we'll see what we can do, he told me. *I've poked around a bit, but I don't run in their circles, and I don't know anything about computers. It's not like we're the damn FBI and we keep IT experts on staff. It's just me and a couple of deputies, and we've got our hands full with DUIs and **actual** flashers and stalkers. But if you can find out who these asshats are, we can show up in force and try to talk some sense into them. Sure you don't want to sic your big brother on them? He sure scared the ever-loving crap out of my son. :) :) Only one who's ever made him see sense.*

I'll keep that tactic in my back pocket, I wrote. *But first I have to find out who they are.*

The most straightforward path ran through Nathan Willoughby. Which meant I needed to go talk to him. I knew he had French class at 9:00am, and according to Chloe, he hung around afterwards trying to catch a glimpse of Taylor, or maybe Miranda, or both. As Darryl had said, for someone who was a self-proclaimed woman-hater, he sure spent a lot of time voluntarily hanging around girls. I wasn't sure if this was a "sour grapes" kind of situation, or a "you beat the one you love" one. Maybe both. Maybe he was just sad and misunderstood, and all he needed was a sympathetic ear and a helping hand. That seemed like an awfully big maybe, but it was worth a shot as an opening tactic.

Accordingly, I hustled out of my first class at 9:50 exactly, and took up a position across the hall from where Chloe's Chinese class and Darryl's French class were about to get out. Chris, I noted out the corner of my eye, had done the same thing, and was now watching me with surreptitious dismay from a post two doors down the hallway.

Chloe's class ended, and a knot of loudly talking students came out, led by Taylor. Chris's face lit up. The expression transformed him from another sullen, slouchy, spotty teenager into someone who was almost handsome, or would be when he finished growing up.

"Taylor!" he called, raising his hand in a wave.

"Taylor!" Now Darryl's French class was getting out, and Nathan was calling from the door. His face had lit up too, just for an instant, before shutting down into an expression of spiteful scorn. *Definitely* sour grapes.

Taylor stopped and looked back and forth between the two boys in indecision. "Um, hi, Nathan," she said. "Hi, Chris! You still up for coffee like we talked about?"

"You told me *we* were going to go get coffee," said Nathan.

"Um..." said Taylor.

"Actually, I need to speak to Nathan for a moment," I said, stepping forward. "Would you mind putting off your coffee date till later?"

Chris's face darkened at the word "date," but lit back up when Taylor said, "Sure, no problem, professor! Come on, Chris, let's go."

"You can't just pull me over and tell me I have to cancel all my plans in order to talk to you!" said Nathan. His arms were folded in a way that he probably hoped was imposing, but really made him look hunched and defensive. The sneer, though, was impressively bold.

"I know. But I was hoping this would be a convenient time to set up a meeting. We need to talk."

"Yeah?" Both the scornful sneer and the insecure hunch deepened. "About what?"

"About—"

"Rowena! There you are! Where have you been?! I've been looking all over for you!" Karen came bustling up at a fast waddle.

"I wanted to talk to Na—"I began.

"What on earth for would you want to talk to *him*? He's not even one of your students! Come on. I really *have* to talk to you about something *important*. Really, Rowena, why you make it so difficult to find you, I don't know! You should be more responsible. What if I had been a student?"

"I have to go now," said Nathan. His sneer had transformed into a smirk, and his arms had uncrossed and were now swinging confidently at his sides. "And I really don't see what you could possibly have to talk to me about, *professor*."

"It's really imp—" But Nathan was already gone. "My next class is about to start," I told Karen. "Can we talk afterwards?"

"Honestly, Rowena, you're *supposed* to make yourself accessible to students *and* your mentors! And this is important! I wanted to talk to you about your contract renewal!"

"Um, okay?" I said. "Of course. But my next class really does start in"—I checked my phone—"four minutes."

"Then what were you doing hanging around here trying to talk to Nathan?"

"I needed to make an appointment to talk to him."

"What on earth for?"

"The Miriam Chen talk."

"What? What on earth could he possibly have to do with that? Well, I suppose I *should* let you go to your class. But come see me right afterwards. We need to talk about your contract."

"Okay," I said, but Karen had already waddled off without waiting for my response.

43

I ASSUMED THAT THE only reason for Karen to demand to talk to me so portentously about my contract was that she had decided to terminate it. I had been bracing myself for this for the past month, but now that it was here, I realized I was in no way ready for it. I already was pretty sure I had no love for Crimson College, but rejection and termination is always hurtful, and I didn't have anything else lined up.

It was still only the second week of October, so application deadlines for most jobs were just now coming due, and interview invitations wouldn't start going out until next month at the earliest. I had no idea what kind of situation I could expect next year, and I certainly had nothing in the pipeline for the spring if Crimson tossed me out on my ear in December. I hadn't even seen any jobs posted for the spring. The fact that I'd gotten one, crappy as it had been, last year had been a stroke of luck that I couldn't possibly expect to be repeated.

Maybe this is the thing that will kick you out of this futile and humiliating job search, and into Alex's arms! I told myself. *Maybe **this** is the thing that will free you from this Sisyphean treadmill, make you choose true love over a parasitical career, and turn your life around!*

But my words sounded hollow in my own head. Maybe all that was true. Maybe it wasn't. Either way, I wanted to go out on my own terms, not be terminated by a dumpy toad-woman who had spent her entire life hoping to become a petty tyrant, and had finally had her dreams come true with me.

My furious thoughts seemed to go unnoticed by the students, and after a very long fifty minutes, I was able to leave the stuffy classroom and go find out my fate.

I passed Mel in the hallway, walking away from Karen's office with a wrathful expression on her face.

"What is it?" I asked.

"Oh." She waved her hand. "You know. Karen." She looked back over her shoulder. "Speaking of which, she's standing in the doorway beckoning at you impatiently. Let's get together afterwards and bitch about her, okay? Maybe during a nice hard run."

"Sounds good," I said.

"Rowena! *There* you are! Let's talk."

I went into Karen's office. She spent a while clearing a space for me to sit down, and taking her own seat in front of her computer, something made more difficult by the ever-larger piles of paperwork all around her.

"Well," she said, once she was finally arranged to her satisfaction. As usual, she was looking at the computer screen instead of at me, although she kept flicking me little glances out of the corner of her eyes, and then looking fearfully away whenever I caught her gaze, like she couldn't bear to register my existence. Probably being a teacher and now a department chair was one of the worst career choices she could have made, since she seemed to be utterly lacking in either empathy or organizational ability. Funny how that turned out.

"Well," she said again. "We have reviewed all your materials—after you *finally* turned them all in—and we—*I*—have decided that, all things considered, we *will* renew your contract. But with certain conditions and stipulations, of course. You should consider next semester to be another probationary semester."

"Really?!" I had been so resigned to being fired that *not* being immediately terminated was vastly more than I could have hoped for. On the other hand, *another* probationary semester was such an egregious piece of bullshit that I didn't know how to respond. "I mean, that's great," I said. "I'm, uh, thrilled to be able to continue here at Crimson."

"Of course." Karen's expression of satisfaction was sickeningly strong for a moment, and then slipped away as my lack of fawning began to penetrate her brain. "Of course," she said again, "we do have a *number* of suggestions for how you can improve your performance and bring it up to the standards we expect from faculty at Crimson."

"Um, sure." Just like last time, I was starting to have the sensation that my spirit was separating from my body and I was watching all this from the outside, or through a thick pain of glass. Torture victims and PTSD sufferers described similar sensations. It seemed ridiculous that something that should have been completely innocuous was triggering the same response in me, but it was. Or maybe it was the nauseatingly musty smell of Karen's office.

"You don't have another class now, do you? Of course not: you're only teaching two courses this semester, aren't you? You'll definitely have to improve your performance by next semester, when you'll be teaching *three* courses, won't you?"

"Um," I said. "Sure."

"I have a list of conditions of improvement for you to go through and sign." She searched around in her various piles of paper for what seemed like several excruciating eternities before she fished out a crumpled print-out of my supposed failings as a teacher, and started going through them.

Some of them were ridiculous, and some of them were outright lies. I tried to counter the outright lies, but let the ridiculous ones slide, in order to save my strength. None of it did any good.

In the end I, feeling rather like someone who'd been dragged off to the basements of Butyrka Prison by the KGB and pressured into a false confession, signed off on everything and agreed that yes, I would *definitely* make all these improvements and stop, e.g., starting and ending class late. Since every single one of my classes at Crimson thus far, not to mention 99% of the classes I had ever taught, had started and ended within two minutes of their official start and end times, and the class Karen had observed had started and ended at exactly 9:00 and 9:50, I didn't even know how to start countering that criticism, so I just signed.

"And what *have* you done to find out what that Miranda is up to?" Karen demanded, once I had signed the form and handed it back to her. "Have you finally realized that she's one of our main troublemakers, or are you still sure she's not part of the Gang of Six?" She was now coming as close as someone like her could to smiling. It made her flabby mouth look even more obscene than usual.

"I mean, I see Miranda four times a week, and she doesn't seem to be up to anything. Other than trying to get an interview with Miriam Chen for the paper. I said I'd see if I could help her out with that, since I'm now on the committee for the talk, and I seem to be taking point on...well, pretty much everything, actually."

"You joined a committee?" Karen was no longer smiling. Her gray skin had developed unhealthy dark purple blotches along her jowl line. "Without consulting me? Perhaps I didn't make myself clear, Rowena, but you have to have permission from your department chair to serve on a committee. What if the department needed you for something?"

"Oh." For a nanosecond I contemplated pointing out that the last time we had met, she had specifically ordered me to do committee work, and told me when I had asked for suggestions that I was responsible for finding and joining a committee myself. But that seemed highly counterproductive.

"If you have any issues with me being on the Miriam Chen committee, you should probably take it up with Sandra DeWitt in Sociology," I said instead. "And Chief Michaels, since I've been working closely with him on security for the event. We have a personal connection—his son served under my brother's command in the Marines—so it made sense for me to be the one to liaise with campus police."

Karen's face went even grayer and blotchier. "Well...well...I suppose I can allow you to continue to sit on that committee for now. But next time you really *must* check with me first before joining any kind of committee or making any kind of service commitment, Rowena."

"Um, okay." I sat there for a moment, waiting for her to say something more, but she had gone back to staring at her computer screen. I decided to take that to mean that I was dismissed.

Unfortunately, that wasn't true. "Oh, and one final thing," said Karen, as I was getting, dizzily, to my feet. "I've signed you up for the Pre-Turkey Trot. I don't know *why* we do this every year, but we do. Theresa *insisted* that I sign you up for it, so I did. Be sure you don't miss it! You may still have a lot to learn about teaching, Rowena, but perhaps you can still serve the department as an"—her voice dripped with so much disgust she sounded in danger of barfing on the spot—"*athlete*. You and that Melissa Wilson. Maybe if you spent less time working out and more time working, you'd be a little more prepared for your classes, but at least this way you'll still be doing us *some* good."

"Um," I said. "Okay." And I stumbled out of the office and away.

44

THE NOT-VERY-BRIGHT lights of the hallway slammed into my eyes as soon as I staggered out of Karen's office, triggering the instant appearance of a big gray blob that danced in the center of my vision, refusing to be dismissed.

"Are you all right?" Mel straightened up from where she had been leaning against the wall, checking her phone. "You've got your hand over your eyes. Did you get something in them?"

"It's nothing," I said. "I've just got a bit of a pre-migraine thing going."

"Pre-migraine—like what?"

"You know," I said. "A scotoma. A blind spot in the center of my vision that turns into a big sparkling thing. Sometimes followed by a sick headache."

"That doesn't sound like nothing to me," she said. "That sounds like you need to go lie down for the rest of the afternoon."

"It'll probably dissipate pretty soon if I can avoid any bright lights."

"Bright lights—like the sun?"

"Um...yeah." It was a bright sunny day outside.

"Look. I know we didn't carpool today, but why don't I drive you home. You really don't look so good, and frankly I'm afraid I'd be committing gross public endangerment or something if I allowed you to drive yourself around in this state."

"It's really no big deal…"

"Yes, it is. Blind spots and visual impairments are a big deal when it comes to driving, so you sit here and let me go get my fucking car, Rowena."

"Can I sit outside?" I asked.

"I thought you said the sunlight would make it worse."

"Yes, but I'd still rather be outside in the fresh air than in here. It always seems like there's never enough oxygen in here or something."

Mel sniffed. "I know what you mean. Okay, you go sit outside, but with sunglasses, okay?"

"I don't have any."

"Well, wear mine, then." She fished a huge pair of aviator sunglasses out of her purse, and waited until I'd put them on, before setting off at a brisk trot in the direction of the faculty parking lot.

I slipped on the sunglasses and followed her more slowly out the building. Now that my eyes were shielded by the dark glasses, the gray blob had morphed to a weird kind of greeny-orange, but it was still amoeba-ing slowly across my field of vision, rendering the familiar surroundings foreign and difficult to navigate.

Sitting outside in the fresh air with my eyes closed helped, and by the time I got into Mel's car, I felt capable of getting around without crashing into something. When I said as much to Mel and suggested that I drive myself home, she refused, however.

"No way," she said. "What if you had a relapse and crashed? Imagine how I'd feel then."

"It's not like I can get up to dangerous speeds on the road between here and home."

"You'd be surprised," she said darkly. "You can have a terrible crash at twenty miles an hour."

"Weren't you in the Air Force?" I said.

The side of her mouth closest to me started to turn up. "Your point?"

"Shouldn't you be swaggering around talking about how you feel the need, the need for speed?"

"First of all, the *Top Gun* guys were Navy. Second of all, I was never a pilot. Actually—don't tell anyone or they'll take away my butch card—I don't even like to fly. I was a linguist, and then I went to college and got a fucking PhD. I might seem pretty macho and tough for academia, but that's only by comparison with the rest of these pansies. I'm really a nerd. And don't tell me that 'pansies' is homophobic. I think as a lesbian, I get to use 'pansies' whenever I please."

"Fair enough," I said. "And I take your point. And I'm happy to have you drive me home, as long as it's no trouble for you."

"Are you kidding? This is the best part of my day so far. After that shit with Karen...I take it she raked you over the coals too? Somehow she managed to turn a simple contract renewal into an hour-long torture session. Now that I know I'm going to be here next semester, I'm not sure I even want to be anymore."

"I know. Same here. Considering that she didn't even fire me, I should be feeling better. But instead I feel like I've been horribly violated. There's nothing that would be actionable in a court of law, or even sounds that bad when you describe it, and I didn't lose my job—in fact, I don't think I was actually ever in any danger of losing my job; it was all a big mind game—but right now I think I hate Karen more than I hate anyone else in the world. I hate her precisely because she's so petty. I thought I hated those guys who held me at gunpoint in Moscow, but at least they were serious opponents, opponents I could fight back against—and did. Whereas the evil thing about Karen is that you can't even fight back against her."

"Yeah," said Mel. "What guys in Moscow?"

"Oh...you know, the guy...my boyfriend...fiancé, actually...the one in Russia, the one who was wounded in Ukraine recently, was investigating something that some 'serious people' took exception to, and they decided to put a stop to it by going through me."

"Oh, shit," said Mel. "But you're not with him anymore, right? You're with this Alex guy at the DLI, right?"

"Right," I said. "And that's probably the right thing to be doing. But I hate that it ended the way it did between me and Dima."

"Yeah," said Mel. "Do you love him? This Alex guy, I mean?"

I leaned back against the car seat. "I think so. In a way. That sounds awful, doesn't it? But before him there was really only Dima, and the way I feel for them is so different that it's hard for me to say which one is love and which one isn't. Probably they both are, just very different kinds of love. I always feel better when I'm around Alex, or when I even think about him. I always feel like he's a good friend, and someone I can trust. I could easily see myself making a life with him, and probably a happy one."

"That's all very nice, but is he someone you can fuck?"

"That too," I said. "That part's pretty great too. The only part that's not great is that he's three thousand miles away."

"Yeah," said Mel. "That part sucks. But this Dima guy was even farther away, right?"

"Right," I said. "A whole ocean away, and he never could manage to get on a plane and fly to me. I did all the flying to him. But I always felt like I had no choice. Like I was caught up in something bigger than myself, and I had to be with him, whether I wanted it or not. I'm not sure if it could exactly be called love at first sight, but within half an hour of talking to him I got this *feeling*, like a voice in my soul, like the hand of God coming down out of the sky and laying itself on my forehead and telling me, 'You WILL be with this man.' Not because I liked him or because he was a good choice, but because I *had* to. I suppose it sounds pretty unhealthy, doesn't it?"

"A bit," said Mel. "But it also sounds like the kind of thing most people spend their whole lives looking for. Not all great things are good, and happiness isn't the most important thing in life. Most people want more than that, even if they don't know it. So what are you going to do about it?"

"I don't know. I went into the meeting with Karen this morning fully prepared to be fired. Alex had already said I could come live with him if I didn't have anywhere else to go, which sounds worse than how he meant it, but we both agreed that if I ended up unemployed, it would be a sign that I should move in with him, and maybe that would be the best outcome for everyone.

"But now I'm on *another* probationary semester. Another semester of limbo, unable to walk away but unable to make any kind of plans to stay, either. I feel like I'm caught between two men, two coasts. Only one job, unfortunately. But I feel trapped in an untenable situation, without a clear path forward, and every time I try to forge one, something comes up that diverts me from my goal and sends me off in the opposite direction. Which always takes me right back into the heart of the maze. I need to break free, but the more I try, the more stuck I become, like a fly caught in a spider's web."

"Yeah," said Mel. "That sounds all too fucking familiar." She made the turn onto Peachtree Avenue. "How are you feeling?"

"Better. Fresh air helped. And so did the sunglasses, so thanks for loaning them to me."

"No problem." She rubbed her left eye. "And you're not the only one having eye problems. I've got this weird twitch in my lower eyelid that won't go away. Probably just stress, but it's annoying as fuck."

"Sounds like it. Oh, by the way. Did Karen tell you that you've been signed up for the 'Pre-Turkey Trot'? Because she gave me this whole spiel about how the department might as well get *some* use out of me, since I was such a shit teacher."

"Oh. Yeah. Under other circumstances I would have been fine with it, but since it came from Karen, I wanted to stuff my refusal down her fat—wait, I probably shouldn't be using 'fat' as an insult, should I?—her ugly throat. But I didn't. I guess we should train for it, or something. You probably don't feel like running today, do you?"

"Actually, a run might do me good. It might clear my head enough for me to actually get some work done this afternoon."

Mel rubbed her eye again. "Dammit! Not you; this damn twitch. Maybe a run will make it go away too. What do you say? We could meet by the front entrance in half an hour, put in a quick run, and then get back down to applying for jobs we're not going to get."

"Sounds like a plan," I said.

45

OUR RUN WAS SHORT, and not as brisk as we had originally planned. My head started to pound after half a mile, and Mel's knees were, she said, "Annoyingly twingey."

"It's not even pain, really," she said. "It just feels like they're...messed up. They've been messed up ever since that weird flu I got, and just when I think they're finally back to normal, they start acting up again. Or maybe I'm just getting old. I'll be thirty-six next week."

"Happy birthday ahead of time!"

"Yeah. To be honest, I'm not that happy about it. I was really hoping that by thirty-six I'd at the very least have steady employment, and hopefully a steady girlfriend as well. Instead I have neither. I'm like a sixteen-year-old stuck in a thirty-six-year-old's decaying body."

"I don't think you're decaying just yet," I said.

"Yeah, but sure as hell *feels* like it. Are you supposed to feel this bad at this age? I know old people complain all the time about how bad they feel, but it seems a little early for it to be this bad. But what the hell do I know? Maybe it's this sucky for everyone." She shook her head. "Well, enough whining. I hear job applications calling."

"Good luck," I said. "And thanks for the ride, and everything else."

"Any time. Is that your phone?"

It was my phone. It was a text from Alex, asking me how I was.

Okay, I texted back. *What's going on? Isn't it still just midmorning there?*

And I need a special reason to text you in the middle of the morning? :) :) Can't it just be because I was thinking about you?

Of course. You just don't normally do it during class hours.

I think I'm going crazy with pent-up lust. I was sitting around watching the students take a test, and all I could think about was you. In, you know, a sexy way. I thought I was going to get a hard-on in the middle of class.

Embarrassing!

Yeah, no fucking kidding. So I thought I'd text you, although now I feel even more frustrated.

What if you called me this evening? I suggested. *Maybe I could, you know, help ease some of that frustration.*

Are you suggesting what I think you're suggesting? :):):)

I think it's time, don't you? I wrote. *We've been having fun with texting, so I think we need to take this next step in our relationship :):):)*

Gulp Will you still respect me if I tell you I've never actually, you know, gone all the way over the phone?

Phone? You think I'm going to be satisfied with just the phone?!? I want video, baby!

The three dots that meant Alex was writing appeared and disappeared on my screen for several minutes before Alex finally responded. *Fuck! I don't know if I'm up for that. No, wait, I am *definitely* up for something, lol, and this is what's on offer. Maybe it's time for me to lose my video sex cherry. Oh shit. My students are coming back from break. Better put the phone away before they figure out what's going on.*

Think about what you want to do later! I told him. *I expect a list of requests and suggestions when we reconvene this evening!*

Yes MA'AM!

That left me with a smile on my face, which kept breaking out even in the middle of formatting my teaching portfolio for the current job application.

Once I got the application sent off, I did what I'd been promising myself for months I would do, and started making a list of academic publishers to whom I could send my book proposal. Once I had a book proposal, that is, but in order to make a book proposal, I had to know what went into a book proposal, which I didn't.

I discovered with glum resignation that a book proposal would involve a lot more writing, most of which would have little to no return on investment. Each publisher had their own requirements, of course, but on top of the expected CV and cover letter, there was some version of a multi-page proposal for the actual book, a chapter-by-chapter outline, a market analysis and list of comparable titles, and a proposed completion date. I could understand why the publishing houses requested this information. But it would be a lot of work to pull together, even if I knew how to do it, which I didn't (yet), and I would probably have to send out dozens of proposals in order to get one acceptance, and that only if I were very lucky.

Alex's call after dinner disrupted my melancholy musings. I treated him to a half-hour rant about life, the universe, and everything, until I remembered the original purpose of this call.

"But enough about me," I said. "As I recall, before I so selfishly derailed it, this call was about doing something to ease your sexual frustration."

"No problem. I know how it goes. And the situation you're in with organizing the Miriam Chen talk sounds like a mess, and that Karen sounds like a real fucking pain in the ass. I'd be ranting about it too, and probably I will be ranting about my own job-related problems soon enough. And it sounds like *you* need to ease some sexual frustration too."

"I guess," I said. "Maybe that's my problem. Although God knows I'm used to long stretches of enforced celibacy."

"Yes, but"—Alex's voice took on a cautious tone—"I gathered from some hints you've let drop that that enforced celibacy was punctuated by, uh, video intimacy."

"Perhaps. Are you ready to try it out?"

"I'm afraid. But I'm so fucking desperate I'm willing to go through with it anyway."

"What do you have on your phone? Skype? WhatsApp? Google HangOut? FaceTime?"

After three dropped calls, we settled on FaceTime as the best carrier for what Alex called his "foray into internet porn." The connection was still weak and the picture kept breaking up, but our faces were recognizably faces more than half the time, which was better than anything else we'd tried.

"Okay," said Alex, once we'd established a decent-enough connection. "What do I do now?"

"Um...whatever you want to do? Get comfortable, I suppose. Whatever you'd do in a regular situation."

"In a regular situation I'd be in bed with my arms around you, asking you how you wanted me to help you cum."

"So get in bed, then. Try to find a comfortable position where you can still hold the phone."

"This is so fucking unsatisfying. And I'm afraid I'm going to jizz all over my multi-hundred-dollar phone, if I don't drop it on the floor first."

"Repetition is the mother of learning," I told him sternly. "Do you want to do this or not?"

"I do, God help me. But next month, which currently seems like a long, *long* time away, we're doing this the right way."

"And what's the right way?" I demanded.

"Skin to skin, not like some kind of awful *Demolition Man* VR-sex."

"Okay. You have a point. But this is what we have right now, so it's virtual sex, or none at all. Think of it as exploring a new facet of your sexuality."

"Or sinking to new depths of sad depravity," said Alex. "All right, all right, I'll stop, I promise! I'm perfectly aware that I'm being a grumpy shit when you're trying to do something nice for me. I just...did you just take your shirt off?"

"And my bra," I said. "So what are you going to do to keep pace?"

46

DESPITE ALEX'S COMPLAINTS about how unsatisfying long-distance sex was, he found it tolerable enough to try it two more times over fall break. This, he said, was obviously a sign that I was corrupting him, but what could he do? Debauchery was a slippery slope, and I'd shoved him down it headfirst.

"Sure, sure," I told him. "You're an innocent little lamb, like every man ever. It's the woman who's always the sexual aggressor."

"Well...maybe a seductress. I guess you're trying to tell me I should own my own sexual neediness, or something?"

"Or something," I agreed.

"Fair enough. Speaking of sexual neediness, have you talked to that Nathan kid you were telling me about yet?"

"No." I groaned. "After Karen interrupted me when I was trying to set up an appointment with him, I tried sending him an email, but he never responded. And I'm not really sure what to do. I don't actually have any official standing here, other than being a professor. I'm not *his* professor, or his advisor, or anything like that, and I'm not from campus police either. All I have are some rumors that he's the one behind the MPA website."

"Are they an official campus organization? Surely in that case they'd be registered somewhere, with officers and contact information and all that."

"I thought of that," I said. "But no. I checked, and they're not actually an officially registered campus organization. They're just a website that seems to be run by someone or someones from campus, and the word on the street is that the person in charge is Nathan Willoughby. Who doesn't want to have anything to do with me."

"Maybe you should try collaring him in the hallway again. That's a lot harder to dodge than an email."

"I know. That's what I'm planning to do first thing Monday, as soon as fall break is over."

Accordingly, the next morning I went and lurked outside of Nathan's French class in the break between my first and second classes. Just like last time, Chris was also lurking nearby, waiting for Taylor to be released.

Nathan caught sight of him as soon as he stepped out of the classroom, and made a face. He made an even bigger face when I stepped in front of him, blocking him from going over to Chris, who was now asking Taylor if she still wanted to go grab some coffee, and told him I wanted to talk to him.

"What about?" He craned his neck, trying to see around me, to where Chris and Taylor were now moving off in the direction of the quad.

"The Miriam Chen talk," I told him.

"I don't see *why*. *I'm* certainly not going! There's no way I'd spend an hour looking at that fat hog, let alone listening to her!"

"Did you write the post?" I asked.

"What post?"

"The post on the MPA blog about Miriam's, um, current appearance. The one that called her a fat hog. The one full of rape threats."

"I never wrote any of those threats!"

"But you wrote the post?"

He shuffled uneasily from foot to foot, not meeting my eyes. He was an inch or so shorter than me, and much less fit. The remnants of teenage acne dotted his face, and the wispy facial hair he was trying to cultivate into a mustache and goatee made him look even younger and less manly than he would have clean-shaven. By his smell and the greasiness of his hair, I guessed he hadn't showered or changed in at least two days, maybe three. My maternal side wanted to take him in hand and tell him that if he wanted female attention, he should start with some basic grooming and personal hygiene, followed by some lessons in charm and deportment. But somehow I doubted that would go down well, and it still wouldn't solve his underlying problem of being terminally self-centered. I wasn't sure what *would* solve that problem, but, looking at him, I could see the attraction of quarterdeck.

"It's a free country!" he said. "The First Amendment says I can write whatever I want!"

"Well," I said. "Not exactly. Incitement and hate speech are not protected. It's like selling secrets to the enemy: it's just too dangerous to be allowed. And especially given the number of threats that have been made against Miriam Chen, the college is taking this very seriously. I've been asked to look into it and find out who the perpetrators are, and you seem like the obvious person to go to for help."

"I have the right to remain silent! That's the Fifth Amendment," he added smugly.

"I'm not arresting you or putting you on trial," I told him. "I'm asking you for help."

"Why should I help *you*?"

"Because I'm a lot nicer than Chief Michaels?"

"Who's that?"

"The chief of campus police."

"Oh." Nathan wrinkled his nose up in a sneer. "Campus police are a *joke*. What're they going to do to *me*?"

"Nothing, if you help us out."

"Sorry. There's no way. I'm not going to do anything to Miriam Chen myself, but I'm not going to go out of my way to make things easier for that bitch to come to campus and spread her poison. If she stays away, lots of students will thank me."

"Nathan." I exhaled sharply through my nose, arresting him in mid-walk-off. I was more pleased than I should have been to see the touch of fear that flashed in his eyes when he saw my irritation. "Have you ever gotten in trouble with the authorities? With the police?"

"Seems like I'm getting harassed pretty good right now!"

I laughed. He stopped from walking away or saying whatever it was he was going to say, too taken aback to respond.

"This," I said, "is not harassment. Police harassment is when they hit you with riot sticks and drag you off by your legs and toss you into an isolation cell and hold you there for days, beating the crap out of you and denying you food and medical care and legal representation. And then there's private harassment, when regular citizens stalk you on the street and follow you home and spraypaint death threats across your door. You've never even seen the first kind, and you'd like to inflict the second kind on others, except you don't have the nerve. But the thing is, Nathan, *I'm* a lot less nice than most people think I am. Because I've experienced both kinds of harassment, and I would be okay with dishing it out if I had to."

"Is that a threat?" he cried.

"No. It's a statement of fact. I don't want to threaten you, Nathan, because that's not my style. But I'm here to tell you that the world is a much darker and more dangerous place than you think it is. You're playing around with being a bad guy, or a victim, or both, but you don't seem to have any conception of what it actually means to be either. So ask yourself: how would you feel if something terrible happened to Miriam Chen? Something that you were, even if indirectly, responsible for? Because I think you'd feel pretty fucking terrible. I think you're smart enough, and sensitive enough, that it would ruin the rest of your life. Being a bad guy is a lot less fun than you think it is, Nathan. Bad guys tend to live short, unhappy lives.

"But you don't *have* to be a bad guy. You want respect and admiration from women? Fine. You know how you could get that? Be a hero. Women *love* heroes. And maybe you feel like you've been denied the chance at heroism, but here it is, staring you right in the face. Tell me—or Chief Michaels, if you'd prefer—who you think is behind the threats to Miriam Chen. If you *really* want to be a hero, take it one step further and denounce the MPA and everything it stands for."

"That doesn't sound like heroism." Nathan was trying to sneer and avoid looking at me at the same time, and it was making him look even less mature than before. "That sounds like snitching."

"The path of the hero is strewn with thorns. I have to go teach my class now, but I'll be waiting to hear from you, Nathan. And I'll be monitoring the MPA's website. If the posts about Miriam Chen are taken down and replaced with a statement denouncing all violence against women and particularly any threats aimed at Miriam Chen, I'll consider that a good first step. Come tell me who made the threats, and I'll get off your back entirely. But this is very serious, Nathan. Don't let it ruin your life as well as Miriam's."

"Um..." Nathan swallowed convulsively. "Um..."

"You have the chance to do something really good," I told him. "I wouldn't let it pass me by, if I were you. I'll be waiting to hear from you." I left before he could say anything more.

47

MY LOW HOPES FOR NATHAN'S cooperation were fulfilled, as he did not email me or request another meeting, and in fact took to avoiding me in the hallways whenever he happened to encounter me. The only sign that my talk with him had had any effect whatsoever was a lengthy post on the MPA website, complaining about the suppression of freedom of speech and how women always seemed to think they could manipulate men into doing whatever they wanted them to. This provoked a number of similar complaints in the comments section, but no threats against Miriam Chen.

I thought about commenting myself and pointing out that the sensation so many men had of being controlled by women was mainly a self-generated illusion, but I decided that would be more trouble than it was worth. All these people seemed like bundles of selfish unhappiness, who would only be shaken out of their self-absorbed misery and into some kind of recognition of the truth and the real world by...what? What would break through their self-absorption and their delusions? Only something wonderful or something terrible. They needed to fall in love, or go through a dreadful ordeal, in order to crack their shells open and penetrate the real person who was still hiding there somewhere underneath. And for some of them, even that wouldn't be enough.

Especially Nathan. Nathan, I guessed, yearned to distinguish himself, just like Miranda—or me. He wanted to help people and devote himself to a cause, just like we did. This would be the point at which many of my feminist friends would start bemoaning the cruel societal pressures that prevented men from developing their nurturing, selfless side and devoting themselves to social causes.

I, however, was a lot more judgmental. Lots of men managed to devote themselves to all kinds of "nurturing" things like homelessness, environmentalism, and animal welfare, and if that didn't suit their fancy, they could always go down John's route and join the Marines. But nooooo. Nathan and his brethren had to go around making some kind of topsy-turvy, Looking Glass social movement in which the oppressors moaned on and on about being oppressed. Which they were. By their own stupid selves. Maybe I should drop a link to Hegel's "Lordship and Bondage" in the MPA comments section...nah. Rather than being enlightened, they'd probably twist that to suit their own purposes too. I needed to put the squeeze on Nathan even harder, or maybe start spying on him. If only he didn't turn tail and run every time he caught sight of me.

Nathan may have been avoiding me, but he seemed to have struck up a friendship with Chris. I saw them palling around campus together, engaged in earnest conversations that sick curiosity made me want to eavesdrop on. My guess was that Nathan was trying to recruit Chris for the MPA, and that Chris, with his poor social graces and probably abusive parents, would be an easy target.

By the end of October, I was no nearer to finding out who had posted those threats against Miriam Chen, but they hadn't been repeated, either. I, optimistically, suggested to both Miriam and Brian Michaels that maybe it was all blowing over and things would calm down by the time the talk actually rolled around. Brian said he sure hoped so but he didn't want to count on it, and Miriam accused me of not taking her safety seriously, so I had walk that statement back and assure her that yes, I was taking her safety very seriously.

And I was. I just hadn't seen anything to make me think that the threat was escalating.

It was good that things were calming down on that front, because I still had plenty of job applications I had to submit, and that book proposal I kept telling myself I was going to get cracking on, but that kept getting derailed. I would *definitely* finish it, or at least start it, the weekend before Thanksgiving, I promised myself. Thanksgiving break was out of the question, since Alex was coming and even I could see that it was inappropriate to ignore him for hours at a time so that I could work, after he'd flown all the way out from California.

But the weekend before Thanksgiving I had nothing but the Pre-Turkey Trot to look forward to. Unless a sudden invitation for an interview at the ASEEES (Association for Slavic, East European, and Eurasian Studies) convention, which was being held that same weekend, appeared in my inbox.

No such invitation, alas, appeared. Since I hadn't known where I would be, or if I would even be employed, last January when panel proposals for the convention were due, I had ended up electing not to submit one at all, and to skip the convention unless I got an interview invitation. My current position at Crimson included $1,000 in conference travel money per academic year, but I'd already committed to going to the AATSEEL (American Association of Teachers of Slavic and East European Languages) conference in Vancouver in January. $1,000 would cover maybe half of that. I was no longer as broke as I'd been the past academic year, but I was still far from rich, and I was still paying off the credit card debt I'd racked up supporting myself and my employment habit. So I would only go to the ASEEES convention in Philadelphia if invited for an interview for a tenure-track job.

By the middle of November, though, I had not received a single interview invitation for any type of job, let alone a tenure-track one.

But I was distracted from my woes by twin releases of explosive posts by both the MPA and the Gang of Six.

48

WHEN I CHECKED, AS I had gotten in the habit of doing, the Gang of Six's website Monday afternoon, a new headline screamed out at me:

COLLEGE DOES NOTHING WHILE THREATS RAIN DOWN ON MIRIAM CHEN'S HEAD FREEDOM OF SPEECH THREATENED

Just when we thought that Crimson couldn't sink any lower they stand by while blatant threats to her health and safety rain down on Miriam Chen's head.

If you've been reading these posts regularly you'll remember that the Men's Protection Alliance threatened to protest the Miriam Chen talk that was originally scheduled for this October but has been pushed back to December maybe out of fear maybe because the faculty and staff here can't get it together enough to organize a simple guest speaker event. The MPA has continued to make threats against Miriam Chen or at least some of their guest posters have. We won't repeat what was said but there were disgusting threats in the comments section of one of the MPA's posts.

Well it's happened again and this time there are even more threats and more disgusting threats. Meanwhile the college has failed to even issue a statement condemning them and the talk is still scheduled to go forward.

While **WE** *condemn these threats we understand why they were made. The college has a stifling atmosphere that makes any kind of expression of thoughts and feelings and serious ideals impossible, it's no wonder that some students are choosing to lash out.*

In fact we have it on good authority that some members of the MPA have come under pressure from campus police and certain faculty members to give up the names of the poster of the threats, that is unacceptable. Journalistic integrity demands that they protect their sources! Shame on campus police and faculty for trying to get them to break the journalistic code! Police and faculty should figure this out on their own without resorting to police state tactics but that's how things are done here it seems. Instead of creating a safe environment where diverse ideas and viewpoints can flourish they're creating a police state where free speech is policed and repressed, they're doubling down on the tactics this college has always used to sweep controversy under the rug without doing anything to solve the underlying problems.

WE CRY FOUL! DO YOUR JOB, CAMPUS POLICE! MAKE SURE MIRIAM CHEN IS SAFE WITHOUT OPPRESSING FREE SPEECH!

I debated between groaning, rolling my eyes, or smacking my forehead, and settled for all three. Then I seriously considered commenting on the post and pointing out that every single comma there was misused. They'd left them out when they needed them, and inserted comma splices when they shouldn't. That was probably not a productive approach to take. Although in the long term it might do these students more good than any other step I might take. At least that way some of them might start using commas correctly...no! I needed to stop worrying about the commas and start worrying about the meat of the matter, which was that I had just become the Gang of Six's Public Enemy Number One. It didn't take much of a leap to guess that the "certain faculty members" who had been threatening members of the MPA referred to me.

I wasn't even going to get into all the contradictory impulses behind this article: did they want the MPA to stop issuing their threats, or did they want them to boldly speak their minds? The problem with free speech is that a lot of what people want to say would really be better off left unsaid.

I wondered what would happen when Karen got wind of this, and if she'd figure out they were referring to me. Then the shit would really hit the fan...but why was I worrying about this when I hadn't even read the MPA's post yet? Their bad behavior and Miriam's safety should be my primary concern, not my own inconvenience.

There was a lively debate going on in the comments section. LostAndFoundBoy, who had been faithfully commenting on every post in a way that made me think he was one of the writers, got into an explosive argument with three other commenters. None of them could decide whether they wanted campus to cancel the talk or arrest the members of the MPA, and the argument eventually devolved into a heated disagreement over the pros and cons of anarchy vs. totalitarianism.

My whole face scrunched up in involuntary distaste as I navigated over to the MPA's website, and I found myself literally turning away and reading out of the corner of my eye as I started on their latest post.

FREEDOM OF SPEECH OPPRESSED! COLLEGE REFUSES TO LISTEN TO STUDENT OBJECTIONS, MIRIAM CHEN TALK GOES FORWARD

Not only is the college insisting on bringing infamous Social Justice Warrior Miriam Chen to campus in spite of student objections, they've threatened to break up any legitimate protests we might make, they say we should confine ourselves to a "free speech area" that we hear will be nowhere near the *new* venue for the talk that keeps getting moved and rescheduled probably to avoid legitimate student protests and expressions of outrage that our legitimate wishes are going unheard.

Not only that but we can now reveal after keeping it quiet for a month that one of our leaders has been repeatedly threatened, harassed and stalked by a female faculty member who is determined to block free speech and bring Miriam Chen to campus despite student objections to having propaganda forced on us. This female faculty member and probably all the other female faculty members are determined to silence and oppress us while claiming harassment themselves! This is just another example of the way so-called feminism has been used as a weapon against men and used to empower women even more even though they've historically manipulated and used men for their own gain while whining about how they're being mistreated and exploited.

MEN, WE HAVE TO SPEAK UP FOR OURSELVES AND NOT GIVE IN TO THIS HARASSMENT AND MANIPULATION!

AND MIRIAM CHEN WILL *NOT* COME TO CAMPUS! WE'LL DO WHATEVER WE HAVE TO TO STOP HER SPREADING HER POISON!

Underneath was a string of comments, even though the post was only a few hours old. Breathing shallowly, as if I were standing over an open cesspit, I read through them with one eye.

Most of them were generic expressions of appreciation to the poster for coming forward and so "bravely" telling the story of his persecution. Even LostAndFoundBoy, who seemed to hang out on the site mainly to act as devil's advocate, thanked the poster for sharing his story of persecution and oppression like a true hero for justice.

For a moment, I couldn't help but imagine Dima's face if I told him about this. While even many apparently decent, sensible men were surprisingly susceptible to the incel message—after all, as Mel had said, the incels were only expressing what most people in their heart of hearts really believed—I was pretty sure that Dima's macho pride would revolt at the idea of calling what these boys were

experiencing "persecution," and his acute sense of the ridiculous
would cause more than a little laughter at the idea of them being
"brave." But I needed to stop thinking about Dima, especially as my
confidant of first resort. If I told anyone about this, it should be Alex.

The fourth comment down was a repeat of Nottagirl's wish to see
Miriam Chen raped by hogs. The commenter had even put in a jolly
animated GIF of hogs having sex. There were a couple of comments
in support of that, and then a comment from "Nottagirl" himself
that said:

*Id like to put all these woman professors in there place! Walking
around liek they own the place and know everythign and cant be
bothered iwth studpid lowlife men like US. Imagine if we showed them
how we REALLY feel! Id never stick my dick in any of THEM cause
im afraid it would drop off from all the toxic manhating poison but
id sure love to stick there broomsticks up there asses only I dont think
theres any room with all the other sticks already up there. That female
faculty member whos harrasing you wonder who shes fucking probably
somebody rich of course unless she cant get anyone to give it to her cause
shes such a bitch itd be sweet to see her begging for it and refusing to
give it to her itd be fun to choke her while giving it to her till her eyes
rolled back in her head they like it you know chokign makes them cum
sometimes they die form it but thats okay they like that too maybe we
should kidnap her and show her what she really wants and needs what
do you say? Killing a stuck-up Becky like her would be doing us all a
favor.*

The comment already had six likes and four subcomments
expressing support.

49

AFTER SOME INTERNAL debate over how he would respond, I sent the link to the post to Brian Michaels, and asked him what he thought we should do.

I don't want to overreact, I wrote. *But the rape and death threats aimed at Miriam and, I'm guessing, me, are pretty ugly, and the statement that "Miriam Chen will *not* come to campus" is worrying.*

Very worrying, Brian wrote back. *I'm going to issue a statement condemning the post and requesting that anyone with any information about the posters come forward. And I think it's time I paid l'il ole Nathan a visit in an official capacity.*

Sounds good, I wrote back. *Keep me posted, and let me know if there's anything I can do.*

Brian said he would, but when he contacted me again on Friday, it was to say that Nathan had, in an astonishing display of resolution, refused to crack and reveal the names of any of the other boys involved. Instead, he had complained to his mother, who had retained a lawyer who had immediately started making threatening statements about police harassment and sexual harassment by faculty members—apparently aimed at me—and the First Amendment, and this had worked the campus administration into such a tizzy that they had ordered Brian to drop it immediately.

So I guess we're back where we started, he wrote. *I still think the free speech zone is a good idea, and I'll plan on having everyone I can muster on security duty that night, but I'm liking this less and less. You sure you don't want your big brother to come give Nathan a good talking-to? :)*

I'm seriously considering it, I wrote back. Which I was. Kind of. The problem was that I wasn't convinced it would work. Aside from any moral qualms I might have felt about using violence and threats to solve my problems, not to mention bringing in a man to fight my fights, Nathan and his ilk were the kind of stinging insect that the more you tried to swat, the more they buzzed around, stinging and driving you crazy. Nathan needed someone he looked up to and admired to set him straight, but I couldn't think of anyone he looked up to and admired, other than other loathsome incels. He obviously didn't have any decent male role models, and the only power any woman could have over him in his current twisted, overly hormonal state was sexual, and I was certainly not about to go there. Maybe John *could* be a good influence on him, although I was doubtful about John's ability to be a good influence on anyone, but there weren't a lot of good pretexts to engineer a meeting between them.

Thinking about this was giving me a nasty headache. I hoped that inspiration would strike over the weekend, and resolved to stop fretting about it and focus on my more immediate problem. The Pre-Turkey Trot was tomorrow, and I, unfortunately, was running in it.

50

THE TENSION-SICKNESS I'd been feeling didn't dissipate with the arrival of the weekend. Far from it. When I got up Saturday morning, the Pre-Turkey Trot loomed before me in all its hideousness. Under other circumstances, I wouldn't have minded running in it. I'd never been interested in racing before, but I wasn't against the idea. But since Karen had signed me up for it without consulting me, and made it sound as if my employment were conditional on me participating, the main thing I felt for the race was resentment and revulsion.

The revulsion increased when I showed up at 9:45 that morning and saw that the athletic center was overrun with pictures of jolly turkeys, and people dressed up in turkey costumes. While I was skeptical of most claims of human exceptionality, I had to admit that only humans seemed sick enough to celebrate mass killing by making cartoons depicting how happy the victims were.

"You eat the one you love," I muttered to myself.

"What's that?" Mel had come up behind me while I had been staring in horror at the happy turkeys.

"It's a play on words. There's a Russian saying about how 'you beat the one you love.' I was just rewording it to fit with the macabre event we're participating in."

Mel took in all the turkey paraphernalia around us. "Good point. At least there aren't a lot of students around. God! I can't believe I'm doing this shit. I mean, if anyone other than Karen had asked me, I'd have been all over it, but as it is...well, shall we go line up at the start?"

We mosied reluctantly over to where a bunch of people in a mixture of running clothes and turkey costumes were milling around on the track.

"What do you think?" Mel said out of the side of her mouth. "Can we take them?"

I surveyed the competition. While faculty as a rule tended towards the profoundly un-athletic, there were always a few health nuts at any college, and right now they'd gathered all of us together and lined us up at the start line on the track. A paranoid person would wonder if our fatter, less fit peers had decided to gather us all together in order to take us out.

"I hear Evelyn from Math is tough to beat," I said. "But frankly, my main concern is just trying to get through this without reinjuring my knee."

"Yeah, know what you mean—is that woman trying to talk to us?"

I looked over to where a vaguely familiar-looking woman was waving from the other side of the lineup.

"I think it's Olena," I said. "The Ukrainian woman. I'll just go over to say hello."

I wove my way through the warming up runners to where Olena, dressed in a distinctively post-Soviet tracksuit, was doing an energetic series of stretches.

"Are you running?" I asked.

"Yes! I am not much of a sportswoman, but they had no one else, so..." She shrugged. "Here I am. I will probably be last."

"Well...I hope not." In truth, Olena was overweight, and didn't appear to be particularly fit. But since she was Ukrainian, it was entirely possible that her base level of fitness was enough to allow her to jog her way through a 5k. One of the many things that astonished

Americans when they went to Eastern Europe was how strong and fit everyone was, even city-dwellers with no interest in sports.

"I have been looking for you," she told me. "One of your students is also my student. Do you know Miranda, from the newspaper? She talks all the time about how she is taking Russian."

"Yes, of course."

"A good student, even with her silly hair," said Olena. "Well, she was a good student. Now she has become a bad student. Has she become a bad student for you?"

"Well...she's been a little preoccupied recently..."

"I know!" Olena snorted. "What does she have to be preoccupied about, I ask? Well, the most usual thing, of course. Men. She has *two* men now, and it's distracting her from what she *should* be focusing on!"

"*Two* men?" I asked. "That's, um, surprising. And I don't really see how that's my business."

Olena snorted again. "Because it is affecting her studies! She is in danger of failing my class if she does not straighten out, and most likely her other classes as well! You are her favorite professor; I know because she told me. I do not think she likes me very much at all, even though she does try to speak Russian with me. She speaks Russian very badly. That's probably not your fault, though. I suppose it is not bad for an American in their first year of study. Well, anyway. *You* need to talk to her and make her understand that she can't go running around like this if she wants to get good grades and graduate from university."

"Um," I said. "Okay." I had no intention of talking to Miranda about her love life unless she broached the subject first, but agreeing seemed the easiest way to get Olena off my back.

"Good," said Olena. "And pass on to her from me that if she *does* want to run around with men, she should pick some better men to run around with. Do you know whom she's dating?"

"No, whom?"

"That Nathan Willoughby!" Olena struggled with the name, which was full of unfriendly sounds like "th" and "w."

"Really?!" Now I didn't have to feign interest.

"Yes," said Olena with satisfaction. "That snot-nosed little boy! He is also my student. He is very impudent, is he not? He tried to argue with me once. I set him straight! But now he sits in the corner and glares at me. I do not see what Miranda sees in him. He is not even handsome, is he?"

"Not really," I agreed. "I'm very surprised that they're dating."

"I am too, but I have seen them together more than once! And Miranda is always flirting with him when they are together, and now she sits next to him during class. At first she sat at the opposite side of the room from him, but now she sits right next to him, and talks and flirts and acts like a frivolous little girl instead of a serious young woman. It is a shame. I do not care about Nathan at all; he is doomed. But I do not want him to take Miranda down with him."

"Yeah," I said. "And, ah, what about the second man?"

"The second man is not so bad, but still unexpected! He is not in the same class as Miranda and Nathan, but he is in my other class, and he is also studying Russian. It is Chris."

"Chris! But Chris..."

"Should not be able to attract the attention of any woman, let alone an intelligent young woman like Miranda," Olena finished for me.

"Well...maybe," I said. "But I also thought he was interested in another girl."

"Perhaps he is," said Olena. "Perhaps they are all dating two or three different people at once. You know how college students are."

"Yes," I said. "Well, that's, ah, very interesting. I'll definitely talk to her."

"Good," said Olena. "Oh, and I wanted to ask: what about your friend? Is he still in the Donbass?"

"Oh," I said. "Yes. He, ah, was just covering what has been happening in Zaitsevo." There had been a short but intense battle the day before outside of Zaitsevo (or Zaitseve in Ukrainian), a village in the Donetsk region that had become a fiercely contested point between the two sides. Dima had texted me afterwards to let me know that he had been observing it—I hoped he had just been observing, and not participating—and had escaped unscathed.

Olena frowned. "It is all very bad," she said. "I have been trying for months to convince my parents to leave Lugansk, but they absolutely refuse. For years we were Ukrainian, and now all of a sudden they are Russian, they say. Meanwhile, my cousins in Kiev spent their whole lives talking—in Russian—about how they were Russian, but suddenly now they are Ukrainian. Sometimes I wish the Soviet Union would return, so that we would stop having these stupid arguments over who we are. But when I tell that to Americans, they refuse to understand. I tell them it is like if your New England became a different country, and took your Boston with it. Now what would happen to your history? To your families? I am tired of *both* sides, especially since it is splitting my family apart. What side is your friend on?"

"He's kind of on his own side," I said. "He's a journalist."

"Akha." She nodded in understanding. "Good. Maybe he will tell some truth that people will—"

The sound of a gunshot made us both do very creditable standing leaps and clutch at each other in sudden terror.

"My God!" said Olena. "I thought...but it's just the start. Damn it! We missed the start!"

"Let's go!"

We took off at a brisk jog after the other runners, who had lined up and set off while we had been talking.

"I thought..." Olena was already out of breath. "I thought...that was a real gun...I thought we were being shot at...too much talk about war...you obviously run faster than I do. You go ahead."

"Are you sure? I don't mind staying back here."

She shook her head. "Go on. I told you: I will finish last. You should go to the front. Maybe you will win!"

"I doubt it," I said, but, shooed onwards by her impatient hand gestures, I took off towards the front of the pack.

51

THE RACE COURSE HAD us run around the track, and then take off across the campus. We were supposed to wind our way through all the dorms, across the back quad, across the front quad, and out the front entrance to the little shopping center down the street. We would turn around there and run back to the athletics center, circling the track again and crossing the finish line. It was an easy, flat five kilometers that conveniently routed us past the greatest number of onlookers possible. I had been skeptical that anyone would care to watch a bunch of professors run a slow 5k, but I had underestimated the attraction of seeing professors run themselves to the point of collapse. It was a wonder that the college didn't make us run the race in full regalia, to add to the spectacle. I decided to keep that thought to myself, just in case it gave anyone ideas.

By the time we made it around the track and out of the athletic center, I had worked my way to the front of the pack, and rejoined Mel. "Sorry," I panted when I caught up with her. "Got distracted. What's happening?"

"Nothing much yet, although things could get exciting when we hit the sand." We were routed to go straight through all the beach volleyball courts.

"Ugh, yes. Oh my God. Are those students?"

"Oh *fuck*," muttered Mel. What looked like the entire student body had turned out to watch us. Some were leaning out their dorm room windows, but the majority had come outside and were lining the race route. Many had whistles and horns and homemade signs.

"This is payback for us standing out by the entrance with our signs at the beginning of the semester," said Mel.

"I don't see why it's *payback*. That was its own payback. This is just further humiliation." I don't know why I found it so humiliating. Under other circumstances I probably would have enjoyed running in a race past a crowd of cheering spectators. But the whole thing was so obviously staged as goofy and undignified entertainment, a way to make faculty look silly for the gratification of the students, that it set my teeth on edge.

"HALL-EY! WIL-SON! HALL-EY! WIL-SON!"

"Oh my God," I said. A group of students was gathered together on the edge of the volleyball court we were about to slog through. Some of them, led by Miranda, had a big poster with my name on it and a Russian flag with the red and blue reversed. Others had a big green poster with a crescent symbol and wobbly Arabic lettering.

"They didn't even spell my name right," said Mel under her breath.

"They're almost in front! They're almost in front!" Our crowd of supporters was pointing at us excitedly. "Go, go, go!" they screamed. "You can do it! Get in front!"

Mel looked over at me and raised an eyebrow.

"Let's do it," I said. "Might as well give someone some pleasure out of this. And it's not like we're going to win."

Mel nodded and put on a burst of speed. I followed close behind her as she wove around the half-dozen people in front of us. By the time we were through the volleyball courts, we were leading the pack. Our fans cheered ecstatically and flapped their posters. I turned and waved at them, triggering more excited shrieking. Miranda held the poster high up over her head and shook it, while Taylor, who was standing next to her and appeared to have switched her allegiance from China to Russia for the race, did a quick cheerleading dance with white, blue, and red pompoms.

The back of my neck prickled. Oh no. Not a migraine. They almost never hit me while I was running, but of course today would be the day. No, wait. It wasn't a migraine. It was the creepy feeling you get when someone is staring at you. I looked past Miranda, Taylor, and the other girls who had joined in on the cheer step that Taylor was leading. Half-hidden behind them was a skinny, dark-haired figure. Nathan Willoughby was staring in my direction...no, he wasn't. He was staring at Taylor with an expression of naked desire that transformed his face from a little boy's into a dangerous animal's.

52

AFTER WE HAD FOUGHT our way through the volleyball courts and escaped the labyrinth of the dorms, we ran along one side of the back quad. The departments in the classroom buildings there had organized cheering sections too, including one from Modern Languages right in front of Bedford Hall. There were no signs or chants for "Halley" or "Wilson" there, just a general sign lying on the ground that said "Modern Languages" and inspirational phrases in all the languages other than Russian and Arabic, which were conspicuously absent. The faculty were gathered around chatting and checking their phones and not watching the race until Mel and I drew level with them.

"They're in front!" Darryl shouted as we passed him. "Hey, everyone, Rowena and Mel are in front!"

The group hastily pulled itself to attention, with a couple of them holding up the poster while the rest clapped and cheered. I waved as we swept past them. Karen, I noted out of the corner of my eye, joined in neither the cheering nor the sign-holding, but watched us—me—silently, her expression disturbingly similar to Nathan's.

Then we were past Bedford Hall and circling around Lee Hall, which separated the front and back quads, before we did a loop of the front quad and headed off to the front entrance. By this time Mel and I were no longer in front. A group of wiry-looking men overtook us as we passed the bookstore, and we decided not to bother giving chase.

"My knee's already starting to twinge a bit," I said, when Mel asked me if I wanted to try to catch up with them.

"Yeah, mine too, actually. Let's just take it easy. No point in killing ourselves for a race we didn't even want to run. And winning would probably be a major faux pas anyway. Probably contingent faculty aren't supposed to finish in the medals."

"Good point," I said, and slowed down even more.

Despite our avowed non-interest in winning, by the time we reached the front entrance, we had caught up with a couple of the stragglers from the breakaway group, who were having problems with their turkey costumes. Then once we were out on College Drive, we passed another of the leaders, who had had a catastrophic footwear malfunction and was crouched on the sidewalk, tying knots in his broken shoelaces. By the time we reached the turnaround point at College Center, we were just a few paces behind the remaining two frontrunners.

"What do you think?" Mel hissed. "Catch up, or drop back?"

"I'm for dropping back," I said. "My knee is really starting to bother me."

"Do you need to stop?"

"If I did, I'd just have to walk back anyway."

"I'd come and pick you up."

"That's okay. Might as well finish the race at this point. But let's take it easy on the pavement."

We eased up some more, but the two frontrunners remained just a few paces ahead of us, as if they, too, had slowed down.

We remained in that formation all the way down College Drive and back through the front entrance. Then one of the men slowed down even more, and turned his head to speak to us.

"Go ahead and take the lead," he said.

"Um..." Mel and I shared a look. "That's okay," I said. "We're nursing injuries and trying to be conservative."

"Yeah, us too," the man said. "I'm Jake, by the way. Physics. And that's Zach. Chemistry. " He craned his head to look further back, where the main pack was now making its way down College Drive. "Wow," he said. "Evelyn's nowhere near us. Normally she's always the frontrunner for the women's group."

"I heard she was nursing a sore Achilles," said Zach.

"That's great!" said Jake. "I mean...for you two, that is. You've got a good shot at winning the whole women's division!"

"Wow," I said, trying to inject the appropriate amount of enthusiasm into my voice. "That's great."

"You know..." said Zach. He and Jake shared a look. Then they slowed down even more.

"Why don't you pass us," suggested Jake. "We've won the overall race every year for the past five years running. Time to let someone else take a turn."

"Oh, no need," I said, slowing down too. "We're not in it to win it."

"Yeah," said Mel. "Because we're afraid that if a couple of VAPs like us win, we'll have our contracts terminated in retaliation."

"Oh, surely not," said Jake. "I'm sure everyone in your department would be thrilled. What department are you from, anyway?"

"Modern Languages," I told him.

"In that case, they'll be *beside* themselves. Modern Languages doesn't even normally field any runners, let alone have winners. You should *definitely* win. It'll be just the boost your department needs. Besides, my groin strain is playing up. I'm going to have to drop back anyway."

"And my ACL's acting up," said Zach. "Seems like a perfect opportunity to avoid winning for a change. Have fun, ladies!" He gave us a bright smile, and then both men slowed to a shuffling jog.

"God damn it," said Mel. "It's going to look pretty strange if we *all* come limping in, obviously trying not to win. How's your knee doing?"

"It's hanging in there. How about yours?"

"My knees aren't too bad, but honestly I'm starting to feel a little sick. Maybe I'm coming down with something again. But I'll be damned if I quit in front of everyone."

"Yeah." We were now running down the other side of the front quad. Staff members were lining the sidewalk, cheering us on. Quitting in front of them would be embarrassing. Instead, we put on a burst of speed, eliciting cheers.

"Someone's comin' for ya!" someone from Facilities Services shouted, as we circled around Lee Hall and crossed into the back quad.

We looked back. The man who'd had the catastrophic footwear malfunction had successfully fixed his shoelaces, and was gaining on us, an expression of determination on his face.

Mel instinctively picked up her pace. I instinctively kept level with her. All our talk about not being in it to win it had been a big lie, and we both knew it. At heart, I liked to win, and I was guessing that Mel liked to win even more.

We pounded past the physics and chemistry buildings, and came to the dorms. The man behind us disappeared into the labyrinth as we wound our way back and forth on the narrow paths between the buildings.

When we broke free of the dorms and came out into the sandpits of the volleyball courts, the man had gained on us again, and was now close enough that I could hear his heavy breathing.

"WIL-SON! HALL-EY! WIL-SON! HALL-EY! OH MY GOD, THEY'RE IN FRONT!" Taylor, Miranda, and our other cheerleaders were still there, and jumping up and down and screaming in excitement to see us leading. Behind them, Chris, wearing an expression of lost bewilderment, was standing next to Nathan, who was watching us with a mixture of open-mouthed surprise and murderous hatred. Not even bothering to share a look, Mel and I both pushed forward even faster.

The man was no longer gaining on us, but he wasn't falling back, either. If he had any reserves once we left the volleyball courts, he was sure to pass us on the homestretch, because my lungs were on fire, and sharp stabs of pain were lancing through my knee with every step. The sensible thing to do would be to slow down, or maybe stop entirely. But I kept pressing forward, trying to squeeze the last drops of speed out of myself.

"Oh fuck!"

I looked back. The man had caught his shoe on a clump of grass on the edge of the last volleyball court, ripping his shoelaces loose again. There was a gasp of shock from the students, quickly followed by an explosion of laughter at the sound of a professor using the f-word.

Mel had seen the same thing, and took off even faster. I stuck just behind her as we raced across the street, into the athletic center, onto the track, and down the homestretch, until we crossed the finish line in first and second place.

"Congratulations! Congratulations! Congratulations!" People were descending on us from every side. Many of them were dressed as turkeys.

"Melissa! Rowena! I knew you could do it!" Theresa pushed her way through all the turkeys to come shake our sweaty hands. "Congratulations! I couldn't be more thrilled. Tanika! Dorothy! Where are those turkey costumes?"

Tanika, looking nervous, and Dorothy, looking worrisomely smug, came scuttling up. Each of them had a big bag in their hands.

"Congratulations again on winning!" said Theresa. "Melissa, you were the overall winner, and Rowena, you were the winner of the women under fifty category. Now, maybe you didn't know this, but now comes the *best* part of being a Pre-Turkey Trot winner! You see, the tradition is that the winner of each division gets a turkey costume, which they then wear to class and around campus on Monday and Tuesday."

She beamed at us. Or maybe she was laughing at us. I strongly suspected she was laughing at us, at least a little.

"Oh wow," I said. "That's...fun."

"Yeah," said Mel, and threw up at Theresa's feet.

53

MEL INSISTED THAT SHE was fine, and had just run too hard.

"Or maybe it was the excitement," she said. "I had a dog who used to vomit whenever she got really excited and happy. Maybe I was just so thrilled at winning that turkey costume that I spontaneously started vomiting."

"Vomiting does seem to be a legitimate response," I said. We were now sitting in the stands, watching the rest of the runners come in. Shayne from Math, the man with the footwear malfunctions, had managed to limp in on one shoe and snag first place in the men's under fifty category, and was now sitting one bleacher below us, looking at his turkey costume with an expression of shock.

"No one told me that this was the prize," he said, when I congratulated him. "If I'd known, I think I might have lost. This is my first year here, and my department let me know they really wanted me to do well, but now I'm questioning my life choices. I mean, is tenure worth dressing up like a giant turkey?"

"I don't know," said Mel. "We're both visiting faculty."

"Jeez. That's really harsh." Shayne wrinkled his nose, and went back to contemplating the turkey costume morosely.

Soon we were joined by Will from Anthropology, who had won the men's over fifty category, and Arlene from Religion, who had won the women's over fifty division. We had been told to stick around for the official awards ceremony, and in the meantime to don our turkey costumes, so that we could parade around the infield in them on the way to the podium.

"It's not too late," said Mel, as she opened her bag full of turkey parts. "There's still plenty of time for me to take up a career standing by the side of the road and holding up a sign that says 'Homeless Iraq Vet, Please Help.'"

"Yeah, but what are the rest of us going to do?" I asked.

Mel shrugged. "Streetwalking?"

"I wonder how difficult it is to get a job as a hotel maid," I said.

"For you? Very difficult. They'd never hire someone with such a posh voice for a job like that. Maybe you could be a high-class nanny."

"True. And maybe being a high-class nanny wouldn't be so bad. I generally get along well with children. There are probably agencies for things like that, aren't there?"

"Probably," said Mel. "Might be worth looking into. And maybe it would pay well enough to actually pay off some loans, while working as a hotel maid sure as hell wouldn't." She held up the turkey head. "How the fuck do you put this damn thing on?"

Jake, Zach, and Evelyn came strolling over. None of them appeared to be favoring a groin, ACL, or Achilles injury.

"Thank God," said Evelyn. "Good going, Shayne. I was afraid I was going to have to uphold the honor of the Math department by winning once again, but you took the pressure off me."

"The costume is in three parts," Zach told Mel. "There's the jumper, which is just a jumpsuit that zips up the back, the headpiece, and the shoe toppers. You step into the jumper and zip it up, and then put on the shoe toppers and the headpiece. You want to finish with that, because it's really hard to do anything once the headpiece is on. Take it from one who knows."

Mel grimaced. "I really do still feel nauseated," she told me. "And maybe kind of feverish. I hope I don't puke again once I put this thing on."

"Maybe if you puke on it, you won't have to wear it," I said.

She brightened. "Worth a try. Okay, let's get this over with."

We started to struggle into our turkey costumes. They were even more awkward and ugly than I had expected, especially the giant yellow turkey-foot shoe toppers. And I had two days of class time wearing this obscene celebration of mass murder to look forward to, too.

The final runners were straggling in. True to her prediction, Olena was the very last to cross the finish line. She looked around the stadium as she did so, and, without breaking stride, came jogging straight over to me.

"I heard you won," she said in Russian. "Congratulations."

"Yeah." I had struggled into the jumper and shoe toppers, but was waiting to put on the headpiece until I absolutely had to. "Thanks."

"I talked to our Miranda," she told me. "That's why I finished last. I stopped and talked to her about her grades and her performance in our classes, and how she needs to take herself in hand and stop running after men."

"Oh," I said. "That's, um, good. What did she say?"

Olena sniffed dismissively. "She just said okay, and then walked off with that Nathan boy. Speaking frankly, I don't know what she sees in him."

"No," I said. "Neither do I."

54

A LOT OF THE STUDENTS had gathered to watch us parade out onto the infield in our turkey costumes. Miranda, looking not at all bad-ass the way she probably wanted to, and Taylor led another cheer for me and Mel as we marched over to the podium. There was also a delegation, led by Karen, from the Modern Languages department. Most of them looking equally stunned and delighted. Karen looked sickeningly self-important, like she had personally orchestrated our victory and run both our races herself.

"I don't feel very good," Mel said as we climbed off the podium. "I hope I don't barf again. And fuck, my knees are killing me. And the rest of me as well."

"Shall we head out now?" I asked.

She shuddered and rubbed the back of her neck, turning her head this and way and that as if trying to release something pinched. "Yeah," she said. "But I must be getting really fucking old and soft, if a little 5k knocks me out like this."

"Come on," I said. "I think we can escape now."

I had considered stopping to talk to Miranda, but Mel really did look bad, and the turkey costumes were a serious impediment to any kind of a meaningful conversation, so, pausing only to remove our foot toppers, we strode off to the parking lot with as much dignity as we could muster.

Mel was feeling even worse that evening, and said she must be coming down with something. I deposited some cans of soup on her doormat, and told her to text me if she needed anything else.

By Monday she was, she said, recovered enough to teach.

"Weird that I keep catching stuff and you don't," she said, when I picked her up Monday morning. "I think I've had, like, three bouts of the flu already this semester. It feels like I can't even get over one before the next one comes along. I went and got the flu shot last month, and I was all like, 'Come and get me, motherfucker! I'm safe now!' But here I am, sick again. And it's weird, too. It's not like any flu I've ever had before. Not a lot of vomiting or coughing or anything like that. I just feel crazy tired, like tireder than I ever have in my life, and I hurt all over. I'm still so sore from that race that I can barely stand to walk. And now my neck is all stiff, and keeps cracking and popping all the time, along with my knees. And this damn eye twitch won't go away."

"Have you seen a doctor?"

"No, but I'm starting to think maybe I should. But what am I going to tell them? I keep coming down with the flu? They're going to tell me that's what you get for going into education. My knees hurt after a hard race? They're going to tell me that's what you get for running on hard pavement, especially once you're over 35. I've got an eye twitch that just won't quit? They'll lecture me about 'stress' and probably tell me I have to start counseling again for fucking PTSD. I've done so much fucking counseling for fucking PTSD I can recite the whole therapy song and dance backwards and forwards. Besides, that's hardly my worst problem. Who gives a shit about PTSD from something that happened ten years ago, when I'm looking at a lifetime of rejection and poverty in the here and now. And that's not something I can just meditate and yoga away. All the meditation in the world won't put food on the table. Agh! God damn it!"

She had jerked in the car seat, bouncing against the seatbelt and snapping her head back against the headrest.

"Are you okay?!" I cried.

She rubbed her neck. "I feel okay right now, but Jesus fucking Christ, that hurt. It was like being fucking tased."

"Was that, um...a seizure?" I asked.

"Um...maybe?"

"Have you ever had any before?"

"No."

"I think we should go to Urgent Care right now," I said.

"I feel fine now. Well, not fine, but not like I'm about to pass out or anything."

"Yeah, but...a seizure. That's serious."

"We don't know that it was a seizure. It was probably just a tic, like with my eye."

"Yeah, but..."

"Tell you what," she said. "I'll make an appointment to go see a doctor this afternoon. How's that?"

"Well..."

"If you take me to Urgent Care right now, we'll both miss class, just for me to get lectured on stress and self-care."

"Yeah, but what if it's...something serious?"

She was quiet as I turned onto College Drive. "I know," she said, as we approached the campus entrance. "I keep thinking about that too. Like, what if it's..." Her voice dropped to a whisper, "leukemia or something? What if the reason I've been feeling so tired and coming down with the flu so much is because I have leukemia?"

"If it's leukemia, then you need to get treatment started immediately," I said. "But I've never heard of leukemia causing seizures."

"Well, what if it's a brain tumor? Or an aneurysm?"

"Then you really need to get treatment started immediately."

"I know," said Mel, in a much smaller voice than I'd ever heard her use before. "But I keep hoping it'll go away. I keep hoping that if I hide under the blankets, the monster won't find me."

"I know," I said. "But a lot of times, the thing to do with monsters is to slay them."

"Yeah. Oh fuck. And it has to be this week as well. I'm supposed to leave tomorrow straight after class to go spend Thanksgiving with my family. Which is going to suck on an epic scale, with or without a brain tumor."

"Yuck," I said. "Do you want me to drive you to your appointment?"

"Let's see if I can actually get one first," said Mel.

55

MEL MADE IT TO HER classroom without any further neurological malfunctions, and told me to stop hovering, and go teach. So I did.

I had meant to corner Miranda after class and demand to know what was going on with her and Nathan. Technically it wasn't any of my business, but since I was still trying to badger him into giving up the names of the people threatening Miriam Chen, I decided that gave me a reason to try to get at him from any angle possible.

After some dithering, though, I decided Mel's potentially life-threatening situation took precedence over Miriam's, and went to check on her between my classes.

"I'm fine," she told me. "Well, I mean, my knees are killing me, but I haven't had any more weird seizure-y things. But Daryll gave me the name of a local doctor, so I'm going to call and see if they can fit me in today."

"Great," I said. "Let me know if you need me to drive you to the appointment. And if the only time they can fit you in is during class, then cancel class."

"I've already had to cancel class a bunch of times this semester."

"Whatever."

"Is that what you'd do if it were you?"

"I hope so," I said. In truth, I was pretty sure I'd be dragging my feet on it at least as badly as Mel, both because I wouldn't want to cancel class and because I would be afraid of what the doctor's visit would tell me. So it was a good thing that Mel had me to nag her into doing this.

When I got out of my second class, I found her heading towards her own second class.

"I got an appointment," she told me. "Darryl recommended his doctor—well, it's the only clinic in town—and I called, and they said they had a cancellation and could fit me in. But it's at 12:30."

"That's perfect," I said. "I'll drive you over right after you get out of class."

"You sure you don't mind?"

"I'm sure. In fact, I insist. I'll meet you here at 11:50."

"Melissa! Rowena! *What* are you doing?!?"

Karen was bearing down on us, her expression as horrified as if she'd caught us engaging in lewd indecency in the hallway.

"Um...going to class?" said Mel.

"*Where* are your turkey costumes!?!"

"Oh fuck!" muttered Mel. I suppressed a groan. In all the excitement of the morning, we'd left our turkey costumes in the back of my car.

"I'm afraid we forgot them," I said. "You see..."

"*How* could you forget your turkey costumes?!? This is the first time anyone from the department has *ever* won anything in the Pre-Turkey Trot, and you *forget* your turkey costumes! You *need* to be showing your commitment to the department! This kind of behavior really makes me question whether you have a future here at Crimson!"

A vision of my fist smashing into Karen's jowly face rose up before me, blotting out everything else.

Don't do it! I ordered myself. I glanced over at Mel. Her hands were clenched, and she was already moving as if to throw herself at Karen.

"I'm afraid Mel isn't feeling well," I said loudly, taking her by the arm. "Winning the race really took a lot out of her. We'll be sure to wear the costumes tomorrow. Meanwhile, Mel has to get to class."

"Yeah." Mel unbunched her fists. "I gotta get to class." A shudder ran through her, a milder version of whatever had made her convulse like a torture victim in the front seat of my car.

"Sick *again*?" said Karen. "Since there's no one to fill in for you, you know we need a fully fit person in your position, Melissa."

"Uh-huh," said Mel, and turned and walked away.

"Well!" Karen sniffed. "What's gotten into *her*?! She doesn't seem to have a lot of Crimson spirit, I must say!"

"She really isn't feeling well," I said.

"That's no excuse!"

I gave Karen a long look. I thought about pointing out to her that when she'd gotten a mild head cold a few weeks earlier, she'd whined and moaned and complained about it for days, as well as snapping at everyone she encountered, claiming her illness as an excuse for her foul mood.

"Happy Thanksgiving," I said instead, and went off in search of Miranda.

56

I STROLLED SEMI-AIMLESSLY around Bedford Hall, and when that failed to turn up Miranda, I headed over in the direction of the food court. Sure enough, there she was, standing in line to get an early lunch. Nathan was standing next to her.

I had seen them together a couple of times before, and Olena had told me her suspicions about their relationship, but it was still a surprise to see Miranda so obviously flirting with Nathan. She was smiling and listening to him, her head cocked to the side, one hand fiddling with the long point of purple hair that fell over her left ear.

I went and got into the end of the same line. Both appeared oblivious to me.

"Yeah, it's, like, *so* unfair," Nathan was saying. "The court gave full custody to my mom, wouldn't give my dad custody at all. They said he was 'unstable' and had 'violent tendencies'"—he made ironic quote marks with his fingers—"and he 'couldn't be trusted to be a good role model for a teenage boy.' Bullshit! I mean, my mom *said* he knocked her around, but *I* never saw any sign of it. I mean, nothing serious. And he'd never hurt *me*. They shoulda left me with *him*. That's what they did with Chris! It's not right that I didn't have my father with me! I could *kill* my mom for taking that away from me, you know what I'm saying?"

"Uh-huh." Miranda was turned to look at him, so I could see her face in profile. For a moment an expression of sharp interrogation peeked out, but then she said, with every evidence of sincere sympathy, "That must have been really difficult."

"Yeah. It's no wonder I'm so fucked up, with no dad around for, like, the most formative years of my life! That's something I'll, like, never get over!"

"That's tough," said Miranda. Overhearing her sympathize with a nasty but also genuinely fucked-up little shit like Nathan, I had the weird sensation of listening to myself.

"So you don't blame your father for his part in it?" she asked. "I mean, for doing stuff that would cause him to lose the right to custody?" I had to hand it to her: I might not have had the courage to ask such a blunt question. Or maybe she had not yet gained my level of finesse.

"No, of course not! I told you: it was all stacked against him! He never had a chance."

"So do you see him now? I mean, you're legally an adult now, right? You could spend time with him whenever you wanted."

"Yeah, well..." Nathan hunched his shoulders. "He's awfully busy. And he lives all the way up in Charlottesville. Virginia, you know. That's, like, too far a drive for him to come down and visit, or for me to go up that often."

"Uh-huh," said Miranda. "Are you going to spend Thanksgiving with him?"

"No." Nathan hunched his shoulders even more. "He's, like, going to, like, New York. To spend it with his second wife's family. What a bitch! My own mom couldn't wait to get rid of him, and now his new wife won't let him go anywhere or do anything without her! If it weren't for her, he'd be able to spend a lot more time with me."

"Uh-huh," said Miranda again. "So you're going to your mom's place, then?"

"Yeah. Bitch! And *her* new husband is a real asshole, too. It's all about my little brother with them. They don't give a shit about me. I might as well not exist as far as they're concerned. The good news is, they'll ignore me the whole time, so I'll have plenty of time to work on my next blog post."

"Oh, yeah?" said Miranda. "Do you have an idea for it, then?"

"Yeah. Didn't I tell you about it? We've got a new member, someone with ties to the Gang of Six, actually, and he's going to introduce himself and write about that Miriam Chen thing, and freedom of speech. You know, it's disgusting the kind of pressure I'm getting about that. Did you know..."

My phone *pinged*. Miranda and Nathan both turned around. "Oh, hi, Professor Halley!" said Miranda, looking awkward. Nathan just stared at me in disgust.

"Hi," I said. I looked at my phone. It was a text from Mel.

You ready to go? she had written. *I'm really not feeling so hot, so I ended class early.*

"I better go," I told Miranda. "Have a nice day!" I shoved my phone back in my pocket and set off towards Bedford Hall at a brisk jog.

57

WHEN I SHOWED UP IN Bedford Hall, the first person I ran into was not Mel, but Chloe.

"Gosh," I said. "You, um, don't look so good." She was sitting on one of the benches outside the classrooms, her head in her hands. Students were eyeing her sideways and then hurrying past.

She lifted her head out of her hands and looked at me. She was visibly trembling.

"Panic attack," she explained through chattering teeth. "Bad one."

"Oh. Do you need any help?"

She shook her head. "I-I j-just w-want t-to r-run aw-way," she said. "I-I j-just w-want t-to g-go r-running f-for m-my l-life out-t of-f th-the b-building, s-screaming 'g-get out-t, g-get out-t!' t-to ev-veryone ar-round m-me, b-but I-I kn-now th-that's j-just th-the p-panic att-ttack t-talking, s-so I-I'm t-trying t-to t-train m-myself t-to s-sit h-here and-d s-stay c-calm instead-d." She hugged her arms around her torso and rocked back and forth on the bench. A bead of sweat trickled down her left temple and onto her cheek.

"Maybe you should get out of here," I said. "If you feel that bad." Right now I wanted to get out of there too. That weird out-of-body sensation I'd had a few times before had washed over me as soon as I'd come up to Chloe's bench, and it wasn't retreating.

"I-I c-can't l-let th-this b-beat m-me!" she said.

"Yeah, but..."

"Hi, Professor Taylor!" It was Taylor, shadowed by Chris. "Are you all right?" she asked. "Do you, like, need anything? You weren't looking too good during class either. Maybe you should go home."

Chloe gave her a look of deep dislike. "That's not an appropriate thing to say to your professor," she said, her outrage overcoming her panic and stopping her teeth from chattering.

"Oh. Um. Sorry. I didn't mean...I just wanted to help..."

"That's very kind of you," I said, before Chloe could have another outburst. "I'll let you know if I need anything, but right now I'm just going to help Professor Taylor home. Oh, by the way: have you seen Professor Wilson?"

Taylor frowned. "Last I saw she was in the ladies' room, even though I thought she had class now. She didn't look too good either. Is something going around?"

"Maybe," I said. "Do you mind going and seeing if Professor Wilson is still in the ladies' room, and if she is, telling her that I'm out here waiting for her?"

"Sure thing, Professor Halley!" Taylor gave me a bright smile and headed off in the direction of the ladies' room. Chris shuffled to the other side of the hallway, where he leaned against the wall, looking awkward and lost.

"I think you should go home," I told Chloe. Her flash of outrage had passed, and she had gone back to hugging herself and shaking. "I'm happy to drive you home myself if you need me to. I have to take Mel to the doctor, but we probably have time to drop you off first."

Chloe shook her head. "N-nuh-uh. I-I c-can t-take c-care of-f m-myself. And-d I-I'm s-stronger th-than th-this. I-I c-can't l-let th-this b-beat m-me."

"Um, okay. Here comes Mel, so I'm going to take her to the doctor now, but if you need anything, text me, okay?"

Chloe made a face that was sort of a grimace and sort of a snarl. Taylor, who had come back with Mel, gave her a nervous look and retreated to Chris. They both, after a whispered consultation, left, giving Chloe several backwards glances on the way.

"How are you feeling?" I asked Mel as we followed them out of the building. As soon as I stepped outside, what I thought of as my "true self" washed over me, and I felt like I was back inside my body once more.

Mel shrugged. "I haven't had any more of that weird twitching. But I feel feverish and bad. In a really weird way. It's like someone's hooked a taser to the base of my neck, and is slowly turning up the power."

"Ugh," I said. "That's awful. Torture, in fact. Not dissimilar to a common interrogation method used by the Russian military."

"Yeah. Maybe this is karma. Not that I ever tortured anyone. But I was associated with people who did. And people who killed dogs for fun or ran children down on the road or shot into crowds of civilians, or did all kinds of other bad things. Maybe now I have to pay for my sins, and theirs too."

"Or maybe it's just bad luck," I said.

"You don't believe in karma?"

"Actually, I do," I said. "But I don't believe in telling you that you deserve...whatever it is you're dealing with. I don't believe in blaming people for their illnesses. And I certainly don't believe that you should have to suffer for what other people did. You shouldn't have to carry the guilt for the US invasion of Iraq on your shoulders. Besides, you can't, no matter how strong you are."

"And if that's what gives...whatever this is...meaning?" she said. "If that's what makes...whatever I'm going to have to go through bearable?"

"If you decide to bear that cross, that's your choice," I said. "Although, to be perfectly honest, I'm not sure how much good it will do. It won't undo anything that's already been done."

"Yeah." Mel shivered her shoulders and shook her head like a dog trying to shake water out of her ears. "Fuck! This is so fucking annoying! Do you know how to get to the doctor's office?"

"You'll have to give me directions."

Fifteen minutes later—Greenfields was not a very big town—Mel's name was being called to go into the back of the Greenfields Family Clinic. She disappeared, and I sat there for another hour and dealt with email on my phone.

I was contemplating the dual nature of smartphones, and how they meant that I could be working even while sitting in a doctor's office, when Mel came out, a bandage on the crook of her elbow and a peeved expression on her face.

"All done?" I asked.

"Just a second." She went over to the desk and got directions for Peachtree Radiology.

"They want me to get a CAT scan," she said, as we left the clinic.

"That sounds reasonable," I said.

"Yeah, so they did a blood draw and said they'd do a workup, check for leukemia, shit like that, and I should probably get a CAT scan of my brain. They said the radiology clinic is walk-in and I can go over there this afternoon, if I want to."

"Do you want to go right now?" I asked. "I'm happy to drive you."

Mel hesitated. "I don't want to bother you."

"You won't be. I don't think you should be driving yourself to something like this. To be honest, I don't know if you should be driving at all right now."

She made a face. "Yeah, me too. Well, thanks. But do you think we can get some lunch first?"

"Sure. So what did the doctor say?"

During the drive to O'Reilly's, Mel filled me in on the appointment. Doctor Blake, she said, was an older guy who looked kind of like a "pedophile Santa Claus."

"And he spent waaaay too long examining my breasts," she said. "He wanted to do a full pelvic exam too, but I said I'd make an appointment with a gynecologist for that. So he just lectured me about ovarian cancer for a while instead. And then he said it was all almost certainly stress—unless I already had terminal ovarian cancer—but if it would set my mind at ease, they could do the blood draw and the CAT scan."

"Gosh," I said. "I don't know whether that's good news or bad."

"Yeah," said Mel. "Neither do I."

58

WHEN WE GOT TO O'REILLY'S, Mel attacked her sandwich with gusto—until she got two bites into it. Then she picked at it, taking tiny bites with so much nervous energy I could hear her teeth snap together with a sharp *click*, and then struggling to swallow.

"You don't have to finish it," I said, once I was done with mine and Mel still had half of hers left. "You can take it home and have it for supper or something. Or throw it out, if you don't like it."

"Wasting food is a sin," Mel answered automatically. "I may have shed most of my upbringing, but I remember how much trouble my family had putting food on the table too well to throw away a perfectly good sandwich."

"So take it home and eat it later," I said. "I bet you'll feel better once you get the CAT scan over with."

"Yeah. Although the scan itself isn't anything to be afraid of. It's the results...they said they're going to have to send the blood draw out for testing, since they're too small a clinic to do it in-house, so I probably won't get the results back from that until next week. And probably not the CAT scan results either. So I'll have that hanging over my head all Thanksgiving break. As if I didn't have enough to worry about."

"I know," I said. I wanted to tell her it was all going to be okay, but I didn't. There was no way that I could know that it would, in fact, be okay, so saying so now would just ring false in both our ears.

"I mean..." She picked at her sandwich some more. "Doctor Blake kept going on about how it was almost certainly stress, but stress can cause some awfully bad things. If you have a heart attack from stress, you're just as dead as if it's from anything else. And then he went on for a while about how it was probably just allergies, since I'd moved to a new area, and most newcomers aren't prepared for the South."

"I thought you were from South Carolina," I said.

"I am. So the allergy thing sounds like bullshit to me. And I never heard of allergies causing weird neurological problems."

"Have you ever had any head injuries?" I asked.

She shrugged uneasily. "Actually, yeah," she said. "You know. One of those stupid war things. We were driving from one supposedly safe base to another, and we hit an IED. I was blown clear, but I got a concussion. But it cleared up pretty quick and I've never noticed any problems from it since then."

"Maybe stress is reaggravating it," I said.

"Or maybe I'm developing an aneurysm or a brain tumor because of it."

"Let's go get that CAT scan," I said, standing up. "And maybe you should see about getting a full workup with the VA soon."

"Oh joy," said Mel, putting the rest of her sandwich in a napkin and standing up too.

Greenfields Radiology was in the same strip mall as O'Reilly's. We walked the three shops down to it, Mel checked in, and we sat down to wait for her number to be called.

There are a lot of downsides to the smalltown South, but one of the upsides is that you rarely have to wait in line long. Mel was in and out in under half an hour.

"Piece of cake," she said when she came out. "Now I just have to wait for the results."

"Yeah," I said. "I hope they get them to you quickly. How do you feel?"

She shrugged. "I'm glad to get all this over with. Now I feel like I can sort of put it off to one side until next week. The bad news is that I'm probably in good enough shape to wear my turkey costume to class tomorrow."

"Oh joy," I said.

59

WHEN I PICKED HER UP the next morning, Mel said she was feeling a lot better.

"Maybe it was the healing rays of the CAT scan," she said. "Or some therapeutic bleeding from the blood draw. Or maybe it really is just allergies or stress, and whatever bad juju was bothering me yesterday is gone. Anyway, I went ahead and put on the jumper of the turkey costume so that I wouldn't forget it today. And I see you did the same."

"Yeah," I said. "I figured I'd put on the rest in the parking lot. Boy, is this going to be awesome."

"You're telling me."

Campus was half-empty when we showed up at 8:30. This meant only about a hundred people saw us as we trekked from faculty parking to Bedford Hall in full turkey regalia.

Karen was waiting by the entrance to Bedford when we showed up at 8:45. This was surprising, since she rarely managed to make it to campus before 9:00, or frequently 9:30.

"Oh, *good*," she said when she saw us. "I wanted to make *sure* you both remembered to wear your turkey costumes today, after yesterday's oversight. Really, you two require *so much* overseeing."

"Yes, massah," Mel muttered under her breath. "Oh shit," she said to me as we stepped into Bedford and let the door close behind us, leaving Karen out on the dreary, November quad. "That was probably racist, or cultural appropriation, or some shit like that, right?"

"I won't tell if you won't tell," I said. "And besides, I think we need to explore the fact that we're working on a modern-day, very genteel and upscale, plantation of knowledge, which was built on the site of an old-school cotton plantation. The outer forms are different, but the underlying relationships are remarkably similar."

"Except that we're more like sharecroppers or day laborers than slaves," Mel said. "Since we're constantly hanging around begging to be given more work, instead of trying to run away."

"Yeah," I said. "Agh!"

"What is it?!"

"I just got this crazy stabbing pain in my eye. And now I've got a big blurry blob in my vision. It's okay. It's just a migraine coming on."

"Maybe *you* need to a get a CAT scan," said Mel. Even underneath the headpiece of her turkey costume, her face looked serious.

"I had one before, when I first started getting migraines back in undergrad."

"Yeah, but that was, what, like fifteen years ago? A lot can change in fifteen years."

"Gee, thanks," I said. "Now *I'm* going to be stressing out about that all Thanksgiving break, too."

"Happy to spread it around. See you after class, all right?"

Mel set off to her classroom, her turkey costume looking even more ludicrous from behind, if such a thing were possible. I trudged over to my own classroom. The gray blob in the middle of my vision was already the size of my fist, and morphing into something that looked kind of like a castle or the pattern on a deck of cards. After the initial stabbing sensation when I'd stepped into the building, the pain had receded, but I could feel it hovering around the edges of my consciousness, like the little blue flashes on the edge of my vision, letting me know that it was coming for me.

"Oh, hey, Miranda," I said, to distract myself.

Miranda, who was about to step into the classroom, stopped and did a double-take.

"Gosh, Professor Halley, I didn't even recognize you there for a moment. That's right! You won your division in the race! So now you get to wear a turkey costume! Why weren't you wearing it yesterday?"

"Selective memory loss," I said. "What do they do in the spring, by the way?"

"The Lamb Chop Trot, the weekend before Easter."

"Um...is Crimson a Satanic cult, and I just didn't get the memo?" I asked.

She laughed. "Probably, but why do you say that, Professor?"

"The Lamb Chop Trot? Before Easter? When Jesus is supposed to be the Paschal Lamb? I suppose eating lamb for Easter is traditional, but jeez, that's sick."

"Oh. Right." Miranda looked uncertain. "I never thought about that before. It's pretty fun, actually. Everyone dresses up as lambs and bunnies and stuff."

"I'm sure," I said.

"Oh, and...there's something I wanted to talk to you about, Professor..."

"Sure."

She looked around. No one else from our class had shown up yet. "It's about...It's about Nathan," she said. "And what Professor Bondarenko"—she struggled over the Ukrainian name—"talked to me about. She said she was going to talk to you about it too."

"Oh," I said. "Um, yeah, she did. But it's really none of my business."

"Yeah, actually, it is, Professor. See, I'm not actually going out with Nathan. Well, I guess I kinda am. But not because I, like, like him." She made a face. "I guess that makes it sound like I'm a really bad person, huh? But the thing is, I really want to find out more about what the MPA is up to, and their connection with the Gang of Six. I'd been hearing rumors that there is one, so I thought I could, like, go undercover or something, see if I could get something out of Nathan."

"And have you?" I asked.

She shrugged. "He was just about say something about it yesterday when we ran into you."

"Yeah. Sorry about that."

"It's okay. I'll try again soon. If I can take listening to more crap about how his mom and his stepmom are evil bitches who turned his father against him. Sounds to me like his father didn't need much turning, but boy is he burned up about it. And boy was he pissed when you and Professor Wilson won the race outright. He's been ranting on and on about how it must be sabotage and no woman could beat a man in a running race in a fair competition, blah blah blah. But nothing specific that I can use to figure out who's making the threats against Miriam Chen."

"Oh," I said. "That's brave of you. And, uh, good luck with that. And if you find out anything, let me know, okay? Miriam Chen is scheduled to arrive next week, and we still don't know who's making these threats and how dangerous they really are."

"I know, Professor. And as soon as I find anything out, I'll let you know."

60

THE MIGRAINE AURA SPREAD out across my vision, leaving me half blinded for my first class. The turkey costume headpiece did not help matters. Nor did it do much to improve the nauseating pain that descended on me during the second class. When I met Mel after our classes were over and told her what was going on, she insisted on driving us home.

"We're a great driving duo," I said. "Seizures and migraines."

"Hush your mouth," said Mel. "Maybe if we're real quiet, they won't hear us and they'll leave us alone. And I have to drive to South Carolina this afternoon."

"You sure you're okay to make the drive?"

"As okay as I'll ever be. You driving anywhere?"

"Just to Atlanta tomorrow to pick up Alex at the airport."

"You'll probably feel better by then, right?"

"Right," I said.

I was a little bit better by the next day, but I felt drained and unfocused, and those annoying blue flashes kept flitting around the edges of my vision as I drove through pre-Thanksgiving Atlanta traffic.

Alex's plane was only delayed by an hour, which for the Wednesday before Thanksgiving was hardly any delay at all.

"Gosh," I said, when he came up to me by the carousel in baggage claim. Actually, I might have jogged over from the neighboring carousel to meet him just that little bit faster. "I'd forgotten how good-looking you are."

"Oh my God," said Alex. "Come here. I'm so desperate to hold you, I can't even appreciate the symmetry of you greeting me the way I once greeted you." He put his arms around me and buried his face in my hair.

"This is nice," I said into his ear. "But I think we might be making a bit of a spectacle of ourselves."

"I don't fucking care."

"I know. But the sooner we get out of here, the sooner we can get home."

"I hope you're implying what I'm thinking you're implying," said Alex.

"I also hope our implications are in sync. Come on." I pulled away from him. "I have plans for you that involve being somewhere other than the middle of baggage claim at a major airport. Let's get your stuff and go."

He held up his carry-on. "You think I was going to risk having checked baggage on Thanksgiving? I've got everything I need right here. Come on. Let's go. I can't wait to hear all about your plans for me."

"They may have to wait for a while to be put into action," I warned him. "Traffic is fierce."

"No doubt. Well, you can fill me in on everything that's been going on with you, and I'll just have to savor the anticipation a little while longer."

"I might be able to slip you some tidbits of what's on my mind while we're waiting in traffic," I said.

"Oh boy. Lead the way."

Rather than outlining my sexual fantasies, however, I spent the 45 minutes we were trapped in airport traffic venting about the Miriam Chen situation.

"It's just so *stupid*," I said. "That little twerp Nathan Willoughby is claiming the First *and* the Fifth Amendments, and journalistic integrity or some nonsense like that as well, and meanwhile, things have upped from teenagers mouthing off, to rape threats, to death threats. I've offered to call the whole thing off and hold a panel on freedom of speech instead, but Miriam won't agree to that. But she won't commit to showing up either. It's like no one involved can grasp the seriousness of the situation, so they keep fretting and wringing their hands and hoping it will go away instead."

"Probably they *can't* grasp the severity of the situation," said Alex. "I mean, why should they? The rest of the country can't seem to come to grips with the fact that we have people strolling into public places and gunning down everyone in sight. So what are you going to do?"

"At this point I just want to call it off, like I said. No one involved seems like decent martyr material, and I don't want to have a school shooting on my head. And Brian Michaels—the chief of campus police—agrees with me. But Miriam won't commit to it, and the rest of the committee and the Dean's office and the Provost's office are very against calling it off. They're afraid it would make Crimson look bad."

"Worse than a shooting would?"

"I don't think they think there's actually going to be a shooting."

"And what about you? Do you think there's going to be a shooting?"

A space opened up ahead of me. A car coming up from the merge ramp signaled desperately. I paused to let it pull in front of me, triggering a furious burst of honking from the car behind me.

"I don't know," I said, once the ruckus had calmed down. "On the one hand, these are all just kids playing make-believe. Even Miriam Chen is just a kid playing make-believe. She can't seem to grasp that actions, even good ones, have real consequences, and that she's signed herself up for something much more dangerous than she ever intended to. And as for Nathan and those twerps posting on the MPA blog—they're in a complete fantasy world. This is all just another RPG to them. So on the one hand, I'd say they don't have the gumption to pull off a shooting, and even if they did, they don't have the real-world know-how. But it's *so* easy to get your hands on a gun in America. Even a complete space cadet like these guys could probably manage it, if nothing else by taking one from their father's gun cabinet. And if they did, they wouldn't understand that it fired real bullets, or what that even means. I could see one of them pulling the trigger just for fun, and unloading an entire clip into a crowd of innocent bystanders before they even realized what they'd done."

"Yeah," said Alex. "I'm afraid your assessment of the situation is all too fucking true. And if you want my opinion, I think you should pull the plug on the whole thing. Cancel Miriam's talk, and don't even hold that panel you were talking about. Do it next semester, when things have cooled down a little."

"I hate to back down and knuckle under to pressure..."

"I know, but you'd sure as fuck hate to have someone get shot on your watch even more. And you're not knuckling under to pressure."

"Yes, I am. They've threatened to commit a shooting if Miriam comes, so if I cancel the talk, I'm giving in to their threats."

"What I meant was that you should give yourself—or rather, the authorities—a little more time to find these guys and do something about them. I mean, for fuck's sake, faculty members are getting put on administrative leave for posting pictures of their kids wearing *Game of Thrones* t-shirts on social media. Seems like you should be able to come down like a ton of bricks on a group of self-proclaimed incels, AKA a known hate movement that has been responsible for multiple mass killings already, who've issued unambiguous threats to commit rape and murder."

"Yeah," I said. "I'll make that argument again on Monday. I just don't think it'll fly. I think the college is too concerned with looking good to take the kind of action necessary. I mean, if they really cared, surely they could bring in IT experts who could, I don't know, comb through the website and find out who these posters actually are. Instead they've just told me, a complete amateur, to see what I can do about it in my spare time."

"I know," said Alex. "But that's not your fault, and ultimately it's not really your problem."

"It *feels* like my problem."

"I know it does. But it's much too big a problem for one person to solve, especially when your hands are tied like this. And I think traffic is moving again."

"Oh good," I said. "In that case, let's stop worrying about all this depressing stuff, and discuss what we're going to do when we get home."

"Now you're talking," said Alex.

I had to concentrate on my driving too much to have a truly satisfying discussion of my plans for Alex, but I made up for it, he said, once we got home.

"Fuck," he said, as we were lying on my bed, taking what he said was only a temporary break. "That was *so* much better than virtual sex. I don't know if I can take much more of this long-distance relationship shit. You know I love to talk to you, Rowena, but talking, even sexy talking, is no substitute for, shall we say, body language."

"Maybe by spending so much time apart and having to communicate primarily through language instead of less verbal forms of expression, we've been getting to know each other as intellectual beings," I said.

"Maybe," said Alex. "But I think I'd still prefer a little less texting and a little more non-verbal communication."

"Well...yeah. Me too, to be honest. But I do feel like this way we know we're not rushing into things just because of, you know, pure animal lust. And I feel like I've gotten to know you better than I might have otherwise."

Alex went silent for so long I thought maybe he'd fallen asleep. "I know," he said after a while. "And I'm glad of that, but there's still a lot you don't know about me, Rowena."

"So tell it to me, then."

"Maybe someday." This time his silence stretched on and on, and when I pulled myself up to look in his face, I saw that he really had fallen asleep.

61

WHEN I WOKE UP AT TWO in the morning, I found him sitting at my table, staring at his phone.

"Is something the matter?" I whispered, padding over to him, still in a state of complete nudity.

He jumped. "Fuck, you startled me. Although looking like that, I'd be happy to have you startle me whenever you want. No, nothing's wrong. I'm just still on California time. Why don't you go back to bed, Rowena."

"Are you going to come join me?"

"Maybe in a bit."

That was not a very satisfying answer, but after I realized that it was the only answer I was going to get, I went back to bed alone.

When I woke up at a more reasonable hour the next morning, Alex was asleep on the far side of the bed. Turned away from me. Not that there was anything wrong with that. Sleeping all cuddled up tended to give me a crick in my neck. But somehow, something about his posture and the way he was all the way on the far edge of the bed felt like rejection. Or maybe like he was protecting himself from me.

When he got up a couple of hours later, though, he was cheerful and amorous. I had to fend him off while I made the rhubarb pie I'd promised my grandmother I'd bring.

"Wow," he said, as I put it together. "You really can cook."

"Of course I can. Although this hardly qualifies as 'cooking.' I'm using a store-bought crust."

"Still seems pretty impressive to me. Can I do anything?"

"Just keep me company. And we can go for a run while it's cooling, if you like."

"A run? You really want to go for a run with me? Didn't you just run in a race this weekend?"

"Yeah," I said. "But that was five days ago. And believe me, once you see all the food my grandmother has out, you'll be glad to have gone for a run beforehand."

"Okay. As long as you promise not to laugh at my glacial, sloth-like running pace."

Alex's running pace was not, of course, glacial or sloth-like. In fact, he gave me a good run for my money, which I made sure to tell him. He was disappointed to hear that we would only have time to shower afterwards, with no extracurricular activities, before setting off for my grandparents' place in Macon, but he perked up when I promised him there would be more fun and good times when we came home tonight.

By 1:00pm we were on our way, with Alex cradling the still-warm pie in his lap.

"Okay," he said, once we had set off. "Time for a briefing. What's the most critical piece of information I should know about your grandparents."

"Um. Well, they're actually pretty easy to get along with. At least I think so. They're, you know, your typical Southerners, so super friendly and hospitable. And they're thrilled to be meeting you. So your main problem will probably be fending off all that friendliness and, of course, force-feeding."

"So what should I call them? Mrs. and Mr. Halley?"

"Actually, these are my mother's parents, so they're, um, the O'Malleys."

Alex took a beat to respond to that. "So you're saying," he said eventually, "that your parents' wedding was the O'Malley-Halley wedding?"

"You're trying not to laugh, aren't you?"

His cheek nearest me was twitching. "Maybe," he said. "But I swear to God, I'm not laughing *at* you."

"Well, that's something. And yes, it's funny to me too. Just, you know, try not to burst out laughing when you meet them. Although they might like you better for it. They like a good laugh themselves."

"In that case, I like them already," said Alex. "Even if I might not know how to act around them. My own grandparents were all so prim and grim that I have no idea how to handle a cheerful old person. I expect them to purse their lips and lecture me on following in my father's footsteps as soon as they see me."

"My grandmother can also do a fine line in lip pursing," I said. "But she's unlikely to turn it your way, at least not on first meeting, and she also likes a good joke. And my grandfather's practically a comedian. Although you should watch out: sometimes his jokes get a little too practical for most people's tastes."

"Forewarned is forearmed," said Alex. "And I take it John's going to be there too?"

"Yes, God help us all."

"How's he doing? Still chasing after a different married woman every night?"

"He says he's gone through all the married women in Jacksonville, and all the good-looking ones at least twice, and now he's left sitting on his ass and twiddling his thumbs."

"I doubt it's just his thumbs he's twiddling," said Alex. "But as long as he keeps it to himself, who am I to judge? Especially now that I've become an internet porn star."

"You're only a star to me," I told him.

"That's good—I think. By the way, speaking of such things, do your grandparents know that I'll be staying with you while I'm here? Or should we maintain some fiction that I'm staying in a hotel or something? Because I know the one time I brought Erin home for Thanksgiving, she wasn't even allowed to stay in the house. I had to get a hotel room for her, and my parents and grandparents were waiting up for me to come home after I dropped her off. This was *after* we both got home from fucking Iraq, too, so I was, like, twenty-eight years old and had been in a fucking *war*, and they were still policing my behavior like I was fourteen or something. While also dropping lots of hints about how much they were hoping for a grandson. Too bad Erin took one look at them and said no fucking way was she being saddled with in-laws like that."

"Um," I said. "No. I doubt they'll inquire too deeply about our sleeping arrangements, but if they do, I'm just planning to tell them you're staying with me. I'm a big girl and I get to decide whom to invite into my bedroom. Plus, these are John's grandparents, remember? Anything we do is going to seem welcomely wholesome by comparison. And, um..." I swallowed. Why was I nervous? Or was I jealous. Both, I decided. "Is Erin the, um, person you've mentioned before? The one you have a past with?"

"Oh. Shit. Yeah. Have I not told you about her?"

"You've mentioned some things. I just didn't know her name. And it's okay. You can tell me as much or as little about her as you want."

"You probably don't want me smoking in your car, right? Because I think this is at least a two-cigarette conversation."

"I thought you quit."

"I did. And then, as per fucking usual, I un-quit. Are you going to give me shit about it?"

"No. Of course not. That's your decision to make."

"Fuck." Alex turned away from me and leaned his head against the car window for a moment. "Why do you have to be so fucking nice about it?"

"Um...would you rather I nagged?"

"Do you even know how to nag?"

"Not really, no."

"It's just..." Alex was still looking out the car window, rather than at me. "It's just...my relationship with Erin isn't something I'm very proud of. I met her...we were in the service together. We met in Iraq. Doing bad things."

He went silent. I waited for a while, but nothing else was forthcoming.

"You don't have to talk about it if you don't want to," I said eventually.

"Yeah, but now that I've brought her up, I feel like I need to come clean."

I had to concentrate on the sharp turn into my grandparents' neighborhood. "Come clean about what?" I asked, once I had straightened the car out.

"Oh, well...you know what? Never mind. Just, you know, like I said, I did a lot of stuff I'm not proud of, and a lot of it was with Erin."

I had to be quiet while I made another sharp turn, this one onto my grandparents' street. The hundred-year-old houses, with their deep front porches and white picket fences and American flags, made an incongruously homey background to our conversation. My grandparents' house was already coming into view

"It's okay," I said. I put my free hand on his thigh. I could feel the muscles jumping under my fingers. "We can talk about it, whenever you're ready. You can tell me anything, you know that, right? Just not right now, because right now we have to socialize. But before we do, I'll just say this. You're already getting free of all that bad stuff, aren't you? I mean, you're no longer in the service. You're no longer seeing Erin. You're putting all that behind you."

"No, I'm not," said Alex. "And I see Erin almost every day. Who the fuck do you think got me my fucking job?"

62

"OH," I SAID. "WELL, um...that's nice."

"How the fuck can you say that? Didn't you hear a word I just said?!"

"Yes," I said. "I did. But we're pulling into my grandparents' driveway right now, and they're already standing out on the front porch, waiting for us. And, oh look, John's already here as well. So now is maybe not the best time to have a big discussion about your other women and dark past."

"I'm not fucking cheating on you, Rowena, if that's what you're wondering."

"I know," I said. "And the rest can be discussed later, okay? This doesn't change anything. You've just told me a little bit more about yourself. Now smile and act nice, because I'm sure my grandparents will be delighted to meet you, and they really do want to like you."

"Oh Jesus. I'm not good at this, you know."

"At what?"

"Socializing. Smiling and being nice to people."

"You're good enough," I said firmly. "And besides, there *could* be a reward for you later if you do it well."

Alex started to smile. "That sounds intriguing." He stopped smiling. "But for fuck's sake, Rowena, how can you say stuff like that after what I just told you?"

"Very easily," I said. "Now let's get out of the car before my grandparents come and drag us out by main force."

In fact, both my grandparents had already descended from the porch and were striding purposefully towards the car. I hopped out, hoping that Alex would take the hint and follow.

"Weena! Darling!" My grandmother threw her arms around me and kissed both my cheeks. My grandfather followed suit as soon as she released me.

"Good to see you, darling," he said. "And where's this man we keep hearing so much about?" His gaze shifted over to where Alex had gotten out of the car and was standing by the passenger door. "Not from her, you understand," my grandfather said, speaking simultaneously to me and Alex. "You've been awfully close-lipped about him, haven't you, sweetheart? But John's been bending our ears about him ever since he arrived."

"Oh." Alex looked like he didn't know what to say to that.

"Ro! Miller!" John jumped off the porch and came jogging over. He was smiling, which I hoped had more to do with seeing me than with the bottle of beer in his hand. Probably that was a vain hope.

"Christ, Ro, what happened to you? You look exhausted."

"Just the aftermath of a migraine. It's gone now."

John grimaced. "You've been having those again? I thought they went away when you finished undergrad."

"Yeah, so did I. But they're back now."

"Well, Jesus, Miller, why aren't you taking better care of my kid sister? At the very least you coulda driven."

"I offered," said Alex. "But she preferred to drive her own car herself."

"Of course she did," said my grandmother. "But now that you're here, maybe you should go lie down for a bit, darling. But first—introductions!" She turned to Alex. "I believe your name is Alex? Alex Miller, according to Vannie here."

"*John*," I whispered to Alex. "*My grandparents call him Vannie.*" Our romantic, hippy parents had originally given John the name Ivanhoe. At the age of eighteen he had legally changed his first name to John, as part of his rebellion that had also seen him put himself through The Citadel on an ROTC scholarship with the Marines. But my grandparents still called him Vannie.

Alex's lips quirked. "That's right," he said to my grandmother. "Alex Miller. Very pleased to meet you. And you must be Mrs. O'Malley."

"Well, look at you! Such nice manners. I never would have expected it from a Yankee."

"Ummm..." said Alex.

"Oh, don't mind me, honey! I just say whatever's on my mind, as I'm sure Weena—Rowena—and Vannie have told you."

"Mostly they just told me how nice you are," said Alex.

"Well! You hear that, Archie? He's Archie," my grandmother told Alex, indicating my grandfather, "and I'm Edith."

"Nice to meet you too, Mr. O'Malley," said Alex, shaking my grandfather's hand.

"Good handshake for a Yankee, too," my grandfather said. "I think you might have done good, Weena. But enough standing around here. I'm sure your grandmother is dying to feed you. She'd better do something before the kitchen counter collapses under all the food she's made. I hope you like pecan pie, Alex. Or is that not something you eat up North?"

"I'm sure I'll love it," said Alex. "But I've been holding the rhubarb pie Rowena made in my lap the whole drive over, so I'm going to have to have at least one piece of that before I go crazy."

"You made your rhubarb pie, Weena? Now we *are* in for a feast. Vannie! Don't just stand there, boy. Get the pie and whatever else they've brought over and let's get into the house before we all freeze to death."

"Why don't I help, *Vannie*," said Alex. "I know Rowena brought a bunch of Christmas presents for you to put under the tree, too. Too much for you to carry on your own."

"Fuck you, Miller," said John.

"Vannie! Language!" said my grandmother. "Come on, Weena darling, let's leave them to...whatever nonsense they're going to get up to, and go inside. You can help me with the potatoes."

My grandfather watched while Alex and John unloaded the car, bickering happily as they did so. "Your grandfather is *so* happy," my grandmother told me, stopping on the porch and turning back to watch them for a moment. "He's always wanted a grandson-in-law, you know. And now you've *finally* brought us one! He seems like a fine young man, even if he is a Yankee."

"Um, yeah," I said, stepping into the house in order to avoid having this conversation overheard. "Although you know we're not actually engaged, right? We're just, um..."

"Oh, don't give me that nonsense about how you're 'just good friends,' darling. He's staying with you, isn't he?"

"Um, yeah..."

"And I take it he's not sleeping on the floor, is he?" She winked and nudged me with her elbow.

"Um, well..."

"Oh, don't look so prudish, Weena."

"I'm not...it's just a bit, well..."

"It's not anything I haven't heard before, darling—or done. What did they call me back in the day? 'A bit of a goer'—and a lot of other things, too. Your mother always was a disappointment in that department, darling, if you don't mind me saying so, although she did finally manage to find your father and produce you two, so all credit to her there. But I had such *high hopes* for you, and then you ran off to Russia and got engaged to that boy over there, which, once I saw his picture, I couldn't blame you for at all, but then you just *wouldn't* get married, and then...but this Alex seems lovely, darling, he really does."

"I mean, I suppose so."

"Don't sound so glum about it, darling! Unless"—her gaze sharpened—"you two had a fight on the way over."

"No. I mean, not really."

"Which means yes, darling."

"It wasn't a fight," I said. "He was just...it's his own business, really, and it's all in the past, anyway. I probably shouldn't be talking about it."

"Telling you about some other woman, was he?" asked my grandmother. "Don't look so surprised, darling! You had that look on your face."

"What look?"

"The look of a woman whose man has just told her about some woman in his past."

"It's uncanny how good you are at guessing sometimes," I said.

She tapped the side of her nose. "Not uncanny, darling. Just lots of years of watching people. So what do you think? Is this other woman a threat? Do we need to do something about her?"

"I'm sure it will be fine," I said.

"Mmmm-hmmmm," said my grandmother skeptically. "Really, darling, maybe you should go lie down. You look *very* tired, and not just like that handsome man of yours has been keeping you up at night."

"It's fine," I said. "And there's no way I'm going to leave Alex alone with you. Let's go check on the potatoes."

63

SOON THE POTATOES, along with the dozen other dishes my grandmother had prepared, were ready, and we sat down to a table so overloaded, I was concerned that the end leaves would collapse, dumping the gingered carrots and cornbread, not to mention my grandparents' heaping plates, onto the floor. But this year, as with every year previously, that disaster failed to happen.

There was almost a moment of awkwardness when Alex passed on the turkey, but it was smoothed over when he explained he was doing it out of solidarity with me. Both my grandparents lit up with joy at that statement, and John declared that meant more for him, and went back for a second drumstick.

Afterwards, my grandfather and John went off to watch the Panthers play the Cowboys. Alex offered to help clean up the kitchen, but my grandmother, with a look of mingled delight and horror, shooed him off to go watch football with the other men.

"And don't tell them you don't like football, hon," she ordered him. "They'll forgive a lot of things, but not a disrespect for football."

"I can watch football," Alex said. "Although by rights in that case I should be watching the Iggles."

"The who, hon?"

"The Philadelphia Eagles," he clarified. "In the local accent they're called 'Iggles.'"

"Oh! That's right. Vannie said you were from Philadelphia. Are the Eagles playing today? Do you need us to find you another television? We could set you up in the guest room."

"It's fine," said Alex. "I'll watch whatever they're watching. Although I'd better check first: Which team should I be supporting?"

"Well, aren't you the clever one. The Panthers, hon, the Panthers. Although Vannie keeps threatening to support the Cowboys out of sheer cussedness. I swear, that boy will be the death of his grandfather someday—*and* his father. He's always been *such* a hellraiser, and cantankerous as a mule with shingles. Although"—my grandmother gave me a pat on the arm—"I think Rowena might be the real troublemaker."

"Um," said Alex. "I suppose..."

"You always *do* have to do what you think is the right thing, no matter what the rest of us think, don't you, darling? Although I suppose 'troublemaker' isn't exactly the right term. More like...you'd probably be running messages for the Americans during the Revolution, or working the Underground Railroad, or chaining yourself to railings with the suffragettes, or hiding Jews from the Nazis, or something like that. But since you don't have those opportunities here and now, you have to go looking for trouble, don't you, darling? You know, I'm simply thrilled to bits that you're at Crimson, darling, but the more I think about it, the more I don't know that Crimson knows what's hit it. It was always a, well, I suppose you could say it's always been a *staid* place, and here comes Hurricane Rowena, bent on stirring up trouble. How *is* that going, by the way, darling? Have you found out anything more about those boys? The ones making all the threats?"

"I'm not bent on stirring up trouble," I said. "*They're* the ones stirring up trouble."

"Yes, but darling, there are always naughty boys like that, and most of the time they just get ignored. It's when people stand up to them that the real trouble happens."

"So, what: you think I should just do nothing?" I asked. "Let them get away with it? Boys will be boys?"

"No, darling," said my grandmother soberly. "I think you're doing a good thing. Heaven knows *someone* needs to do something about them. But there's going to be trouble because of it, you mark my words. From them, and also from all those other people there who never did anything about it, and are going to look and feel mighty foolish when *you* put a stop to it."

"Yeah," I said. "I think you may be right."

"I know Crimson, dear, and I know people, and I know I'm right. But no point in worrying about it now. You"—she pointed at Alex—"go watch the Panthers with Archie and Vannie, and Weena and I will clean up. Then you can decide whether you want to stay here for a little while longer, or rush home to make up whatever it is you need to make up over."

"We don't..." Alex said.

"Nonsense, dear." She winked at him. "I'm giving you an excuse to slip away early."

"Well," said Alex. "I appreciate that. And I'll go root for the Panthers now, but just let me know when you want to go, Rowena."

"Now, darling, you just sit down here and rest while I clean up," said my grandmother, once Alex had disappeared into the den where John was already shouting in semi-sober outrage over a ref's call.

"I can help."

"I know you can, darling, but honestly, you look so bad I don't know I could stand to see you standing over my sink. Are you getting another one of your migraines?"

"Maybe a bit." I rubbed my temples. A dull but sickening pain was spreading from my eyes across my scalp to the back of my neck, although I thought it might be just a garden-variety tension headache rather than a migraine.

"Do you want me to send the rest of the rhubarb pie home with you, darling, or take it out and wash the pan?"

"Um. Whatever you want."

"Are you going to eat it if I send it back with you?"

"Probably. Alex sure seemed to like it. I hope he wasn't just being polite."

"Even if he was just being polite, it sure seemed like he enjoyed doing so. I'll send the rest of the pie back with you, still in its pan. And a whole bunch of leftovers. I know you can cook for yourself, sweetheart, but right now you shouldn't have to. Concentrate on resting up, and taking care of your handsome man. Even if he *is* seeing another woman, although I can't believe that."

I looked around furtively. "He's not," I said, speaking in a half-whisper, even though I was sure no one could overhear us over the sound of the game and John and my grandfather's yells of approbation and disappointment at the Panther's play. "He just...well, I hope this isn't too much information..."

"Your secret is safe with me, darling."

"He just told me that he's currently working with a woman with whom he used to have a relationship," I whispered. "He says there's nothing going on between them, and I believe that, but it was a bit of a shock to have that blurted out to me on the drive over. And he's got...other problems. John-type problems."

My grandmother raised an eyebrow. "John has so many problems, darling. You'll have to narrow it down for me."

"Well, it turns out they were both in Iraq at the same time, which is one of the reasons John will actually tolerate him. But it sounds like Alex maybe had an even worse time of it over there than John. He wouldn't tell me exactly what happened, but I can make some good guesses. And it was all...it was a pretty heavy conversation to have while driving over to Thanksgiving dinner."

"I'm sure. But at least he told you."

"I know. And it's not even that. It's mainly work that's bothering me. I don't know what to do about this talk I'm organizing, and about the boys I told you about, the ones issuing threats to the speaker."

"Yes," said my grandmother. "That *is* serious." Her mouth was set in a firm line. A proper steel magnolia, that was Edith O'Malley. "You know, darling, maybe I can do something about it," she said.

"You can? I mean, that would be great if you could, but what could you do?"

"Well, you know that Irene Collins goes to our church, and she and I go way back, and she's an alum of Crimson just like I am."

"Uh-huh." Irene Collins was old money who had parlayed her family fortune into a successful business as an attorney at a time when women didn't do that sort of thing, especially not in small-town Georgia, and her husband was a judge.

"She's on the board at Crimson. Not just the alumni board, like your mother and I"—Crimson had a largely ceremonial board composed of alumni, to which both my mother and grandmother belonged, and also a "real" board of directors, composed of rich and/or influential people—"but the one that calls the shots. Why don't I give her a call and, shall we say, express my concerns about what's going on there. Maybe she can make something happen. At the very least, Alan"—Alan was Irene's husband—"might be able to do something about finding out who these boys are. He's just a good ol' boy, not a touch of class or brains to him even if he *is* a judge, but he's one of those good ol' boys who doesn't put up with boys messing around, and certainly not with threatening women. Between the two of them they might be able to do something."

"That's certainly worth trying," I said. "And thanks."

"Of course, darling. Now why don't you go have a little lie-down in the guest bedroom—I'm sure John won't mind—and then you and Alex go home and make up whatever you need to make up. As long as you make sure he takes good care of you tonight!"

"I'm sure he'll do his best," I said, and went to lie down.

64

LYING DOWN IN THE GUEST bedroom didn't really make me feel any better, but at least I got some quiet downtime. I was almost dozing off when Alex came and sat down next to me on the bed.

"The game can't be over yet," I said.

"Oh God no. It's only halftime. I think I've just had about all the football I can handle for one day. Please tell me you're ready to go home, so I can have a legitimate excuse to leave. Shit. I didn't mean for that to sound so bad."

I sat up. "It didn't sound bad. I'm more than ready to go home too. Although we might have to come back tomorrow or Saturday. My grandmother always puts up her Christmas tree right after Thanksgiving, and that's a big deal."

"No problem. Just as long as we have some 'alone time' in between then."

"We will. Let's go."

I got up and found my grandmother sitting at the kitchen island, talking on the phone.

"Anyway, Irene, Rowena's coming in right now. Rowena, honey?" She held out the phone. "Irene's on the phone right now, and she'd love to talk to you about your 'situation.'"

"Sure," I said. "If it's no trouble."

I heard Irene laugh over the phone. "Alan and the boys are all trying to get me to bring them beers during halftime. This is the perfect excuse to tell them to get their lazy heinies over to the fridge themselves and get their own beers. Do you have speakerphone, Edith? Put it on so that we can all put our heads together."

"*Should I leave?*" Alex whispered to me. "*I'd hate to listen in on anything above my security clearance.*"

"Alex wants to know if he's allowed to stay, or if this is above his security clearance," I said out loud.

Irene laughed over the speakerphone. "Is that your new man, Rowena? And he's there with you instead of watching the Panthers? Of course he can stay, then. Edith and I are too old to have any secrets anymore, and much as we both love Crimson, we don't want to cover up anything that should be uncovered. Edith's been filling me in on what's going on over there, but why don't you give me your take on it, Rowena."

I gave her a quick recap of the MPA and the Gang of Six, and the Miriam Chen talk and the escalating series of threats aimed her way on the MPA blog.

"Well, for goodness' sake," said Irene when I was done. "That's even worse than I thought. I'd like to say we never had anything like that happen while we were there, but that was only because we hadn't invented the internet yet. You remember the trouble those frat boys caused, don't you, Edith? I swear, sometimes I think they should have kept Crimson a women's college. Or is that not allowed anymore?"

"It's still allowed," I said. "Sort of. Anyway, we've got Nathan and his ilk there now, so we've got to deal with them. I want to cancel the event, or at least hire extra security, but the higher-ups won't hear of it. Not out of principle, but because they're afraid it will make the college look bad."

Irene snorted. "A little late for that, if you ask me. Haven't we already made the national news at least twice about this, and this Miriam girl hasn't even arrived yet? And I have to say I agree that cancelling the event sends the wrong message."

"It does," I agreed. "But a guest speaker getting shot would send an even worse message."

"Have they said why they won't pony up for the extra security?"

"They said it would create a hostile atmosphere for the students. Again, that might be true, but getting shot would create an even more hostile atmosphere, in my humble opinion. I think, other than a general reluctance to acknowledge the problem, they might just not have the money."

"Nonsense," said Irene briskly. "They just got more money than they know what to do with from the good folks, and I say that with extreme sarcasm, at Security Solutions. And"—I could hear an idea bubbling up in her voice—"maybe Security Solutions could do at least a *little* good. You know, I voted against taking the money from them when it came before the board, and I know your mother and grandmother voted against it when it came up before the alumni board, but we were overruled. Not that I was surprised, because I could see the way the wind was blowing from a mile off, but I still felt I had to make my stance known. Still, now that we've got them, we may as well get some benefit out of them. Surely they can come up with some security personnel for the event. They might even provide it pro bono. Let me make some calls, and I'll see what I can do."

"Wow," I said. "If it's, um, no trouble."

"I hope it *is* trouble, Rowena, because to tell the truth, I'm bored out of my skull. Being old and retired is a tedious business, and I don't even have any grandchildren to spoil. Raising some Cain over this will give me something to do. And, as Edith will tell you, I do enjoy a good fight!"

"Well, in that case, thank you," I said.

"Thank me once I get you some results, hon," she said. "And now I'll let you go so you can get back to your Thanksgiving." There was a round of formalities, and then she hung up.

"Well, that went even better than I'd expected," said my grandmother. "I knew if we could get Irene on our side, she'd go after them like a bulldog. And getting Security Solutions to provide extra security isn't half bad an idea. She was that mad when the vote to take their money went through, but now it's a done deal, you can be sure she'll be looking for every way she can to turn it to her advantage. And I think you've had enough beer." The last was to John, who had come wandering into the kitchen.

He held up his hands. "I wasn't here for a beer, I swear. Although I *was* here for Miller. I'll bet you could make a pretty good joke out of that, couldn't you, Ro? Is that what you and Miller do when you're alone together? Tell each other language jokes?"

"There is a certain amount of lingual activity," I said primly.

John grinned. "I'm not entirely sure what you just said, but it sounds dirty. Anyway, the second half's starting, Miller, if you want to watch it."

"I'd love to, but I think Rowena is ready to go home," said Alex. "You know, what with her headache and all."

"She's pleading headaches already? You *are* in trouble, Miller. Your choice, though. Hey, what are you up to tomorrow? A couple of my buddies and I are getting together to go hunting. You wanna join us? Oh shit, I shouldn't have said that in front of you and your delicate sensibilities, Ro. Pretend you didn't hear that."

"I don't have delicate sensibilities," I said. "I have convictions. And it's not about my feelings, it's about theirs."

"By 'theirs' I assume you mean the deer's?"

"Yes," I said.

"But they're totally overrunning the place! We've got to do *something* about them!"

"One might say that *we're* overrunning the place," I said. "Maybe *they* should do something about *us*."

"Well, they're giving it a damn good try. Jase got his truck totaled last month when he hit one. And it seems like people are coming down with Lyme disease left, right, and center in Jacksonville, and they say it's deer bringing all the ticks in."

"That is unfortunate," I said. "But I would guess that in both those cases, the deer are rather worse off than the humans. After all, they're collateral victims in a human-caused problem."

"Well, shit, sis. Would it make you feel better if I told you we go all Native American and say a prayer and commune with nature and all that shit?"

"I don't know," I said. "Did you care whether the insurgents trying to shoot you had thrice-shriven themselves and dedicated themselves to Allah beforehand?"

John threw up his hands again. "There's just no fucking—oops, sorry, Grandma—arguing with you, Ro. You seem all girly-girly and goody-goody, but talking to you is like dealing with a goddamn—shit, sorry Grandma—brick wall."

"I think you should go back and watch the game before you dig yourself into an even deeper hole, Vannie," said my grandmother. "As I was just saying, you're the hellraiser, but Weena is the real troublemaker. But right now she's a troublemaker with a migraine, so let's let her go home in peace."

65

"DO YOU WANT ME TO DRIVE?" Alex offered when we got to the car.

I rubbed my temples. "Sure. I think my eyes are starting to act up now, so it would probably be better if someone else were behind the wheel. But I should warn you that second gear can be tricky."

"As you might recall, my piece-of-shit car can't shift into third half the time, so I'm used to it. Just promise you won't laugh if I stall out."

"It happens to me all the time, so it would be hypocritical of me if I did."

Alex got us home with only one minor stall-out, which we agreed was good going for a first try. As soon as we got back into the apartment, I said I was going to go take a hot shower and see if that would help my head. So far, I had developed neither the scotoma of a visual migraine, nor the crushing pain of a regular migraine, but I could feel both flirting with me, hanging around on the edges of my consciousness and threatening to let loose as soon as the right trigger came along.

"You go take a shower," Alex said. "And when you get out, I can give you a neck rub if you'd like and you think it'd help."

"It's certainly worth trying," I said. "In any case, I'm sure I'll enjoy it."

But when I got out of the shower, Alex was sitting on the bed staring at his phone, a frown etched into his face.

"What is it?" I asked. "Is it your parents?"

"What? Oh, no." He put the phone facedown on the floor. "Although that reminds me that I should give them a call this evening."

I looked at the facedown phone. Every instinct in my body screamed that he had just gotten a message from the mysterious Erin. An almost insane urge to run over and snatch up the phone and confront him about it bubbled up inside me. Fortunately, my natural state of repression rose to the fore and saved me.

I went and sat down beside him on the bed. "So, what's this I hear about the possibility of a neck rub?"

He flexed his fingers. "You still want one?"

"I do." Instead of sitting at easy massage distance, though, I found myself snuggling up against him, burying my face in his chest.

"Wow." He put his arms around me. "What brought this on?"

"I don't know. I just...I guess I've been thinking about, you know, what you told me on the drive over today."

He went still. "Do I even want to know what it is you've been thinking?"

"Probably not all of it. A lot of it has been jealousy that I'm too ashamed to admit to."

He shifted, pulling me closer and holding me tighter. "Jealousy is okay. I like the idea of jealousy. Better than rejection."

"Well, that's good, because I've been feeling a lot of it."

He kissed the top of my head. "I'm flattered to be the one to have brought that out in you. I think."

"That's good. And...if there's other stuff you want to tell me, you should...just go ahead and tell me. Even if you think I won't like it. I understand, really well, that everyone is a mixed bag. Everyone's got at least a little evil in them. I've learned to accept that, and forgive them, just like I hope they can forgive me.

"And, you know, John is my brother. Pretty much everything he does, from his hobby of hunting to the fact that he's a Marine, is something that I abhor. I mean, I really do believe that he has done and will continue to do a lot of genuinely evil things, whether that's killing for fun, or killing for duty—and worse than that, arranging for other people to kill or be killed for duty. On some level, he's a genuinely bad person who probably makes the world a worse place just by existing. Plus, he's a drama queen and a pain in the ass.

"But he's still my brother. The only brother I'll ever have. And I love him even so, both because of the blood bond we share, and because I made a conscious choice a long time ago that he was my brother and I was going to stick by him and forgive him, no matter what. And not just him. What I said to him back there was true. I don't have delicate sensibilities, I have convictions. Convictions that most people break most of the time, including sometimes me. But I can't turn my back on them, cut them off, because that would mean turning my back on *everybody*. So instead I forgive people. Not because I think that what they're doing is okay. Far from it. Because, much as I hate this cliché, sometimes the best thing to do is to love the sinner, even as you hate the sin."

I stopped. I could feel Alex taking a deep breath, his chest rising against my cheek. His skin was almost feverishly warm against mine, and his heart was beating triple time in my ear

"So what you're saying," he said after a while, "is that you love me?"

Now my heart started beating triple time. *Did* I love Alex? As I'd told Mel, probably so—but now that the words were out there, hanging in the air over our heads like a Sword of Damocles, I felt like the thing they were poised to cut was not our relationship, but the

last threads of my love for Dima, that I'd nurtured so carefully for so
many years in such stony ground.

"Would that be a bad thing?" I asked.

"No," said Alex. "It wouldn't be a bad thing at all."

66

AFTER THAT, THE REST of Alex's visit was more relaxed. We spent Friday at my place, making a conscious effort not to talk about work or anything heavy. The closest we got to that was a lengthy discussion of what it would be like if Alex stayed in California and I moved out there with him. Both of us thought that would be pretty great, although Alex reiterated several times that he didn't want me to have to give up my career.

"Maybe I could find a new career," I said. "Maybe even something completely outside of academia."

"You'd do that?"

"Heck yeah. At least I think so. Maybe I could go back into nonprofit work. Maybe something with immigrants and immigration law, or prison reform; it wouldn't be that much different from what I was doing in Russia. Or maybe I could branch out and do something with environmental justice. None of that pays well, of course, but neither does what I'm doing now."

"Yeah. I'd bet there'd be tons of opportunities for immigration-related work in California. And, you know, if we were living together, making money wouldn't be so important. Our housing costs would halve."

"Yeah," I said. "Something to think about. And, speaking of thinking..."

"Yes?"

"I was thinking of visiting you out in California again."

"That'd be great! Over Christmas break?"

"If you're going to be around, and you'd want me to come."

Alex smiled. "Oh, I'd want you to fucking come. In both senses of the word. I should probably spend at least a couple of days with my parents back in Pennsylvania, but the rest of the time, I'd be all yours. It'd be great if you could come and spend a couple of weeks with me, see how you liked the place. Maybe you could even start looking for jobs in the area."

"Yeah," I said. "That sounds like a great idea."

By Friday evening we were so enthused about the plan that I went ahead and bought plane tickets. Buying the tickets wiped out all the forward progress I'd made in paying off my credit card debt, but I considered it worth the cost. I even started looking into non-academic jobs in the area. It was the first time I'd ever regretted not going to law school. I knew that the law student market was at least as glutted as the academic market, but maybe it would be pretty easy for a JD to get a low-paying job with an NGO.

"Or maybe you could look into teaching English as a second language, or tutoring," Alex said.

"Yeah...somehow that feels like I'd still be in academia, but as a failure. I think I'd only want to do that if I could make a lot of money doing it. Or if I had nothing else going for me."

"We'll figure something out," Alex said, kissing my ear. "And I can assure you that you're not a failure. Maybe the real failures are the ones who stay in."

"Yeah," I said. "Maybe."

On Saturday we drove out and visited my grandparents and John again. We trimmed my grandmother's enormous Christmas tree, and I carefully avoided picking an argument with John about the deer corpse he had hanging out in the backyard. John, who most certainly did have delicate sensibilities, or at least a profound need to hide his own insecurities by harassing others about things he was ashamed of, tried to pick one with me. Eventually even our grandfather, who generally had the patience of a saint, told him to stop being an ass and go watch tv or something until he could straighten up and act right.

"I swear," he said, after John had left the room. "I love that boy, but...How on God's green earth did you put up with him for a solid two weeks this spring, Weena?"

"With difficulty," I said. "Alex helped."

"And we appreciate it," said my grandfather. "Most men woulda turned tail and run at the first sniff of Vannie. The fact that you stuck around speaks highly of you. Even if you *are* a Yankee."

"Uh," said Alex. "Thanks. Although it's looking like I might be morphing into a Californian. And maybe Rowena too."

"Is that *so*?" My grandmother gave us both an elated look. "*Do* tell!"

"Um," I said. "There's not much to tell. I just got tickets to go out to California for two weeks over winter break. That's all."

"Well..." My grandmother appeared to be choosing her words carefully. "Well, darling, California *is* a long way away, and I'll be sorry to have you gone during your break, since we hardly ever see you during the semester, even though you're just down the road, but that *does* sound like a lovely thing to do. I hope you two have a *wonderful* time."

"I'm sure we will," said Alex, and put his hand on my leg. It was, clear as clear, a gesture meant to lay claim to me publicly. Not in a bad way, but to show my grandparents what his intentions were. I tried to tell myself that I was pleased about it. And on one level I was. The weight of his hand on my thigh seemed to lift a much bigger weight off my mind, the weight of worrying about him and his intentions and our future and *my* future and whether I was doomed to spend the rest of it sad and alone. The thought of living with Alex, in

California, and maybe working some kind of a meaningful, even if low-paying, job outside of academia, was very attractive. Part of me was already certain that it was the right choice, the right future, for both of us.

But part of me felt like his heart wasn't entirely where his hand was. Part of me felt like he was just going through the motions because he didn't know what else to do. And while we'd known each other for over a year, how much time had we actually spent together? Not very much. Time was slipping away from us, and we needed to catch it and make sure we didn't let it get away from us and spend the next few months or years floating along in a long-distance sort-of serious relationship. But right now I felt like if we were already talking about me moving out to California and moving in with him, we were rushing into things. Maybe these two weeks together over break would bring some clarity.

"I'm sure we'll have a lovely time," I said.

67

SUNDAY MORNING SAW me driving Alex back to the airport. I offered to park the car and walk with him to security, but he said no, he'd probably cause another scene with an excessively amorous goodbye, and we didn't want that, did we?

"Speak for yourself," I said.

"I'd really fucking love to hold you one last time before getting back on that plane, Rowena. But I know how expensive parking is, and what a pain it is to deal with airport traffic, and I feel bad about making you go out of your way as much as you already have, and...shit, I'm not sure I want our goodbye to be public. So just drop me off at the curb and drive away, okay?"

"Okay," I said. "If you're sure that's what you want."

"I don't want to be saying goodbye at all. But at least this way it'll be quick."

I couldn't argue with that, so I did as he requested, and headed off home to my apartment, which I knew from experience was going to seem empty and lonely for the next couple of days without him.

Not that I would have that much time for moping about it. Tuesday was Miriam Chen's talk. I had volunteered, by which I mean I had been volunteered, to be the one to go pick her up at the airport Tuesday morning. She was supposed to arrive at midday, which would leave me just enough time to teach both classes and then rush back over to my new favorite stomping grounds of ATL.

Then I was supposed to entertain her/guard her all afternoon, personally escort her to and from the talk, and drive her back to the airport on Wednesday. Looked like I was going to get really, really familiar with I-75 before this was over.

The good news was that both the MPA and the Gang of Six had gone quiet over Thanksgiving. I had been monitoring the MPA's most recent post, the one that had had those threats against both Miriam and me, and the comments had dried up to a trickle and then stopped altogether, and there hadn't been any more posts since then. Presumably all those big tough men had had to go home and visit their moms over Thanksgiving, and hadn't had the time to engage in much online whining. I just had to keep my fingers crossed that they would be too busy during the pre-finals buildup to get around to issuing any more threats this week.

Sunday afternoon I got a call from Irene Collins.

"Rowena? Is that you? Edith gave me your number. Did I get you at a bad time?"

"Not at all," I said.

"Oh, that's great. And I have good news! I spent the past few days leaning on the rest of the Board, on the administration, and the fine folks at Security Solutions—thank you for this little project, by the way; I haven't had this much fun since I retired—and I'm delighted to say that Security Solutions has agreed to provide a security team for the event. In exchange for having a big banner up at the entrance, and being publicly thanked for it at the beginning and end of the talk. The feeling I got is that they're desperately trying to whitewash their reputation, and they've agreed to help out because they think this is the way to do it. Which we knew would be the case all along."

"Yeah," I said. "Thanks a ton. This is great."

"Anytime, Rowena. Like I said, this has been the most fun I've had since I retired. I think I need to be more involved in the college—what do you think?"

"I think it would do the college good, even if they wouldn't agree," I said.

Irene laughed and said she'd email over the information from Security Solutions about their security team.

As soon as I got off the phone with her I emailed Brian Michaels with the news. He emailed right back to say that he'd already heard from "some a—hole" from Security Solutions who had told him that he, the a—hole, was now in charge.

Don't worry, we'll figure it out, he wrote. *But first we're going to have to have a pissing contest over jurisdiction. Not that I'm complaining, mind. We need all the help we can get. But these big-city private boys need to be put in their place sometimes.*

I wished him luck and emailed Sandra and the rest of the committee to let them know what was going on. Some of them immediately got into a snit over the situation and over the fact that I had decided a lot of this unilaterally, but since I was the one doing 90% of the work to actually organize the event, they didn't snit about it for too long. Especially once I offered to let one of them go pick up Miriam in my stead. Funnily enough, they all had urgent prior engagements.

I went to bed Sunday evening thinking that things were as well in hand as they were going to be. When I got up Monday morning, I was greeted by another post from the MPA, with a frantic email from Miriam right on its heels.

68

MIRIAM CHEN MUST NOT BE ALLOWED TO SPEAK!
I BIT BACK A GROAN. Then, since there was no one there to hear it, I let it loose. It didn't do anything to get rid of the headline screaming at me from the MPA website.

I scrolled through the actual post. It was just one paragraph.

Against the express wishes of the student body the college has decided to go ahead with the Miriam Chen talk, in fact she is arriving here tomorrow and will be giving her talk **at the basketball arena** *which has been commandeered for a purpose far different from what it was originally intended for.* *WE MUST STAND UP AGAINST THIS PERVERSION OF STUDENT WISHES! BOYCOTT THE TALK AND JOIN US IN PROTEST OUTSIDE THE BASKETBALL ARENA INSTEAD! *DON'T GO TO THE FREE SPEECH ZONE IN THE BACK QUAD!* WE'LL SHOW THEM WHAT WE THINK ABOUT THEIR OPPRESSION OF OUR SPEECH! DROWN OUT THEIR THREATS WITH OUR PROTESTS! IF THEY WANT TO SILENCE US WE'LL SILENCE THEM!*

Well, that didn't sound too threatening. And they were telling us exactly what they were planning to do and where they were planning to do it. I would just drop Brian Michaels a note about this post, in case he hadn't seen it yet, and he and the team from Security Solutions could decide what they wanted to do about it. Probably they wouldn't actually arrest the protesters, since the college would never go for that. Maybe they could be herded to the other side of the road from the basketball arena. Of course, if any of them actually knew how to shoot and had any kind of a decent rifle, they could drop Miriam—and me, since I would be escorting her into the building—from the far side of the street no problem. Maybe we needed to sneak in the back entrance.

I opened up my email to tell Brian Michaels exactly that, and found a panic-stricken email from Miriam waiting for me.

*Have you seen what those maniacs have written this time? Is anyone keeping an eye on them?!? Is anyone **doing** anything about them?!? I don't know if I can go through with this now.*

I ground my teeth a little. Not that I blamed her. The more I thought about being dropped by a sniper while walking Miriam into the basketball arena, the less I liked the idea. The problem was that I thought Miriam needed to make a resolute decision one way or the other. Either she needed to say she wasn't going to put others in danger (because hey, she was an activist, so her primary concern should be other people) and would therefore stay away, or she needed to say that freedom of speech and standing up to misogynistic bullies who fantasize about raping and killing women was a cause worth risking her life for.

I saw, I wrote back. *I'm forwarding it to the chief of campus police right now. As I mentioned yesterday, we'll be bringing in extra security for the event. Of course you shouldn't do it if you feel it's unacceptably dangerous, but security will be **very tight**, and I'll be escorting you personally, so it's in my best interests to keep you safe :) I was thinking that, if you prefer, we can skip the campus tour and the dinner and sneak in and out through the back entrance of the basketball arena when they're least expecting it.*

Didn't you say that the extra security would be provided by Security Solutions? she wrote back. Miriam Chen might not be very brave, but she wasn't stupid, either. *Aren't they a for-profit prison and security company? With ties to Blackwater, or whatever it's called now?*

Yes. I'm not saying I'm happy about it, I told her. *But they're the best we've got right now.*

We exchanged emails for the rest of the day. By the evening I had convinced both her and Brian Michaels that if she was going to go ahead and come, she should slip into the arena from the back, when we hoped no one would be expecting her, and slip away just as anonymously afterwards. I just hoped I was right about how safe that would be.

69

TUESDAY, DECEMBER 1st. Miriam's flight was scheduled to arrive in Atlanta at 1:13pm. It was a little under two hours to get from Greenfields to the airport. This meant I had just barely enough time to teach my two classes, and then rush off to Atlanta. I hoped the traffic gods would smile upon me.

The traffic gods didn't exactly smile upon me, but they didn't frown on me too badly either, so I was in position in baggage claim by 1:15. I had told Miriam I wouldn't be holding up a sign with her name. I didn't think there were any suspicious-looking people lurking nearby, waiting to jump us as soon as Miriam appeared, but why take chances? I'd learned about security in a hard school, and I might as well put those lessons to good use.

I recognized Miriam as soon as she came into baggage claim. Even in a giant airport like Atlanta, there weren't that many grossly overweight Asian women.

I caught her eye and made a miniscule movement of my head, trying to indicate that she should come over to me without drawing any attention to either of us. She squinted at me in confusion, then stopped and stared openly. Looked like neither of us had much of a future as undercover intelligence agents. I gave her a tiny wave. She gave a tiny wave back, and then, looking around in a way that drew curious stares from everyone around her, came over.

Up close and in person, she was even fatter than she'd appeared on Skype. Or maybe she'd continued to gain weight all semester. Her hair, in contrast, was thin and stringy. Angry red pimples had broken out on her forehead and in the folds beside her nose, and fine black hair was growing on her upper lip and the edge of her jaw.

Something in me snapped at the sight. Mostly what I'd felt for Miriam so far had been disappointment and irritation. But I'd seen pictures of her from just last year, and they hadn't had any of this. As recently as a year ago she'd been slim and pretty, with no sign of what I guessed was the acne and hair problems of polycystic ovarian syndrome. I didn't know exactly what had caused her to change like this, but it was clear that the ordeal she'd been through had taken a terrible toll. Even if no one so much as flashed a knife at her, she could end up infertile and ill because of what had been done to her.

"It's great to see you in person," I said. "Do you have any bags?"

She lifted up an elegant leather backpack that had probably been suitable for her previous self, but looked ludicrous next to her current fleshy body. "Just this."

"Great. I'm parked in short-term parking. Do you want to stop and get anything while we're here? It's about two hours back to Greenfields, FYI, so if you want lunch, now's your chance. I was just going to take you straight to your hotel from here. You can rest there a little bit, have an early supper in the hotel—the restaurant's supposed to be good—and then I'll bring you over to the arena and walk you in the back entrance, stay with you until it's time to go onstage, and walk onstage with you."

"I'll be in the hotel by myself?"

"Well. That was the plan. Although we were thinking of taking you out for drinks afterwards."

"I can't drink alcohol. It interferes with my meds."

"Of course. Obviously you wouldn't have to drink alcohol. It's more a way to, you know, celebrate the talk and socialize."

"I think I'll just want to go straight to bed afterwards. I can't handle crowds. But I don't want to be left by myself all afternoon in the hotel. I get panic attacks, especially in hotels. And what if someone stalks me there and attacks me?"

"Well..." I said. "I suppose that's possible. Although we haven't made where you'll be staying public knowledge."

"Yeah, but how many people know about it? You and Sandra and everyone else on the committee, right? Plus the police guy. Plus what's-her-name, the secretary who made the reservations. And it's a small town, right? How many hotels are there? Not that many, and I'll bet the college always uses the same one."

"You're right," I said. "At least you're right about there not being that many hotels, and I'll bet you're right about the college always using the same one. Um...I suppose you could come spend the afternoon at my place..."

Miriam made a face. Clearly she wasn't any more thrilled at the idea of spending the afternoon at my place than I was thrilled at the idea of her doing so. But after a little more discussion, we both agreed it was the safest option, so that's what we'd do.

70

MIRIAM STARED FEARFULLY out the car window the whole way to Greenfields.

"I don't think we're in much danger in the car," I said. "Well, not from being attacked. Maybe from a car accident. But I sincerely doubt any students have the wherewithal to tail us and, I don't know, try to gun us down on a deserted road."

Miriam gave me an alarmed look. "I hadn't even thought of that."

"Good," I said. "Because we're probably safe from that. I mean, not to dwell on morbid things, but that's not really the style of these kinds of punks, you know what I mean? They're not sophisticated government hit men, or even reasonably competent kidnappers. The MO for people like this is to stroll into a populated area and just start blowing people away. Or running them over with a car. But we're already in a car. Doing something to us now would be a lot of work, and not cause the sensation they want to achieve. In Russia you might have to resort to suicide bombings and professional assassins, but in the US any school kid with the key to his dad's gun cabinet can commit mass murder."

"Oh. I hadn't thought about it like that. I've never thought about it in relation to other dangerous countries. I've never actually been out of the US."

"Well, I can tell you from personal experience that America's pretty freaking scary," I said. "I mean, I worried about getting hit by a terrorist attack in Russia—or about being mistaken for a terrorist, since I have dark hair—and I worried about being the target of assassination, but in the latter case it's normally expected. I mean, it's not random. You generally know if you're doing something that's going to get you on someone's shit list, and they normally give you a number of warnings, plenty of chances to back off, before they take you out. And even suicide bombers have an obvious agenda. While here it's just...random and mysterious. Although in your case, maybe not so much. I mean, you *are* a political activist who's drawn down outrage on herself through her activism. Which is one of the reasons, frankly, that it seems unlikely that anything really bad will actually happen. Not that we should slack off and be careless. But that's not how these people normally seem to operate. They're amateurs. They're unlikely to go after someone who has even a token guard."

"Oh." Miriam gave me a sideways look. "I don't know whether that makes me feel better or worse."

"I meant for it to make you feel better. Also to vent a little. You know, when I lived in Russia at least the people threatening my life were worth fearing. I might not agree with FSB hitmen and hardened jihadists, but I could respect them. While here it's mainly just a bunch of spotty teenagers with poor social skills and delusions of grandeur."

"Yeah. I guess," said Miriam. "But what I was going to say was that I've never been to the South before. It all seems kind of...scary. Like I'm expecting to see some gap-toothed kid playing the banjo around every corner."

"You're probably pretty safe from that," I said. "Although we don't take kindly to stuck-up Yankees who go around mouthing negative stereotypes."

"That's right. You're from here, aren't you?"

"Yep," I said. "Georgia, born and bred."

"I never thought about someone from Georgia getting a PhD and becoming a professor before."

"The world is a wild place," I said.

Miriam relaxed enough to ask me advice about grad school, which she was considering. She tensed up again when we got to Greenfields. Apparently small towns in general were exotic and scary to her.

She tensed up even more when I drove her on a quick tour through campus. It was now almost 3:30, and the "free speech zone" was being set up on the back quad. Miriam slouched down until she was almost slumped on the floor of the car when she saw it.

"I don't see anyone other than workers around it," I said as we drove past.

"What if one of the workers is part of the plot?!"

"I *suppose* that's possible," I said. "But it seems very unlikely. Like I said, plotting is a lot of work, and to be honest, I doubt most of these people have ever even heard of you, or would give a crap if they had."

"Yeah...can we get out of here?"

We drove on to the Greenfields Inn & Suites, the most upscale hotel (of three) in town. At first Miriam refused to check in. Then she wanted me to drop her off in the back so she could sneak in. When we discovered that all the back doors required a keycard for entrance, she wanted me to go around to the front desk and have them let her in that way, but I refused to leave her lurking by herself in the back alley behind the hotel. In the end I got the doorman to come and walk us both into the lobby while the valet watched over my car.

We made it to the front desk unaccosted, but as soon as Miriam checked in, a short but extremely buff-looking guy in a sort of uniform-y looking outfit with "Security Solutions" stitched on the front pocket of his shirt came over and said his name was Carl and he was Miriam's personal security detail for the evening.

"No one told me anything about this," Miriam and I both said.

Carl gave us that kind of flat look that security-related people give you when you're being difficult. "Then I suggest you ladies check your emails," he said. "It was just decided. You were supposed to be informed."

We pulled out our phones and checked our emails. Both of us had gotten identical emails from Brian Michaels telling us that Security Solutions had decided to provide Miriam with a personal bodyguard for the evening. The email included the official ID photo for a Carl Baker. I wasn't very good at identifying people from their photos, but both that Carl and the Carl standing in front of me were extremely fit black men with bald heads and severe expressions, so I decided to take him at his word. After all, as I'd told Miriam, any conspiracy we were dealing with was extremely unlikely to involve enough planning and sophistication to infiltrate another organization. It was unlikely to involve any planning or sophistication at all. Which made it potentially even more dangerous.

"Miriam wants to go rest at my place for a little while," I told Carl. "She'll feel safer there."

"I don't have authorization to allow you to do that, ma'am," said Carl. "And it's already 4:00pm, and my instructions are to have Ms. Chen seated in the restaurant and ordering dinner by 5:30pm sharp. I suggest that she remain in her room until then."

"I *can't*," said Miriam. "I *hate* hotel rooms. I get awful panic attacks from them...in fact, I think I'm about to get one now..."

"Is this *Miriam Chen*? How *wonderful* to see you! Welcome to Crimson! Oh. And it's you. Regina, was it? I suppose you were on airport pickup duty? Well, *thank* you for all your help, Regina, but you can go now. I'll take over things from here."

A chill went up my spine. I turned around. Bearing down on us with the inexorable menace of an iceberg in an Arctic shipping lane was Dorothy, with Tanika Scott firmly in tow.

71

CARL, BLESS HIS HEART, immediately moved to intercept Dorothy and stop her in her tracks. A short but intense argument followed, in which Carl demanded to see some ID from both Dorothy and Tanika, and confirmation that they were indeed authorized to be here.

"Oh, Regina can vouch for us," said Dorothy, with breezy certainty.

"I don't have a Regina on my list of authorized personnel here, ma'am," said Carl.

"Well, then, why is she still here? Send her away!"

"I just have a Rowena, ma'am," said Carl. "Doctor Rowena Halley." It was difficult to tell in a face as impassive as his, but I thought he was suppressing a laugh. Carl didn't seem to like Dorothy any better than I did, which suggested he was at least a good judge of character.

"Oh, well..." Dorothy looked momentarily flustered, but then regained her composure. "Rowena, of course, that's what I meant. But Tanika and I are here from the Dean's office to give Miriam a *proper* welcome. Rowena was just picking her up from the airport. Now *we're* here to show her around."

"I just want to rest," said Miriam.

"Oh, well, *of course* you're tired after your *big trip* today, but you're only here for a few hours! We have to show you all the sights

337

of Greenfields! We've booked reservations in the *nicest* restaurant in town! We'll go visit the downtown—you know, we have the most *charming* little historic district, including an old courthouse from the 19th century—walk around there a bit, and then have a *delightful* little supper and get you to your talk well-fed and in *plenty* of time to blow us all away!"

Dorothy beamed at Miriam. She didn't seem to notice how the rest of us flinched at the phrase "blow us all away."

"That was not the agreed-upon plan, ma'am," said Carl.

"Maybe not when *you* were brought on board, but we've come up with it now, and it's a *delightful* plan, don't you agree?"

There was some wrangling, but eventually it was decided to go along with Dorothy's plan. Carl and I agreed that it was probably safe enough, especially since it was spur-of-the-moment, and Miriam was eager for anything that would keep her out of her hotel room.

"And now you can go, Regi—Rowena," said Dorothy.

"I want Rowena with me," said Miriam. "I feel safer with her with me."

"Yes, but you *see*, Miriam, we only have reservations for the three of us—I suppose your, ah, *bodyguard* isn't going to eat anyway, is he?—and it's *quite* an exclusive restaurant, so we couldn't squeeze an extra person in, even if we could get budget authorization for it, which we probably couldn't, so I'm afraid that Reg—Rowena can't join us. Besides, there isn't room in Tanika's car."

"I'll be driving Ms. Chen wherever she needs to go, ma'am," Carl interjected at this point. "I have an official Security Solutions SUV that seats eight. And Doctor Halley is supposed to walk Ms. Chen into the arena and onto the stage." He looked at his watch. "Given the time constraints we're working with, I recommend that we do what needs to be done to keep Doctor Halley with us."

"Oh, didn't anyone tell you? The Dean's office has decided it would be more fitting to have, well, a *dean* walk Miriam onto the stage. Reg—Rowena is welcome to *attend* the talk, of course, if she wishes, but *I'll* be Miriam's escort for the rest of the evening. And, I mean, it's not as if Reg—Rowena is any kind of a *bodyguard*, is she? She's just a driver, but now we have a *proper* chauffeur, so Reg—Rowena can go."

Dorothy beamed at us some more. Miriam and I exchanged helpless glances.

"Ladies?" said Carl, looking at me and Miriam. "It's your call."

For a moment I was tempted to ask him to throw Dorothy out of the hotel on her ass.

"I suppose it *is* more fitting to have someone from the Dean's office walk Miriam onto the stage," I said.

Miriam nodded in mournful agreement.

"*Excellent*," said Dorothy. "Goodbye, Reg—Rowena. What did you say your name was—Carl? You go get your car. Tanika and I will walk Miriam to her room so that she can drop off her things and freshen up, and then we'll be ready to go."

I left to the sound of Carl trying with increasing impatience to explain to Dorothy that he had to be with Miriam at all times. I hurried off, feeling like a coward but leaving as fast as possible anyway.

72

I DROVE HOME FOR A check on Fevronia and a quick supper, and then headed back to campus. I felt bad about abandoning Miriam to Dorothy, but relieved at not having to deal with her. I was, though, looking forward to the talk. Miriam was a pill in person, but everything I'd heard was that she was a good writer and speaker. I could just sit back and enjoy the show without any further bother.

Even in Georgia night was coming early, now that it was December, so it was already dark as I parked and headed over to the basketball arena. My plan was to check out the security arrangements and see if I could find Brian Michaels and ask him how things were going.

I was distracted by the sound of chanting coming from the sidewalk by the arena entrance. The protesters, I guessed, refusing to take their place in the "free speech zone" in the back quad across the street.

When I came around the arena, I saw that my surmise had been correct. A group of about a dozen students, all male, were gathered near the entrance, waving signs with things like "No to Chen!" and "Yes to Free Speech!" on them. They were chanting "Free Speech! Free Speech!" in unison.

I looked around. No sign of either campus police or anyone from Security Solutions. For a moment I considered going over and confronting the protesters myself. Then I rejected the idea. They weren't going to go away just because a lone female faculty member went over and asked them to. They didn't look like they were about to carry out a terrorist attack, but there was still something about their unified chanting, and their faces distorted in anger and passion, that made them seem much more menacing than a group of teenage boys. Although teenage boys could be pretty damn menacing. Their presence here was transforming the movie-set cuteness of campus into something much scarier, as if the welcoming mask had been ripped off, revealing the dark passions below.

I started to retreat, backing up rather than turning around out of an instinctive desire not to turn my back on them.

"Hey!"

I froze. One of the protesters had broken formation and taken a couple of steps towards me.

"Hey!" he shouted again. He stepped into the pool of light from the streetlight above the arena entrance. It was, surprise surprise, Nathan.

"It's *her*!" he shouted, pointing dramatically at me, as if we were in the final drawing room/courtroom scene in a murder mystery and the detective was finally unmasking the cunning murderer. "The one who's been stalking and harassing me!"

The heads of the rest of the group whipped around in unison and stared at me. Their synchronization was eerie. There was something primal about it, like that of a hunting pack. The hair on the back of my neck stood up in response, and my body issued two simultaneous and conflicting directives: stand tall, bare my teeth, and growl; or turn tail and run.

"She's the one who's been stalking me, trying to get me in trouble—trying to get me to *betray* the rest of you!" Nathan cried, still pointing at me dramatically. "She's complaining that *I'm* the danger, when she's really the dangerous one! She's been using her position of authority to harass me while she pretends to be the victim!"

The pack, as one acne-spotted, badly-dressed, unwashed, lank-haired beast, began moving in unison in my direction. The ones with signs switched their grips on them, transforming them in an instant from political statements to weapons. As they drew closer, the light over the entrance caught their eyes, giving them a feral gleam.

I glanced at the entrance. I could probably make it to the doors before the pack could. But what if the doors were still locked? I had arrived early, with the express purpose of checking out the security. Well, I had checked it out, and found it lacking. The doors were supposed to be opened to admit guests starting at 6:30. I had arrived at 6:00. Maybe the people setting up the metal detectors and bag checks had already unlocked the doors, and maybe they hadn't. If I ran for the doors and couldn't get through them, I would be trapped between them and the pack. One-on-one, I was sure I could take any of them out in either a footrace or a hand-to-hand fight. But this would be twelve-on-one, and some of them might be carrying weapons more dangerous than their silly signs on flimsy sticks.

I started to back away, in the direction I'd come from. The pack quickened their step. Some of them, I was sure, were growling under their breath, probably not even aware of what they were doing.

Try to talk to them or not? Retreating like I was doing might only encourage them to pursue. Maybe I could talk some sense into them. Maybe trying to talk some sense into them would only enrage them further. Maybe it would put me in a better legal position if the beat-down they were determined to administer was going to be inevitable anyway.

"I'm not here to bother you," I said, holding up my hands. "I'm just going to go on my way, and you can too."

"She's lying!" shouted Nathan. "She's trying to trick us!"

The growl from the rest of the pack deepened in tone. "Get her!" one of the boys shouted. "Let's show her not to mess with *us!* We have to stand up for ourselves!"

There was a soft clanking from inside the arena, and the doors swung open.

"What the hell is going on?" a loud and angry male voice demanded.

73

THE PACK SWUNG THEIR attention from me to the voice. Their steps faltered. Brian Michaels stepped out of the building, followed by two more equally large men, also in police uniforms, and a couple of very fit-looking men in Security Solutions uniforms.

"Nathan Willoughby!" said Brian Michaels. "I done *tole* you to stay away from here!"

"You can't stop us from holding a legal protest!" said Nathan. "It's our First Amendment right!" He tried to say it defiantly, but his voice cracked halfway through. Behind him, the pack began to break up, transforming back into a bunch of awkward teenage boys, shuffling their feet and looking at the ground.

"Which is why you got the 'free speech zone,'" Brian Michaels said. "You can protest your little hearts out there. But you were specifically told to stay away from the entrance to the basketball arena!"

"You can't deny us our First Amendment rights! And...and besides, the real problem is *her*!" Nathan pointed dramatically at me again. "She's been harassing and stalking me! *Threatening* me! *She's* the one you should be going after!"

Brian Michaels turned and looked at me consideringly. "Rowena Halley?" he asked. "John Halley's little sister?"

"Uh-huh," I said.

"Thought so. You look just like him, though a far sight prettier, if you don't mind me sayin'." He winked at me. "You been stalkin' and harassin' these boys, Doctor Halley?"

"Well," I said. "I did have a couple of meetings with Nathan, and try to set up a couple more, to try to convince him to give us the names of the people making the threats against Miriam Chen. And I did point out to Nathan the potential consequences of his actions. But telling someone that something bad might happen if they do something stupid is different from a threat, I'd say."

"Yeah," said Brian Michaels. "That's what I figured. Well, boys." He turned to look back at Nathan. "It's my lucky day. I've been waitin' for you to do something that would allow me to arrest you, and you've finally gone and obliged me. The way I see it, you boys were disturbin' the peace, *and* threatenin' an unarmed bystander. With weapons." He reached over and took one of the signs out of its holder's suddenly nerveless grip. "These little things might look pathetic, but they're still dangerous enough in the wrong hands," he said. "So I think I need to arrest you before you go and do somethin' *really* stupid. And I think we need to do a search of your rooms. Wonder what we'll find?"

He grinned. The boys shuffled their feet even more nervously than before.

"You can't do that!" cried Nathan.

With surprising quickness for such a big man, Brian Michaels . whipped out his cuffs and snapped them onto Nathan's wrists before Nathan had time to react.

"I think you'll find I can, son," Brian Michaels said.

74

ARRESTING ALL TWELVE of the boys and disposing of them took quite a while. Since the entire campus police force consisted of Brian Michaels and two deputies, they were stretched thin dealing with twelve miscreants. The men from Security Solutions called in for reinforcements, and once they arrived the boys were all put in the kind of hand-and-leg shackles you see dangerous prisoners being transported in on TV, packed into black SUVs with big SSs (I wondered how intentional that was) stenciled on them, and driven off to the Greenfields police station.

By then there was a large crowd milling around the entrance, staring at the proceedings with undisguised curiosity and demanding to know what was going on and when they would be allowed to get in.

"I guess we better start lettin' these folks in," said Brian Michaels. "I've let the town boys know what's going on, and they're gonna process our little hellraisers and hold 'em overnight, or until we figure out what to do with 'em. 'Course, I'm sure some of 'em have rich mommies and daddies who're gonna call in a bunch of bigshot lawyers who'll get 'em out by first thing tomorrow mornin'. But I've said they can't be released until we search their rooms, and we can't do that till we get everyone safely through the talk. We just arrested one bunch o' troublemakers, but that don't mean there won't be more. You wanna go in first? You're gonna have to come down to the

346

station and give a statement, but you're gonna have to hold off till they get all those boys processed and locked up, so you might as well go enjoy this talk that you worked so hard to organize."

"Um," I said. "Okay." So I led the way through the metal detectors and bag search, and onto the floor of the basketball arena, which had been transformed into what looked like a political rally, with a stage for the speaker, and folding chairs in rows on the floor.

Turnout was so high that the folding chairs all filled up in minutes. People were still filing in and finding seats in the bleachers when, at 7:15, Brian Michaels came over and said that Dorothy was demanding that we get started because she couldn't wait around all evening.

"Thought I'd run that by you first, though," he said. "Seein' as how this is really your event, even though looks like they kicked you out o' it at the last minute."

"That's okay," I said. "And maybe give it another five or ten minutes, until things slow down a bit at the entrances, and then go ahead and start the introductions? I think they might take a while."

"If Dorothy's doing 'em, you bet it will," said Brian Michaels, and went off to give the orders.

Dorothy only waited three minutes before bustling herself, Miriam, and Tanika Scott onto the stage. But she spent so long introducing herself and talking about why we were all here, and forcing Tanika to talk about diversity and inclusion on the Crimson campus, that by the time Miriam herself actually stepped up to the microphone, the influx of attendees had slowed almost to a halt.

"Hello," said Miriam hesitantly. I clenched all over. What if there really were an assassination attempt planned on her, and the protest outside had just been a diversion? Or—and this seemed the most likely disaster scenario—what if, after all this time and trouble, it turned out that Miriam was just plain bad?

I scanned the crowd for would-be shooters. Nothing. No one had any yard-long packages that they were unwrapping to reveal a sniper rifle. No one was moving stealthily through the crowd, trying to get close to the stage in order to shoot Miriam at point-blank range with a homemade pistol. The only thing that was happening was that the crowd was smiling and laughing.

Because Miriam was good. She was, just as promised, a brilliant public speaker. All that self-centered neuroticism was melting away under the spotlights and the audience's gaze, and she was talking, with humor and passion, about why she'd decided to speak out against sexism in gaming, and why we, too, should care about it. She even managed to work in a few gentle self-deprecating jokes about her recent weight gain.

"You look beautiful to me, Miriam!" several people shouted from the bleachers.

"Yeah, Miriam, we love you no matter how you look—but you look great!" more people shouted from the opposite side of the stadium.

"Thanks. Thank you. I'm, uh...I'm actually choking up now," said Miriam. She stopped for a moment and wiped her face. "I, uh...um..."

"Don't you worry, honey!" people were shouting from the audience. "You take all the time you need!"

Miriam's heavy shoulders started to shake. *Oh God,* I thought. *She's about to have a public breakdown.*

"It might look like I'm sobbing," she said, her voice thick. "And I am. But I'm also laughing. Because I was so afraid to come here, but instead of all the terrible things I was imagining, you're all being so kind to me. Which reminds me of all the good things about gaming that got me into it in the first place." Her voice was sounding stronger and clearer. "You know, people make fun of us for not 'living in the real world,'" she said. "We're 'just playing games.' But games are how we all learn how to deal with the 'real world.' Without games, there would be no 'real world.' Games both express our conception of the 'real world,' and shape it. And so yes, games and gaming can be ugly, cruel, corrupt—all those things. But it can also be a space—a space of 'pure imagination,' to quote one of my favorite movies when I was a kid—where we can try to change how we do things, where we can learn to be better people than we can in the 'real world.' Games can be a space for us to imagine what kind of society we want to live in, and then work to build that society, first in imagination, then in reality. And that, everyone, is why I will never stop fighting for the right of girls everywhere to play."

She left the stage in tears, to a standing ovation. There was not a gunman in sight.

75

DOROTHY, BASKING IN the success of Miriam's talk, insisted that she should be the one to take her to the airport the next morning. Sandra and I agreed. In a separate email, Sandra warned me that "this is how Dorothy is. Always taking credit for other people's good deeds."

I said that I'd noticed, but as long as Miriam wasn't too upset by the change in plans, it wasn't worth fighting over. Miriam told me when I emailed her about it that she was grateful for everything I'd done to organize the talk and help her out, but that Dorothy seemed like a really interesting person who'd had a lot of good advice for her, and she was looking forward to the opportunity to talk to her more on the ride back to the airport.

I thought about telling Miriam she was sadly mistaken in Dorothy's character. Then I decided there was no point. If Dorothy had managed to be helpful and charming for the single evening she had spent with Miriam, and could make an entire 90-minute drive to the airport without blowing it, then that was all to the good. Let Miriam leave with happy memories of Crimson.

My classes were buzzing with the news of the arrest of twelve Crimson students. Arguments kept breaking out over the ethics and legality of the move.

"If they were the ones making those disgusting posts, then they deserve to be arrested!" Miranda said hotly during the first class.

"There's no law against making blog posts. Freedom of speech, y'all," mumbled Chris into the table. Even though he hadn't been one of the boys arrested, he was looking even more bedraggled than usual, and his eyes were puffy and had dark circles under them.

"Yeah, but did you read what they wrote? It was absolutely disgusting!"

"Yeah, but..."

"What they wrote was disgusting, but it probably only became illegal when they started making direct threats against Miriam Chen—and me," I said, breaking up the incipient argument. "And yeah, I get it. It's a tricky situation. One I've been on both sides of now. In Russia I've seen freedom of speech curtailed, and people engaged in peaceful political activism jailed, in the name of 'keeping the peace.' Here I've been threatened and almost attacked in the name of 'free speech.'"

"Almost attacked!" exclaimed several of the students together.

I gave them a short description of the confrontation in front of the basketball arena the night before.

"And they didn't actually hurt me, but they were definitely about to," I finished. "If they hadn't been arrested then, they probably would have done something really bad. Doing something really bad is surprisingly easy, when you're in a big mob. Now, shall we get back to our review of case endings?"

Afterwards, Miranda asked if she could interview me about the incident.

"I've already gotten dibs on doing a big piece on it for the paper," she said. "An eyewitness account would be great!"

"Sure," I said. "But first I have to go give an official statement to Chief Michaels."

"Oh wow! I'm hoping to get an interview with him too."

"I'll put in a good word for you," I promised her.

Brian Michaels had asked me to come by in the afternoon. A very tired-looking deputy, who introduced himself as Officer O'Hare, took my statement. Then when I was done, he told me that Chief Michaels wanted to talk to me.

When I came into his office, Brian Michaels was sitting behind his desk, looking at a laptop that he had perched awkwardly in front of the desktop computer. "Come on in, have a seat." He rubbed his eyes, which were red and bruised. Looked like no one had been getting much sleep recently.

"You want anythin'?" he asked. "Coffee? I'm tryin' to decide whether to have that tenth cup. I'm gettin' too old to be pullin' all-nighters these days."

"I'm good," I said. "But you go ahead."

He thought about it, then shook his head. "Nah," he said. "My heart can't take it like it used to. Back in the day I could drink it from a firehose, and it only did me good. Now I start gettin' palpitations after cup five. Gettin' old is BS."

"That's what I hear," I said.

"Yeah. But that's not what I called you here for. I thought you'd like to know what we found when we raided the boys' rooms."

"I take it you found something good?" I said.

"Well, of course we found a ton o' bootleg hooch, a bunch o' grass, and some baggies of white stuff we're sending away for analysis to see if they're coke like we think they are. Some o' those boys are gonna get in a world o' trouble for possession with intent to deal, and the rest are goin' down for underage drinking."

"Do you really think they're drug dealers?" I asked.

Brian Michaels shrugged. "Depends on what you mean by 'dealers.' They're not out cruisin' the playgrounds of Atlanta, lookin' to get preschoolers hooked on crack, if that's what you mean. But some of 'em had way more than what they could go through on their own li'l selves. So yeah, they were probably doin' a little dealin' on the side. Half the kids here do. Hell, *you* probably did when you were in school."

"Low-level drug dealing wasn't really my style," I said. "Instead I ran away to Russia and worked to bring down the government. Well, according to the government, that is."

He smiled and rubbed his face. "Yeah. Sounds 'bout right, from everythin' I've heard from your brother. I'd wish my own boy could be a little more like you, but maybe not. Anyway. That's not what I brought you here to see. Scoot your chair over here and have a look at this."

I rolled my chair around the desk so that I was sitting next to him. He angled the laptop, which was covered with the kind of stickers that college students liked to festoon all over their computers, so that we could both see it.

"Take a look at that," he said.

He had an internet browser up, and was showing its history. It showed multiple visits to the MPA website, plus several more sites that, judging by the names, were other incel gathering places and manifestos.

"Some of this is real sick shit," said Brian. "I've been readin' through it, but I ain't gonna show it to you. 'Less you wanna see it."

"That's okay," I said. "I can imagine. Is this Nathan's computer?"

Brian shook his head. "No, although our boy Nathan's computer ain't that different. This belongs to some kid named Haley Parker. If he wasn't such a little shit, I'd half feel sorry for him, since Haley sure sounds like a girl's name. Bet he got teased half to death when he was a kid."

"Hence the need to lash out at women, I suppose," I said.

"Yeah. Like I said, I'd feel sorry for him, except he's a little creep. I'm not the most tech-savvy guy out there, but I know a few things, and I've been pokin' around, goin' onto these sites with his profile. Guess who sent Miriam some inappropriate emails, and then when she told him where to get off, started makin' threats against her—and you?"

"Haley Parker?" I guessed. "Who went by Nottagirl?"

"Got it in one. But that's not the best part."

"What's the best part?" I asked.

"Our good friend Haley here also kept a diary on his computer. You know, pourin' out all his thoughts and feelins' to the one person who'd really understand him—himself." Brian gave me a sideways look. "Is it just me, or are these boys sure actin' girly? Talkin' 'bout their feelins' and gettin' together for little parties and keepin' diaries and all?"

"It's not just you," I said.

"Yeah, thought so. So anyway, our pal Haley here's been keepin' a little journal o' his innermost thoughts and feelins', and it sounds like he *was* plannin' on maybe doin' somethin'. Sounds like he had a huge crush on Miriam Chen, and when it turned sour, he wanted to get his revenge on her. Only we arrested him, and Miriam's already been and gone."

"Wow," I said. "Did you find any weapons or anything in his room?"

Brian shook his head. "Nope. Looks like he didn't get that far in his plannin'. You ask me, he's not the mastermind he thinks he is. Couldn't even get his hands on a shotgun."

"Well," I said. "That's a good thing. What do you think is going to happen to him? And the others?"

Brian shrugged. "Best guess? The ones with the drugs'll get the book thrown at 'em. The rest'll get citations for disturbin' the peace, pay a slap-on-the-wrist fine, and walk free. Includin' Haley here. He was clean. No drugs or alcohol, just death threats, and we don't do much about death threats. And Nathan Willoughby's already been sprung. His momma had the fanciest lawyer this side o' DC down at the courthouse at eight o'clock this mornin', arguin' that her little boy was the victim, not the perp, of a terrible crime. They're already threatenin' to sue us. There was even talk o' suin' you for harassment and stalkin.'"

"Um..." I said. "Do you think they have a case?"

He shrugged. "I wouldn't worry 'bout it too much, I was you. It's pure BS, and you and I both know that, and so would any reasonable judge. But they gotta play the victim card to the hilt, try and get him to come outta this smellin' o' roses 'stead o' shit."

"I'm afraid that's what we're all going to end up smelling like," I said.

"Yeah," said Brian. "Well, I'll let you go now, but I thought you'd wanna know. And I'll let you know if anythin' else comes up. And if Nathan gives you too much shit, you let *me* know, okay?"

"Sure," I said.

"Now, if only these computers'd tell me who the Gang o' Six is," said Brian, rubbing his tired eyes. "I've been lookin', and there are some private messages between some o' the guys about the 'Sixer,' but they never say who it is. Sounds like there was someone hangin' out with 'em sometimes who had somethin' to do with the Gang o' Six, but it wasn't anyone in the inner circle. Not that the Gang o' Six's done anythin' illegal, but I got deans ridin' my ass, demandin' to know who they are. I'd love to be able to get rid of 'em all in one blow."

"Well, I'll keep my eyes open," I said. "Oh, and by the way, my student Miranda is doing a feature about the case for the *Champion*. She's hoping to be able to interview you."

"Well, tell her to come around," said Brian. "Not tonight, but in a day or two. We'll give her some good sound bites, let everyone know what we think 'bout students who go around makin' threats and causin' trouble."

"Will do," I said. "Meanwhile, get some rest."

"Thanks," said Brian, and went back to staring at the laptop.

76

FRIDAY WAS THE LAST day of classes. Mel came and picked me up that morning at 8:20, looking cheerful.

"Finally got the last of the results from all those tests back," she said. "Everything normal. No sign of leukemia in the blood draw, and the CAT scan showed no tumors or anything like that. They said I could do an MRI if I wanted to, but insurance wouldn't cover it, and it'll cost at least a thousand dollars."

"Wow, that's a lot," I said. "But it's good that they don't think it's leukemia or a brain tumor. How do you feel?"

She shrugged, looking less cheerful. "Not great, actually. I really thought I was coming down with the flu after Thanksgiving, but it turned into nothing. But I still feel sort of like I've got this nagging flu that I can't kick, and my knees and hands and neck hurt all the time and keep popping and making funny noises, and that twitch in my eye keeps coming back. I'm hoping it'll go away over break."

"Yeah," I said. "You might want to get it checked out with the VA even so. Maybe they'll spring for the MRI. Especially since you had that concussion."

"Yeah. Maybe. But right now I just want to be happy about not having leukemia or some shit like that. It feels like a monster was creeping out from under the bed, but I fought it off. Maybe it'll come out again later, but right now I'm going to focus on getting through the last day of class and then finals. That's enough for one week."

"Yeah," I said.

When I walked into Bedford Hall, Miranda, Chris, Nathan, and Taylor were all standing in a knot in front of my classroom. An unhappy, confrontational knot.

"You're both just a couple of teasing sluts!" Nathan was saying, jabbing his finger at Taylor and then Miranda. "You both led me on! Just to dump me and make fun of me!"

"I never led you on," Miranda said sharply. "I just had lunch with you a couple of times. You led yourself on."

"I...I never meant to lead you on," said Taylor. Her lips were quivering like she was about to cry. "I didn't...I didn't know that's what you wanted. I thought you just wanted to be my friend!"

"Yeah." Nathan snorted. "Like who's gonna want to be *your* friend? The only reason any guy'd ever have anything to do with a stupid Stacy like you is to get in your pants."

"That's not...that's not true!" Taylor's whole face was now screwed up in a pre-sobbing spasm. She turned towards Chris. "It's not true, is it?" she asked him, her voice full of naked appeal. "*You* wanted to be my friend, didn't you?"

He shuffled from foot to foot. "I dunno," he said, looking at the floor. "I...it was like Nathan said. You're just...you're just so goddam hot!" he burst out. "I can't think about anything else when I'm around you! Face it, Taylor: no guy is ever gonna want to be your friend. You're just too painful to be around."

"But that's...that's just not *fair*," wailed Taylor. "That's not *my* fault!"

"Yeah, it is," said Nathan. "You know what you're doing and you do it on purpose."

Chris nodded in silent agreement.

"Well...well...in that case..." Taylor furiously scrubbed the tears from her face, and gave them both hard stares. "In that case I don't ever want to have anything to do with you, ever again! I wanted to be your friend, Chris, I really did, but now you're just as bad as *him*!" She nodded towards Nathan. "Worse, actually, because you were nice at first. It's like getting stabbed in the back by someone I thought I could trust!" She spun around on her heel and marched out of Bedford Hall, angrily brushing tears away as she went.

"That was a dick move, Chris," said Miranda. "I didn't expect any better from Nathan here, but I thought *you* had a little more class. Guess you're the same as all the other assholes, though."

"And you're a slut, just like all the others!" Chris spat out. "You *did* lead Nathan on, I know you did!"

She shrugged. "Like I said, it was just lunch a couple of times. For the story. How was I to know that a misogynistic little creep like him would even be interested?"

"You flirted with me! You know you did!" said Nathan.

"Weren't you the one who said journalistic integrity was more important than anything else?" demanded Miranda. "I was chasing a story."

"That's different!"

"What's sauce for the goose is sauce for the gander," said Miranda. "Oh, hi, Professor." She brushed past Chris and into the classroom, her head held high.

Chris gave me an uncertain look. Nathan gave me a look of deep loathing. I raised my eyebrows at both of them. Chris, his eyes fixed firmly on the ground, bolted and fled out the front of Bedford Hall.

"Yeah, you run on out of here!" Nathan yelled after him. "Like the little lost boy you say you are!" He turned back to me. "Proud of yourself?" he demanded. "I spent the night in jail, and a bunch of my friends are still there, and it's all your fault!"

I thought of a lot of responses to that. Since I was pretty angry myself by then, what came out was, "Real men take responsibility for their actions."

Nathan's mouth fell open. Then he snapped it shut, but just a little too late to pretend it hadn't happened. "Yeah, well...you're just a bitch!" he muttered, and turned and fled too, almost knocking down Chloe, who was coming over from where she'd been standing on the other side of the seating area.

"Looks like we might not have a lot of students for our last class of the semester," I said.

"Yeah." She shook her head. "That Taylor! I said she was trouble, didn't I? At least someone finally put her in her place."

"Um," I said. "I have to go teach." I retreated into the classroom before I could give her a piece of my mind, too.

I incautiously looked up at the ceiling light as I stepped into the room, triggering an instant visual migraine. So instead of lecturing I had the students—the few that had shown up—write practice sentences on the board.

"And don't forget!" I said, as the class dispersed. "The final exam is eight o'clock Monday morning. Be there or be square. I've posted review materials on Sakai; don't hesitate to email me with any questions."

"If we're still *alive* then," moaned Camden. "I've got so much studying to do between now and then, I don't know how I'm gonna make it."

"You'll make it," I said. "Remember to take breaks and get plenty of rest. All-nighters are counterproductive."

Camden and the others gave me skeptical looks. All-nighters, I knew, were the favored study style of many students because they gave the illusion of dedicated test prep, without almost any actual learning taking place.

Miranda hung back after the others had left. "I wanted to thank you," she said. "For, you know, putting in a good word with Chief Michaels for me. He gave me a really long interview yesterday afternoon. Said he was happy to do it. I think he's pretty pissed about the whole thing."

"Yeah," I said. "I got that impression too."

"And, you know...I don't know...I *do* feel kinda bad about what I did to Nathan," she burst out. "I mean, I never promised to sleep with him or anything like that. We really did just have lunch a few times. But I guess I was a little nicer to him than I would have been if I hadn't wanted to get something from him. I guess that *was* kinda slutty, huh?"

"Calculating, not slutty," I said. "And welcome to being a journalist—or a lot of other things. There's a lot of being nice to people you wouldn't otherwise be nice to in a lot of professions. And like you said, Nathan led himself on."

"I know. And you know, I went into it thinking that maybe he really was just misunderstood, and we could be friends once we got to know each other. I was actually kinda hoping that would be the case, you know what I mean? Like I'd find out he really wasn't that bad, and he'd find out that he could be friends with a girl.

"But the more I got to know him, the less I liked him. I feel kinda sorry for him, though. You know, his mom arranged to get him out of jail right away, paid a ton of money to a really fancy lawyer, and all he'll talk about is how his dad is gonna come help him out real soon. Only from I've gathered, his dad hasn't come help him out for a good fifteen years. But that's all Nathan thinks about. How much he wants his dad to, you know, act like a dad, and how much he wants girls to be nice to him and, you know, sleep with him. Only he's a complete pain in the neck. Most girls aren't gonna want to have anything to do with him, and probably his dad too."

"Yeah," I said. "Poor Nathan. But like I said to him, real men take responsibility for their actions—and real women do, too."

"Yeah. So does that mean I should take responsibility for leading Nathan on?"

"Like you said, he led himself on," I repeated. "But you could take responsibility for being the agent of hurt feelings, even if inadvertently. Deceiving people, even if you don't mean to, can be very hurtful."

"Yeah, well...that's a part of getting a story I'm not so sure I like."

"Yeah," I said.

"Although it kinda worked, so I can see why people do it. I mean, I got all kinds of deep background from Nathan that he never would have given me otherwise. Now if only I could use it to find out more about the Gang of Six. I *still* don't know who's behind it, dammit."

"Maybe Nathan knows," I said. "According to Chief Michaels, the MPA kids knew someone from the Gang of Six. We just don't know who it is, and he doesn't really care, since the Gang of Six hasn't done anything illegal."

"Yeah," said Miranda. "Well, maybe I'll try to make up with Nathan. If he knows something and he'll tell me, it would be worth it."

"Good luck," I said.

77

I SPENT SATURDAY BASKING in the glorious realization that I only had two final exams next week, and no classes. Well, I basked for about half an hour, and then I got back to work on my next round of job applications. Several were due December 15th and December 31st. This seemed silly, since who was going to review job applications over the holidays? Overworked faculty who didn't have a life and were desperate for tenure, that's who.

Sunday morning I was greeted with an email from Miranda.

OMG you have to read the new Go6 post!

I opened up the Gang of Six website. A red headline screamed at me:

THIS IS THE END!

For the past year we have worked tirelessly to shed light on the injustices of Crimson College. We got some momentum going earlier this semester especially once new members joined and started writing more but now things have stalled out again or even gone backward.

Worse than that we have learned that injustice is committed not just by organizations like the college but by individuals including individuals we counted as friends. We don't want to talk about personal betrayals but they HURT! Even worse than institutional betrayals.

But we do want to talk about institutional betrayals like the arrest of members of the Men's Protection Alliance last week. Regular readers will know that we didn't support the agenda of the MPA but we DID support their right to free speech and express their opinions. Last week they were ARRESTED while carrying out a peaceful protest as guaranteed by the First Amendment. It turns out a lot of what the MPA was saying about harassment and oppression was TRUE!

THAT WAS THE LAST STRAW! How can we have any faith in an institution that blatantly violates First Amendment rights? How can we have any faith in friends that turn their backs on us as soon as trouble happens?

WE CAN'T! IN PROTEST WE WILL NOT BE TAKING FINAL EXAMS AND NEITHER WILL THE BETRAYERS!

We always posted these things anonymously but this time we're going to sign off on this ourselves. This post was by LostAndFoundBoy, you might recognize me as a prolific commenter on both the Go6 and MPA blogs.

LostAndFoundBoy

I was just sending the link to Brian Michaels to see what he thought when I got an outraged email from Karen.

Rowena, why are we *still* getting posts like this from the Gang of Six? I thought I told you to take care of this! But now they're making threats! At least now they *have* to arrest Miranda.

I've already forwarded this to Chief Michaels, I wrote back. *But I don't know that there's anything actionable about the post. Any threat there is pretty vague and veiled. And it seems pretty likely that this particular post was written by a boy, since it was signed off by LostandFoundBoy.*

Karen sent back an email saying that Miranda was cunning and was probably hiding behind a masculine-looking username to throw us off the scent. I said I was going to leave it up to Brian, since campus security was his business, not mine. Karen told me I was being irresponsible and not showing the right attitude and Crimson spirit.

By this time Brian Michaels had gotten back to me to say that he'd had a look at it and couldn't decide if it was a threat or not, so he was tossing it in the lap of the senior administration to decide what they wanted to do about it. I forwarded that email to Karen to let her know that things were being taken care of, and told myself I was done with the matter.

Despite my intention not to worry about it anymore, I found myself going through old posts on both the Gang of Six and MPA websites, reading the comments from LostAndFoundBoy to try to piece together some kind of a profile for him. All I could make out about him, though, was that he had started posting about six weeks into the current semester, and that his comments were mostly low-key complaints. He'd called the other MPA commenters to task more than once when they'd made particularly offensive comments or threats, but he'd also defended the MPA from its detractors on the Gang of Six website. I wanted him to be Nathan, but that didn't really seem like Nathan's style.

After an hour of that, I decided I was wasting my time. It was probably just some kid mouthing off, right? Who cared who LostAndFoundBoy was, anyway? Probably nothing would come of it, or if it did, a few kids would boycott their finals and we would find out who the Gang of Six was. Which would satisfy our curiosity, at least, although I would be sad to see them unmasked and, most likely, muzzled.

78

SUNDAY EVENING THE Dean's office issued a statement saying that a blog post of a potentially threatening nature, which indicated the possibility of a disruption to final exams, had been brought to their attention, but they had decided to hold finals anyway. However, extra security would be on hand during finals week, and everyone was exhorted to be vigilant and notify campus police of anything suspicious.

Mel and I were both silent and grim as we carpooled over to campus at 7:30am. Not because we were particularly apprehensive that something bad might happen, but because 8:00am finals were never any fun. They involved dragging in early in the morning, and then hunting down the students who inevitably slept through their alarms or had other catastrophes that always seemed to happen twice as often for the 8:00am slot as for the midday and afternoon exam periods.

Miranda was already waiting at the classroom door when I showed up at 7:45. Another strike against Karen's insistence that Miranda was the mastermind behind the Gang of Six.

"You ready for the test?" I asked her as I let us into the classroom.

She yawned. "Not really. I feel like shit, honestly."

"Too much studying for finals?"

"Yeah. And also..." She looked around. No one else had shown up yet. "I had a big fight with Chris this weekend. About all the shitty things he said to Taylor. I mean, I don't even like Taylor that much, but he shouldn't have said that, should he? She was really upset about it. And then..." She looked around again. Still no one else there. She lowered her voice to a stage whisper even so. "Then he said he was, like, you know, in love with *me*."

"I'm not surprised," I said.

"Yeah, but he seemed really into Taylor!"

"I know," I said. "But it's not unheard of for someone to be in love with two people at once."

"Yeah. I guess. And I felt, like, really bad for him, but I told him I just wasn't interested in him that way, and he started accusing me of dropping him for Nathan, which is, like, totally untrue. But now they're both convinced that Taylor and I both, like, played them and are like, laughing about it or something. They both told me separately it must be, like, a plot between us. Taylor and I don't even talk! I didn't even know who she was until Chris introduced us last month."

"That sounds messy," I said.

"Yeah. And I think..."

Whatever Miranda thought was interrupted by the arrival of Camden, followed by the rest of the class. By 8:02 everyone was assembled except for Chris.

"Let's go ahead and get started," I said. "Any latecomers can join us when they get here."

By the time I had explained all the sections of the exam and read through the listening comprehension questions, it was 8:20, and Chris still wasn't there.

I opened up my Crimsonmail and tried to compose an email to him. Crimsonmail had a feature that allowed you to start typing a person's name or email address into the "to" field and it would autofill the rest. But I couldn't get Chris's name to come up. Typing in "Chris" or "Christopher" brought up a dozen other Christophers and Christines, but not Christopher Atherstone. Frustrating, and it also showed how little I'd emailed Chris. I felt a pang of guilt over ignoring him for a solid sixteen weeks.

"Does anyone know Chris's email address?" I asked the class. I could go into my course roster and look it up, but that was a multi-step process that I was hoping to skip.

"It's cadarl15@crimson.edu," said Miranda.

"Thanks," I said. "I never would have guessed that."

"Yeah," she said. "He went into the system and changed his name to Atherstone, his dad's name, but his legal last name is Darling, his mom's name, and they'd already assigned his email by the time he was able to change his name."

"So..." I said. "You're saying his legal name is Christopher Darling?"

"Yeah. Christopher Anthony Darling."

I laughed, that special joy that comes from a sudden insight bubbling up inside of me until it had to overflow.

All the students stopped writing and looked up at me.

"It's nothing," I said.

"No, tell us, Professor!" said Camden. "I guess Darling's a pretty funny name, huh?"

"It's not that," I said. "It's just...sometimes it pays to be well-read."

"How so, Professor?" asked Camden.

"Oh, well...this is just a guess...but you know the Gang of Six? You know their latest post?"

Everyone nodded.

"Well, I just started wondering if Chris is LostAndFoundBoy."

There was a lot of forehead wrinkling in response.

"The Darlings were the family that ran off with Peter Pan," I explained. "Wendy kept house for him, and her brothers became Lost Boys. And St. Christopher is the patron saint of travelers, and St. Anthony is the patron saint of lost things. You'd pray to St.

Christopher if you were lost, and St. Anthony if you wanted to find something. So Christopher Anthony Darling could be a Lost Boy who was found."

There was a moment of silence while everyone tried to work through that. Then everyone's faces split into grins.

"Day-um, Professor, that's clever," said Camden.

"I might be wrong," I said, already regretting having told them my guess.

"No, I think you're right, Professor," said Miranda. "I think Chris has been trying to hint to me for a couple of months now that he's the latest member of the Gang of Six. But I thought he was just, you know, making stuff up to show off."

"Huh," I said. "Well...maybe he's boycotting his finals, then. I'll send him an email just in case, though. The rest of you get back to your exams. Sorry for interrupting you."

"No problem, Professor," said Camden. "That was way cooler than an exam...what was that?!"

A piercing scream had come from the front of the building. Followed by what was either a jackhammer, or a burst of gunfire.

79

"*Stay here!*" I ordered the students. There were more screams coming from the building entrance. Everything had taken on that sensation of unreality again. A head that didn't feel like mine peeked out the classroom and looked down the hallway towards the front door.

A figure in a black ski mask was coming into the building. It was holding an automatic rifle in one hand, and struggling with the door with the other. I could feel hysterical laughter threaten to bubble up and spill out of me, just like the joy had a moment ago.

I pulled back into the classroom, shut the door, and stared at it in horrified befuddlement. Did it lock? There had to be a way to lock it from the inside. It was a heavy, sturdy door—except for that damn glass window in the top half. And the walls were just light plasterboard. My eyes, frantically flicking over the room, noticed all the stains from roof leaks past I had never noticed before. Rotten, falling-apart plasterboard. But still better than nothing at all.

"*Get under the table,*" I hissed at the students, who were still frozen over their exams.

"Is it an active shooter?" asked Camden. His face had gone dead white, something I'd heard of but never seen before.

"It's someone with an automatic rifle," I said. "It's *Chris* with automatic rifle, I'm sure of it. Maybe coming for us. So get under the fucking table! Why the fuck doesn't this door have a lock! Where is this door's lock!"

Screams were coming down the hall in our direction. I could track Chris's progress through the building by them. He was moving slowly but steadily in our direction. Still no gunfire. Maybe he'd spent all his ammunition in that original burst. Maybe he was saving his entire magazine for us, the final exam he'd said he was going to put a stop to.

The students started scrambling to get away from the door. *"None of the doors can be locked from the inside,"* Miranda whispered to me. *"The administration was afraid of students occupying the rooms in protest when they built the building, so they made it so classrooms can only be locked from the outside."*

"Fuck!" I hissed back.

"Maybe we should make a barricade with the table and our bookbags," whispered Camden, his eyes so big it looked like his pupils were disappearing into the whites surrounding them.

"Good thinking," I whispered.

I took hold of the doorhandle and braced myself against the doorframe, in a feeble attempt to hold the outward-opening door closed while the students got the table into position. All the hair on my body was standing on end, trying to scare off a predator that would never even see my pathetic defiance. My body felt tiny and weak and yet huge at the same time, and I wanted to crawl into one of the cracks in the wall and hide, even as I seemed to make an enormous, unmissable target. Electric shocks were running up and down my back, telling me to *run, run, run away* and leave the students as bait to slow my pursuer down.

Amber and Crystal were curled up in the corner, their arms around each other, sobbing and reciting garbled fragments of the Lord's Prayer and Psalm 23 together.

Hallowed be thy name...thou art with me...thy will be done...I will fear no evil...the valley of the shadow of death...deliver us from evil...deliver us from evil...deliver us from evil...

In the other corner, Isobel was crouched behind the rolling suitcase she used as a bookbag, whispering frantically into her phone, "Mommy? Mommy, are you there? Mommy...someone's trying to shoot us...I love you, Mommy, I love you..."

Instead of running, I dug my heels into the dirty carpet and braced myself against the doorframe harder. *Please, somebody, stop him*, I thought. I found myself fantasizing that some brave hero would jump him and knock him down and take away his gun before he got to us. Someone much bigger and stronger and smarter and braver than me would stop him before he reached us, and we would escape unscathed without ever having to confront him.

Camden, Miranda, and a hitherto unremarkable student named Jackson flipped the table on its side. I jumped over it and we pushed it up against the door.

"*Everyone come and hide behind the table*," I hissed. "*That way he won't be able to aim at you through the window.*"

The students in the corners whimpered, but crawled over and huddled together against the table.

"*The door opens outwards*," I hissed at them. "*So we have to try and hold onto the handle and brace it closed if he tries to get in. He won't be able to pull it open if we all work together to keep it closed.*"

"*What if he shoots through the door?*" whispered Isobel tearfully.

"*The table will help protect us*," I whispered back. In fact, I thought that if Chris opened fire on the door, half of us would be dead in seconds. But if he got into the room and opened fire, all of us would be dead, so I was determined to keep the door closed no matter what.

The screams had gone silent. It was quiet enough that I could hear slow footsteps approaching our door. Isobel whimpered again. Camden put one hand over her mouth, and shoved his other hand into his own mouth and bit down, probably to keep from whimpering too.

The footsteps paused outside our door. I could sense, as if I had magical extra senses, the presence of someone just a foot away, on the other side of the flimsy wall. I could sense both his own insignificant presence, and the presence of Death itself looming behind him, cloaking him in its vast power.

"Deliver us from evil," Amber whispered. *"Deliver us from evil, deliver us from evil, deliver us from evil."*

The footsteps moved on.

80

AMBER, CRYSTAL, AND Isobel burst into tears.

"*Sssssh!*" I whispered. *"He might come back!"*

"Taylor!"

Chris was shouting. It was his voice, but it wasn't. It was louder and scarier and more scared all mixed together.

"Taylor, come out right now! Or I'm coming to get you. Come out now, Taylor, and I won't hurt anyone."

"Don't do it, Taylor!"

Miranda had, with more courage than sense, stood up and shouted that. I grabbed at her shirt and tried to yank her back down behind the table, but she shook me off.

"Miranda!" I hissed. *"Don't draw his attention!"*

"And what?" she hissed back. *"Let him go after Taylor? Besides, he's at least as mad at me as he is at her. And he hasn't started shooting yet. I bet he doesn't even have any bullets."*

"I haven't forgotten what you did either, Miranda!" Chris shouted. "You come out here too!"

"Do NOT go out there!" I whisper-shouted at Miranda.

"I can't let him come in here and get me!" she whisper-shouted back. *"And the more we talk with him, the longer we have for help to arrive."*

That was true. I stood up too. "Chris!" I called. Or tried to. What came out was a kind of strangled cough. "Chris!" I tried again.

"Chris, Miranda and I are going to come out, okay? We're going to come out and talk to you, okay? So why don't you put the gun down so we can talk?"

There was a long silence.

"Okay," Chris said eventually. "I'm putting the gun down. Come out and talk."

Still feeling like this wasn't really happening, I cracked open the door and stepped over the table, almost tripping and falling flat on my face onto the floor.

When I had pulled myself upright against the door, Chris was standing in the middle of the hallway, halfway between my classroom and Chloe's. He was facing in my direction, and had the gun aimed straight at me.

"CLOSE THE DOOR!" I shouted, and slammed the door shut as hard as I could. I could feel Miranda on the other side trying to push it open.

"*Close the goddam door!*" I hissed at her. "*He's still got his gun!*"

Miranda stopped scrabbling at the door. Thank God.

Students who had been in the hallway studying or taking bathroom breaks and hadn't made it to a classroom in time had taken cover behind the benches. Nathan was kneeling behind the bench on the other side of the corridor, half-hidden from me but not nearly hidden enough from Chris. On the far end of the hallway I could see Taylor and Chloe in the doorway to Chloe's classroom. Chloe had her hand on Taylor's shoulder, like she wasn't sure whether to pull her to safety or push her out into the open. Chris started to turn in their direction.

"Why don't you put your gun down, Chris," I said.

He turned back to face me. "You can't keep me away from Miranda," he said. "I'm going to make them both listen to me!"

"Okay," I said. "I'm sure we'd all be happy to talk. Especially if you put the gun down."

He whirled around, aiming the gun at Taylor and Chloe. "Come out here!" he ordered. "Come out where I can talk to you!"

Taylor, with Chloe half-pushing her, half-holding her up, stumbled out into the hallway. Chris raised up his gun.

"HEY ASSHOLE!"

Chris's head whipped around. Chloe wavered, indecision written on her face as plain as day. Then her expression firmed. She jerked Taylor back into the classroom. As the door closed behind them, I could see her pushing Taylor to the floor and throwing herself on top of her, covering her with her own body.

"WHAT ARE YOU LOOKING AT? YOU LOOK AT ME WHEN I'M TALKING TO YOU!"

Mel had come out of her classroom and was shouting at Chris at the top of her lungs. Chris looked at her, and then back at where Taylor and Chloe had disappeared into Chloe's classroom.

"DON'T!" I screamed, just as his finger tightened on the trigger.

81

MEL WAS LYING ON TOP of me. She had thrown herself onto me so fast it was as if the transition from us standing side-by-side to her lying on top of me had never happened.

"You okay?" she whispered in my ear.

I nodded with as tiny a movement as I could make.

"I'm going to try to draw his fire."

I shook my head, trying to indicate vigorous disagreement without making any obvious movements.

"I have to, Rowena. We can't take him down. No one's coming to save us, at least not in time. But if I draw his fire, maybe you can crawl into one of the classrooms and pull the door shut behind you. Stay low and stay moving, understand? As soon as I roll off you, you roll as fast as you can towards the door, and slide through it and close it and get under a desk, and...*he's coming.*"

The shots had stopped. Instead there were footsteps, coming our way, which was a hundred times worse. And funny clicking noises, like metal being banged against metal.

"He's trying to change his clip," Mel whispered to me. "*This is it.* Hey! HEY ASSHOLE!" Her weight suddenly lifted off me. "HEY ASSHOLE! OVER HERE!"

I knew I should do what she had told me and crawl for the door like a startled lizard bolting for safety. But I couldn't make myself move. I couldn't make myself leave her. Fear or protectiveness, I couldn't tell, but I couldn't leave her side. I looked up.

Chris was standing there in front of us, fiddling awkwardly with his automatic rifle, trying to get the clip in and failing. He must not have practiced enough beforehand, believing the reality would be as fun and easy as it was in his imagination. Or maybe he was more upset than he thought he would be.

"Chris," I said softly. He looked up from his gun. His eyes looked scared and confused and angry and scared and exultant and scared all in one.

"Chris," I said again softly. I sat up a bit more and raised my hands, showing him my empty palms. "Chris, why don't you put down the gun."

He shook his head furiously, then stopped and grabbed at his ear. His new earring must have caught on his ski mask. He pawed at it for a moment before giving up and focusing on reloading. His shoulders jerked, and the magazine made an ominous *click*. Mel, who was still standing by my side, grabbed me by the shoulder and heaved me behind her.

There was another click. Both Mel and Chris cried out in fury and fear. I didn't want to look up, but I did. No blood. Chris was staring at his gun with a puzzled expression.

Misfire. Misfire. He must have loaded it wrong.

"Chris," I said again. "Chris, just put down the gun and let's talk."

"You're so much like her," he said. "Like Miranda. I can't bear to look at you." He threw the jammed AR-15 onto the floor. It fired as it hit the ground.

Get him away from the gun. He doesn't have the gun anymore. Oh thank God, he doesn't have the gun anymore. "Thank you for putting down the gun," I said. "That was really good of you, Chris. Now let's just...let's just talk, okay?" I put my hands over my head again. "I'm not going to try anything. I just want to talk to you. I know you're going through a hard time. You can tell me about it. You can tell me anything."

"That's what *she* said. She told me I could tell her anything. She told me she was my friend. I thought she loved me." Chris reached into the pocket of his camouflage jacket. An electric shock of terror burst through my chest before I even consciously registered what he was pulling out.

It's a semi-automatic. I was thinking more clearly than I had when I had taken my doctoral exams, or defended my dissertation, or any moment in my life when I hadn't had a gun pointed at me. *Maybe it will jam too.*

He pointed it at me. "You're just like her," he repeated. "I loved her so much, and she threw me away! And you're just like her! Only older! You could be her mom!"

"I know," I said. The barrel of the handgun seemed like such a small thing. You read about how gun barrels are supposed to look enormously big, swallowing up your whole world, when they're pointed at you, but this time, just like last time, the gun barrel pointed at me seemed much too tiny to do serious damage. Something that small and mundane shouldn't be able to kill. But it could. And a fraction of a second from now, it might kill me.

"All I wanted was for her to love me," he said, in a small little-lost-boy voice. "But she laughed in my face."

"Hey ASSHOLE!" Mel's foot flashed out and caught Chris's leg, making him stumble and fall to one knee.

He gave her a look of hurt confusion. Then he lifted up the handgun, his finger moving for the trigger.

"NO!" Mel and I both screamed. He paused. Mel kicked him hard in the leg again. He groaned. Hurt filled his eyes, the only part of his face I could see through the black ski mask.

"All I wanted was for her to love me," he said. "But she wouldn't. *You* ruined that." He paused for thought. "And Nathan," he added.

"Let's just leave Nathan out of this," I said. "Let's not worry about Nathan. Why don't you put that gun down like you did the other one, and we can talk about it."

"NO!" He shook his head angrily. "Where's Nathan? I saw him here earlier, I'm sure of it."

A whimper came from the bench behind him. Chris turned around and caught sight of Nathan.

"You!" said Chris. "You said you were my friend too, and look what you did."

"I never...I never did nothing, man."

Chris strode over and jerked Nathan to his feet by the collar. "I think you're the real problem," he said to Nathan. "You kept blaming everything on the girls, but the real snake in the grass was always you!"

"Hey man...hey man, it wasn't me..."

Chris raised the gun and pointed it at Nathan. Nathan, with the desperation of a cornered animal, grabbed at the gun. They both wrestled for it, grunting and swearing and crying like two little boys in a play-fight. Until the gun went off four times in rapid succession.

82

THE FIRST RESPONDERS showed up as people started creeping warily out of their classrooms. Mel and I were on the floor, trying to stanch the blood that was pouring from Nathan and Chris's bodies. She had Nathan, and I had Chris. So much blood was pouring out of his chest that I would have said he must have long since died, but the blood kept coming, which meant he was still alive.

"I can't feel my legs," Nathan was whispering urgently to Mel. "I can't feel my legs!"

"Don't move," she told him. "Help is coming real fast. Just stay still till they get here."

Campus police showed up first, followed by EMTs, and then the town police. Mel and I were checked out quickly and then pushed out of the way while they worked frantically over Chris and Nathan to stabilize them and secure them before loading them up in ambulances and taking them away.

Campus was put on lockdown for the rest of the day, and exams were cancelled for the rest of the week. Mel and I gave brief statements to the police, and were told we could go home, but that they would want more in-depth statements later. I told Brian Michaels what I had guessed about Chris being LostandFoundBoy. He nodded tightly and said he'd look into it after they searched his room.

By the afternoon, the media had gotten wind of what had happened, and descended on Greenfields. I messaged my parents, grandparents, John, Alex, and—after some hesitation—Dima to let them know what had happened and that I was okay.

My family and Alex all responded to say that it was horrible but they were glad I was okay. Dima only got back to me the next morning.

What is wrong with you, Inna? Why do you get into these situations?!?

I don't know, I wrote back. *Bad luck? The fact that I'm living in a violent society?*

No. You get into these situations because you seek them out. You want to be a martyr, and so you go searching for martyrdom.

I don't want to be a martyr, I wrote. *But I can't stand by or run and hide when other people need help.*

Maybe you should learn how.

And what about you? I asked.

We're not talking about me.

Yeah, we are, I wrote him. *We're talking about how I'm the same as you.*

I'm a bad influence, you mean.

No. We're just drawn together because we're alike.

There was a long wait until the next text.

Maybe you're right, he wrote. *This is why we need to stay away from each other.*

Or maybe we need each other, I wrote back. *At least as friends.*

There was another long wait until the next text came.

I don't think we can be together, Inna, it said. *Not even as friends, and certainly not as something more. I've tried, but...it's too painful. And I think I make you do dangerous things.*

So, what: You want to quit?

Yes.

No! Please! Not again!

That got no reply, so after a few minutes I sent another text:

Can we at least talk about this on video?

After ten minutes the reply came:

The last time we did video was very painful, Inna. Seeing you, even over such a bad connection, was too painful to stand. And we're bad for each other. We need to stop pretending we can be friends, Inna. We need to stop writing to each other.

Please don't do this, I wrote. *Not again.*

But there was no reply.

83

THERE WAS STILL NO reply when Brian Michaels showed up at my apartment at noon.

"I wanted to come check on you, get a more detailed statement and let you know what's goin' on," he said. He looked me up and down. "You don't look so good. You sure you're okay? We can do this later if you want."

"It's okay," I told him. "Let's do it now."

I gave a detailed statement of what had happened, and signed off on it.

"You were right," Brian said when I was done. "About Chris being LostAndFoundBoy. Jus' between you an' me, I got a peek at his computer before the big boys from Atlanta came and took it away, and yep, there it was. His profile on both those sites. From what we can gather, the Gang of Six was started last year by just one kid, Liam Jones. He'd been writin' for the *Champion* till he got fired for bein' a little too loudmouthed 'bout what he thought o' the college. So he decided to freelance. He wanted to get the other kids from the *Champion* to join him, but none o' them did, so the Gang of Six was only ever Liam, till he got assigned to be Chris's Senior Mentor this fall. He decided to bring Chris on board, and accordin' to him, Chris pretty much took over.

"Meanwhile, sounds like Chris was also pallin' around with Nathan, who was his RA. He got caught up in both things, and, well, it all went to hell. Gettin' told to take a hike this weekend by both the girls he had crushes on was the final straw. Looks like he went home and broke into his dad's gun cabinet, and, well...we all know what happened next."

"Yeah," I said. "Any updates on him?"

Brian shrugged. "As of this mornin' he was still alive, but he hadn't yet regained consciousness. He lost a lot of blood, and they're saying he might end up with permanent brain damage."

"How awful," I said.

"Some might call it justice," said Brian. "And if he wakes up, we're gonna do everything we can to make sure he goes away for a long time."

"What about Nathan?"

"Nathan got hit in the spine, had emergency surgery last night. Now they're keepin' him stable. Best guess is that he'll survive but'll never walk again."

"Also awful," I said. "Is he going to be charged with anything?"

"Right now it's not lookin' like it. Far as we can tell, he never did anythin' actually illegal. But I ain't cryin' too hard at the thought of him in a wheelchair. Nathan spent this whole past year sowin' the wind. Now he's reapin' the whirlwind."

"Yeah," I said.

"Anyway, I'm sure it'll be all over the news, but I'll keep you posted as well, let you know if I have any more questions. Meanwhile, I'll let you get some rest, try and relax after all of this."

Brian left. I mooned around the apartment for a while, trying to concentrate on doing something productive, and failing. Then, gripped by an intense spasm of loneliness and neediness, I texted Alex.

How are you doing? he texted back. *I wish I were there with you right now.*

Yeah, me too. But really soon I'll be with you. I just wish I were already there.

I do too. More and more each day. Counting down the minutes until I see you!

Me too :) :)

If you're okay for a bit, I've gotta go soon, but I'll check in with you later, okay?

I'm fine, I assured him. *Looking forward to hearing from you again later, though!*

Me too :) :) You know, when I heard about what had happened, I felt sick. And now I'm so happy that you're still alive and with me that I want to laugh and cry all at the same time. I guess this is love, huh?

Very likely, I wrote.

In that case, love you!

I love you too, I wrote back. I realized as I typed them that that was the first time I'd ever written those words. After all the sad endings of the year, it felt like a hopeful beginning.

THE END

THE NEXT BOOK IN THE series, **Honor Court***, is available now! Get it by scanning the QR code below:*

AND AS A SPECIAL EXCLUSIVE freebie to readers of **Trigger Warning***, I'm giving away* **Winter Break***, a novelette set a few weeks after the events of* **Trigger Warning** *and told from Dima's point of view.*

*You can get it and sign up for my mailing list (but only if you want to!)
by scanning the QR code below:*

About the author

SID STARK LIVES A LIFE very similar to her characters', only with more grading and fewer exciting chase scenes. She did once get held up in Heathrow on suspicion of being a Russian criminal traveling on an American passport, though, which was fun. She loves to hear from her readers, and can be reached by email at **sidstark@sidstarkauthor.com,** at her website at **https://sidstarkauthor.com/,** on Facebook at **https://www.facebook.com/SidStarkAuthor/,** and Twitter at **@SidStarkAuthor.**